THE NEW YORK TRILOGY

Paul Auster was born in New Jersey in 1947. After attending Columbia University he lived in France for four years. Since 1974 he has published poems, essays, novels and translations. He lives in Brooklyn, New York.

by the same author

The New York Trilogy
In the Country of Last Things
The Invention of Solitude
Moon Palace
The Music of Chance
Leviathan
Mr Vertigo
Art of Hunger
Hand to Mouth
Selected Poems
Lulu on the Bridge

PAUL AUSTER

The New York Trilogy

City of Glass

Ghosts

The Locked Room

faber and faber

The New York Trilogy was originally published in the USA as
City of Glass (1985), *Ghosts* and *The Locked Room* (1986) by
Sun & Moon Press, Los Angeles

First published in 1987
by Faber and Faber Limited
3 Queen Square London WC1N 3AU
This edition first published in 1999

Photoset by Parker Typesetting Service, Leicester
Printed and bound in Great Britain by
Mackays of Chatham PLC, Chatham, Kent

© Paul Auster, 1985, 1986, 1987

Paul Auster is hereby identified as author of this work
in accordance with Section 77 of the Copyright,
Designs and Patents Act 1988.

A CIP record for this book is
available from the British Library
ISBN 0–571–20058–3

2 4 6 8 10 9 7 5 3 1

Contents

City of Glass
1

Ghosts
133

The Locked Room
197

City of Glass

1

It was a wrong number that started it, the telephone ringing three times in the dead of night, and the voice on the other end asking for someone he was not. Much later, when he was able to think about the things that happened to him, he would conclude that nothing was real except chance. But that was much later. In the beginning, there was simply the event and its consequences. Whether it might have turned out differently, or whether it was all predetermined with the first word that came from the stranger's mouth, is not the question. The question is the story itself, and whether or not it means something is not for the story to tell.

As for Quinn, there is little that need detain us. Who he was, where he came from, and what he did are of no great importance. We know, for example, that he was thirty-five years old. We know that he had once been married, had once been a father, and that both his wife and son were now dead. We also know that he wrote books. To be precise, we know that he wrote mystery novels. These works were written under the name of William Wilson, and he produced them at the rate of about one a year, which brought in enough money for him to live modestly in a small New York apartment. Because he spent no more than five or six months on a novel, for the rest of the year he was free to do as he wished. He read many books, he looked at paintings, he went to the movies. In the summer he watched baseball on television; in the winter he went to the opera. More than anything else, however, what he liked to do was walk. Nearly every day, rain or shine, hot or cold, he would leave his apartment to walk through the city – never really going anywhere, but simply going wherever his legs happened to take him.

New York was an inexhaustible space, a labyrinth of endless steps, and no matter how far he walked, no matter how well he came to know its neighbourhoods and streets, it always left him with the feeling of being lost. Lost, not only in the city, but within himself as well. Each time he took a walk, he felt as though he were leaving himself behind, and by giving himself up to the movement of the streets, by reducing himself to a seeing eye, he was able to escape the obligation to think, and this, more than anything else, brought him a measure of peace, a salutary emptiness within. The world was outside of him, around him, before him, and the speed with which it kept changing made it impossible for him to dwell on any one thing for very long. Motion was of the essence, the act of putting one foot in front of the other and allowing himself to follow the drift of his own body. By wandering aimlessly, all places became equal and it no longer mattered where he was. On his best walks, he was able to feel that he was nowhere. And this, finally, was all he ever asked of things: to be nowhere. New York was the nowhere he had built around himself, and he realized that he had no intention of ever leaving it again.

In the past, Quinn had been more ambitious. As a young man he had published several books of poetry, had written plays, critical essays, and had worked on a number of long translations. But quite abruptly, he had given up all that. A part of him had died, he told his friends, and he did not want it coming back to haunt him. It was then that he had taken on the name of William Wilson. Quinn was no longer that part of him that could write books, and although in many ways Quinn continued to exist, he no longer existed for anyone but himself.

He had continued to write because it was the only thing he felt he could do. Mystery novels seemed a reasonable solution. He had little trouble inventing the intricate stories they required, and he wrote well, often in spite of himself, as if without having to make an effort. Because he did not consider himself to be the author of what he wrote, he did not feel responsible for it and therefore was not compelled to defend it in his heart. William Wilson, after all, was an invention, and even though he had been born within Quinn himself, he now led an independent life.

Quinn treated him with deference, at times even admiration, but he never went so far as to believe that he and William Wilson were the same man. It was for this reason that he did not emerge from behind the mask of his pseudonym. He had an agent, but they had never met. Their contacts were confined to the mail, for which purpose Quinn had rented a numbered box at the post office. The same was true of the publisher, who paid all fees, monies, and royalties to Quinn through the agent. No book by William Wilson ever included an author's photograph or biographical note. William Wilson was not listed in any writers' directory, he did not give interviews, and all the letters he received were answered by his agent's secretary. As far as Quinn could tell, no one knew his secret. In the beginning, when his friends learned that he had given up writing, they would ask him how he was planning to live. He told them all the same thing: that he had inherited a trust fund from his wife. But the fact was that his wife had never had any money. And the fact was that he no longer had any friends.

It had been more than five years now. He did not think about his son very much anymore, and only recently he had removed the photograph of his wife from the wall. Every once in a while, he would suddenly feel what it had been like to hold the three-year-old boy in his arms – but that was not exactly thinking, nor was it even remembering. It was a physical sensation, an imprint of the past that had been left in his body, and he had no control over it. These moments came less often now, and for the most part it seemed as though things had begun to change for him. He no longer wished to be dead. At the same time, it cannot be said that he was glad to be alive. But at least he did not resent it. He was alive, and the stubbornness of this fact had little by little begun to fascinate him – as if he had managed to outlive himself, as if he were somehow living a posthumous life. He did not sleep with the lamp on anymore, and for many months now he had not remembered any of his dreams.

It was night. Quinn lay in bed smoking a cigarette, listening to the rain beat against the window. He wondered when it would stop and whether he would feel like taking a long walk or a short walk in the morning. An open copy of Marco Polo's *Travels* lay face down on the pillow beside him. Since finishing the latest William Wilson novel two weeks earlier, he had been languishing. His private-eye narrator, Max Work, had solved an elaborate series of crimes, had suffered through a number of beatings and narrow escapes, and Quinn was feeling somewhat exhausted by his efforts. Over the years, Work had become very close to Quinn. Whereas William Wilson remained an abstract figure for him, Work had increasingly come to life. In the triad of selves that Quinn had become, Wilson served as a kind of ventriloquist. Quinn himself was the dummy, and Work was the animated voice that gave purpose to the enterprise. If Wilson was an illusion, he nevertheless justified the lives of the other two. If Wilson did not exist, he nevertheless was the bridge that allowed Quinn to pass from himself into Work. And little by little, Work had become a presence in Quinn's life, his interior brother, his comrade in solitude.

Quinn picked up the Marco Polo and started reading the first page again. 'We will set down things seen as seen, things heard as heard, so that our book may be an accurate record, free from any sort of fabrication. And all who read this book or hear it may do so with full confidence, because it contains nothing but the truth.' Just as Quinn was beginning to ponder the meaning of the sentences, to turn their crisp assurances over in his mind, the telephone rang. Much later, when he was able to reconstruct the events of that night, he would remember looking at the clock, seeing that it was past twelve, and wondering why someone should be calling him at that hour. More than likely, he thought, it was bad news. He climbed out of bed, walked naked to the telephone, and picked up the receiver on the second ring.

'Yes?'

There was a long pause on the other end, and for a moment Quinn thought the caller had hung up. Then, as if from a great distance, there came the sound of a voice unlike any he had ever heard. It was at once mechanical and filled with feeling, hardly more than a whisper and yet perfectly audible, and so even in tone that he was unable to tell if it belonged to a man or a woman.

'Hello?' said the voice.

'Who is this?' asked Quinn.

'Hello?' said the voice again.

'I'm listening,' said Quinn. 'Who is this?'

'Is this Paul Auster?' asked the voice. 'I would like to speak to Mr Paul Auster.'

'There's no one here by that name.'

'Paul Auster. Of the Auster Detective Agency.'

'I'm sorry,' said Quinn. 'You must have the wrong number.'

'This is a matter of utmost urgency,' said the voice.

'There's nothing I can do for you,' said Quinn. 'There is no Paul Auster here.'

'You don't understand,' said the voice. 'Time is running out.'

'Then I suggest you dial again. This is not a detective agency.'

Quinn hung up the phone. He stood there on the cold floor, looking down at his feet, his knees, his limp penis. For a brief moment he regretted having been so abrupt with the caller. It might have been interesting, he thought, to have played along with him a little. Perhaps he could have found out something about the case – perhaps even have helped in some way. 'I must learn to think more quickly on my feet,' he said to himself.

Like most people, Quinn knew almost nothing about crime. He had never murdered anyone, had never stolen anything, and he did not know anyone who had. He had never been inside a police station, had never met a private detective, had never spoken to a criminal. Whatever he knew about these things, he had learned from books, films, and newspapers. He did not, however, consider this to be a handicap. What interested him about the stories he wrote was not their relation to the world but their relation to other stories. Even before he became William Wilson, Quinn had been a devoted reader of mystery novels. He knew that most of them were poorly written, that most could not stand up to even the vaguest sort of examination, but still, it was the form that appealed to him, and it was the rare, unspeakably bad mystery that he would refuse to read. Whereas his taste in other books was rigorous, demanding to the point of narrow-mindedness, with these works he showed almost no discrimination whatsoever. When he was in the right mood, he had little trouble reading ten or twelve of them in a row. It was a kind of hunger that took hold of him, a craving for a special food, and he would not stop until he had eaten his fill.

What he liked about these books was their sense of plenitude and economy. In the good mystery there is nothing wasted, no sentence, no word that is not significant. And even if it is not significant, it has the potential to be so – which amounts to the same thing. The world of the book comes to life, seething with possibilities, with secrets and contradictions. Since everything seen or said, even the slightest, most trivial thing, can bear a connection to the outcome of the story, nothing must be overlooked. Everything becomes essence; the centre of the book shifts with each event that propels it forward. The centre, then, is everywhere, and no circumference can be drawn until the book has come to its end.

The detective is the one who looks, who listens, who moves through this morass of objects and events in search of the thought, the idea that will pull all these things together and make sense of them. In effect, the writer and the detective are interchangeable. The reader sees the world through the detective's eye, experiencing the proliferation of its details as if for the first time. He has become awake to the things around him, as if they might speak to him, as if, because of the attentiveness he now brings to them, they might begin to carry a meaning other than the simple fact of their existence. Private eye. The term held a triple meaning for Quinn. Not only was it the letter 'i,' standing for 'investigator,' it was 'I' in the upper case, the tiny life-bud buried in the body of the breathing self. At the same time, it was also the physical eye of the writer, the eye of the man who looks out from himself into the world and demands that the world reveal itself to him. For five years now, Quinn had been living in the grip of this pun.

He had, of course, long ago stopped thinking of himself as real. If he lived now in the world at all, it was only at one remove, through the imaginary person of Max Work. His detective necessarily had to be real. The nature of the books demanded it. If Quinn had allowed himself to vanish, to withdraw into the confines of a strange and hermetic life, Work continued to live in the world of others, and the more Quinn seemed to vanish, the more persistent Work's presence in that world became. Whereas Quinn tended to feel out of place in his own skin, Work was aggressive, quick-tongued, at home in whatever spot he happened to find himself. The very things that caused problems for Quinn, Work took for granted, and he walked through the mayhem of his adventures with an ease and indifference that never failed to impress his creator. It was not precisely that Quinn wanted to be Work, or even to be like him, but it reassured him to pretend to be Work as he was writing his books, to know that he had it in him to be Work if he ever chose to be, even if only in his mind.

That night, as he at last drifted off to sleep, Quinn tried to imagine what Work would have said to the stranger on the phone. In his dream, which he later forgot, he found himself alone in a room, firing a pistol into a bare white wall.

The following night, Quinn was caught off guard. He had thought the incident was over and was not expecting the stranger to call again. As it happened, he was sitting on the toilet, in the act of expelling a turd, when the telephone rang. It was somewhat later than the previous night, perhaps ten or twelve minutes before one. Quinn had just reached the chapter that tells of Marco Polo's journey from Peking to Amoy, and the book was open on his lap as he went about his business in the tiny bathroom. The ringing of the telephone came as a distinct irritation. To answer it promptly would mean getting up without wiping himself, and he was loath to walk across the apartment in that state. On the other hand, if he finished what he was doing at his normal speed, he would not make it to the phone in time. In spite of this, Quinn found himself reluctant to move. The telephone was not his favourite object, and more than once he had considered getting rid of his. What he disliked most of all was its tyranny. Not only did it have the power to interrupt him against his will, but inevitably he would give in to its command. This time, he decided to resist. By the third ring, his bowels were empty. By the fourth ring, he had succeeded in wiping himself. By the fifth ring, he had pulled up his pants, left the bathroom, and was walking calmly across the apartment. He answered the phone on the sixth ring, but there was no one at the other end. The caller had hung up.

The next night, he was ready. Sprawled out in his bed, perusing the pages of *The Sporting News*, he waited for the stranger to call a third time. Every now and then, when his nerves got the better of him, he would stand up and pace about the apartment. He put on a record – Haydn's opera, *The Man in the Moon* – and listened to it from start to finish. He waited and waited. At two-thirty, he finally gave up and went to sleep.

He waited the next night, and the night after that as well. Just as he was about to abandon his scheme, realizing that he had been wrong in all his assumptions, the telephone rang again. It was May nineteenth. He would remember the date because it was his parents' anniversary – or would have been, had his parents been alive – and his mother had once told him that he had been conceived on her wedding night. This fact had always appealed to him – being able to pinpoint the first moment of his existence – and over the years he had privately celebrated his birthday on that day. This time it was somewhat earlier than on the other two nights – not yet eleven o'clock – and as he reached for the phone he assumed it was someone else.

'Hello?' he said.

Again, there was a silence on the other end. Quinn knew at once that it was the stranger.

'Hello?' he said again. 'What can I do for you?'

'Yes,' said the voice at last. The same mechanical whisper, the

10

same desperate tone. 'Yes. It is needed now. Without delay.'

'What is needed?'

'To speak. Right now. To speak right now. Yes.'

'And who do you want to speak to?'

'Always the same man. Auster. The one who calls himself Paul Auster.'

This time Quinn did not hesitate. He knew what he was going to do, and now that the time had come, he did it.

'Speaking,' he said. 'This is Auster speaking.'

'At last. At last I've found you.' He could hear the relief in the voice, the tangible calm that suddenly seemed to overtake it.

'That's right,' said Quinn. 'At last.' He paused for a moment to let the words sink in, as much for himself as for the other. 'What can I do for you?'

'I need help,' said the voice. 'There is great danger. They say you are the best one to do these things.'

'It depends on what things you mean.'

'I mean death. I mean death and murder.'

'That's not exactly my line,' said Quinn. 'I don't go around killing people.'

'No,' said the voice petulantly. 'I mean the reverse.'

'Someone is going to kill you?'

'Yes, kill me. That's right. I am going to be murdered.'

'And you want me to protect you?'

'To protect me, yes. And to find the man who is going to do it.'

'You don't know who it is?'

'I know, yes. Of course I know. But I don't know where he is.'

'Can you tell me about it?'

'Not now. Not on the phone. There is great danger. You must come here.'

'How about tomorrow?'

'Good. Tomorrow. Early tomorrow. In the morning.'

'Ten o'clock?'

'Good. Ten o'clock.' The voice gave an address on East 69th Street. 'Don't forget, Mr Auster. You must come.'

'Don't worry,' said Quinn. 'I'll be there.'

11

2

The next morning, Quinn woke up earlier than he had in several weeks. As he drank his coffee, buttered his toast, and read through the baseball scores in the paper (the Mets had lost again, two to one, on a ninth inning error), it did not occur to him that he was going to show up for his appointment. Even that locution, *his appointment*, seemed odd to him. It wasn't his appointment, it was Paul Auster's. And who that person was he had no idea.

Nevertheless, as time wore on he found himself doing a good imitation of a man preparing to go out. He cleared the table of the breakfast dishes, tossed the newspaper on the couch, went into the bathroom, showered, shaved, went on to the bedroom wrapped in two towels, opened the closet, and picked out his clothes for the day. He found himself tending toward a jacket and tie. Quinn had not worn a tie since the funerals of his wife and son, and he could not even remember if he still owned one. But there it was, hanging amidst the debris of his wardrobe. He dismissed a white shirt as too formal, however, and instead chose a grey and red check affair to go with the grey tie. He put them on in a kind of trance.

It was not until he had his hand on the doorknob that be began to suspect what he was doing. 'I seem to be going out,' he said to himself. 'But if I am going out, where exactly am I going?' An hour later, as he climbed from the number 4 bus at 70th Street and Fifth Avenue, he still had not answered the question. To one side of him was the park, green in the morning sun, with sharp, fleeting shadows; to the other side was the Frick, white and austere, as if abandoned to the dead. He thought for a moment of Vermeer's *Soldier and Young Girl Smiling*, trying to remember the expression on the girl's face, the exact position of her hands around the cup, the red back of the faceless man. In his mind, he caught a glimpse of the blue map on the wall and the sunlight pouring through the window, so like the sunlight that surrounded him now. He was walking. He was crossing the street and moving eastward. At Madison Avenue he turned right and went south for a block, then turned left and saw where he was. 'I seem to have arrived,' he said to himself. He stood before the building and paused. It suddenly did not seem to matter any more. He felt remarkably calm, as if everything had already happened to him. As he opened the door that would lead him into the lobby, he gave himself one last word of advice. 'If all this is really happening,' he said, 'then I must keep my eyes open.'

It was a woman who opened the apartment door. For some reason, Quinn had not been expecting this, and it threw him off track. Already, things were happening too fast. Before he had a chance to absorb the woman's presence, to describe her to himself and form his impressions, she was talking to him, forcing him to respond. Therefore, even in those first moments, he had lost ground, was starting to fall behind himself. Later, when he had time to reflect on these events, he would manage to piece together his encounter with the woman. But that was the work of memory, and remembered things, he knew, had a tendency to subvert the things remembered. As a consequence, he could never be sure of any of it.

The woman was thirty, perhaps thirty-five; average height at best; hips a touch wide, or else voluptuous, depending on your point of view; dark hair, dark eyes, and a look in those eyes that was at once self-contained and vaguely seductive. She wore a black dress and very red lipstick.

'Mr Auster?' A tentative smile; a questioning tilt to the head.

'That's right,' said Quinn. 'Paul Auster.'

'I'm Virginia Stillman,' the woman began. 'Peter's wife. He's been waiting for you since eight o'clock.'

'The appointment was for ten,' said Quinn, glancing at his watch. It was exactly ten.

'He's been frantic,' the woman explained. 'I've never seen him like this before. He just couldn't wait.'

She opened the door for Quinn. As he crossed the threshold and entered the apartment, he could feel himself going blank, as if his brain had suddenly shut off. He had wanted to take in the details of what he was seeing, but the task was somehow beyond him at that moment. The apartment loomed up around him as a kind of blur. He realized that it was large, perhaps five or six rooms, and that it was richly furnished, with numerous art objects, silver ashtrays, and elaborately framed paintings on the walls. But that was all. No more than a general impression – even though he was there, looking at those things with his own eyes.

He found himself sitting on a sofa, alone in the living room. He remembered now that Mrs Stillman had told him to wait there while she went to find her husband. He couldn't say how long it had been. Surely no more than a minute or two. But from the way the light was coming through the windows, it seemed to be almost noon. It did not occur to him, however, to consult his watch. The smell of Virginia Stillman's perfume hovered around him, and he began to imagine what she looked like without any clothes on. Then he thought about what Max Work might have been thinking, had he been there. He decided to light a cigarette. He blew the smoke into the room. It pleased him to watch it leave his mouth in gusts, disperse, and take on new definition as the light caught it.

He heard the sound of someone entering the room behind him. Quinn stood up from the sofa and turned around, expecting to see Mrs Stillman. Instead, it was a young man, dressed entirely in white, with the white-blond hair of a child. Uncannily, in that first moment, Quinn thought of his own dead son. Then, just as suddenly as the thought had appeared, it vanished.

Peter Stillman walked into the room and sat down in a red velvet armchair opposite Quinn. He said not a word as he made his way to his seat, nor did he acknowledge Quinn's presence. The act of moving from one place to another seemed to require all his attention, as though not to think of what he was doing would reduce him to immobility. Quinn had never seen anyone move in such a manner, and he realized at once that this was the same person he had spoken to on the phone. The body acted almost exactly as the voice had: machine-like, fitful, alternating between slow and rapid gestures, rigid and yet expressive, as if the operation were out of control, not quite corresponding to the will that lay behind it. It seemed to Quinn that Stillman's body had not been used for a long time and that all its functions had been relearned, so that motion had become a conscious process, each movement broken down into its component submovements, with the result that all flow and spontaneity had been lost. It was like watching a marionette trying to walk without strings.

Everything about Peter Stillman was white. White shirt, open at the neck; white pants, white shoes, white socks. Against the pallor of his skin, the flaxen thinness of his hair, the effect was almost transparent, as though one could see through to the blue veins behind the skin of his face. This blue was almost the same as the blue of his eyes: a milky blue that seemed to dissolve into a mixture of sky and clouds. Quinn could not image himself addressing a word to this person. It was as though Stillman's presence was a command to be silent.

Stillman settled slowly into his chair and at last turned his attention to Quinn. As their eyes met, Quinn suddenly felt that Stillman had become invisible. He could see him sitting in the chair across from him, but at the same time it felt as though he was not there. It occurred to Quinn that perhaps Stillman was blind. But no, that did not seem possible. The man was looking at him, even studying him, and if recognition did not flicker across his face, it still held something more than a blank stare. Quinn did not know what to do. He sat there dumbly in his seat, looking back at Stillman. A long time passed.

'No questions, please,' the young man said at last. 'Yes. No. Thank you.' He paused for a moment. 'I am Peter Stillman. I say this of my own free will. Yes. That is not my real name. No. Of course, my mind is not all it should be. But nothing can be done about that. No. About that. No, no. Not anymore.

'You sit there and think: who is this person talking to me? What are these words coming from his mouth? I will tell you. Or else I will not tell you. Yes and no. My mind is not all it should be. I say this of my own free will. But I will try. Yes and no. I will try to tell you, even if my mind makes it hard. Thank you.

'My name is Peter Stillman. Perhaps you have heard of me, but more than likely not. No matter. That is not my real name. My real name I cannot remember. Excuse me. Not that it makes a difference. That is to say, anymore.

'This is what is called speaking. I believe that is the term. When words come out, fly into the air, live for a moment, and die. Strange, is it not? I myself have no opinion. No and no again. But still, there are words you will need to have. There are many of them. Many millions I think. Perhaps only three or four. Excuse me. But I am doing well today. So much better than usual. If I can give you the words you need to have, it will be a great victory. Thank you. Thank you a million times over.

'Long ago there was mother and father. I remember none of that. They say: mother died. Who they are I cannot say. Excuse me. But that is what they say.

'No mother, then. Ha ha. Such is my laughter now, my belly burst of mumbo jumbo. Ha ha ha. Big father said: it makes no difference. To me. That is to say, to him. Big father of the big muscles and the boom, boom, boom. No questions now, please.

'I say what they say because I know nothing. I am only poor Peter Stillman, the boy who can't remember. Boo hoo. Willy nilly. Nincompoop. Excuse me. They say, they say. But what does poor little Peter say? Nothing, nothing. Anymore.

'There was this. Dark. Very dark. As dark as very dark. They say: that was the room. As if I could talk about it. The dark, I mean. Thank you.

'Dark, dark. They say for nine years. Not even a window. Poor Peter Stillman. And the boom, boom, boom. The caca piles. The pipi lakes. The swoons. Excuse me. Numb and naked. Excuse me. Anymore.

'There is the dark then. I am telling you. There was food in the dark, yes, mush food in the hush dark room. He ate with his hands. Excuse me. I mean Peter did. And if I am Peter, so much

the better. That is to say, so much the worse. Excuse me. I am
Peter Stillman. That is not my real name. Thank you.

'Poor Peter Stillman. A little boy he was. Barely a few words of
his own. And then no words, and then no one, and then no, no,
no. Anymore.

'Forgive me, Mr Auster. I see that I am making you sad. No
questions, please. My name is Peter Stillman. That is not my real
name. My real name is Mr Sad. What is your name, Mr Auster?
Perhaps you are the real Mr Sad, and I am no one.

'Boo hoo. Excuse me. Such is my weeping and wailing. Boo
hoo, sob sob. What did Peter do in that room? No one can say.
Some say nothing. As for me, I think that Peter could not think.
Did he blink? Did he drink? Did he stink? Ha ha ha. Excuse me.
Sometimes I am so funny.

'Wimble click crumblechaw beloo. Clack clack bedrack. Numb
noise, flacklemuch, chewmanna. Ya, ya, ya. Excuse me. I am the
only one who understands these words.

'Later and later and later. So they say. It went on too long for
Peter to be right in the head. Never again. No, no, no. They say
that someone found me. I do not remember. No, I do not
remember what happened when they opened the door and the
light came in. No, no, no. I can say nothing about any of this.
Anymore.

'For a long time I wore dark glasses. I was twelve. Or so they
say. I lived in a hospital. Little by little, they taught me how to be
Peter Stillman. They said: you are Peter Stillman. Thank you, I
said. Ya, ya, ya. Thank you and thank you. I said.

'Peter was a baby. They had to teach him everything. How to
walk, you know. How to eat. How to make caca and pipi in the
toilet. That wasn't bad. Even when I bit them, they didn't do the
boom, boom, boom. Later, I even stopped tearing off my clothes.

'Peter was a good boy. But it was hard to teach him words. His
mouth did not work right. And of course he was not all there in
his head. Ba ba ba, he said. And da da da. And wa wa wa. Excuse
me. It took more years and years. Now they say to Peter: you can
go now, there's nothing more we can do for you. Peter Stillman,

you are a human being, they said. It is good to believe what doctors say. Thank you. Thank you so very much.

'I am Peter Stillman. That is not my real name. My real name is Peter Rabbit. In the winter I am Mr White, in the summer I am Mr Green. Think what you like of this. I say it of my own free will. Wimble click crumblechaw beloo. It is beautiful, is it not? I make up words like this all the time. That can't be helped. They just come out of my mouth by themselves. They cannot be translated.

'Ask and ask, It does no good. But I will tell you. I don't want you to be sad, Mr Auster. You have such a kind face. You remind me of a somesuch or a groan, I don't know which. And your eyes look at me. Yes, yes. I can see them. That is very good. Thank you.

'That is why I will tell you. No questions, please. You are wondering about all the rest. That is to say, the father. The terrible father who did all those things to little Peter. Rest assured. They took him to a dark place. They locked him up and left him there. Ha ha ha. Excuse me. Sometimes I am so funny.

'Thirteen years, they said. That is perhaps a long time. But I know nothing of time. I am new every day. I am born when I wake up in the morning, I grow old during the day, and I die at night when I go to sleep. It is not my fault. I am doing so well today. I am doing so much better than I have ever done before.

'For thirteen years the father was away. His name is Peter Stillman too. Strange, is it not? That two people can have the same name? I do not know if that is his real name. But I do not think he is me. We are both Peter Stillman. But Peter Stillman is not my real name. So perhaps I am not Peter Stillman, after all.

'Thirteen years I say. Or they say. It makes no difference. I know nothing of time. But what they tell me is this. Tomorrow is the end of thirteen years. That is bad. Even though they say it is not, it is bad. I am not supposed to remember. But now and then I do, in spite of what I say.

'He will come. That is to say, the father will come. And he will try to kill me. Thank you. But I do not want that. No, no. Not anymore. Peter lives now. Yes. All is not right in his head, but still

he lives. And that is something, is it not? You bet your bottom
dollar. Ha ha ha.

'I am mostly now a poet. Every day I sit in my room and write
another poem. I make up all the words myself, just like when I
lived in the dark. I begin to remember things that way, to pretend
that I am back in the dark again. I am the only one who knows
what the words mean. They cannot be translated. These poems
will make me famous. Hit the nail on the head. Ya, ya ya.
Beautiful poems. So beautiful the whole world will weep.

'Later perhaps I will do something else. After I am done being a
poet. Sooner or later I will run out of words, you see. Everyone
has just so many words inside him. And then where will I be? I
think I would like to be a fireman after that. And after that a
doctor. It makes no difference. The last thing I will be is a
high-wire walker. When I am very old and have at last learned
how to walk like other people. Then I will dance on the wire, and
people will be amazed. Even little children. That is what I would
like. To dance on the wire until I die.

'But no matter. It makes no difference. To me. As you can see, I
am a rich man. I do not have to worry. No, no. Not about that.
You bet your bottom dollar. The father was rich, and little Peter
got all his money after they locked him up in the dark. Ha ha ha.
Excuse me for laughing. Sometimes I am so funny.

'I am the last of the Stillmans. That was quite a family, or so
they say. From old Boston, in case you might have heard of it. I
am the last one. There are no others. I am the end of everyone, the
last man. So much the better, I think. It is not a pity that it should
all end now. It is good for everyone to be dead.

'The father was perhaps not really bad. At least I say so now.
He had a big head. As big as very big, which meant there was too
much room in there. So many thoughts in that big head of his. But
poor Peter, was he not? And in terrible straits indeed. Peter who
could not see or say, who could not think or do. Peter who could
not. No. Not anything.

'I know nothing of any of this. Nor do I understand. My wife is
the one who tells me these things. She says it is important for me

to know, even if I do not understand. But even this I do not understand. In order to know, you must understand. Is that not so? But I know nothing. Perhaps I am Peter Stillman, and perhaps I am not. My real name is Peter Nobody. Thank you. And what do you think of that?

'So I am telling you about the father. It is a good story, even if I do not understand it. I can tell it to you because I know the words. And that is something, is it not? To know the words I mean. Sometimes I am so proud of myself! Excuse me. This is what my wife says. She says the father talked about God. That is a funny word to me. When you put it backwards, it spells dog. And a dog is not much like God, is it? Woof woof. Bow wow. Those are dog words. I think they are beautiful. So pretty and true. Like the words I make up.

'Anyway. I was saying. The father talked about God. He wanted to know if God had a language. Don't ask me what this means. I am only telling you because I know the words. The father thought a baby might speak it if the baby saw no people. But what baby was there? Ah. Now you begin to see. You did not have to buy him. Of course, Peter knew some people words. That could not be helped. But the father thought maybe Peter would forget them. After a while. That is why there was so much boom, boom, boom. Every time Peter said a word, his father would boom him. At last Peter learned to say nothing. Ya ya ya. Thank you.

'Peter kept the words inside him. All those days and months and years. There in the dark, little Peter all alone, and the words made noise in his head and kept him company. This is why his mouth does not work right. Poor Peter. Boo hoo. Such are his tears. The little boy who can never grow up.

'Peter can talk like people now. But he still has the other words in his head. They are God's language, and no one else can speak them. They cannot be translated. That is why Peter lives so close to God. That is why he is a famous poet.

'Everything is so good for me now. I can do whatever I like. Any time, any place. I even have a wife. You can see that. I mentioned her before. Perhaps you have even met her. She is beautiful, is she not? Her name is Virginia. That is not her real name. But that makes no difference. To me.

'Whenever I ask, my wife gets a girl for me. They are whores. I put my worm inside them and they moan. There have been so many. Ha ha. They come up here and I fuck them. It feels good to fuck. Virginia gives them money and everyone is happy. You bet your bottom dollar. Ha ha.

'Poor Virginia. She does not like to fuck. That is to say, with me. Perhaps she fucks another. Who can say? I know nothing of this. It makes no difference. But maybe if you are nice to Virginia she will let you fuck her. It would make me happy. For your sake. Thank you.

'So. There are a great many things. I am trying to tell them to you. I know that all is not right in my head. And it is true, yes, and I say this of my own free will, that sometimes I just scream and scream. For no good reason. As if there had to be a reason. But for none that I can see. Or anyone else. No. And then there are the times when I say nothing. For days and days on end. Nothing, nothing, nothing. I forget how to make the words come out of my mouth. Then it is hard for me to move. Ya ya. Or even to see. That is when I become Mr Sad.

'I still like to be in the dark. At least sometimes. It does me good, I think. In the dark I speak God's language and no one can hear me. Do not be angry, please. I cannot help it.

'Best of all, there is the air. Yes. And little by little, I have learned to live inside it. The air and the light, yes, that too, the light that shines on all things and puts them there for my eyes to see. There is the air and the light and this best of all. Excuse me. The air and the light. Yes. When the weather is good, I like to sit by the open window. Sometimes I look out and watch the things below. The street and all the people, the dogs and cars, the bricks of the building across the way. And then there are the times when I close my eyes and just sit there, with the breeze blowing on my face, and the light inside the air, all around me and just beyond my eyes, and the world all red, a beautiful red inside my eyes, with the sun shining on me and my eyes.

'It is true that I rarely go out. It is hard for me, and I am not always to be trusted. Sometimes I scream. Do not be angry with me, please. I cannot help it. Virginia says I must learn how to behave in public. But sometimes I cannot help myself, and the screams just come out of me.

'But I do love going to the park. There are the trees, and the air and the light. There is good in all that, is there not? Yes. Little by little, I am getting better inside myself. I can feel it. Even Dr Wyshnegradsky says so. I know that I am still the puppet boy. That cannot be helped. No, no. Anymore. But sometimes I think I will at last grow up and become real.

'For now, I am still Peter Stillman. That is not my real name. I cannot say who I will be tomorrow. Each day is new, and each day I am born again. I see hope everywhere, even in the dark, and when I die I will perhaps become God.

'There are many more words to speak. But I do not think I will speak them. No. Not today. My mouth is tired now, and I think the time has come for me to go. Of course, I know nothing of time. But that makes no difference. To me. Thank you very much. I know you will save my life, Mr Auster. I am counting on you. Life can last just so long, you understand. Everything else is in the room, with darkness, with God's language, with screams. Here I am of the air, a beautiful thing for the light to shine on. Perhaps you will remember that. I am Peter Stillman. That is not my real name. Thank you very much.'

3

The speech was over. How long it had lasted Quinn could not say. For it was only now, after the words had stopped, that he realized they were sitting in the dark. Apparently, a whole day had gone by. At some point during Stillman's monologue the sun had set in the room, but Quinn had not been aware of it. Now he could feel the darkness and the silence, and his head was humming with them. Several minutes went by. Quinn thought that perhaps it was up to him to say something now, but he could not be sure. He could hear Peter Stillman breathing heavily in his spot across the room. Other than that, there were no sounds. Quinn could not decide what to do. He thought of several possibilities, but then, one by one, dismissed them from his mind. He sat there in his seat, waiting for the next thing to happen.

The sound of stockinged legs moving across the room finally broke the silence. There was the metal click of a lamp switch, and suddenly the room was filled with light. Quinn's eyes automatically turned to its source, and there, standing beside a table lamp to the left of Peter's chair, he saw Virginia Stillman. The young man was gazing straight ahead, as if asleep with his eyes open. Mrs Stillman bent over, put her arm around Peter's shoulder, and spoke softly into his ear.

'It's time now, Peter,' she said. 'Mrs Saavedra is waiting for you.'

Peter looked up at her and smiled. 'I am filled with hope,' he said.

Virginia Stillman kissed her husband tenderly on the cheek. 'Say goodbye to Mr Auster,' she said.

Peter stood up. Or rather, he began the sad, slow adventure of manoeuvring his body out of the chair and working his way to his feet. At each stage there were relapses, crumplings, catapults back, accompanied by sudden fits of immobility, grunts, words whose meaning Quinn could not decipher.

At last Peter was upright. He stood in front of his chair with an expression of triumph and looked Quinn in the eyes. Then he smiled, broadly and without self-consciousness.

'Goodbye,' he said.

'Goodbye, Peter,' said Quinn.

Peter gave a little spastic wave of the hand and then slowly turned and walked across the room. He tottered as he went, listing first to the right, then to the left, his legs by turns buckling and locking. At the far end of the room, standing in a lighted doorway, was a middle-aged woman dressed in a white nurse's uniform. Quinn assumed it was Mrs Saavedra. He followed Peter Stillman with his eyes until the young man disappeared through the door.

Virginia Stillman sat down across from Quinn, in the same chair her husband had just occupied.

'I could have spared you all that,' she said, 'but I thought it would be best for you to see it with your own eyes.'

'I understand,' said Quinn.

'No, I don't think you do,' the woman said bitterly. 'I don't think anyone can understand.'

Quinn smiled judiciously and then told himself to plunge in. 'Whatever I do or do not understand,' he said, 'is probably beside the point. You've hired me to do a job, and the sooner I get on with it the better. From what I can gather, the case is urgent. I make no claims about understanding Peter or what you might have suffered. The important thing is that I'm willing to help. I think you should take it for what it's worth.'

He was warming up now. Something told him that he had captured the right tone, and a sudden sense of pleasure surged through him, as though he had just managed to cross some internal border within himself.

'You're right,' said Virginia Stillman. 'Of course you're right.'

The woman paused, took a deep breath, and then paused again, as if rehearsing in her mind the things she was about to say. Quinn noticed that her hands were clenched tightly around the arms of the chair.

'I realize,' she went on, 'that most of what Peter says is very confusing – especially the first time you hear him. I was standing in the next room listening to what he said to you. You mustn't assume that Peter always tells the truth. On the other hand, it would be wrong to think he lies.'

'You mean that I should believe some of the things he said and not believe others.'

'That's exactly what I mean.'

'Your sexual habits, or lack of them, don't concern me, Mrs Stillman,' said Quinn. 'Even if what Peter said is true, it makes no difference. In my line of work you tend to meet a little of everything, and if you don't learn to suspend judgement, you'll never get anywhere. I'm used to hearing people's secrets, and I'm also used to keeping my mouth shut. If a fact has no direct bearing on a case, I have no use for it.'

Mrs Stillman blushed. 'I just wanted you to know that what Peter said isn't true.'

Quinn shrugged, took out a cigarette, and lit it. 'One way or the other,' he said, 'it's not important. What I'm interested in are the other things Peter said. I assume they're true, and if they are, I'd like to hear what you have to say about them.'

'Yes, they're true.' Virginia Stillman released her grip on the chair and put her right hand under her chin. Pensive. As if searching for an attitude of unshakeable honesty. 'Peter has a child's way of telling it. But what he said is true.'

'Tell me something about the father. Anything you think is relevant.'

'Peter's father is a Boston Stillman. I'm sure you've heard of the family. There were several governors back in the nineteenth century, a number of Episcopal bishops, ambassadors, a Harvard president. At the same time, the family made a great deal of money in textiles, shipping, and God knows what else. The details are unimportant. Just so long as you have some idea of the background.

'Peter's father went to Harvard, like everyone else in the family. He studied philosophy and religion and by all accounts was quite brilliant. He wrote his thesis on sixteenth- and seventeenth-century theological interpretations of the New World, and then he took a job in the religion department at Columbia. Not long after that, he married Peter's mother. I don't know much about her. From the photographs I've seen, she was very pretty. But delicate – a little like Peter, with those pale blue eyes and white skin. When Peter was born a few years later, the family was living in a large apartment on Riverside Drive. Stillman's academic career was prospering. He rewrote his dissertation and turned it into a book – it did very well – and was made a full professor when he was thirty-four or thirty-five. Then Peter's mother died. Everything about that death is unclear. Stillman claimed that she had died in her sleep, but the evidence seemed to point to suicide. Something to do with an overdose of pills, but of course nothing could be proved. There was even some talk that he had killed her. But those were just rumours, and nothing ever came of it. The whole affair was kept very quiet.

'Peter was just two at the time, a perfectly normal child. After his wife's death, Stillman apparently had little to do with him. A nurse was hired, and for the next six months or so she took complete care of Peter. Then, out of the blue, Stillman fired her. I forget her name – a Miss Barber, I think – but she testified at the trial. It seems that Stillman just came home one day and told her that he was taking charge of Peter's upbringing. He sent in his resignation to Columbia and told them he was leaving the university to devote himself full-time to his son. Money, of course, was no object, and there was nothing anyone could do about it.

'After that, he more or less dropped out of sight. He stayed on in the same apartment, but he hardly ever went out. No one really knows that happened. I think, probably, that he began to believe in some of the far-fetched religious ideas he had written about. It made him crazy, absolutely insane. There's no other way to describe it. He locked Peter in a room in the apartment, covered up the windows, and kept him there for nine years. Try to imagine it, Mr Auster. Nine years. An entire childhood spent in darkness, isolated from the world, with no human contact except an occasional beating. I live with the results of that experiment, and I can tell you the damage was monstrous. What you saw today was Peter at his best. It's taken thirteen years to get him this far, and I'll be damned if I let anyone hurt him again.'

Mrs Stillman stopped to catch her breath. Quinn sensed that she was on the verge of a scene and that one more word might put her over the edge. He had to speak now, or the conversation would run away from him.

'How was Peter finally discovered?' he asked.

Some of the tension went out of the woman. She exhaled audibly and looked Quinn in the eyes.

'There was a fire,' she said.

'An accidental fire or one set on purpose?'

'No one knows.'

'What do you think?'

'I think Stillman was in his study. He kept the records of his experiment there, and I think he finally realized that his work had been a failure. I'm not saying that he regretted anything he had done. But even taking it on his own terms, he knew he had failed. I think he reached some point of final disgust with himself that night and decided to burn his papers. But the fire got out of control, and much of the apartment burned. Luckily, Peter's room was at the other end of a long hall, and the firemen got to him in time.'

'And then?'

'It took several months to sort everything out. Stillman's papers had been destroyed, which meant there was no concrete evidence. On the other hand, there was Peter's condition, the room he had been locked up in, those horrible boards across the windows, and eventually the police put the case together. Stillman was finally brought to trial.'

'What happened in court?'

'Stillman was judged insane and he was sent away.'

'And Peter?'

'He also went to a hospital. He stayed there until just two years ago.'

'Is that where you met him?'

'Yes. In the hospital.'

'How?'

'I was his speech therapist. I worked with Peter every day for five years.'

'I don't mean to pry. But how exactly did that lead to marriage?'

'It's complicated.'

'Do you mind telling me about it?'

'Not really. But I don't think you'd understand.'

'There's only one way to find out.'

'Well, to put it simply. It was the best way to get Peter out of the hospital and give him a chance to lead a more normal life.'

'Couldn't you have been made his legal guardian?'

'The procedures were very complicated. And besides, Peter was no longer a minor.'

'Wasn't that an enormous self-sacrifice on your part?'

'Not really. I was married once before – disastrously. It's not something I want for myself any more. At least with Peter there's a purpose to my life.'

'Is it true that Stillman is being released?'

'Tomorrow. He'll be arriving at Grand Central in the evening.'

'And you feel he might come after Peter. Is this just a hunch, or do you have some proof?'

'A little of both. Two years ago, they were going to let Stillman out. But he wrote Peter a letter, and I showed it to the authorities. They decided he wasn't ready to be released, after all.'

'What kind of letter was it?'

'An insane letter. He called Peter a devil boy and said there would be a day of reckoning.'

'Do you still have the letter?'

'No. I gave it to the police two years ago.'

'A copy?'

'I'm sorry. Do you think it's important?'

'It might be.'

'I can try to get one for you if you like.'

'I take it there were no more letters after that one.'

'No more letters. And now they feel Stillman is ready to be discharged. That's the official view, in any case, and there's nothing I can do to stop them. What I think, though, is that Stillman simply learned his lesson. He realized that letters and threats would keep him locked up.'

'And so you're still worried.'

'That's right.'

'But you have no precise idea of what Stillman's plans might be.'

'Exactly.'

'What is it you want me to do?'

'I want you to watch him carefully. I want you to find out what he's up to. I want you to keep him away from Peter.'

'In other words, a kind of glorified tail job.'

'I suppose so.'

'I think you should understand that I can't prevent Stillman from coming to this building. What I can do is warn you about it. And I can make it my business to come here with him.'

'I understand. As long as there's some protection.'

'Good. How often do you want me to check in with you?'

'I'd like you to give me a report every day. Say a telephone call in the evening, around ten or eleven o'clock.'

'No problem.'

'Is there anything else?'

'Just a few more questions. I'm curious, for example, to know how you found out that Stillman will be coming into Grand Central tomorrow evening.'

'I've made it my business to know, Mr Auster. There's too much at stake here for me to leave it to chance. And if Stillman isn't followed from the moment he arrives, he could easily disappear without a trace. I don't want that to happen.'

'What train will he be on?'

'The six forty-one, arriving from Poughkeepsie.'

'I assume you have a photograph of Stillman?'

'Yes, of course.'

'There's also the question of Peter. I'd like to know why you told him about all this in the first place. Wouldn't it have been better to have kept it quiet?'

'I wanted to. But Peter happened to be listening in on the other phone when I got the news of his father's release. There was nothing I could do about it. Peter can be very stubborn, and I've learned it's best not to lie to him.'

'One last question. Who was it who referred you to me?'

'Mrs Saavedra's husband, Michael. He used to be a policeman, and he did some research. He found out that you were the best man in the city for this kind of thing.'

'I'm flattered.'

'From what I've seen of you so far, Mr Auster, I'm sure we've found the right man.'

Quinn took this as his cue to rise. It came as a relief to stretch his legs at last. Things had gone well, far better than he had expected, but his head hurt now, and his body ached with an exhaustion he had not felt in years. If he carried on any longer, he was sure to give himself away.

'My fee is one hundred dollars a day plus expenses,' he said. 'If you could give me something in advance, it would be proof that I'm working for you – which would ensure us a privileged investigator-client relationship. That means everything that passes between us would be in strictest confidence.'

Virginia Stillman smiled, as if at some secret joke of her own. Or perhaps she was merely responding to the possible double meaning of his last sentence. Like so many of the things that happened to him over the days and weeks that followed, Quinn could not be sure of any of it.

'How much would you like?' she asked.

'It doesn't matter. I'll leave that up to you.'

'Five hundred?'

'That would be more than enough.'

'Good. I'll go get my cheque book.' Virginia Stillman stood up and smiled at Quinn again. 'I'll get you a picture of Peter's father, too. I think I know just where it is.'

Quinn thanked her and said he would wait. He watched her leave the room and once again found himself imagining what she would look like without any clothes on. Was she somehow coming on to him, he wondered, or was it just his own mind trying to sabotage him again? He decided to postpone his meditations and take up the subject again later.

Virginia Stillman walked back into the room and said, 'Here's the cheque. I hope I made it out correctly.'

Yes, yes, thought Quinn as he examined the check, everything is tip top. He was pleased with his own cleverness. The cheque, of course, was made out to Paul Auster, which meant that Quinn could not be held accountable for impersonating a private detective without a licence. It reassured him to know that he had somehow put himself in the clear. The fact that he would never be able to cash the cheque did not trouble him. He understood, even then, that he was not doing any of this for money. He slipped the cheque into the inside breast pocket of his jacket.

'I'm sorry there's not a more recent photograph,' Virginia Stillman was saying. 'This one dates from more than twenty years ago. But I'm afraid it's the best I can do.'

Quinn looked at the picture of Stillman's face, hoping for a sudden epiphany, some sudden rush of subterranean knowledge that would help him to understand the man. But the picture told him nothing. It was no more than a picture of a man. He studied it for a moment longer and concluded that it could just as easily have been anyone.

'I'll look at it more carefully when I get home,' he said, putting it into the same pocket where the cheque had gone. 'Taking the passage of time into account, I'm sure I'll be able to recognize him at the station tomorrow.'

'I hope so,' said Virginia Stillman. 'It's terribly important, and I'm counting on you.'

'Don't worry,' said Quinn. 'I haven't let anyone down yet.'

She walked him to the door. For several seconds they stood there in silence, not knowing whether there was something to add or if the time had come to say goodbye. In that tiny interval,

Virginia Stillman suddenly threw her arms around Quinn, sought out his lips with her own, and kissed him passionately, driving her tongue deep inside his mouth. Quinn was so taken off guard that he almost failed to enjoy it.

When he was at last able to breathe again, Mrs Stillman held him at arm's length and said, 'That was to prove that Peter wasn't telling you the truth. It's very important that you believe me.'

'I believe you,' said Quinn. 'And even if I didn't believe you, it wouldn't really matter.'

'I just wanted you to know what I'm capable of.'

'I think I have a good idea.'

She took his right hand in her two hands and kissed it. 'Thank you, Mr Auster. I really do think you're the answer.'

He promised he would call her the next night, and then he found himself walking out the door, taking the elevator downstairs, and leaving the building. It was past midnight when he hit the street.

4

Quinn had heard of cases like Peter Stillman before. Back in the days of his other life, not long after his own son was born, he had written a review of a book about the wild boy of Aveyron, and at the time he had done some research on the subject. As far as he could remember, the earliest account of such an experiment appeared in the writings of Herodotus: the Egyptian pharaoh Psamtik isolated two infants in the seventh century BC and commanded the servant in charge of them never to utter a word in their presence. According to Herodotus, a notoriously unreliable chronicler, the children learned to speak – their first word being the Phrygian word for bread. In the Middle Ages, the Holy Roman Emperor Frederick II repeated the experiment, hoping to discover man's true 'natural language' using similar methods, but the children died before they ever spoke any words. Finally, in what was undoubtedly a hoax, the early sixteenth-century King of Scotland, James IV, claimed that Scottish children isolated in the same manner wound up speaking 'very good Hebrew.'

Cranks and ideologues, however, were not the only ones interested in the subject. Even so sane and sceptical a man as Montaigne considered the question carefully, and in his most important essay, the *Apology for Raymond Sebond*, he wrote: 'I believe that a child who had been brought up in complete solitude, remote from all association (which would be a hard experiment to make), would have some sort of speech to express his ideas. And it is not credible that Nature has denied us this resource that she has given to many other animals . . . But it is yet to be known what language this child would speak; and what has been said about it by conjecture has not much appearance of truth.'

Beyond the cases of such experiments, there were also the cases of accidental isolation – children lost in the woods, sailors marooned on islands, children brought up by wolves – as well as the cases of cruel and sadistic parents who locked up their children, chained them to beds, beat them in closets, tortured them for no other reason than the compulsions of their own madness – and Quinn had read through the extensive literature devoted to these stories. There was the Scottish sailor Alexander Selkirk (thought by some to be the model for Robinson Crusoe) who had lived for four years alone on an island off the coast of Chile and who, according to the ship captain who rescued him in 1708, 'had so much forgot his language for want of use, that we could scarce understand him.' Less than twenty years later, Peter of Hanover, a wild child of about fourteen, who had been discovered mute and naked in a forest outside the German town of Hamelin, was brought to the English court under the special protection of George I. Both Swift and Defoe were given a chance to see him, and the experience led to Defoe's 1726 pamphlet, *Mere Nature Delineated*. Peter never learned to speak, however, and several months later was sent to the country, where he lived to the age of seventy, with no interest in sex, money, or other worldly matters. Then there was the case of Victor, the wild boy of Aveyron, who was found in 1800. Under the patient and meticulous care of Dr Itard, Victor learned some of the rudiments of speech, but he never progressed beyond the level of a small child. Even better known than Victor was Kaspar Hauser, who appeared one afternoon in Nuremberg in 1828, dressed in an outlandish costume and barely able to utter an intelligible sound. He was able to write his name, but in all other respects he behaved like an infant. Adopted by the town and entrusted to the care of a local teacher, he spent his days sitting on the floor playing with toy horses, eating only bread and water. Kaspar nevertheless developed. He became an excellent horseman, became obsessively neat, had a passion for the colours red and white, and by all accounts displayed an extraordinary memory, especially for names and faces. Still, he preferred to remain indoors, shunned bright light and, like Peter of Hanover, never showed any interest in sex or money. As the memory of his past gradually came back to him, he was able to recall how he had spent many years on the floor of a darkened room, fed by a man who never spoke to him or let himself be seen. Not long after these disclosures, Kaspar was murdered by an unknown man with a dagger in a public park.

It had been years now since Quinn had allowed himself to think of these stories. The subject of children was too painful for him, especially children who had suffered, had been mistreated, had died before they could grow up. If Stillman was the man with the dagger, come back to avenge himself on the boy whose life he had destroyed, Quinn wanted to be there to stop him. He knew he could not bring his own son back to life, but at least he could prevent another from dying. It had suddenly become possible for him to do this, and standing there on the street now, the idea of what lay before him loomed up like a terrible dream. He thought of the little coffin that held his son's body and how he had seen it on the day of the funeral being lowered into the ground. That was isolation, he said to himself. That was silence. It did not help, perhaps, that his son's name had also been Peter.

5

At the corner of 72nd Street and Madison Avenue, he waved
down a cab. As the car rattled through the park toward the West
Side, Quinn looked out the window and wondered if these were
the same trees that Peter Stillman saw when he walked out into
the air and the light. He wondered if Peter saw the same things he
did, or whether the world was a different place for him. And if a
tree was not a tree, he wondered what it really was.

After the cab had dropped him off in front of his house, Quinn
realized that he was hungry. He had not eaten since breakfast
early that morning. It was strange, he thought, how quickly time
had passed in the Stillman apartment. If his calculations were
correct, he had been there for more than fourteen hours. Within
himself, however, it felt as though his stay had lasted three or
four hours at most. He shrugged at the discrepancy and said to
himself, 'I must learn to look at my watch more often.'

He retraced his path along 107th Street, turned left on Broadway, and began walking uptown, looking for a suitable place to
eat. A bar did not appeal to him tonight – eating in the dark, the
press of boozy chatter – although normally he might have welcomed it. As he crossed 112th Street, he saw that the Heights
Luncheonette was still open and decided to go in. It was a
brightly lit yet dreary place, with a large rack of girlie magazines
on one wall, an area for stationery supplies, another area for
newspapers, several tables for patrons, and a long Formica
counter with swivel stools. A tall Puerto Rican man in a white
cardboard chef's hat stood behind the counter. It was his job to
make the food, which consisted mainly of gristle-studded hamburger patties, bland sandwiches with pale tomatoes and wilted
lettuce, milkshakes, egg creams, and buns. To his right, ensconced behind the cash register, was the boss, a small balding man

with curly hair and a concentration camp number tattooed on his forearm, lording it over his domain of cigarettes, pipes, and cigars. He sat there impassively, reading the night owl edition of the next morning's *Daily News*.

The place was almost deserted at that hour. At the back table sat two old men in shabby clothes, one very fat and the other very thin, intently studying the racing forms. Two empty coffee cups sat on the table between them. In the foreground, facing the magazine rack, a young student stood with an open magazine in his hands, staring at the picture of a naked woman. Quinn sat down at the counter and ordered a hamburger and a coffee. As the counterman swung into action, he spoke over his shoulder to Quinn.

'Did you see game tonight, man?'

'I missed it. Anything good to report?'

'What do you think?'

For several years Quinn had been having the same conversation with this man, whose name he did not know. Once, when he had been in the luncheonette, they had talked about baseball, and now, each time Quinn came in, they continued to talk about it. In the winter, the talk was of trades, predictions, memories. During the season, it was always the most recent game. They were both Mets fans, and the hopelessness of that passion had created a bond between them.

The counterman shook his head. 'First two times up, Kingman hits solo shots,' he said. 'Boom, boom. Big mothers – all the way to the moon. Jones is pitching good for once and things don't look too bad. It's two to one, bottom of the ninth. Pittsburgh gets men on second and third, one out, so the Mets go to the bullpen for Allen. He walks the next guy to load them up. The Mets bring the corners in for a force at home, or maybe they can get the double play if it's hit up the middle. Peña comes up and chicken-shits a little grounder to first and the fucker goes through Kingman's legs. Two men score, and that's it, bye-bye New York.'

'Dave Kingman is a turd,' said Quinn, biting into his hamburger.

'But watch out for Foster,' said the counterman.

'Foster's washed up. A has-been. A mean-faced bozo.' Quinn chewed his food carefully, feeling with his tongue for stray bits of bone. 'They should ship him back to Cincinnati by express mail.'

'Yeah,' said the counterman. 'But they'll be tough. Better than last year, anyway.'

'I don't know,' said Quinn, taking another bite. 'It looks good on paper, but what do they really have? Stearns is always getting hurt. They have minor leaguers at second and short, and Brooks can't keep his mind on the game. Mookie's good, but he's raw, and they can't even decide who to put in right. There's still Rusty, of course, but he's too fat to run anymore. And as for the pitching, forget it. You and I could go over to Shea tomorrow and get hired as the top two starters.'

'Maybe I make you the manager,' said the counterman. 'You could tell those fuckers where to get off.'

'You bet your bottom dollar,' said Quinn.

After he finished eating, Quinn wandered over to the stationery shelves. A shipment of new notebooks had come in, and the pile was impressive, a beautiful array of blues and greens and reds and yellows. He picked one up and saw that the pages had the narrow lines he preferred. Quinn did all his writing with a pen, using a typewriter only for final drafts, and he was always on the lookout for good spiral notebooks. Now that he had embarked on the Stillman case, he felt that a new notebook was in order. It would be helpful to have a separate place to record his thoughts, his observations, and his questions. In that way, perhaps, things might not get out of control.

He looked through the pile, trying to decide which one to pick. For reasons that were never made clear to him, he suddenly felt an irresistible urge for a particular red notebook at the bottom. He pulled it out and examined it, gingerly fanning the pages with his thumb. He was at a loss to explain to himself why he found it so appealing. It was a standard eight and a half by eleven notebook with one hundred pages. But something about it seemed to call out to him – as if its unique destiny in the world was to hold the words that came from his pen. Almost embarrassed by the intensity of his feelings, Quinn tucked the red notebook under his arm, walked over to the cash register, and bought it.

Back in his apartment a quarter of an hour later, Quinn removed the photograph of Stillman and the cheque from his jacket pocket and placed them carefully on his desk. He cleared the debris from the surface – dead matches, cigarette butts, eddies of ash, spent ink cartridges, a few coins, ticket stubs, doodles, a dirty handkerchief – and put the red notebook in the centre. Then he drew the shades in the room, took off all his clothes, and sat down at the desk. He had never done this before, but it somehow seemed appropriate to be naked at this moment. He sat there for twenty or thirty seconds, trying not to move, trying not to do anything but breathe. Then he opened the red notebook. He picked up his pen and wrote his initials, DQ (for Daniel Quinn), on the first page. It was the first time in more than five years that he had put his own name in one of his notebooks. He stopped to consider this fact for a moment but then dismissed it as irrelevant. He turned the page. For several moments he studied its blankness, wondering if he was not a bloody fool. Then he pressed his pen against the top line and made the first entry in the red notebook.

Stillman's face. Or: Stillman's face as it was twenty years ago. Impossible to know whether the face tomorrow will resemble it. It is certain, however, that this is not the face of a madman. Or is this not a legitimate statement? To my eyes, at least, it seems benign, if not downright pleasant. A hint of tenderness around the mouth even. More than likely blue eyes, with a tendency to water. Thin hair even then, so perhaps gone now, and what remains gray, or even white. He bears an odd familiarity: the meditative type, no doubt high-strung, someone who might stutter, fight with himself to stem the flood of words rushing from his mouth.

Little Peter. Is it necessary for me to imagine it, or can I accept it on faith? The darkness. To think of myself in that room, screaming. I am reluctant. Nor do I think I even want to understand it. To what end? This is not a story, after all. It is a fact, something happening in the world, and I am supposed to do a job, one little thing, and I have said yes to it. If all goes well, it should even be quite simple. I have not been hired to understand – merely to act. This is something new. To keep it in mind, at all costs.

And yet, what is it that Dupin says in Poe? 'An identification of the reasoner's intellect with that of his opponent.' But here it would apply to Stillman senior. Which is probably even worse.

As for Virginia, I am in a quandary. Not just the kiss, which might be explained by any number of reasons; not what Peter said about her, which is unimportant. Her marriage? Perhaps. The complete incongruity of it. Could it be that she's in it for the money? Or somehow working in collaboration with Stillman? That would change everything. But, at the same time, it makes no sense. For why would she have hired me? To have a witness to her apparent good intentions? Perhaps. But that seems too complicated. And yet: why do I feel she is not to be trusted?

Stillman's face, again. Thinking for these past few minutes that I have seen it before. Perhaps years ago in the neighbourhood – before the time of his arrest.

To remember what it feels like to wear other people's clothes. To begin with that, I think. Assuming I must. Back in the old days, eighteen, twenty years ago, when I had no money and friends would give me things to wear. J's old overcoat in college, for example. And the strange sense I would have of climbing into his skin. That is probably a start.

And then, most important of all: to remember who I am. To remember who I am supposed to be. I do not think this is a game. On the other hand, nothing is clear. For example: who are you? And if you think you know, why do you keep lying about it? I have no answer. All I can say is this: listen to me. My name is Paul Auster. That is not my real name.

6

Quinn spent the next morning at the Columbia library with Stillman's book. He arrived early, the first one there as the doors opened, and the silence of the marble halls comforted him, as though he had been allowed to enter some crypt of oblivion. After flashing his alumni card at the drowsing attendant behind the desk, he retrieved the book from the stacks, returned to the third floor, and then settled down in a green leather armchair in one of the smoking rooms. The bright May morning lurked outside like a temptation, a call to wander aimlessly in the air, but Quinn fought it off. He turned the chair around, positioning himself with his back to the window, and opened the book.

The Garden and the Tower: Early Visions of the New World was divided into two parts of approximately equal length, 'The Myth of Paradise' and 'The Myth of Babel'. The first concentrated on the discoveries of the explorers, beginning with Columbus and continuing on through Raleigh. It was Stillman's contention that the first men to visit America believed they had accidentally found paradise, a second Garden of Eden. In the narrative of his third voyage, for example, Columbus wrote: 'For I believe that the earthly Paradise lies here, which no one can enter except by God's leave.' As for the people of this land, Peter Martyr would write as early as 1505: 'They seem to live in that golden world of which old writers speak so much, wherein men lived simply and innocently, without enforcement of laws, without quarrelling, judges, or libels, content only to satisfy nature.' Or, as the ever-present Montaigne would write more than half a century later: 'In my opinion, what we actually see in these nations not only surpasses all the pictures which the poets have drawn of the Golden Age, and all their inventions representing the then happy state of mankind, but also the conception and desire of

philosophy itself.' From the very beginning, according to
Stillman, the discovery of the New World was the quickening
impulse of utopian thought, the spark that gave hope to the
perfectibility of human life – from Thomas More's book of 1516 to
Gerónimo de Mendieta's prophecy, some years later, that
America would become an ideal theocratic state, a veritable City
of God.

There was, however, an opposite point of view. If some saw
the Indians as living in prelapsarian innocence, there were others
who judged them to be savage beasts, devils in the form of men.
The discovery of cannibals in the Caribbean did nothing to
assuage this opinion. The Spaniards used it as a justification to
exploit the natives mercilessly for their own mercantile ends. For
if you do not consider the man before you to be human, there are
few restraints of conscience on your behaviour towards him. It
was not until 1537, with the papal bull of Paul III, that the Indians
were declared to be true men possessing souls. The debate
nevertheless went on for several hundred years, culminating on
the one hand in the 'noble savage' of Locke and Rousseau – which
laid the theoretical foundations of democracy in an independent
America – and, on the other hand, in the campaign to exterminate
the Indians, in the undying belief that the only good Indian was a
dead Indian.

The second part of the book began with a new examination of
the fall. Relying heavily on Milton and his account in *Paradise Lost*
– as representing the orthodox Puritan position – Stillman
claimed that it was only after the fall that human life as we know it
came into being. For if there was no evil in the Garden, neither
was there any good. As Milton himself put it in the *Areopagitica*,
'It was out of the rind of one apple tasted that good and evil leapt
forth into the world, like two twins cleaving together.' Stillman's
gloss on this sentence was exceedingly thorough. Alert to the
possibility of puns and word play throughout, he showed how
the word 'taste' was actually a reference to the Latin word
'sapere,' which means both 'to taste' and 'to know' and therefore
contains a subliminal reference to the tree of knowledge: the

source of the apple whose taste brought forth knowledge into the world, which is to say, good and evil. Stillman also dwelled on the paradox of the word 'cleave,' which means both 'to join together' and 'to break apart,' thus embodying two equal and opposite significations, which in turn embodies a view of language that Stillman found to be present in all of Milton's work. In *Paradise Lost*, for example, each key word has two meanings – one before the fall and one after the fall. To illustrate his point, Stillman isolated several of those words – sinister, serpentine, delicious – and showed how their prelapsarian use was free of moral connotations, whereas their use after the fall was shaded, ambiguous, informed by a knowledge of evil. Adam's one task in the Garden had been to invent language, to give each creature and thing its name. In that state of innocence, his tongue had gone straight to the quick of the world. His words had not been merely appended to the things he saw, they had revealed their essences, had literally brought them to life. A thing and its name were interchangeable. After the fall, this was no longer true. Names became detached from things; words devolved into a collection of arbitrary signs; language had been severed from God. The story of the Garden, therefore, not only records the fall of man, but the fall of language.

Later in the Book of Genesis there is another story about language. According to Stillman, the Tower of Babel episode was an exact recapitulation of what happened in the Garden – only expanded, made general in its significance for all mankind. The story takes on special meaning when its placement in the book is considered: chapter eleven of Genesis, verses one through nine. This is the very last incident of prehistory in the Bible. After that, the Old Testament is exclusively a chronicle of the Hebrews. In other words, the Tower of Babel stands as the last image before the true beginning of the world.

Stillman's commentaries went on for many pages. He began with a historical survey of the various exegetical traditions concerning the story, elaborated on the numerous misreadings that had grown up around it, and ended with a lengthy catalogue of

legends from the Aggadah (a compendium of rabbinical interpretations not connected with legal matters). It was generally
accepted, wrote Stillman, that the Tower had been built in the
year 1996 after the creation, a scant three hundred and forty years
after the Flood, 'lest we be scattered abroad upon the face of the
whole earth'. God's punishment came as a response to this
desire, which contradicted a command that had appeared earlier
in Genesis: 'Be fertile and increase, fill the earth and master it.' By
destroying the Tower, therefore, God condemned man to obey
this injunction. Another reading, however, saw the Tower as a
challenge against God. Nimrod, the first ruler of all the world,
was designated as the Tower's architect: Babel was to be a shrine
that symbolized the universality of his power. This was the
Promethean view of the story, and it hinged on the phrases
'whose top may reach unto heaven' and 'let us make a name'. The
building of the Tower became the obsessive, overriding passion
of mankind, more important finally than life itself. Bricks became
more precious than people. Women labourers did not even stop
to give birth to their children; they secured the newborn in their
aprons and went right on working. Apparently, there were three
different groups involved in the construction: those who wanted
to dwell in heaven, those who wanted to wage war against God,
and those who wanted to worship idols. At the same time, they
were united in their efforts – 'And the whole earth was of one
language, and of one speech' – and the latent power of a united
mankind outraged God. 'And the Lord said, Behold, the people
is one, and they have all one language; and this they begin to do:
and now nothing will be restrained from them, which they have
imagined to do.' This speech is a conscious echo of the words God
spoke on expelling Adam and Eve from the Garden: 'Behold, the
man is become one of us, to know good and evil; and now, lest he
put forth his hand, and take also of the tree of life, and eat, and
live forever – Therefore the Lord God sent him forth from the
garden of Eden . . .' Still another reading held that the story was
intended merely as a way of explaining the diversity of peoples
and languages. For if all men were descended from Noah and his

sons, how was it possible to account for the vast differences among cultures? Another, similar reading contended that the story was an explanation of the existence of paganism and idolatry – for until this story all men are presented as being monotheistic in their beliefs. As for the Tower itself, legend had it that one third of the structure sank into the ground, one third was destroyed by fire, and one third was left standing. God attacked it in two ways in order to convince man that the destruction was a divine punishment and not the result of chance. Still, the part left standing was so high that a palm tree seen from the top of it appeared no larger than a grasshopper. It was also said that a person could walk for three days in the shadow of the Tower without ever leaving it. Finally – and Stillman dwelled upon this at great length – whoever looked upon the ruins of the Tower was believed to forget everything he knew.

What all this had to do with the New World Quinn could not say. But then a new chapter started, and suddenly Stillman was discussing the life of Henry Dark, a Boston clergyman who was born in London in 1649 (on the day of Charles I's execution), came to America in 1675, and died in a fire in Cambridge, Massachusetts in 1691.

According to Stillman, as a young man Henry Dark had served as private secretary to John Milton – from 1669 until the poet's death five years later. This was news to Quinn, for he seemed to remember reading somewhere that the blind Milton had dictated his work to one of his daughters. Dark, he learned, was an ardent Puritan, a student of theology, and a devoted follower of Milton's work. Having met his hero one evening at a small gathering, he was invited to pay a call the following week. That led to further calls, until eventually Milton began to entrust Dark with various small tasks: taking dictation, guiding him through the streets of London, reading to him from the works of the ancients. In a 1672 letter written by Dark to his sister in Boston, he mentioned long discussions with Milton on the finer points of Biblical exegesis. Then Milton died, and Dark was disconsolate. Six months later, finding England a desert, a land that offered him nothing, he decided to emigrate to America. He arrived in Boston in the summer of 1675.

Little was known of his first years in the New World. Stillman speculated that he might have travelled westward, foraging out into uncharted territory, but no concrete evidence could be found to support this view. On the other hand, certain references in Dark's writings indicated an intimate knowledge of Indian customs, which led Stillman to theorize that Dark might possibly have lived among one of the tribes for a period of time. Be that as it may, there was no public mention of Dark until 1682, when his name was entered in the Boston marriage registry as having taken one Lucy Fitts as his bride. Two years later, he was listed as heading a small Puritan congregation on the outskirts of the city. Several children were born to the couple, but all them died in infancy. A son John, however, born in 1686, survived. But in 1691 the boy was reported to have fallen accidentally from a second-story window and perished. Just one month later, the entire house went up in flames, and both Dark and his wife were killed.

Henry Dark would have passed into the obscurity of early American life if not for one thing: the publication of a pamphlet in 1690 entitled *The New Babel*. According to Stillman, this little work of sixty-four pages was the most visionary account of the new continent that had been written up to that time. If Dark had not died so soon after its appearance, its effect would no doubt have been greater. For, as it turned out, most of the copies of the pamphlet were destroyed in the fire that killed Dark. Stillman himself had been able to discover only one – and that by accident in the attic of his family's house in Cambridge. After years of diligent research, he had concluded that this was the only copy still in existence.

The New Babel, written in bold, Miltonic prose, presented the case for the building of paradise in America. Unlike the other writers on the subject, Dark did not assume paradise to be a place that could be discovered. There were no maps that could lead a man to it, no instruments of navigation that could guide a man to its shores. Rather, its existence was immanent within man

himself: the idea of a beyond he might someday create in the here
and now. For utopia was nowhere – even, as Dark explained, in
its 'wordhood.' And if man could bring forth this dreamed-of
place, it would only be by building it with his own two hands.

Dark based his conclusions on a reading of the Babel story as a
prophetic work. Drawing heavily on Milton's interpretation of
the fall, he followed his master in placing an inordinate importance on the role of language. But he took the poet's ideas one step
further. If the fall of man also entailed a fall of language, was it not
logical to assume that it would be possible to undo the fall, to
reverse its effects by undoing the fall of language, by striving to
recreate the language that was spoken in Eden? If man could
learn to speak this original language of innocence, did it not
follow that he would thereby recover a state of innocence within
himself? We had only to look at the example of Christ, Dark
argued, to understand that this was so. For was Christ not a man,
a creature of flesh and blood? And did not Christ speak this
prelapsarian language? In Milton's *Paradise Regained*, Satan
speaks with 'double-sense deluding', whereas Christ's 'actions to
his words accord, his words / To his large heart give utterance
due, his heart / Contains of good, wise, just, the perfect shape.'
And had God not 'now sent his living Oracle / Into the World to
teach his final will, / And sends his Spirit of Truth henceforth to
dwell / In pious Hearts, an inward Oracle / To all Truth requisite
for me to know'? And, because of Christ, did the fall not have a
happy outcome, was it not a *felix culpa*, as doctrine instructs?
Therefore, Dark contended, it would indeed be possible for man
to speak the original language of innocence and to recover, whole
and unbroken, the truth within himself.

Turning to the Babel story, Dark then elaborated his plan and
announced his vision of things to come. Quoting from the second
verse of Genesis 11 – 'And it came to pass, as they journeyed from
the east, that they found a plain in the land of Shi-nar; and they
dwelt there' – Dark stated that this passage proved the westward
movement of human life and civilization. For the city of Babel – or
Babylon – was situated in Mesopotamia, far east of the land of the

Hebrews. If Babel lay to the west of anything, it was Eden, the original site of mankind. Man's duty to scatter himself across the whole earth – in response to God's command to 'be fertile . . . and fill the earth' – would inevitably move along a western course. And what more Western land in all Christendom, Dark asked, than America? The movement of English settlers to the New World, therefore, could be read as the fulfilment of the ancient commandment. America was the last step in the process. Once the continent had been filled, the moment would be ripe for a change in the fortunes of mankind. The impediment to the building of Babel – that man must fill the earth – would be eliminated. At that moment it would again be possible for the whole earth to be of one language and one speech. And if that were to happen, paradise could not be far behind.

Just as Babel had been built three hundred and forty years after the Flood, so it would be, Dark predicted, exactly three hundred and forty years after the arrival of the Mayflower at Plymouth that the commandment would be carried out. For surely it was the Puritans, God's newly chosen people, who held the destiny of mankind in their hands. Unlike the Hebrews, who had failed God by refusing to accept his son, these transplanted Englishmen would write the final chapter of history before heaven and earth were joined at last. Like Noah in his ark, they had travelled across the vast oceanic flood to carry out their holy mission.

Three hundred and forty years, according to Dark's calculations, meant that in 1960 the first part of the settlers work would have been done. At that point, the foundations would have been laid for the real work that was to follow: the building of the new Babel. Already, Dark wrote, he saw encouraging signs in the city of Boston, for there, as nowhere else in the world, the chief construction material was brick – which, as set forth in verse three of Genesis 11, was specified as the construction material of Babel. In the year 1960, he stated confidently, the new Babel would begin to go up, its very shape aspiring toward the heavens, a symbol of the resurrection of the human spirit. History would be written in reverse. What had fallen would be raised up; what had been broken would be made whole. Once completed, the Tower would be large enough to hold every inhabitant of the New World. There would be a room for each person, and once he entered that room, he would forget everything he knew. After forty days and forty nights, he would emerge a new man, speaking God's language, prepared to inhabit the second, ever-lasting paradise.

So ended Stillman's synopsis of Henry Dark's pamphlet, dated 20 December 1690, the seventieth anniversary of the landing of the Mayflower.

Quinn let out a little sigh and closed the book. The reading room was empty. He leaned forward, put his head in his hands, and closed his eyes. '1960,' he said aloud. He tried to conjure up an image of Henry Dark, but nothing came to him. In his mind he saw only fire, a blaze of burning books. Then, losing track of his thoughts and where they had been leading him, he suddenly remembered that 1960 was the year that Stillman had locked up his son.

He opened the red notebook and set it squarely on his lap. Just as he was about to write in it, however, he decided that he had had enough. He closed the red notebook, got up from his chair, and returned Stillman's book to the front desk. Lighting a cigarette at the bottom of the stairs, he left the library and walked out into the May afternoon.

7

He made it to Grand Central well in advance. Stillman's train was not due to arrive until six forty-one, but Quinn wanted time to study the geography of the place, to make sure that Stillman would not be able to slip away from him. As he emerged from the subway and entered the great hall, he saw by the clock that it was just past four. Already the station had begun to fill with the rush hour crowd. Making his way through the press of oncoming bodies, Quinn made a tour of the numbered gates, looking for hidden staircases, unmarked exits, dark alcoves. He concluded that a man determined to disappear could do so without much trouble. He would have to hope that Stillman had not been warned that he would be there. If that were the case, and Stillman managed to elude him, it would mean that Virginia Stillman was responsible. There was no one else. It solaced him to know that he had an alternate plan if things went awry. If Stillman did not show up, Quinn would go straight to 69th Street and confront Virginia Stillman with what he knew.

As he wandered through the station, he reminded himself of who he was supposed to be. The effect of being Paul Auster, he had begun to learn, was not altogether unpleasant. Although he still had the same body, the same mind, the same thoughts, he felt as though he had somehow been taken out of himself, as if he no longer had to walk around with the burden of his own consciousness. By a simple trick of the intelligence, a deft little twist of naming, he felt incomparably lighter and freer. At the same time, he knew it was all an illusion. But there was a certain comfort in that. He had not really lost himself; he was merely pretending, and he could return to being Quinn whenever he wished. The fact that there was now a purpose to his being Paul Auster – a purpose that was becoming more and more important to him – served as a kind of moral justification for the charade and absolved him of having to defend his lie. For imagining himself as Auster had become synonymous in his mind with doing good in the world.

He wandered through the station, then, as if inside the body of Paul Auster, waiting for Stillman to appear. He looked up at the vaulted ceiling of the great hall and studied the fresco of constellations. There were light bulbs representing the stars and line drawings of the celestial figures. Quinn had never been able to grasp the connection between the constellations and their names. As a boy he had spent many hours under the night sky trying to tally the clusters of pinprick lights with the shapes of bears, bulls, archers, and water carriers. But nothing had ever come of it, and he had felt stupid, as though there were a blind spot in the centre of his brain. He wondered if the young Auster had been any better at it than he was.

Across the way, occupying the greater part of the station's east wall, was the Kodak display photograph, with its bright, unearthly colors. The scene that month showed a street in some New England fishing village, perhaps Nantucket. A beautiful spring light shone on the cobblestones, flowers of many colors stood in window boxes along the house fronts, and far down at the end of the street was the ocean, with its white waves and blue, blue water. Quinn remembered visiting Nantucket with his wife long ago, in her first month of pregnancy, when his son was no more than a tiny almond in her belly. He found it painful to think of that now, and he tried to suppress the pictures that were forming in his head. 'Look at it through Auster's eyes,' he said to himself, 'and don't think of anything else.' He turned his attention to the photograph again and was relieved to find his thoughts wandering to the subject of whales, to the expeditions that had set out from Nantucket in the last century, to Melville and the opening pages of *Moby Dick*. From there his mind drifted off to the accounts he had read of Melville's last years – the taciturn old man working in the New York customs house, with no readers, forgotten by everyone. Then, suddenly, with great clarity and precision, he saw Bartleby's window and the blank brick wall before him.

Someone tapped him on the arm, and as Quinn wheeled to meet the assault, he saw a short, silent man holding out a green and red ballpoint pen to him. Stapled to the pen was a little white paper flag, one side of which read: 'This good article is the Courtesy of a DEAF MUTE. Pay any price. Thank you for your help.' On the other side of the flag there was a chart of the manual alphabet – LEARN TO SPEAK TO YOUR FRIENDS – that showed the hand positions for each of the twenty-six letters. Quinn reached into his pocket and gave the man a dollar. The deaf mute nodded once very briefly and then moved on, leaving Quinn with the pen in his hand.

It was now past five o'clock. Quinn decided he would be less vulnerable in another spot and removed himself to the waiting room. This was generally a grim place, filled with dust and people with nowhere to go, but now, with the rush hour at full force, it had been taken over by men and women with briefcases, books, and newspapers. Quinn had trouble finding a seat. After searching for two or three minutes, he finally found a place on one of the benches, wedging himself between a man in a blue suit and a plump young woman. The man was reading the sports section of the *Times*, and Quinn glanced over to read the account of the Mets' loss the night before. He had made it to the third or fourth paragraph when the man turned slowly toward him, gave him a vicious stare, and jerked the paper out of view.

After that, a strange thing happened. Quinn turned his attention to the young woman on his right, to see if there was any reading material in that direction. Quinn guessed her age at around twenty. There were several pimples on her left cheek, obscured by a pinkish smear of pancake makeup, and a wad of chewing gum was crackling in her mouth. She was, however, reading a book, a paperback with a lurid cover, and Quinn leaned ever so slightly to his right to catch a glimpse of the title. Against all his expectations, it was a book he himself had written – *Suicide Squeeze* by William Wilson, the first of the Max Work novels.

Quinn had often imagined this situation: the sudden, unexpected pleasure of encountering one of his readers. He had even imagined the conversation that would follow: he, suavely diffident as the stranger praised the book, and then, with great reluctance and modesty, agreeing to autograph the title page, 'since you insist'. But now that the scene was taking place, he felt quite disappointed, even angry. He did not like the girl sitting next to him, and it offended him that she should be casually skimming the pages that had cost him so much effort. His impulse was to tear the book out of her hands and run across the station with it.

He looked at her face again, trying to hear the words she was sounding out in her head, watching her eyes as they darted back and forth across the page. He must have been looking too hard, for a moment later she turned to him with an irritated expression on her face and said, 'You got a problem, mister?'

Quinn smiled weakly. 'No problem,' he said. 'I was just wondering if you liked the book.'

The girl shrugged. 'I've read better and I've read worse.'

Quinn wanted to drop the conversation right there, but something in him persisted. Before he could get up and leave, the words were already out of his mouth. 'Do you find it exciting?'

The girl shrugged again and cracked her gum loudly. 'Sort of. There's a part where the detective gets lost that's kind of scary.'

'Is he a smart detective?'

'Yeah, he's smart. But he talks too much.'

'You'd like more action?'

'I guess so.'

'If you don't like it, why do you go on reading?'

'I don't know.' The girl shrugged once again. 'It passes the time, I guess. Anyway, it's no big deal. It's just a book.'

He was about to tell her who he was, but then he realized that it made no difference. The girl was beyond hope. For five years he had kept William Wilson's identity a secret, and he wasn't about to give it away now, least of all to an imbecile stranger. Still, it was

53

painful, and he struggled desperately to swallow his pride. Rather than punch the girl in the face, he abruptly stood up from his seat and walked away.

At six-thirty he posted himself in front of gate twenty-four. The train was due to arrive on time, and from his vantage in the centre of the doorway, Quinn judged that his chances of seeing Stillman were good. He took out the photograph from his pocket and studied it again, paying special attention to the eyes. He remembered having read somewhere that the eyes were the one feature of the face that never changed. From childhood to old age they remained the same, and a man with the head to see it could theoretically look into the eyes of a boy in a photograph and recognize the same person as an old man. Quinn had his doubts, but this was all he had to go on, his only bridge to the present. Once again, however, Stillman's face told him nothing.

The train pulled into the station, and Quinn felt the noise of it shoot through his body: a random, hectic din that seemed to join with his pulse, pumping his blood in raucous spurts. His head then filled with Peter Stillman's voice, as a barrage of nonsense words clattered against the walls of his skull. He told himself to stay calm. But that did little good. In spite of what he had been expecting of himself at this moment, he was excited.

The train was crowded, and as the passengers started filling the ramp and walking towards him, they quickly became a mob. Quinn flapped the red notebook nervously against his right thigh, stood on his tiptoes, and peered into the throng. Soon the people were surging around him. There were men and women, children and old people, teenagers and babies, rich people and poor people, black men and white women, white men and black women, Orientals and Arabs, men in brown and gray and blue and green, women in red and white and yellow and pink, children in sneakers, children in shoes, children in cowboy boots, fat people and thin people, tall people and short people, each one different from all the others, each one irreducibly himself. Quinn watched them all, anchored to his spot, as if his whole being had

been exiled to his eyes. Each time an elderly man approached, he
braced himself for it to be Stillman. They came and went too
quickly for him to indulge in disappointment, but in each old face
he seemed to find an augur of what the real Stillman would be
like, and he rapidly shifted his expectations with each new face,
as if the accumulation of old men was heralding the imminent
arrival of Stillman himself. For one brief instant Quinn thought,
'So this is what detective work is like.' But other than that he
thought nothing. He watched. Immobile among the moving
crowd, he stood there and watched.

With about half the passengers now gone, Quinn had his first
sight of Stillman. The resemblance to the photograph seemed
unmistakable. No, he had not gone bald, as Quinn had thought
he would. His hair was white, and it lay on his head uncombed,
sticking up here and there in tufts. He was tall, thin, without
question past sixty, somewhat stooped. Inappropriately for the
season, he wore a long, brown overcoat that had gone to seed,
and he shuffled slightly as he walked. The expression on his face
seemed placid, midway between a daze and thoughtfulness. He
did not look at the things around him, nor did they seem to
interest him. He had one piece of luggage, a once beautiful but
now battered leather suitcase with a strap around it. Once or
twice as he walked up the ramp he put the suitcase down and
rested for a moment. He seemed to be moving with effort, a bit
thrown by the crowd, uncertain whether to keep up with it or to
let the others pass him by.

Quinn backed off several feet, positioning himself for a quick
move to the left or right, depending on what happened. At the
same time, he wanted to be far enough away so that Stillman
would not feel he was being followed.

As Stillman reached the threshold of the station, he put his bag
down once again and paused. At that moment Quinn allowed
himself a glance to Stillman's right, surveying the rest of the
crowd to be doubly sure he had made no mistakes. What happened then defied explanation. Directly behind Stillman,
heaving into view just inches behind his right shoulder, another

man stopped, took a lighter out of his pocket, and lit a cigarette. His face was the exact twin of Stillman's. For a second Quinn thought it was an illusion, a kind of aura thrown off by the electromagnetic currents in Stillman's body. But no, this other Stillman moved, breathed, blinked his eyes; his actions were clearly independent of the first Stillman. The second Stillman had a prosperous air about him. He was dressed in an expensive blue suit; his shoes were shined; his white hair was combed; and in his eyes there was the shrewd look of a man of the world. He, too, was carrying a single bag: an elegant black suitcase, about the same size as the other Stillman's.

Quinn froze. There was nothing he could do now that would not be a mistake. Whatever choice he made – and he had to make a choice – would be arbitrary, a submission to chance. Uncertainty would haunt him to the end. At that moment, the two Stillmans started on their way again. The first turned right, the second turned left. Quinn craved an amoeba's body, wanting to cut himself in half and run off in two directions at once. 'Do something,' he said to himself, 'do something now, you idiot.'

For no reason, he went to his left, in pursuit of the second Stillman. After nine or ten paces, he stopped. Something told him he would live to regret what he was doing. He was acting out of spite, spurred on to punish the second Stillman for confusing him. He turned around and saw the first Stillman shuffling off in the other direction. Surely this was his man. This shabby creature, so broken down and disconnected from his surroundings – surely this was the mad Stillman. Quinn breathed deeply, exhaled with a trembling chest, and breathed in again. There was no way to know: not this, not anything. He went after the first Stillman, slowing his pace to match the old man's, and followed him to the subway.

It was nearly seven o'clock now, and the crowds had begun to thin out. Although Stillman seemed to be in a fog, he nevertheless knew where he was going. The professor went straight for the subway staircase, paid his money at the token booth below, and waited calmly on the platform for the Times Square Shuttle.

Quinn began to lose his fear of being noticed. He had never seen anyone so lost in his own thoughts. Even if he stood directly in front of him, he doubted that Stillman would be able to see him.

They travelled to the West Side on the shuttle, walked through the dank corridors of the 42nd Street station, and went down another set of stairs to the IRT trains. Seven or eight minutes later they boarded the Broadway express, careened uptown for two long stops, and got off at 96th Street. Slowly making their way up the final staircase, with several pauses as Stillman set down his bag and caught his breath, they surfaced on the corner and entered the indigo evening. Stillman did not hesitate. Without stopping to get his bearings, he began walking up Broadway along the east side of the street. For several minutes Quinn toyed with the irrational conviction that Stillman was walking toward his house on 107th Street. But before he could indulge himself in a full-blown panic, Stillman stopped at the corner of 99th Street, waited for the light to change from red to green, and crossed over to the other side of Broadway. Halfway up the block there was a small fleabag for down-and-outs, the Hotel Harmony. Quinn had passed it many times before, and he was familiar with the winos and vagabonds who hung around the place. It surprised him to see Stillman open the front door and enter the lobby. Somehow he had assumed the old man would have found more comfortable lodgings. But as Quinn stood outside the glass-panelled door and saw the professor walk up to the desk, write what was undoubtedly his name in the guest book, pick up his bag and disappear into the elevator, he realized that this was where Stillman meant to stay.

Quinn waited outside for the next two hours, pacing up and down the block, thinking that Stillman would perhaps emerge to look for dinner in one of the local coffee shops. But the old man did not appear, and at last Quinn decided he must have gone to sleep. He put in a call to Virginia Stillman from a pay booth on the corner, gave her a full report of what had happened, and then headed home to 107th Street.

8

The next morning, and for many mornings to follow, Quinn
posted himself on a bench in the middle of the traffic island at
Broadway and 99th Street. He would arrive early, never later
than seven o'clock, and sit there with a take-out coffee, a buttered
roll, and an open newspaper on his lap, watching the glass door
of the hotel. By eight o'clock Stillman would come out, always in
his long brown overcoat, carrying a large, old-fashioned carpet
bag. For two weeks this routine did not vary. The old man would
wander through the streets of the neighbourhood, advancing
slowly, sometimes by the merest of increments, pausing, moving
on again, pausing once more, as though each step had to be
weighed and measured before it could take its place among the
sum total of steps. Moving in this manner was difficult for Quinn.
He was used to walking briskly, and all this starting and stopping
and shuffling began to be a strain, as though the rhythm of his
body was being disrupted. He was the hare in pursuit of the
tortoise, and again and again he had to remind himself to hold
back.

What Stillman did on these walks remained something of a
mystery to Quinn. He could, of course, see with his own eyes
what happened, and all these things he dutifully recorded in his
red notebook. But the meaning of these things continued to elude
him. Stillman never seemed to be going anywhere in particular,
nor did he seem to know where he was. And yet, as if by
conscious design, he kept to a narrowly circumscribed area,
bounded on the north by 110th Street, on the south by 72nd
Street, on the west by Riverside Park, and on the east by
Amsterdam Avenue. No matter how haphazard his journeys
seemed to be – and each day his itinerary was different – Stillman
never crossed these borders. Such precision baffled Quinn, for in

all other respects Stillman seemed to be aimless.

As he walked, Stillman did not look up. His eyes were permanently fixed on the pavement, as though he were searching for something. Indeed, every now and then he would stoop down, pick some object off the ground, and examine it closely, turning it over and over in his hand. It made Quinn think of an archaeologist inspecting a shard at some prehistoric ruin. Occasionally, after poring over an object in this way, Stillman would toss it back onto the sidewalk. But more often than not he would open his bag and lay the object gently inside it. Then, reaching into one of his coat pockets, he would remove a red notebook – similar to Quinn's but smaller – and write in it with great concentration for a minute or two. Having completed this operation, he would return the notebook to his pocket, pick up his bag, and continue on his way.

As far as Quinn could tell, the objects Stillman collected were valueless. They seemed to be no more than broken things, discarded things, stray bits of junk. Over the days that passed, Quinn noted a collapsible umbrella shorn of its material, the severed head of a rubber doll, a black glove, the bottom of a shattered light bulb, several pieces of printed matter (soggy magazines, shredded newspapers), a torn photograph, anonymous machinery parts, and sundry other clumps of flotsam he could not identify. The fact that Stillman took this scavenging seriously intrigued Quinn, but he could do no more than observe, write down what he saw in the red notebook, hover stupidly on the surface of things. At the same time, it pleased him to know that Stillman also had a red notebook, as if this formed a secret link between them. Quinn suspected that Stillman's red notebook contained answers to the questions that had been accumulating in his mind, and he began to plot various stratagems for stealing it from the old man. But the time had not yet come for such a step.

Other than picking up objects from the street, Stillman seemed to do nothing. Every now and then he would stop somewhere for a meal. Occasionally he would bump into someone and mumble an apology. Once a car nearly ran over him as he was crossing the street. Stillman did not talk to anyone, did not go into any stores, did not smile. He seemed neither happy nor sad. Twice, when his scavenging haul had been unusually large, he returned to the hotel in the middle of the day and then re-emerged a few minutes later with an empty bag. On most days he spent at least several hours in Riverside Park, walking methodically along the mac-adam footpaths or else thrashing through the bushes with a stick. His quest for objects did not abate amidst the greenery. Stones, leaves, and twigs all found their way into his bag. Once, Quinn observed, he even stooped down for a dried dog turd, sniffed it carefully, and kept it. It was in the park, too, that Stillman rested. In the afternoon, often following his lunch, he would sit on a bench and gaze out across the Hudson. Once, on a particularly warm day, Quinn saw him sprawled out on the grass asleep. When darkness came, Stillman would eat dinner at the Apollo Coffee Shop on 97th Street and Broadway and then return to his hotel for the night. Not once did he try to contact his son. This was confirmed by Virginia Stillman, whom Quinn called each night after returning home.

The essential thing was to stay involved. Little by little, Quinn began to feel cut off from his original intentions, and he won-dered now if he had not embarked on a meaningless project. It was possible, of course, that Stillman was merely biding his time, lulling the world into lethargy before striking. But that would assume he was aware of being watched, and Quinn felt that was unlikely. He had done his job well so far, keeping at a discrete distance from the old man, blending into the traffic of the street, neither calling attention to himself nor taking drastic measures to keep himself hidden. On the other hand, it was possible that Stillman had known all along that he would be watched – had even known it in advance – and therefore had not taken the trouble to discover who the particular watcher was. If being followed was a certainty, what did it matter? A watcher, once discovered, could always be replaced by another.

This view of the situation comforted Quinn, and he decided to believe in it, even though he had no grounds for belief. Either Stillman knew what he was doing or he didn't. And if he didn't, then Quinn was going nowhere, was wasting his time. How much better it was to believe that all his steps were actually to some purpose. If this interpretation required knowledge on Stillman's part, then Quinn would accept this knowledge as an article of faith, at least for the time being.

There remained the problem of how to occupy his thoughts as he followed the old man. Quinn was used to wandering. His excursions through the city had taught him to understand the connectedness of inner and outer. Using aimless motion as a technique of reversal, on his best days he could bring the outside in and thus usurp the sovereignty of inwardness. By flooding himself with externals, by drowning himself out of himself, he had managed to exert some small degree of control over his fits of despair. Wandering, therefore, was a kind of mindlessness. But following Stillman was not wandering. Stillman could wander, he could stagger like a blindman from one spot to another, but this was a privilege denied to Quinn. For he was obliged now to concentrate on what he was doing, even if it was next to nothing. Time and again his thoughts would begin to drift, and soon thereafter his steps would follow suit. This meant that he was constantly in danger of quickening his pace and crashing into Stillman from behind. To guard against this mishap he devised several different methods of deceleration. This first was to tell himself that he was no longer Daniel Quinn. He was Paul Auster now, and with each step he took he tried to fit more comfortably into the strictures of that transformation. Auster was no more than a name to him, a husk without content. To be Auster meant being a man with no interior, a man with no thoughts. And if there were no thoughts available to him, if his own inner life had been made inaccessible, then there was no place for him to retreat to. As Auster he could not summon up any memories or fears, any dreams or joys, for all these things, as they pertained to Auster, were a blank to him. He consequently had to remain solely on his own surface, looking outward for sustenance. To keep his eyes fixed on Stillman, therefore, was not merely a distraction from the train of his thoughts, it was the only thought he allowed himself to have.

For a day or two this tactic was mildly successful, but eventually even Auster began to droop from the monotony. Quinn realized that he needed something more to keep himself occupied, some little task to accompany him as he went about his work. In the end, it was the red notebook that offered him salvation. Instead of merely jotting down a few casual comments, as he had done the first few days, he decided to record every detail about Stillman he possibly could. Using the pen he had bought from the deaf mute, he set about his task with diligence. Not only did he take note of Stillman's gestures, describe each object he selected or rejected for his bag, and keep an accurate timetable for all events, but he also set down with meticulous care an exact itinerary of Stillman's divagations, noting each street he followed, each turn he made, and each pause that occurred. In addition to keeping him busy, the red notebook slowed Quinn's pace. There was no danger now of overtaking Stillman. The problem, rather, was to keep up with him, to make sure he did not vanish. For walking and writing were not easily compatible activities. If for the past five years Quinn had spent his days doing the one and the other, now he was trying to do them both at the same time. In the beginning he made many mistakes. It was especially difficult to write without looking at the page, and he often discovered that he had written two or even three lines on top of each other, producing a jumbled, illegible palimpsest. To look at the page, however, meant stopping, and this would increase his chances of losing Stillman. After a time, he decided that it was basically a questions of position. He experimented with the notebook in front of him at a forty-five degree angle, but he found his left wrist soon tired. After that, he tried keeping the notebook directly in front of his face, eyes peering over it like some Kilroy come to life, but this proved impractical. Next, he tried propping the notebook on his right arm several inches above his elbow and supporting the back of the notebook with his left palm. But this cramped his writing hand and made writing on the bottom half of the page impossible. Finally, he decided to rest the notebook on his left hip, much as an artist holds his palette. This was an improvement. The carrying no longer caused a strain, and his right hand could hold the pen unencumbered by other duties. Although this method also had its drawbacks, it seemed to be the most comfortable arrangement over the long haul. For Quinn was now able to divide his attention almost equally between Stillman and his writing, glancing now up at the one, now down at the other, seeing the thing and writing about it in the same fluid gesture. With the deaf mute's pen in his right hand and the red notebook on his left hip, Quinn went on following Stillman for another nine days.

His nightly conversations with Virginia Stillman were brief. Although the memory of the kiss was still sharp in Quinn's mind, there had been no further romantic developments. At first, Quinn had expected something to happen. After such a promising start, he felt certain that he would eventually find Mrs Stillman in his arms. But his employer had rapidly retreated behind the mask of business and not once had referred to that isolated moment of passion. Perhaps Quinn had been misguided in his hopes, momentarily confusing himself with Max Work, a man who never failed to profit from such situations. Or perhaps it was simply that Quinn was beginning to feel his loneliness more keenly. It had been a long time since a warm body had been beside him. For the fact was, he had started lusting after Virginia Stillman the moment he saw her, well before the kiss took place. Nor did her current lack of encouragement prevent him from continuing to imagine her naked. Lascivious pictures marched through Quinn's head each night, and although the chances of their becoming real seemed remote, they remained a pleasant diversion. Much later, long after it was too late, he realized that deep inside he had been nurturing the chivalric hope of solving the case so brilliantly, of removing Peter Stillman from danger so swiftly and irrevocably, that he would win Mrs Stillman's desire for as long as he wanted it. That, of course, was a mistake. But of all the mistakes Quinn made from beginning to end, it was no worse than any other.

It was the thirteenth day since the case had begun. Quinn returned home that evening out of sorts. He was discouraged, ready to abandon ship. In spite of the games he had been playing with himself, in spite of the stories he had made up to keep himself going, there seemed to be no substance to the case. Stillman was a crazy old man who had forgotten his son. He could be followed to the end of time, and still nothing would happen. Quinn picked up the phone and dialled the Stillman apartment.

'I'm about ready to pack it in,' he said to Virginia Stillman. 'From all I've seen, there's no threat to Peter.'

'That's just what he wants us to think,' the woman answered. 'You have no idea how clever he is. And how patient.'

'He might be patient, but I'm not. I think you're wasting your money. And I'm wasting my time.'

'Are you sure he hasn't seen you? That could make all the difference.'

'I wouldn't stake my life on it, but yes, I'm sure.'

'What are you saying, then?'

'I'm saying you have nothing to worry about. At least for now. If anything happens later, contact me. I'll come running at the first sign of trouble.'

After a pause Virginia Stillman said, 'You could be right.' Then, after another pause, 'But just to reassure me a little, I wonder if we could compromise.'

'It depends on what you have in mind.'

'Just this. Give it a few more days. To make absolutely certain.'

'On one condition,' said Quinn. 'You've got to let me do it in my own way. No more restraints. I have to be free to talk to him, to question him, to get to the bottom of it once and for all.'

'Wouldn't that be risky?'

'You don't have to worry. I'm not going to tip our hand. He won't even guess who I am or what I'm up to.'

'How will you manage that?'

'That's my problem. I have all kinds of tricks up my sleeve. You just have to trust me.'

'All right, I'll go along. I don't suppose it will hurt.'

'Good. I'll give it a few more days, and then we'll see where we stand.'

'Mr Auster?'

'Yes?'

'I'm terribly grateful. Peter has been in such good shape these past two weeks, and I know it's because of you. He talks about you all the time. You're like . . . I don't know . . . a hero to him.'

'And how does Mrs Stillman feel?'

'She feels much the same way.'

'That's good to hear. Maybe someday she'll allow me to feel grateful to her.'

'Anything is possible, Mr Auster. You should remember that.'

'I will. I'd be a fool not to.'

Quinn made a light supper of scrambled eggs and toast, drank a bottle of beer, and then settled down at his desk with the red notebook. He had been writing in it now for many days, filling page after page with his erratic, jostled hand, but he had not yet had the heart to read over what he had written. Now that the end at last seemed in sight, he thought he might hazard a look.

Much of it was hard going, especially in the early parts. And when he did manage to decipher the words, it did not seem to have been worth the trouble. 'Picks up pencil in middle of block. Examines, hesitates, puts in bag . . . Buys sandwich in deli . . . Sits on bench in park and reads through red notebook.' These sentences seemed utterly worthless to him.

It was all a question of method. If the object was to understand Stillman, to get to know him well enough to be able to anticipate what he would do next, Quinn had failed. He had started with a limited set of facts: Stillman's background and profession, the imprisonment of his son, his arrest and hospitalization, a book of bizarre scholarship written while he was supposedly still sane,

HUDSON RIVER

RIVERSIDE PARK

RIVERSIDE DRIVE

WEST END AVENUE

✕ Hotel

BROADWAY

AMSTERDAM AVENUE

and above all Virginia Stillman's certainty that he would now try to harm his son. But the facts of the past seemed to have no bearing on the facts of the present. Quinn was deeply disillusioned. He had always imagined that the key to good detective work was a close observation of details. The more accurate the scrutiny, the more successful the results. The implication was that human behaviour could be understood, that beneath the infinite façade of gestures, tics, and silences, there was finally a coherence, an order, a source of motivation. But after struggling to take in all these surface effects, Quinn felt no closer to Stillman than when he first started following him. He had lived Stillman's life, walked at his pace, seen what he had seen, and the only thing he felt now was the man's impenetrability. Instead of narrowing the distance that lay between him and Stillman, he had seen the old man slip away from him, even as he remained before his eyes.

For no particular reason that he was aware of, Quinn turned to a clean page of the red notebook and sketched a little map of the area Stillman had wandered in.

Then, looking carefully through his notes, he began to trace with his pen the movements Stillman had made on a single day – the first day he had kept a full record of the old man's wanderings. The result was as follows:

Quinn was struck by the way Stillman had skirted around the edge of the territory, not once venturing into the centre. The diagram looked a little like a map of some imaginary state in the Midwest. Except for the eleven blocks up Broadway at the start, and the series of curlicues that represented Stillman's meanderings in Riverside Park, the picture also resembled a rectangle. On the other hand, given the quadrant structure of New York streets, it might also have been a zero or the letter 'O'.

Quinn went on to the next day and decided to see what would happen. The results were not at all the same.

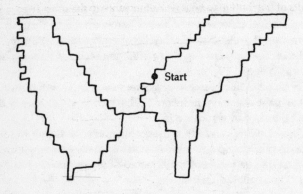

This picture made Quinn think of a bird, a bird of prey perhaps, with its wings spread, hovering aloft in the air. A moment later, this reading seemed far-fetched to him. The bird vanished, and in its stead there were only two abstract shapes, linked by the tiny bridge Stillman had formed by walking west on 83rd Street. Quinn paused for a moment to ponder what he was doing. Was he scribbling nonsense? Was he feeble-mindedly frittering away the evening, or was he trying to find something? Either response, he realized, was unacceptable. If he was simply killing time, why had he chosen such a painstaking way to do it? Was he so muddled that he no longer had the courage to think? On the other hand, if he was not merely diverting himself, what was he actually up to? It seemed to him that he was looking for a sign. He was ransacking the chaos of Stillman's movements for some glimmer of cogency. This implied only one thing: that he continued to disbelieve the arbitrariness of Stillman's actions. He wanted there to be a sense to them, no matter how obscure. This, in itself, was unacceptable. For it meant that Quinn was allowing himself to deny the facts, and this, as he well knew, was the worst thing a detective could do.

Nevertheless, he decided to go on with it. It was not late, not even eleven o'clock yet, and the truth was that it could do no harm. The results of the third map bore no resemblance to the other two.

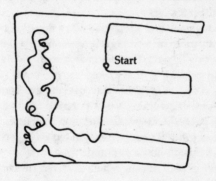

There no longer seemed to be a question about what was happening. If he discounted the squiggles from the park, Quinn felt certain that he was looking at the letter 'E'. Assuming the first diagram had in fact represented the letter 'O,' then it seemed legitimate to assume that the bird wing of the second formed the letter 'W'. Of course, the letters O-W-E spelled a word, but Quinn was not ready to draw any conclusions. He had not begun his inventory until the fifth day of Stillman's travels, and the identities of the first four letters were anyone's guess. He regretted not having started sooner, knowing now that the mystery of those four days was irretrievable. But perhaps he would be able to make up for the past by plunging forward. By coming to the end, perhaps he could intuit the beginning.

The next day's diagram seemed to yield a shape that resembled the letter 'R'. As with the others, it was complicated by numerous irregularities, approximations, and ornate embellishments in the park. Still clinging to a semblance of objectivity, Quinn tried to look at it as if he had not been anticipating a letter of the alphabet. He had to admit that nothing was sure: it could well have been meaningless. Perhaps he was looking for pictures in the clouds, as he had done as a small boy. And yet, the coincidence was too striking. If one map had resembled a letter, perhaps even two, he might have dismissed it as a quirk of chance. But four in a row was stretching it too far.

The next day gave him a lopsided 'O', a doughnut crushed on one side with three or four jagged lines sticking out the other. Then came a tidy 'F', with the customary rococo swirls to the side. After that there was a 'B' that looked like two boxes haphazardly placed on top of one another, with packing excelsior brimming over the edges. Next there was a tottering 'A' that somewhat resembled a ladder, with graded steps on each side. And finally there was a second 'B': precariously tilted on a perverse single point, like an upside-down pyramid.

Quinn then copied out the letters in order: OWEROFBAB. After fiddling with them for a quarter of an hour, switching them around, pulling them apart, rearranging the sequence, he returned to the original order and wrote them out in the following manner: OWER OF BAB. The solution seemed so grotesque that his nerve almost failed him. Making all due allowances for the fact that he had missed the first four days and that Stillman had not yet finished, the answer seemed inescapable: THE TOWER OF BABEL.

Quinn's thoughts momentarily flew off to the concluding pages of *A. Gordon Pym* and to the discovery of the strange hieroglyphs on the inner wall of the chasm – letters inscribed into the earth itself, as though they were trying to say something that could no longer be understood. But on second thought this did not seem apt. For Stillman had not left his message anywhere. True, he had created the letters by the movement of his steps, but they had not been written down. It was like drawing a picture in the air with your finger. The image vanishes as you are making it. There is no result, no trace to mark what you have done.

And yet, the pictures did exist – not in the streets where they had been drawn, but in Quinn's red notebook. He wondered if Stillman had sat down each night in his room and plotted his course for the following day or whether he had improvised as he had gone along. It was impossible to know. He also wondered what purpose this writing served in Stillman's mind. Was it merely some sort of note to himself, or was it intended as a message to others? At the very least, Quinn concluded, it meant that Stillman had not forgotten Henry Dark.

Quinn did not want to panic. In an effort to restrain himself, he tried to imagine things in the worst possible light. By seeing the worst, perhaps it would not be as bad as he thought. He broke it down as follows. First: Stillman was indeed plotting something against Peter. Response: that had been the premise in any case. Second: Stillman had known he would be followed, had known his movements would be recorded, had known his message would be deciphered. Response: that did not change the essential fact – that Peter had to be protected. Third: Stillman was far more dangerous than previously imagined. Response: that did not mean he could get away with it.

This helped somewhat. But the letters continued to horrify Quinn. The whole thing was so oblique, so fiendish in its circum-locutions, that he did not want to accept it. Then doubts came, as if on command, filling his head with mocking, sing-song voices. He had imagined the whole thing. The letters were not letters at all. He had seen them only because he had wanted to see them. And even if the diagrams did form letters, it was only a fluke. Stillman had nothing to do with it. It was all an accident, a hoax he had perpetrated on himself.

He decided to go to bed, slept fitfully, woke up, wrote in the red notebook for half an hour, went back to bed. His last thought before he went to sleep was that he probably had two more days, since Stillman had not yet completed his message. The last two letters remained – the 'E' and the 'L'. Quinn's mind dispersed. He arrived in a neverland of fragments, a place of wordless things and thingless words. Then, struggling through his torpor one last time, he told himself that El was the ancient Hebrew for God.

In his dream, which he later forgot, he found himself in the town dump of his childhood, sifting through a mountain of rubbish.

9

The first meeting with Stillman took place in Riverside Park. It was mid-afternoon, a Saturday of bicycles, dog-walkers, and children. Stillman was sitting alone on a bench, staring out at nothing in particular, the little red notebook on his lap. There was light everywhere, an immense light that seemed to radiate outward from each thing the eye caught hold of, and overhead, in the branches of the trees, a breeze continued to blow, shaking the leaves with a passionate hissing, a rising and falling that breathed on as steadily as surf.

Quinn had planned his moves carefully. Pretending not to notice Stillman, he sat down on the bench beside him, folded his arms across his chest, and stared out in the same direction as the old man. Neither of them spoke. By his later calculations, Quinn estimated that this went on for fifteen or twenty minutes. Then, without warning, he turned his head toward the old man and looked at him point blank, stubbornly fixing his eyes on the wrinkled profile. Quinn concentrated all his strength in his eyes, as if they could begin to burn a hole in Stillman's skull. This stare went on for five minutes.

At last Stillman turned to him. In a surprisingly gentle tenor voice he said, 'I'm sorry, but it won't be possible for me to talk to you.'

'I haven't said anything,' said Quinn.

'That's true,' said Stillman. 'But you must understand that I'm not in the habit of talking to strangers.'

'I repeat,' said Quinn, 'that I haven't said anything.'

'Yes, I heard you the first time. But aren't you interested in knowing why?'

'I'm afraid not.'

'Well put. I can see you're a man of sense.'

Quinn shrugged, refusing to respond. His whole being now exuded indifference.

Stillman smiled brightly at this, leaned toward Quinn, and said in a conspiratorial voice, 'I think we're going to get along.'

'That remains to be seen,' said Quinn after a long pause.

Stillman laughed – a brief, booming 'haw' – and then continued. 'It's not that I dislike strangers *per se*. It's just that I prefer not to speak to anyone who does not introduce himself. In order to begin, I must have a name.'

'But once a man gives you his name, he's no longer a stranger.'

'Exactly. That's why I never talk to strangers.'

Quinn had been prepared for this and knew how to answer. He was not going to let himself be caught. Since he was technically Paul Auster, that was the name he had to protect. Anything else, even the truth, would be an invention, a mask to hide behind and keep him safe.

'In that case,' he said, 'I'm happy to oblige you. My name is Quinn.'

'Ah,' said Stillman reflectively, nodding his head. 'Quinn.'

'Yes, Quinn. Q-U-I-N-N.'

'I see. Yes, yes, I see. Quinn. Hmmm. Yes. Very interesting. Quinn. A most resonant word. Rhymes with twin, does it not?'

'That's right. Twin.'

'And sin, too, if I'm not mistaken.'

'You're not.'

'And also in – one n – or inn – two. Isn't that so?'

'Exactly.'

'Hmmm. Very interesting. I see many possibilities for this word, this Quinn, this . . . quintessence . . . of quiddity. Quick, for example. And quill. And quack. And quirk. Hmmm. Rhymes with grin. Not to speak of kin. Hmmm. Very interesting. And win. And fin. And din. And gin. And pin. And tin. And bin. Even rhymes with djinn. Hmmm. And if you say it right, with been. Hmmm. Yes, very interesting. I like your name enormously, Mr Quinn. It flies off in so many little directions at once.'

'Yes, I've often noticed that myself.'

'Most people don't pay attention to such things. They think of words as stones, as great unmoveable objects with no life, as monads that never change.'

'Stones can change. They can be worn away by wind or water. They can erode. They can be crushed. You can turn them into shards, or gravel, or dust.'

'Exactly. I could tell you were a man of sense right away, Mr Quinn. If you only knew how many people have misunderstood me. My work has suffered because of it. Suffered terribly.'

'Your work?'

'Yes, my work. My projects, my investigations, my experiments.'

'Ah.'

'Yes. But in spite of all the setbacks, I have never really been daunted. At present, for example, I am engaged in one of the most important things I have ever done. If all goes well, I believe I will hold the key to a series of major discoveries.'

'The key?'

'Yes, the key. A thing that opens locked doors.'

'Ah.'

'Of course, for the time being I'm merely collecting data, gathering evidence so to speak. Then I will have to coordinate my findings. It's highly demanding work. You wouldn't believe how hard – especially for a man of my age.'

'I can imagine.'

'That's right. There's so much to do, and so little time to do it. Every morning I get up at dawn. I have to be outside in all kinds of weather, constantly on the move, forever on my feet, going from one place to the next. It wears me out, you can be sure of that.'

'But it's worth it.'

'Anything for the truth. No sacrifice is too great.'

'Indeed.'

'You see, no one has understood what I have understood. I'm the first. I'm the only one. It puts a great burden of responsibility on me.'

'The world on your shoulders.'

'Yes, so to speak. The world, or what is left of it.'

'I hadn't realized it was as bad as that.'

'It's that bad. Maybe even worse.'

'Ah.'

'You see, the world is in fragments, sir. And it's my job to put it back together again.'

'You've taken on quite a bit.'

'I realize that. But I'm merely looking for the principle. That's well within the scope of one man. If I can lay the foundation, other hands can do the work of restoration itself. The important thing is the premise, the theoretical first step. Unfortunately, there is no one else who can do this.'

'Have you made much progress?'

'Enormous strides. In fact, I feel now that I'm on the verge of a significant breakthrough.'

'I'm reassured to hear it.'

'It's a comforting thought, yes. And it's all because of my cleverness, the dazzling clarity of my mind.'

'I don't doubt it.'

'You see, I've understood the need to limit myself. To work within a terrain small enough to make all results conclusive.'

'The premise of the premise, so to speak.'

'That's it, exactly. The principle of the principle, the method of operation. You see, the world is in fragments, sir. Not only have we lost our sense of purpose, we have lost the language whereby we can speak of it. These are no doubt spiritual matters, but they have their analogue in the material world. My brilliant stroke has been to confine myself to physical things, to the immediate and tangible. My motives are lofty, but my work now takes place in the realm of the everyday. That's why I'm so often misunderstood. But no matter. I've learned to shrug these things off.'

'An admirable response.'

'The only response. The only one worthy of a man of my stature. You see, I am in the process of inventing a new language. With work such as that to do, I can't be bothered by the stupidity of others. In any case, it's all part of the disease I'm trying to cure.'

'A new language?'

'Yes. A language that will at last say what we have to say. For our words no longer correspond to the world. When things were whole, we felt confident that our words could express them. But little by little these things have broken apart, shattered, collapsed into chaos. And yet our words have remained the same. They have not adapted themselves to the new reality. Hence, every time we try to speak of what we see, we speak falsely, distorting the very thing we are trying to represent. It's made a mess of everything. But words, as you yourself understand, are capable of change. The problem is how to demonstrate this. That is why I now work with the simplest means possible – so simple that even a child can grasp what I am saying. Consider a word that refers to a thing – "umbrella", for example. When I say the word "umbrella", you see the object in your mind. You see a kind of stick, with collapsible metal spokes on top that form an armature for a waterproof material which, when opened, will protect you from the rain. This last detail is important. Not only is an umbrella a thing, it is a thing that performs a function – in other words, expresses the will of man. When you stop to think of it, every object is similar to the umbrella, in that it serves a function. A pencil is for writing, a shoe is for wearing, a car is for driving. Now, my question is this. What happens when a thing no longer performs its function? Is it still the thing, or has it become something else? When you rip the cloth off the umbrella, is the umbrella still an umbrella? You open the spokes, put them over your head, walk out into the rain, and you get drenched. Is it possible to go on calling this object an umbrella? In general, people do. At the very limit, they will say the umbrella is broken. To me this is a serious error, the source of all our troubles. Because it can no longer perform its function, the umbrella has ceased to be an umbrella. It might resemble an umbrella, it might once have been an umbrella, but now it has changed into something else. The word, however, has remained the same. Therefore, it can no longer express the thing. It is imprecise; it is false; it hides the thing it is supposed to reveal. And if we cannot even name a common, everyday object that we hold in our hands, how can we expect to speak of the things that truly concern us? Unless we can begin to embody the notion of change in the words we use, we will continue to be lost.'

'And your work?'

'My work is very simple. I have come to New York because it is the most forlorn of places, the most abject. The brokenness is everywhere, the disarray is universal. You have only to open your eyes to see it. The broken people, the broken things, the broken thoughts. The whole city is a junk heap. It suits my purpose admirably. I find the streets an endless source of material, an inexhaustible storehouse of shattered things. Each day I go out with my bag and collect objects that seem worthy of investigation. My samples now number in the hundreds – from the chipped to the smashed, from the dented to the squashed, from the pulverized to the putrid.'

'What do you do with these things?'

'I give them names.'

'Names?'

'I invent new words that will correspond to the things.'

'Ah. Now I see. But how do you decide? How do you know if you've found the right word?'

'I never make a mistake. It's a function of my genius.'

'Could you give me an example?'

'Of one of my words?'.

'Yes.'

'I'm sorry, but that won't be possible. It's my secret, you understand. Once I've published my book, you and the rest of the world will know. But for now I have to keep it to myself.

'Classified information.'

'That's right. Top secret.'

'I'm sorry.'

'You shouldn't be too disappointed. It won't be long now before I've put my findings in order. Then great things will begin to happen. It will be the most important event in the history of mankind.'

*

The second meeting took place a little past nine o'clock the
following morning. It was Sunday, and Stillman had emerged
from the hotel an hour later than usual. He walked the two blocks
to his customary breakfast place, the Mayflower Cafe, and sat
down in a corner booth at the back. Quinn, growing bolder now,
followed the old man into the restaurant and sat down in the
same booth, directly opposite him. For a minute or two Stillman
seemed not to notice his presence. Then, looking up from his
menu, he studied Quinn's face in an abstract sort of way. He
apparently did not recognize him from the day before.

'Do I know you?' he asked.

'I don't think so,' said Quinn. 'My name is Henry Dark.'

'Ah,' Stillman nodded. 'A man who begins with the essential. I like that.'

'I'm not one to beat around the bush,' said Quinn.

'The bush? What bush might that be?'

'The burning bush, of course.'

'Ah, yes. The burning bush. Of course.' Stillman looked at
Quinn's face – a little more carefully now, but also with what
seemed to be a certain confusion. 'I'm sorry,' he went on, 'but I
don't remember your name. I recall that you gave it to me not
long ago, but now it seems to be gone.'

'Henry Dark,' said Quinn.

'So it is. Yes, now it comes back to me. Henry Dark.'
Stillman paused for a long moment and then shook his head.
'Unfortunately, that's not possible, sir.'

'Why not?'

'Because there is no Henry Dark.'

'Well, perhaps I'm another Henry Dark. As opposed to the
one who doesn't exist.'

'Hmmm. Yes, I see your point. It is true that two people
sometimes have the same name. It's quite possible that your
name is Henry Dark. But you're not *the* Henry Dark.'

'Is he a friend of yours?'

Stillman laughed, as if at a good joke. 'Not exactly,' he said.

'You see, there never was any such person as Henry Dark. I made him up. He's an invention.'

'No,' said Quinn, with feigned disbelief.

'Yes. He's a character in a book I once wrote. A figment.'

'I find that hard to accept.'

'So did everyone else. I fooled them all.'

'Amazing. Why in the world did you do it?'

'I needed him, you see. I had certain ideas at the time that were too dangerous and controversial. So I pretended they had come from someone else. It was a way of protecting myself.'

'How did you decide on the name Henry Dark?'

'It's a good name, don't you think? I like it very much. Full of mystery, and at the same time quite proper. It suited my purpose well. And besides, it had a secret meaning.'

'The allusion to darkness?'

'No, no. Nothing so obvious. It was the initials, HD. That was very important.'

'How so?'

'Don't you want to guess?'

'I don't think so.'

'Oh, do try. Make three guesses. If you don't get it then, I'll tell you.'

Quinn paused for a moment, trying to give it his best effort. 'HD,' he said. 'For Henry David? As in Henry David Thoreau.'

'Not even close.'

'How about HD pure and simple? For the poet Hilda Doolittle.'

'Worse than the first one.'

'All right, one more guess. HD. H . . . and D . . . Just a moment . . . How about . . . Just a moment . . . Ah . . . Yes, here we are. H for the weeping philosopher, Heraclitus . . . and D for the laughing philosopher, Democritus . . . Heraclitus and Democritus . . . the two poles of the dialectic.'

'A very clever answer.'

'Am I right?'

'No, of course not. But a clever answer just the same.'

'You can't say I didn't try.'

'No, I can't. That's why I'm going to reward you with the correct answer. Because you tried. Are you ready?'

'Ready.'

'The initials HD in the name Henry Dark refer to Humpty Dumpty.'

'Who?'

'Humpty Dumpty. You know who I mean. The egg.'

'As in "Humpty Dumpty sat on a wall?" '

'Exactly.'

'I don't understand.'

'Humpty Dumpty: the purest embodiment of the human condition. Listen carefully, sir. What is an egg? It is that which has not yet been born. A paradox, is it not? For how can Humpty Dumpty be alive if he has not been born? And yet, he is alive – make no mistake. We know that because he can speak. More than that, he is a philosopher of language. "When *I* use a word, Humpty Dumpty said, in rather a scornful tone, it means just what I choose it to mean – neither more nor less. The question is, said Alice, whether you *can* make words mean so many different things. The question is, said Humpty Dumpty, which is to be master – that's all." '

'Lewis Carroll.'

'*Through the Looking Glass*, chapter six.'

'Interesting.'

'It's more than interesting, sir. It's crucial. Listen carefully, and perhaps you will learn something. In his little speech to Alice, Humpty Dumpty sketches the future of human hopes and gives the clue to our salvation: to become masters of the words we speak, to make language answer our needs, Humpty Dumpty was a prophet, a man who spoke truths the world was not ready for.'

'A man?'

'Excuse me. A slip of the tongue. I mean an egg. But the slip is instructive and helps to prove my point. For all men are eggs, in a manner of speaking. We exist, but we have not yet achieved the form that is our destiny. We are pure potential, an example of the not-yet-arrived. For man is a fallen creature – we know that from Genesis. Humpty Dumpty is also a fallen creature. He falls from his wall, and no one can put him back together again – neither the king, nor his horses, nor his men. But that is what we must all now strive to do. It is our duty as human beings: to put the egg back together again. For each of us, sir, is Humpty Dumpty. And to help him is to help ourselves.'

'A convincing argument.'

'It's impossible to find a flaw in it.'

'No cracks in the egg.'

'Exactly.'

'And, at the same time, the origin of Henry Dark.'

'Yes. But there is more to it than that. Another egg, in fact.'

'There's more than one?'

'Good heavens, yes. There are millions of them. But the one I have in mind is particularly famous. It's probably the most celebrated egg of all.'

'You're beginning to lose me.'

'I'm speaking of Columbus's egg.'

'Ah, yes. Of course.'

'You know the story?'

'Everyone does.'

'It's charming, is it not? When faced with the problem of how to stand an egg on its end, he merely tapped slightly on the bottom, cracking the shell just enough to create a certain flatness that would support the egg when he removed his hand.'

'It worked.'

'Of course it worked. Columbus was a genius. He sought paradise and discovered the New World. It is still not too late for it to become paradise.'

'Indeed.'

'I admit that things have not worked out too well yet. But there is still hope. Americans have never lost their desire to discover new worlds. Do you remember what happened in 1969?'

'I remember many things. What do you have in mind?'

'Men walked on the moon. Think of that, dear sir. Men walked on the moon!'

'Yes, I remember. According to the President, it was the greatest event since creation.'

'He was right. The only intelligent thing that man ever said. And what do you suppose the moon looks like?'

'I have no idea.'

'Come, come, think again.'

'Oh yes. Now I see what you mean.'

'Granted, the resemblance is not perfect. But it is true that in certain phases, especially on a clear night, the moon does look very much like an egg.'

'Yes. Very much like.'

At that moment, a waitress appeared with Stillman's breakfast and set it on the table before him. The old man eyed the food with relish. Decorously lifting a knife with his right hand, he cracked the shell of his soft-boiled egg and said, 'As you can see, sir, I leave no stone unturned.'

The third meeting took place later that same day. The afternoon was well advanced: the light like gauze on the bricks and leaves, the shadows lengthening. Once again, Stillman retreated to Riverside Park, this time to the edge of it, coming to rest on a knobby outcrop at 84th Street known as Mount Tom. On this same spot, in the summers of 1843 and 1844, Edgar Allan Poe had spent many long hours gazing out at the Hudson. Quinn knew this because he had made it his business to know such things. As it turned out, he had often sat there himself.

He felt little fear now about doing what he had to do. He circled the rock two or three times, but failed to get Stillman's attention. Then he sat down next to the old man and said hello. Incredibly, Stillman did not recognize him. This was the third time Quinn had presented himself, and each time it was as though Quinn had been someone else. He could not decide whether this was a good sign or bad. If Stillman was pretending, he was an actor like no other in the world. For each time Quinn had appeared, he had done it by surprise. And yet Stillman had not even blinked. On the other hand, if Stillman really did not recognize him, what did this mean? Was it possible for anyone to be so impervious to the things he saw?

The old man asked him who he was.

'My name is Peter Stillman,' said Quinn.

'That's my name,' answered Stillman. 'I'm Peter Stillman.'

'I'm the other Peter Stillman,' said Quinn.

'Oh. You mean my son. Yes, that's possible. You look just like him. Of course, Peter is blond and you are dark. Not Henry Dark, but dark of hair. But people change, don't they? One minute we're one thing, and then another another.'

'Exactly.'

'I've often wondered about you, Peter. Many times I've thought to myself, "I wonder how Peter is getting along."'

'I'm much better now, thank you.'

'I'm glad to hear it. Someone once told me you had died. It made me very sad.'

'No, I've made a complete recovery.'

'I can see that. Fit as a fiddle. And you speak so well, too.'

'All words are available to me now. Even the ones most people have trouble with. I can say them all.'

'I'm proud of you, Peter.'

'I owe it all to you.'

'Children are a great blessing. I've always said that. An incomparable blessing.'

'I'm sure of it.'

'As for me, I have my good days and my bad days. When the bad days come, I think of the ones that were good. Memory is a great blessing, Peter. The next best thing to death.'

'Without a doubt.'

'Of course, we must live in the present, too. For example, I am currently in New York. Tomorrow, I could be somewhere else. I travel a great deal, you see. Here today, gone tomorrow. It's part of my work.'

'It must be stimulating.'

'Yes, I'm very stimulated. My mind never stops.'

'That's good to hear.'

'The years weigh heavily, it's true. But we have so much to be thankful for. Time makes us grow old, but it also gives us the day and the night. And when we die, there is always someone to take our place.'

'We all grow old.'

'When you're old, perhaps you'll have a son to comfort you.'

'I would like that.'

'Then you would be as fortunate as I have been. Remember, Peter, children are a great blessing.'

'I won't forget.'

'And remember, too, that you shouldn't put all your eggs in one basket. Conversely, don't count your chickens before they hatch.'

'No. I try to take things as they come.'

'Last of all, never say a thing you know in your heart is not true.'

'I won't.'

'Lying is a bad thing. It makes you sorry you were ever born. And not to have been born is a curse. You are condemned to live outside time. And when you live outside time, there is no day and night. You don't even get a chance to die.'

'I understand.'

'A lie can never be undone. Even the truth is not enough. I am a father, and I know about these things. Remember what happened to the father of our country. He chopped down the cherry tree, and then he said to his father, "I cannot tell a lie." Soon thereafter, he threw the coin across the river. These two stories are crucial events in American history. George Washington chopped down the tree, and then he threw away the money. Do you understand? He was telling us an essential truth. Namely, that money doesn't grow on trees. This is what made our country great, Peter. Now George Washington's picture is on every dollar bill. There is an important lesson to be learned from all this.'

'I agree with you.'

'Of course, it's unfortunate that the tree was cut down. That tree was the Tree of Life, and it would have made us immune to death. Now we welcome death with open arms, especially when we are old. But the father of our country knew his duty. He could not do otherwise. That is the meaning of the phrase, "Life is a bowl of cherries." If the tree had remained standing, we would have had eternal life.'

'Yes, I see what you mean.'

'I have many such ideas in my head. My mind never stops. You were always a clever boy, Peter, and I'm glad you understand.'

'I can follow you perfectly.'

'A father must always teach his son the lessons he has learned. In that way knowledge is passed down from generation to generation, and we grow wise.'

'I won't forget what you've told me.'

'I'll be able to die happily now, Peter.'

'I'm glad.'

'But you mustn't forget anything.'

'I won't, father. I promise.'

The next morning, Quinn was in front of the hotel at his usual time. The weather had finally changed. After two weeks of resplendent skies, a drizzle now fell on New York, and the streets were filled with the sound of wet, moving tyres. For an hour Quinn sat on the bench, protecting himself with a black umbrella, thinking Stillman would appear at any moment. He worked his way through his roll and coffee, read the account of the Mets' Sunday loss, and still there was no sign of the old man. Patience, he said to himself, and began to tackle the rest of the paper. Forty minutes passed. He reached the financial section and was about to read an analysis of a corporate merger when the rain suddenly intensified. Reluctantly, he got up from his bench and removed himself to a doorway across the street from the hotel. He stood there in his clammy shoes for an hour and a half. Was Stillman sick, he wondered? Quinn tried to imagine him lying in his bed, sweating out a fever. Perhaps the old man had died during the night and his body had not yet been discovered. Such things happened, he told himself.

Today was to have been the crucial day, and Quinn had made elaborate and meticulous plans for it. Now his calculations were for naught. It disturbed him that he had not taken this contingency into account.

Still, he hesitated. He stood there under his umbrella, watching the rain slide off it in small, fine drops. By eleven o'clock he had begun to formulate a decision. Half an hour later he crossed the street, walked forty paces down the block, and entered Stillman's hotel. The place stank of cockroach repellant and dead cigarettes. A few of the tenants, with nowhere to go in the rain, were sitting in the lobby, sprawled out on orange plastic chairs. The place seemed blank, a hell of stale thoughts.

A large black man sat behind the front desk with his sleeves rolled up. One elbow was on the counter, and his head was propped in his open hand. With his other hand he turned the pages of a tabloid newspaper, barely pausing to read the words. He looked bored enough to have been there all his life.

'I'd like to leave a message for one of your guests,' Quinn said.

The man looked up at him slowly, as if wishing him to disappear.

'I'd like to leave a message for one of your guests,' Quinn said again.

'No guests here,' said the man. 'We call them residents.'

'For one of your residents, then. I'd like to leave a message.'

'And just who might that be, bub?'

'Stillman. Peter Stillman.'

The man pretended to think for a moment, then shook his head. 'Nope. Can't recall anyone by that name.'

'Don't you have a register?'

'Yeah, we've got a book. But it's in the safe.'

'The safe? What are you talking about?'

'I'm talking about the book, bub. The boss likes to keep it locked up in the safe.'

'I don't suppose you know the combination?'

'Sorry. The boss is the only one.'

Quinn sighed, reached into his pocket, and pulled out a five dollar bill. He slapped it on the counter and kept his hand on top of it.

'I don't suppose you happen to have a copy of the book, do you?' he asked.

'Maybe,' said the man. 'I'll have to look in my office.'

The man lifted up the newspaper, which was lying open on the counter. Under it was the register.

'A lucky break,' said Quinn, releasing his hand from the money.

'Yeah, I guess today's my day,' answered the man, sliding the bill along the surface of the counter, whisking it over the edge, and putting it in his pocket. 'What did you say your friend's name was again?'

'Stillman. An old man with white hair.'

'The gent in the overcoat?'

'That's right.'

'We call him the Professor.'

'That's the man. Do you have a room number? He checked in about two weeks ago.'

The clerk opened the register, turned the pages, and ran his finger down the column of names and numbers. 'Stillman,' he said. 'Room 303. He's not here anymore.'

'What?'

'He checked out.'

'What are you talking about?'

'Listen, bub, I'm telling you what it says here. Stillman checked out last night. He's gone.'

'That's the craziest thing I ever heard.'

'I don't care what it is. It's all down here in black and white.'

'Did he give a forwarding address.'

'Are you kidding?'

'What time did he leave?'

'Have to ask Louie, the night man. He comes on at eight.'

'Can I see the room?'

'Sorry. I rented it myself this morning. The guy's up there asleep.'

'What did he look like?'

'For five bucks you've got a lot of questions.'

'Forget it,' said Quinn, waving his hand desperately. 'It doesn't matter.'

He walked back to his apartment in a downpour, getting drenched in spite of his umbrella. So much for functions, he said to himself. So much for the meaning of words. He threw the umbrella onto the floor of his living room in disgust. Then he took off his jacket and flung it against the wall. Water splattered everywhere.

He called Virginia Stillman, too embarrassed to think of doing anything else. At the moment she answered, he nearly hung up the phone.

'I lost him,' he said.

'Are you sure?'

'He checked out of his room last night. I don't know where he is.'

'I'm scared, Paul.'

'Have you heard from him?'

'I don't know. I think so, but I'm not sure.'

'What does that mean?'

'Peter answered the phone this morning while I was taking my bath. He won't tell me who it was. He went into his room, closed the shades, and refuses to speak.'

'But he's done that before.'

'Yes. That's why I'm not sure. But it hasn't happened in a long time.'

'It sounds bad.'

'That's what I'm afraid of.'

'Don't worry. I have a few ideas. I'll get to work on them right away.'

'How will I reach you?'

'I'll call you every two hours, no matter where I am.'

'Do you promise?'

'Yes, I promise.'

'I'm so scared, I can't stand it.'

'It's all my fault. I made a stupid mistake, and I'm sorry.'

'No, I don't blame you. No one can watch a person twenty-four hours a day. It's impossible. You'd have to be inside his skin.'

'That's just the trouble. I thought I was.'

'It's not too late now, is it?'

'No. There's still plenty of time. I don't want you to worry.'

'I'll try not to.'

'Good. I'll be in touch.'

'Every two hours?'

'Every two hours.'

He had finessed the conversation rather nicely. In spite of everything, he had managed to keep Virginia Stillman calm. He found it hard to believe, but she still seemed to trust him. Not that it would be of any help. For the fact was, he had lied to her. He did not have several ideas. He did not have even one.

10

Stillman was gone now. The old man had become part of the city. He was a speck, a punctuation mark, a brick in an endless wall of bricks. Quinn could walk through the streets every day for the rest of his life, and still he would not find him. Everything had been reduced to chance, a nightmare of numbers and probabilities. There were no clues, no leads, no moves to be made.

Quinn backtracked in his mind to the beginning of the case. His job had been to protect Peter, not to follow Stillman. That had simply been a method, a way of trying to predict what would happen. By watching Stillman, the theory was that he would learn what his intentions were toward Peter. He had followed the old man for two weeks. What, then, could he conclude? Not much. Stillman's behaviour had been too obscure to give any hints.

There were, of course, certain extreme measures that they could take. He could suggest to Virginia Stillman that she get an unlisted telephone number. That would eliminate the disturbing calls, at least temporarily. If that failed, she and Peter could move. They could leave the neighbourhood, perhaps leave the city altogether. At the very worst, they could take on new identities, live under different names.

This last thought reminded him of something important. Until now, he realized, he had never seriously questioned the circumstances of his hiring. Things had happened too quickly, and he had taken it for granted that he would fill in for Paul Auster. Once he had taken the leap into that name, he had stopped thinking about Auster himself. If this man was as good a detective as the Stillmans thought he was, perhaps he would be able to help with the case. Quinn would make a clean breast of it, Auster would forgive him, and together they would work to save Peter Stillman.

He looked through the yellow pages for the Auster Detective Agency. There was no listing. In the white pages, however, he found the name. There was one Paul Auster in Manhattan, living on Riverside Drive – not far from Quinn's own house. There was no mention of a detective agency, but that did not necessarily mean anything. It could be that Auster had so much work he didn't need to advertise. Quinn picked up the phone and was about to dial when he thought better of it. This was too important a conversation to leave to the phone. He did not want to run the risk of being brushed off. Since Auster did not have an office, that meant he worked at home. Quinn would go there and talk to him face to face.

The rain had stopped now, and although the sky was still grey, far to the west Quinn could see a tiny shaft of light seeping through the clouds. As he walked up Riverside Drive, he became aware of the fact that he was no longer following Stillman. It felt as though he had lost half of himself. For two weeks he had been tied by an invisible thread to the old man. Whatever Stillman had done, he had done; wherever Stillman had gone, he had gone. His body was not accustomed to this new freedom, and for the first few blocks he walked at the old shuffling pace. The spell was over, and yet his body did not know it.

Auster's building was in the middle of the long block that ran between 116th and 119th Streets, just south of Riverside Church and Grant's Tomb. It was a well-kept place, with polished doorknobs and clean glass, and it had an air of bourgeois sobriety that appealed to Quinn at that moment. Auster's apartment was on the eleventh floor, and Quinn rang the buzzer, expecting to hear a voice speak to him through the intercom. But the door buzzer answered him without any conversation. Quinn pushed the door open, walked through the lobby, and rode the elevator to the eleventh floor.

It was a man who opened the apartment door. He was a tall dark fellow in his mid-thirties, with rumpled clothes and a two-day beard. In his right hand, fixed between his thumb and first two fingers, he held an uncapped fountain pen, still poised in a writing position. The man seemed surprised to find a stranger standing before him.

'Yes?' he asked tentatively.

Quinn spoke in the politest tone he could muster. 'Were you expecting someone else?'

'My wife, as a matter of fact. That's why I rang the buzzer without asking who it was.'

'I'm sorry to disturb you,' Quinn apologized. 'But I'm looking for Paul Auster.'

'I'm Paul Auster,' said the man.

'I wonder if I could talk to you. It's quite important.'

'You'll have to tell me what it's about first.'

'I hardly know myself.' Quinn gave Auster an earnest look. 'It's complicated, I'm afraid. Very complicated.'

'Do you have a name?'

'I'm sorry. Of course I do. Quinn.'

'Quinn what.'

'Daniel Quinn.'

The name seemed to suggest something to Auster, and he paused for a moment abstractedly, as if searching through his memory. 'Quinn,' he muttered to himself. 'I know that name from somewhere.' He went silent again, straining harder to dredge up the answer. 'You aren't a poet, are you?'

'I used to be,' said Quinn. 'But I haven't written poems for a long time now.'

'You did a book several years ago, didn't you? I think the title was *Unfinished Business*. A little book with a blue cover.'

'Yes. That was me.'

'I liked it very much. I kept hoping to see more of your work. In fact, I even wondered what had happened to you.'

'I'm still here. Sort of.'

Auster opened the door wider and gestured for Quinn to enter the apartment. It was a pleasant enough place inside: oddly shaped, with several long corridors, books cluttered everywhere,

pictures on the walls by artists Quinn did not know, and a few
children's toys scattered on the floor – a red truck, a brown bear, a
green space monster. Auster led him to the living room, gave him
a frayed upholstered chair to sit in, and then went off to the
kitchen to fetch some beer. He returned with two bottles, placed
them on a wooden crate that served as the coffee table, and sat
down on the sofa across from Quinn.

'Was it some kind of literary thing you wanted to talk about?'
Auster began.

'No,' said Quinn. 'I wish it was. But this has nothing to do with
literature.'

'With what, then?'

Quinn paused, looked around the room without seeing anything, and tried to start. 'I have a feeling there's been a terrible
mistake. I came here looking for Paul Auster, the private
detective.'

'The what?' Auster laughed, and in that laugh everything was
suddenly blown to bits. Quinn realized that he was talking
nonsense. He might just as well have asked for Chief Sitting Bull
– the effect would have been no different.

'The private detective,' he repeated softly.

'I'm afraid you've got the wrong Paul Auster.'

'You're the only one in the book.'

'That might be,' said Auster. 'But I'm not a detective.'

'Who are you then? What do you do?'

'I'm a writer.'

'A writer?' Quinn spoke the word as though it were a lament.

'I'm sorry,' Auster said. 'But that's what I happen to be.'

'If that's true, then there's no hope. The whole thing is a bad
dream.'

'I have no idea what you're talking about.'

Quinn told him. He began at the beginning and went through
the entire story, step by step. The pressure had been building up
in him since Stillman's disappearance that morning, and it came
out of him now as a torrent of words. He told of the phone calls
for Paul Auster, of his inexplicable acceptance of the case, of his

meeting with Peter Stillman, of his conversation with Virginia Stillman, of his reading Stillman's book, of his following Stillman from Grand Central Station, of Stillman's daily wanderings, of the carpet bag and the broken objects, of the disquieting maps that formed letters of the alphabet, of his talks with Stillman, of Stillman's disappearance from the hotel. When he had come to the end, he said, 'Do you think I'm crazy?'

'No,' said Auster, who had listened attentively to Quinn's monologue. 'If I had been in your place, I probably would have done the same thing.'

These words came as a great relief to Quinn, as if, at long last, the burden was no longer his alone. He felt like taking Auster in his arms and declaring his friendship for life.

'You see,' said Quinn, 'I'm not making it up. I even have proof.' He took out his wallet and removed the five hundred dollar cheque that Virginia Stillman had written two weeks earlier. He handed it to Auster. 'You see,' he said. 'It's even made out to you.'

Auster looked the cheque over carefully and nodded. 'It seems to be a perfectly normal cheque.'

'Well, it's yours,' said Quinn. 'I want you to have it.'

'I couldn't possibly accept it.'

'It's of no use to me.' Quinn looked around the apartment and gestured vaguely. 'Buy yourself some more books. Or a few toys for your kid.'

'This is money you've earned. You deserve to have it yourself.' Auster paused for a moment. 'There's one thing I'll do for you, though. Since the cheque is in my name, I'll cash it for you. I'll take it to my bank tomorrow morning, deposit it in my account, and give you the money when it clears.'

Quinn did not say anything.

'All right?' Auster asked. 'Is it agreed?'

'All right,' said Quinn at last. 'We'll see what happens.'

Auster put the cheque on the coffee table, as if to say the matter had been settled. Then he leaned back on the sofa and looked Quinn in the eyes. 'There's a much more important question than the cheque,' he said. 'The fact that my name has been mixed up in this. I don't understand it at all.'

'I wondered if you've had any trouble with your phone lately. Wires sometimes get crossed. A person tries to call a number, and even though he dials correctly, he gets someone else.'

'Yes, that's happened to me before. But even if my phone was broken, that doesn't explain the real problem. It would tell us why the call went to you, but not why they wanted to speak to me in the first place.'

'Is it possible that you know the people involved?'

'I've never heard of the Stillmans.'

'Maybe someone wanted to play a practical joke on you.'

'I don't hang around with people like that.'

'You never know.'

'But the fact is, it's not a joke. It's a real case with real people.'

'Yes,' said Quinn after a long silence. 'I'm aware of that.'

They had come to the end of what they could talk about. Beyond that point there was nothing: the random thoughts of men who knew nothing. Quinn realized that he should be going. He had been there almost an hour, and the time was approaching for his call to Virginia Stillman. Nevertheless, he was reluctant to move. The chair was comfortable, and the beer had gone slightly to his head. This Auster was the first intelligent person he had spoken to in a long time. He had read Quinn's old work, he had admired it, he had been looking forward to more. In spite of everything, it was impossible for Quinn not to feel glad of this.

They sat there for a short time without saying anything. At last, Auster gave a little shrug, which seemed to acknowledge that they had come to an impasse. He stood up and said, 'I was about to make some lunch for myself. It's no trouble making it for two.'

Quinn hesitated. It was as though Auster had read his thoughts, divining the thing he wanted most – to eat, to have an excuse to stay a while. 'I really should be going,' he said. 'But yes, thank you. A little food can't do any harm.'

'How does a ham omelette sound?'

'Sounds good.'

Auster retreated to the kitchen to prepare the food. Quinn would have liked to offer to help, but he could not budge. His body felt like a stone. For want of any other idea, he closed his eyes. In the past, it had sometimes comforted him to make the world disappear. This time, however, Quinn found nothing interesting inside his head. It seemed as though things had ground to a halt in there. Then, from the darkness, he began to hear a voice, a chanting, idiotic voice that sang the same sentence over and over again: 'You can't make an omelette without breaking eggs.' He opened his eyes to make the words stop.

There was bread and butter, more beer, knives and forks, salt and pepper, napkins, and omelettes, two of them, oozing on white plates. Quinn ate with crude intensity, polishing off the meal in what seemed a matter of seconds. After that, he made a great effort to be calm. Tears lurked mysteriously behind his eyes, and his voice seemed to tremble as he spoke, but somehow he managed to hold his own. To prove that he was not a self-obsessed ingrate, he began to question Auster about his writing. Auster was somewhat reticent about it, but at last he conceded that he was working on a book of essays. The current piece was about *Don Quixote*.

'One of my favourite books, said Quinn.

'Yes, mine too. There's nothing like it.'

Quinn asked him about the essay.

'I suppose you could call it speculative, since I'm not really out to prove anything. In fact, it's all done tongue-in-cheek. An imaginative reading, I guess you could say.'

'What's the gist?'

'It mostly has to do with the authorship of the book. Who wrote it, and how it was written.'

'Is there any question?'

'Of course not. But I mean the book inside the book Cervantes wrote, the one he imagined he was writing.'

'Ah.'

'It's quite simple. Cervantes, if you remember, goes to great lengths to convince the reader that he is not the author. The book,

he says, was written in Arabic by Cid Hamete Benengeli. Cervantes describes how he discovered the manuscript by chance one
day in the market at Toledo. He hires someone to translate it for
him into Spanish, and thereafter he presents himself as no more
than the editor of the translation. In fact, he cannot even vouch
for the accuracy of the translation itself.'

'And yet he goes on to say,' Quinn added, 'that Cid Hamete
Benengeli's is the only true version of Don Quixote's story. All
the other versions are frauds, written by impostors. He makes a
great point of insisting that everything in the book really happened in the world.'

'Exactly. Because the book after all is an attack on the dangers
of the make-believe. He couldn't very well offer a work of the
imagination to do that, could he? He had to claim that it was real.'

'Still, I've always suspected that Cervantes devoured those old
romances. You can't hate something so violently unless a part of
you also loves it. In some sense, Don Quixote was just a stand-in
for himself.'

'I agree with you. What better portrait of a writer than to show a
man who has been bewitched by books?'

'Precisely.'

'In any case, since the book is supposed to be real, it follows
that the story has to be written by an eyewitness to the events that
take place in it. But Cid Hamete, the acknowledged author, never
makes an appearance. Not once does he claim to be present at
what happens. So, my question is this: who is Cid Hamete
Benengeli?'

'Yes, I see what you're getting at.'

'The theory I present in the essay is that he is actually a
combination of four different people. Sancho Panza is of course
the witness. There's no other candidate – since he is the only one
who accompanies Don Quixote on all his adventures. But Sancho
can neither read nor write. Therefore, he cannot be the author.
On the other hand, we know that Sancho has a great gift for
language. In spite of his inane malapropisms, he can talk circles
around everyone else in the book. It seems perfectly possible to

me that he dictated the story to someone else – namely, to the barber and the priest, Don Quixote's good friends. They put the story into proper literary form – in Spanish – and then turned the manuscript over to Simon Carasco, the bachelor from Salamanca, who proceeded to translate it into Arabic. Cervantes found the translation, had it rendered back into Spanish, and then published the book, *The Adventures of Don Quixote*.'

'But why would Sancho and the others go to all that trouble?'

'To cure Don Quixote of his madness. They want to save their friend. Remember, in the beginning they burn his books of chivalry, but that has no effect. The Knight of the Sad Countenance does not give up his obsession. Then, at one time or another, they all go out looking for him in various disguises – as a woman in distress, as the Knight of the Mirrors, as the Knight of the White Moon – in order to lure Don Quixote back home. In the end, they are actually successful. The book was just one of their ploys. The idea was to hold a mirror up to Don Quixote's madness, to record each of his absurd and ludicrous delusions, so that when he finally read the book himself, he would see the error of his ways.'

'I like that.'

'Yes. But there's one last twist. Don Quixote, in my view, was not really mad. He only pretended to be. In fact, he orchestrated the whole thing himself. Remember: throughout the book Don Quixote is preoccupied by the question of posterity. Again and again he wonders how accurately his chronicler will record his adventures. This implies knowledge on his part; he knows beforehand that this chronicler exists. And who else is it but Sancho Panza, the faithful squire whom Don Quixote has chosen for exactly this purpose? In the same way, he chose the three others to play the roles he destined for them. It was Don Quixote who engineered the Benengeli quartet. And not only did he select the authors, it was probably he who translated the Arabic manuscript back into Spanish. We shouldn't put it past him. For a man so skilled in the art of disguise, darkening his skin and donning the clothes of a Moor could not have been very difficult. I like to imagine that scene in the marketplace at Toledo. Cervantes hiring Don Quixote to decipher the story of Don Quixote himself. There's great beauty to it.'

'But you still haven't explained why a man like Don Quixote would disrupt his tranquil life to engage in such an elaborate hoax.'

'That's the most interesting part of all. In my opinion, Don Quixote was conducting an experiment. He wanted to test the gullibility of his fellow men. Would it be possible, he wondered, to stand up before the world and with the utmost conviction spew out lies and nonsense? To say that windmills were knights, that a barber's basin was a helmet, that puppets were real people? Would it be possible to persuade others to agree with what he said, even though they did not believe him? In other words, to what extent would people tolerate blasphemies if they gave them amusement? The answer is obvious, isn't it? To any extent. For the proof is that we still read the book. It remains highly amusing to us. And that's finally all anyone wants out of a book – to be amused.'

Auster leaned back on the sofa, smiled with a certain ironic pleasure, and lit a cigarette. The man was obviously enjoying himself, but the precise nature of that pleasure eluded Quinn. It seemed to be a kind of soundless laughter, a joke that stopped short of its punchline, a generalized mirth that had no object. Quinn was about to say something in response to Auster's theory, but he was not given the chance. Just as he opened his mouth to speak, he was interrupted by a clattering of keys at the front door, the sound of the door opening and then slamming shut, and a burst of voices. Auster's face perked up at the sound. He rose from his seat, excused himself to Quinn, and walked quickly towards the door.

Quinn heard laughter in the hallway, first from a woman and then from a child – the high and the higher, a staccato of ringing shrapnel – and then the basso rumbling of Auster's guffaw. The child spoke: 'Daddy, look what I found!' And then the woman explained that it had been lying on the street, and why not, it seemed perfectly okay. A moment later he heard the child running towards him down the hall. The child shot into the living room, caught sight of Quinn, and stopped dead in his tracks. He was a blond-haired boy of five or six.

'Good afternoon,' said Quinn.

The boy, rapidly withdrawing into shyness, managed no more than a faint hello. In his left hand he held a red object that Quinn could not identify. Quinn asked the boy what it was.

'It's a yoyo,' he answered, opening his hand to show him. 'I found it on the street.'

'Does it work?'

The boy gave an exaggerated pantomime shrug. 'Dunno. Siri can't do it. And I don't know how.'

Quinn asked him if he could try, and the boy walked over and put it in his hand. As he examined the yoyo, he could hear the child breathing beside him, watching his every move. The yoyo was plastic, similar to the ones he had played with years ago, but more elaborate somehow, an artifact of the space age. Quinn fastened the loop at the end of the string around his middle finger, stood up, and gave it a try. The yoyo gave off a fluted, whistling sound as it descended, and sparks shot off inside it. The boy gasped, but then the yoyo stopped, dangling at the end of its line.

'A great philosopher once said,' muttered Quinn, 'that the way up and the way down are one and the same.'

'But you didn't make it go up,' said the boy. 'It only went down.'

'You have to keep trying.'

Quinn was rewinding the spool for another attempt when Auster and his wife entered the room. He looked up and saw the woman first. In that one brief moment he knew that he was in trouble. She was a tall, thin blonde, radiantly beautiful, with an energy and happiness that seemed to make everything around her invisible. It was too much for Quinn. He felt as though Auster were taunting him with the things he had lost, and he responded with envy and rage, a lacerating self-pity. Yes, he too would have liked to have this wife and this child, to sit around all day spouting drivel about old books, to be surrounded by yoyos and ham omelettes and fountain pens. He prayed to himself for deliverance.

Auster saw the yoyo in his hand and said, 'I see you've already met. Daniel,' he said to the boy, 'this is Daniel.' And then to Quinn, with that same ironic smile, 'Daniel, this is Daniel.'

The boy burst out laughing and said, 'Everybody's Daniel!'

'That's right,' said Quinn. 'I'm you, and you're me.'

'And around and around it goes,' shouted the boy, suddenly spreading his arms and spinning around the room like a gyroscope.

'And this,' said Auster, turning to the woman, 'is my wife, Siri.'

The wife smiled her smile, said she was glad to meet Quinn as though she meant it, and then extended her hand to him. He shook it, feeling the uncanny slenderness of her bones, and asked if her name was Norwegian.

'Not many people know that,' she said.

'Do you come from Norway?'

'Indirectly,' she said. 'By way of Northfield, Minnesota.' And then she laughed her laugh, and Quinn felt a little more of himself collapse.

'I know this is sort of last minute,' Auster said, 'but if you have some time to spare, why don't you stay and have dinner with us?'

'Ah,' said Quinn, struggling to keep himself in check. 'That's very kind. But I really must be going. I'm late as it is.'

He made one last effort, smiling at Auster's wife and waving goodbye to the boy. 'So long, Daniel,' he said, walking towards the door.

The boy looked at him from across the room and laughed again. 'Goodbye myself!' he said.

Auster accompanied him to the door. He said, 'I'll call you as soon as the cheque clears. Are you in the book?'

'Yes,' said Quinn. 'The only one.'

'If you need me for anything,' said Auster, 'just call. I'll be happy to help.'

Auster reached out to shake hands with him, and Quinn realized that he was still holding the yoyo. He placed it in Auster's right hand, patted him gently on the shoulder, and left.

11

Quinn was nowhere now. He had nothing, he knew nothing, he knew that he knew nothing. Not only had he been sent back to the beginning, he was now before the beginning, and so far before the beginning that it was worse than any end he could imagine.

His watch read nearly six. Quinn walked home the way he had come, lengthening his strides with each new block. By the time he came to his street, he was running. It's June second, he told himself. Try to remember that. This is New York, and tomorrow will be June third. If all goes well, the following day will be the fourth. But nothing is certain.

The hour had long since passed for his call to Virginia Stillman, and he debated whether to go through with it. Would it be possible to ignore her? Could he abandon everything now, just like that? Yes, he said to himself, it was possible. He could forget about the case, get back to his routine, write another book. He could take a trip if he liked, even leave the country for a while. He could go to Paris, for example. Yes, that was possible. But anywhere would do, he thought, anywhere at all.

He sat down in his living room and looked at the walls. They had once been white, he remembered, but now they had turned a curious shade of yellow. Perhaps one day they would drift further into dinginess, lapsing into grey, or even brown, like some piece of ageing fruit. A white wall becomes a yellow wall becomes a gray wall, he said to himself. The paint becomes exhausted, the city encroaches with its soot, the plaster crumbles within. Changes, then more changes still.

He smoked a cigarette, and then another, and then another. He looked at his hands, saw that they were dirty, and got up to wash them. In the bathroom, with the water running in the sink, he

decided to shave as well. He lathered his face, took out a clean
blade, and started scraping off his beard. For some reason, he
found it unpleasant to look in the mirror and kept trying to avoid
himself with his eyes. You're getting old, he said to himself,
you're turning into an old fart. Then he went into the kitchen, ate
a bowl of cornflakes, and smoked another cigarette.

It was seven o'clock now. Once again, he debated whether to
call Virginia Stillman. As he turned the question over in his mind,
it occurred to him that he no longer had an opinion. He saw the
argument for making the call, and at the same time he saw the
argument for not making it. In the end, it was etiquette that
decided. It would not be fair to disappear without telling her first.
After that, it would be perfectly acceptable. As long as you tell
people what you are going to do, he reasoned, it doesn't matter.
Then you are free to do what you want.

The number, however, was busy. He waited five minutes and
dialled again. Again, the number was busy. For the next hour
Quinn alternated between dialling and waiting, always with the
same result. At last he called the operator and asked whether the
phone was out of order. There would be a charge of thirty cents,
he was told. Then came a crackling in the wires, the sound of
further dialling, more voices. Quinn tried to imagine what the
operators looked like. Then the first woman spoke to him again:
the number was busy.

Quinn did not know what to think. There were so many
possibilities, he could not even begin. Stillman? The phone off
the hook? Someone else altogether?

He turned on the television and watched the first two innings
of the Mets game. Then he dialled once again. Same thing. In the
top of the third St Louis scored on a walk, a stolen base, an infield
out, and a sacrifice fly. The Mets matched that run in their half of
the inning on a double by Wilson and a single by Youngblood.
Quinn realized that he didn't care. A beer commercial came on,
and he turned off the sound. For the twentieth time he tried to
reach Virginia Stillman, and for the twentieth time the same thing
happened. In the top of the fourth St Louis scored five runs, and

Quinn turned off the picture as well. He found his red notebook, sat down at his desk, and wrote steadily for the next two hours. He did not bother to read over what he had written. Then he called Virginia Stillman and got another busy signal. He slammed the receiver down so hard that the plastic cracked. When he tried to call again, he could no longer get a dial tone. He stood up, went into the kitchen, and made another bowl of cornflakes. Then he went to bed.

In his dream, which he later forgot, he found himself walking down Broadway, holding Auster's son by the hand.

Quinn spent the following day on his feet. He started early, just after eight o'clock, and did not stop to consider where he was going. As it happened, he saw many things that day he had never noticed before.

Every twenty minutes he would go into a phone booth and call Virginia Stillman. As it had been the night before, so it was today. By now Quinn expected the number to be busy. It no longer even bothered him. The busy signal had become a counterpoint to his steps, a metronome beating steadily inside the random noises of the city. There was comfort in the thought that whenever he dialled the number, the sound would be there for him, never swerving in its denial, negating speech and the possibility of speech, as insistent as the beating of a heart. Virginia and Peter Stillman were shut off from him now. But he could soothe his conscience with the thought that he was still trying. Whatever darkness they were leading him into, he had not abandoned them yet.

He walked down Broadway to 72nd Street, turned east to Central Park West, and followed it to 59th Street and the statue of Columbus. There he turned east once again, moving along Central Park South until Madison Avenue, and then cut right, walking downtown to Grand Central Station. After circling haphazardly for a few blocks, he continued south for a mile, came to the juncture of Broadway and Fifth Avenue at 23rd Street, paused to look at the Flatiron Building, and then shifted course, taking a

westward turn until he reached Seventh Avenue, at which point
he veered left and progressed further downtown. At Sheridan
Square he turned east again, ambling down Waverly Place,
crossing Sixth Avenue, and continuing on to Washington
Square. He walked through the arch and made his way south
among the crowds, stopping momentarily to watch a juggler
perform on a slack rope stretched between a light pole and a tree
trunk. Then he left the little park at its downtown east corner,
went through the university housing project with its patches of
green grass, and turned right at Houston Street. At West Broadway he turned again, this time to the left, and proceeded onward
to Canal. Angling slightly to his right, he passed through a vest
pocket park and swung around to Varick Street, walked by
number 6, where he had once lived, and then regained his
southern course, picking up West Broadway again where it
merged with Varick. West Broadway took him to the base of the
World Trade Centre and on into the lobby of one of the towers,
where he made his thirteenth call of the day to Virginia Stillman.
Quinn decided to eat something, entered one of the fast food
places on the ground floor, and leisurely consumed a sandwich
as he did some work in the red notebook. Afterwards, he walked
east again, wandering through the narrow streets of the financial
district, and then headed further south, towards Bowling Green,
where he saw the water and the seagulls above it, careening in
the midday light. For a moment he considered taking a ride on
the Staten Island Ferry, but then thought better of it and began
tracking his way to the north. At Fulton Street he slid to his right
and followed the north-eastward path of East Broadway, which
led through the miasma of the Lower East Side and then up into
Chinatown. From there he found the Bowery, which carried him
along to Fourteenth Street. He then hooked left, cut diagonally
through Union Square, and continued uptown along Park
Avenue South. At 23rd Street he jockeyed north. A few blocks
later he jutted right again, went one block to the east, and then
walked up Third Avenue for a while. At 32nd Street he turned
right, came upon Second Avenue, turned left, moved uptown

another three blocks, and then turned right one last time, whereupon he met up with First Avenue. He then walked the remaining seven blocks to the United Nations and decided to take a short rest. He sat down on a stone bench in the plaza and breathed deeply, idling in the air and the light with closed eyes. Then he opened the red notebook, took the deaf mute's pen from his pocket, and began a new page.

For the first time since he had bought the red notebook, what he wrote that day had nothing to do with the Stillman case. Rather, he concentrated on the things he had seen while walking. He did not stop to think about what he was doing, nor did he analyse the possible implications of this uncustomary act. He felt an urge to record certain facts, and he wanted to put them down on paper before he forgot them.

Today, as never before: the tramps, the down-and-outs, the shopping-bag ladies, the drifters and drunks. They range from the merely destitute to the wretchedly broken. Wherever you turn, they are there, in good neighbourhoods and bad.

Some beg with a semblance of pride. Give me this money, they seem to say, and soon I will be back there with the rest of you, rushing back and forth on my daily rounds. Others have given up hope of ever leaving their tramphood. They lie there sprawled out on the sidewalk with their hat, or cup, or box, not even bothering to look up at the passerby, too defeated even to thank the ones who drop a coin beside them. Still others try to work for the money they are given: the blind pencil sellers, the winos who wash the windshield of your car. Some tell stories, usually tragic accounts of their own lives, as if to give their benefactors something for their kindness – even if only words.

Others have real talents. The old black man today, for example, who tap-danced while juggling cigarettes – still dignified, clearly once a vaudevillian, dressed in a purple suit with a green shirt and a yellow tie, his mouth fixed in a half-remembered stage smile. There are also the pavement chalk artists and musicians: saxaphonists, electric guitarists, fiddlers. Occasionally, you will even come across a genius, as I did today:

A clarinettist of no particular age, wearing a hat that obscured his face, and sitting cross-legged on the sidewalk, in the manner of a snake-charmer. Directly in front of him were two wind-up monkeys, one with a tambourine and the other with a drum. With the one shaking and the other banging, beating out a weird and precise syncopation, the man would improvise endless tiny variations on his instrument, his body swaying stiffly back and forth, energetically miming the monkeys' rhythm. He played jauntily and with flair, crisp and looping figures in the minor mode, as if glad to be there with his mechanical friends, enclosed in the universe he had created, never once looking up. It went on and on, always finally the same, and yet the longer I listened the harder I found it to leave.

To be inside that music, to be drawn into the circle of its repetitions: perhaps that is a place where one could finally disappear.

But beggars and performers make up only a small part of the vagabond population. They are the aristocracy, the elite of the fallen. Far more numerous are those with nothing to do, with nowhere to go. Many are drunks – but that term does not do justice to the devastation they embody. Hulks of despair, clothed in rags, their faces bruised and bleeding, they shuffle through the streets as though in chains. Asleep in doorways, staggering insanely through traffic, collapsing on sidewalks – they seem to be everywhere the moment you look for them. Some will starve to death, others will die of exposure, still others will be beaten or burned or tortured.

For every soul lost in this particular hell, there are several others locked inside madness – unable to exit to the world that stands at the threshold of their bodies. Even though they seem to be there, they cannot be counted as present. The man, for example, who goes everywhere with a set of drumsticks, pounding the pavement with them in a reckless, nonsensical rhythm, stooped over awkwardly as he advances along the street, beating and beating away at the cement. Perhaps he thinks he is doing important work. Perhaps, if he did not do what he did, the city would fall apart. Perhaps the moon would spin out of its orbit and come crashing into the earth. There are the ones who talk to themselves, who mutter, who scream, who curse, who groan, who tell themselves stories as if to someone else. The man

I saw today, sitting like a heap of garbage in front of Grand Central Station, the crowds rushing past him, saying in a loud, panic-stricken voice: 'Third Marines ... eating bees ... the bees crawling out of my mouth.' Or the woman shouting at an invisible companion: 'And what if I don't want to! What if I just fucking don't want to!'

There are the women with their shopping bags and the men with their cardboard boxes, hauling their possessions from one place to the next, forever on the move, as if it mattered where they were. There is the man wrapped in the American flag. There is the woman with a Hallowe'en mask on her face. There is the man in a ravaged overcoat, his shoes wrapped in rags, carrying a perfectly pressed white shirt on a hanger – still sheathed in the dry-cleaner's plastic. There is the man in a business suit with bare feet and a football helmet on his head. There is the woman whose clothes are covered from head to toe with Presidential campaign buttons. There is the man who walks with his face in his hands, weeping hysterically and saying over and over again: 'No, no, no. He's dead. He's not dead. No, no, no. He's dead. He's not dead.'

Baudelaire: Il me semble que je serais toujours bien là où je ne suis pas. In other words: It seems to me that I will always be happy in the place where I am not. Or, more bluntly: Wherever I am not is the place where I am myself. Or else, taking the bull by the horns: Anywhere out of the world.

It was almost evening. Quinn closed the red notebook and put the pen in his pocket. He wanted to think a little more about what he had written but found he could not. The air around him was soft, almost sweet, as though it no longer belonged to the city. He stood up from the bench, stretched his arms and legs, and walked to a phone booth, where he called Virginia Stillman again. Then he went to dinner.

In the restaurant he realized that he had come to a decision about things. Without his even knowing it, the answer was already there for him, sitting fully formed in his head. The busy signal, he saw now, had not been arbitrary. It had been a sign, and it was telling him that he could not yet break his connection with the case, even if he wanted to. He had tried to contact Virginia Stillman in order to tell her that he was through, but the fates had not allowed it. Quinn paused to consider this. Was 'fate' really the word he wanted to use? It seemed like such a ponderous and old-fashioned choice. And yet, as he probed more deeply into it, he discovered that was precisely what he meant to say. Or, if not precisely, it came closer than any other term he could think of. Fate in the sense of what was, of what happened to be. It was something like the word 'it' in the phrase 'it is raining' or 'it is night.' What that 'it' referred to Quinn had never known. A generalized condition of things as they were, perhaps; the state of is-ness that was the ground on which the happenings of the world took place. He could not be any more definite than that. But perhaps he was not really searching for anything definite.

It was fate, then. Whatever he thought of it, however much he might want it to be different, there was nothing he could do about it. He had said yes to a proposition, and now he was powerless to undo that yes. That meant only one thing: he had to go through with it. There could not be two answers. It was either this or that. And so it was, whether he liked it or not.

The business about Auster was clearly a mistake. Perhaps there had once been a private detective in New York with that name. The husband of Peter's nurse was a retired policeman – therefore not a young man. In his day there had no doubt been an Auster with a good reputation, and he had naturally thought of him when called upon to provide a detective. He had looked in the telephone book, had found only one person with that name and assumed he had the right man. Then he gave the number to the Stillmans. At that point, the second mistake had occurred. There had been a foul-up in the lines, and somehow his number had got crossed with Auster's. That kind of thing happened every day. And so he had received the call – which anyway had been destined for the wrong man. It all made perfect sense.

One problem still remained. If he was unable to contact Virginia Stillman – if, as he believed, he was meant *not* to contact her

– how exactly was he to proceed? His job was to protect Peter, to make sure that no harm came to him. Did it matter what Virginia Stillman thought he was doing as long as he did what he was supposed to do? Ideally, an operative should maintain close contact with his client. That had always been one of Max Work's principles. But was it really necessary? As long as Quinn did his job, how could it matter? If there were any misunderstandings, surely they could be cleared up once the case was settled.

He could proceed, then, as he wished. He would no longer have to telephone Virginia Stillman. He could abandon the oracular busy signal once and for all. From now on, there would be no stopping him. It would be impossible for Stillman to come near Peter without Quinn knowing about it.

Quinn paid up his cheque, put a mentholated toothpick in his mouth, and began walking again. He did not have far to go. Along the way, he stopped at a twenty-four hour Citibank and checked his balance with the automatic teller. There were three hundred and forty-nine dollars in his account. He withdrew three hundred, put the cash in his pocket, and continued uptown. At 57th Street he turned left and walked to Park Avenue. There he turned right and went on walking north until 69th Street, at which point he turned onto the Stillmans' block. The building looked the same as it had on the first day. He glanced up to see if there were any lights on in the apartment, but he could not remember which windows were theirs. The street was utterly quiet. No cars drove down it, no people passed. Quinn stepped across to the other side, found a spot for himself in a narrow alleyway, and settled in for the night.

12

A long time passed. Exactly how long it is impossible to say. Weeks certainly, but perhaps even months. The account of this period is less full than the author would have liked. But information is scarce, and he has preferred to pass over in silence what could not be definitely confirmed. Since this story is based entirely on facts, the author feels it his duty not to overstep the bounds of the verifiable, to resist at all costs the perils of invention. Even the red notebook, which until now has provided a detailed account of Quinn's experiences, is suspect. We cannot say for certain what happened to Quinn during this period, for it is at this point in the story that he began to lose his grip.

He remained for the most part in the alley. It was not uncomfortable once he got used to it, and it had the advantage of being well hidden from view. From there he could observe all the comings and goings at the Stillmans' building. No one left and no one entered without his seeing who it was. In the beginning, it surprised him that he saw neither Virginia nor Peter. But there were many delivery men constantly coming and going, and eventually he realized that it was not necessary for them to leave the building. Everything could be brought to them. It was then that Quinn understood that they, too, were holing up, waiting inside their apartment for the case to end.

Little by little, Quinn adapted to his new life. There were a number of problems to be faced, but one by one he managed to solve them. First of all, there was the question of food. Because utmost vigilance was required of him, he was reluctant to leave his post for any length of time. It tormented him to think that something might happen in his absence, and he made every effort to minimize the risks. He had read somewhere that between 3.30 and 4.30 am there were more people asleep in their beds than at any other time. Statistically speaking, the chances were best that nothing would happen during that hour, and therefore Quinn chose it as the time to do his shopping. On Lexington Avenue not far north there was an all-night grocery, and at three-thirty every morning Quinn would walk there at a brisk pace (for the exercise, and also to save time) and buy whatever he needed for the next twenty-four hours. It turned out not to be much – and, as it happened, he needed less and less as time went on. For Quinn learned that eating did not necessarily solve the problem of food. A meal was no more than a fragile defence against the inevitability of the next meal. Food itself could never answer the question of food: it only delayed the moment when the question would have to be asked in earnest. The greatest danger, therefore, was in eating too much. If he took in more than he should, his appetite for the next meal increased, and thus more food was needed to satisfy him. By keeping a close and constant watch on himself, Quinn was gradually able to reverse the process. His ambition was to eat as little as possible, and in this way to stave off his hunger. In the best of all worlds, he might have been able to approach absolute zero, but he did not want to be overly ambitious in his present circumstances. Rather, he kept the total fast in his mind as an ideal, a state of perfection he could aspire to but never achieve. He did not want to starve himself to death – and he reminded himself of this every day – he simply wanted to leave himself free to think of the things that truly concerned him. For now, that meant keeping the case uppermost in his thoughts. Fortunately, this coincided with his other major ambition: to make the three hundred dollars last as long as he could. It goes without saying that Quinn lost a good deal of weight during this period.

His second problem was sleep. He could not stay awake all the time, and yet that was really what the situation required. Here, too, he was forced to make certain concessions. As with eating, Quinn felt that he could make do with less than he was accustomed to. Instead of the six to eight hours of sleep he was used to getting, he decided to limit himself to three or four. Adjusting to this was difficult, but far more difficult was the problem of how to distribute these hours so as to maintain maximum vigilance. Clearly, he could not sleep for three or four hours in a row. The risks were simply too great. Theoretically, the most efficient use of the time would be to sleep for thirty seconds every five or six minutes. That would reduce his chances of missing something almost to nil. But he realized that this was physically impossible. On the other hand, using this impossibility as a kind of model, he tried to train himself into taking a series of short naps, alternating between sleeping and waking as often as he could. It was a long struggle, demanding discipline and concentration, for the longer the experiment went on, the more exhausted he became. In the beginning, he tried for sequences of forty-five minutes each, then gradually reduced them to thirty minutes. Towards the end, he had begun to manage the fifteen-minute nap with a fair amount of success. He was helped in his efforts by a near-by church, whose bells rang every fifteen minutes – one stroke on the quarter-hour, two strokes on the half-hour, three strokes on the three-quarter-hour, and four strokes on the hour, followed by the appropriate number of strokes for the hour itself. Quinn lived by the rhythm of that clock, and eventually he had trouble distinguishing it from his own pulse. Starting at midnight, he would begin his routine, closing his eyes and falling asleep before the clock had struck twelve. Fifteen minutes later he would wake, at the half-hour double stroke fall asleep, and at the three-quarter-hour triple stroke wake once more. At three-thirty he would go off for his food, return by four o'clock, and then go to sleep again. His dreams during this period were few. When they did occur, they were strange: brief visions of the immediate – his hands, his shoes, the brick wall beside him. Nor was there ever a moment when he was not dead tired.

His third problem was shelter, but this was more easily solved than the other two. Fortunately, the weather remained warm, and as late spring moved into summer, there was little rain. Every now and then there was a shower, and once or twice a downpour with thunder and lightning, but all in all it was not bad, and

Quinn never stopped giving thanks for his luck. At the back of the alley there was a large metal bin for garbage, and whenever it rained at night Quinn would climb into it for protection. Inside, the smell was overpowering, and it would permeate his clothes for days on end, but Quinn preferred it to getting wet, for he did not want to run the risk of catching cold or falling ill. Happily, the lid had been bent out of shape and did not fit tightly over the bin. In one corner there was a gap of six or eight inches that formed a kind of air hole for Quinn to breathe through – sticking his nose out into the night. By standing on his knees on top of the garbage and leaning his body against one wall of the bin, he found that he was not altogether uncomfortable.

On clear nights he would sleep under the bin, positioning his head in such a way that the moment he opened his eyes he could see the front door of Stillmans' building. As for emptying his bladder, he usually did this in the far corner of the alley, behind the bin and with his back to the street. His bowels were another matter, and for this he would climb into the bin to ensure privacy. There were also a number of plastic garbage cans beside the bin, and from one of these Quinn was usually able to find sufficiently clean newspaper to wipe himself, although once, in an emergency, he was forced to use a page from the red notebook. As for washing and shaving, these were two of the things that Quinn learned to live without.

How he managed to keep himself hidden during this period is a mystery. But it seems that no one discovered him or called his presence to the attention of the authorities. No doubt he learned early on the schedule of the garbage collectors and made sure to be out of the alley when they came. Likewise the building superintendent, who deposited the trash each evening in the bin and the cans. Remarkable as it seems, no one ever noticed Quinn. It was as though he had melted into the walls of the city.

The problems of housekeeping and material life occupied a certain portion of each day. For the most part, however, Quinn had time on his hands. Because he did not want anyone to see him, he had to avoid other people as systematically as he could.

He could not look at them, he could not talk to them, he could not think about them. Quinn had always thought of himself as a man who liked to be alone. For the past five years, in fact, he had actively sought it. But it was only now, as his life continued in the alley, that he began to understand the true nature of solitude. He had nothing to fall back on anymore but himself. And of all the things he discovered during the days he was there, this was the one he did not doubt: that he was falling. What he did not understand, however, was this: in that he was falling, how could he be expected to catch himself as well? Was it possible to be at the top and the bottom at the same time? It did not seem to make sense.

He spent many hours looking up at the sky. From his position at the back of the alley, wedged in between the bin and the wall, there were few other things to see, and as the days passed he began to take pleasure in the world overhead. He saw that, above all, the sky was never still. Even on cloudless days, when the blue seemed to be everywhere, there were constant little shifts, gradual disturbances as the sky thinned out and grew thick, the sudden whitenesses of planes, birds, and flying papers. Clouds complicated the picture, and Quinn spent many afternoons studying them, trying to learn their ways, seeing if he could not predict what would happen to them. He became familiar with the cirrus, the cumulus, the stratus, the nimbus, and all their various combinations, watching for each one in its turn, and seeing how the sky would change under its influence. Clouds, too, introduced the matter of colour, and there was a wide range to contend with, spanning from black to white, with an infinity of greys between. These all had to be investigated, measured, and deciphered. On top of this, there were the pastels that formed whenever the sun and the clouds interracted at certain times of day. The spectrum of variables was immense, the result depending on the temperatures of the different atmosphere levels, the types of clouds present in the sky, and where the sun happened to be at that particular moment. From all this came the reds and pinks that Quinn liked so much, the purples and vermilions, the oranges and lavenders, the golds and feathery persimmons. Nothing lasted for long. The colours would soon disperse, merging with others and moving on or fading as the night appeared. Almost always there was a wind to hasten these events. From where he sat in the alley, Quinn could rarely feel it, but by watching its effect on the clouds, he could gauge its intensity and the nature of the air it carried. One by one, all weathers passed over his head, from sunshine to storms, from gloom to radiance. There were the dawns and dusks to observe, the midday transformations, the early evenings, the nights. Even in its blackness, the sky did not rest. Clouds drifted through the dark, the moon was forever in a different form, the wind continued to blow. Sometimes a star even settled into Quinn's patch of sky, and as he looked up he would wonder if it was still there, or if it had not burned out long ago.

The days therefore came and went. Stillman did not appear. Quinn's money ran out at last. For some time he had been steeling himself for this moment, and towards the end he hoarded his funds with maniacal precision. No penny was spent without first judging the necessity of what he thought he needed, without first weighing all the consequences, pro and con. But not even his most stringent economies could halt the march of the inevitable.

It was some time in mid-August when Quinn discovered that he no longer could hold out. The author has confirmed this date through diligent research. It is possible, however, that this moment occurred as early as late July, or as late as early September, since all investigations of this sort must make allowances for a certain margin for error. But, to the best of his knowledge, having considered the evidence carefully and sifted through all apparent contradictions, the author places the following events in August, somewhere between the twelfth and twenty-fifth of the month.

Quinn had almost nothing now – a few coins that amounted to less than a dollar. He was certain that money had arrived for him during his absence. It was simply a matter of retrieving the cheques from his mailbox at the post office, taking them to the bank, and cashing them. If all went well, he could be back to East 69th Street within a few hours. We will never know the agonies he suffered at having to leave his spot.

He did not have enough money to take the bus. For the first time in many weeks, then, he began to walk. It was odd to be on his feet again, moving steadily from one place to the next, swinging his arms back and forth, feeling the pavement under the soles of his shoes. And yet there he was, walking west on 69th Street, turning right on Madison Avenue, and beginning to make his way north. His legs were weak, and he felt as though his head were made of air. He had to stop every now and then to catch his breath, and once, on the brink of falling, he had to grab hold of a lamp post. He found that things went better if he lifted his feet as little as possible, shuffling forward with slow, sliding steps. In this way he could conserve his strength for the corners, where he had to balance himself carefully before and after each step up and down from the curb.

At 84th Street he paused momentarily in front of a shop. There was a mirror on the façade, and for the first time since he had begun his vigil, Quinn saw himself. It was not that he had been afraid to confront his own image. Quite simply, it had not occurred to him. He had been too busy with his job to think about himself, and it was as though the question of his appearance had ceased to exist. Now, as he looked at himself in the shop mirror, he was neither shocked nor disappointed. He had no feeling about it at all, for the fact was that he did not recognize the person he saw there as himself. He thought that he had spotted a stranger in the mirror, and in that first moment he turned around sharply to see who it was. But there was no one near him. Then he turned back to examine the mirror more carefully. Feature by feature, he studied the face in front of him and slowly began to notice that this person bore a certain resemblance to the man he had always thought of as himself. Yes, it seemed more than likely that this was Quinn. Even now, however, he was not upset. The transformation in his appearance had been so drastic that he could not help but be fascinated by it. He had turned into a bum. His clothes were discoloured, disheveled, debauched by filth. His face was covered by a thick black beard with tiny flecks of grey in it. His hair was long and tangled, matted into tufts behind his ears, and crawling down in curls almost to his shoulders. More than anything else, he reminded himself of Robinson Crusoe, and he marvelled at how quickly these changes had taken place in him. It had been no more than a matter of months, and in that time he had become someone else. He tried to remember himself as he had been before, but he found it difficult. He looked at this new Quinn and shrugged. It did not really matter. He had been one thing before, and now he was another. It was neither better nor worse. It was different, and that was all.

He continued uptown for several more blocks, then turned left, crossed Fifth Avenue, and walked along the wall of Central Park. At 96th Street he entered the park and found himself glad to be among the grass and trees. Late summer had exhausted much of the greenness, and here and there the ground showed through in brown, dusty patches. But the trees overhead were still filled with leaves, and everywhere there was a sparkling of light and shade that struck Quinn as miraculous and beautiful. It was late morning, and the heavy heat of the afternoon lay several hours off.

Halfway through the park Quinn was overtaken by an urge to rest. There were no streets here, no city blocks to mark the stages of his progress, and it seemed to him suddenly that he had been walking for hours. Making it to the other side of the park felt as though it would take another day or two of dogged hiking. He went on for a few more minutes, but at last his legs gave out. There was an oak tree not far from where he stood, and Quinn went for it now, staggering in the way a drunk gropes for his bed after an all-night binge. Using the red notebook as a pillow, he lay down on a grassy mound just north of the tree and fell asleep. It was the first unbroken sleep he had had in months, and he did not wake until it was morning again.

His watch said that it was nine-thirty, and he cringed to think of the time he had lost. Quinn stood up and began loping towards the west, amazed that his strength was back, but cursing himself for the hours he had wasted in getting it. He was beyond consolation. No matter what he did now, he felt that he would always be too late. He could run for a hundred years, and still he would arrive just as the doors were closing.

He emerged from the park at 96th Street and continued west. At the corner of Columbus Avenue he saw a telephone booth, which suddenly reminded him of Auster and the five hundred dollar cheque. Perhaps he could save time by collecting the money now. He could go directly to Auster, put the cash in his pocket, and avoid the trip to the post office and the bank. But would Auster have the cash on hand? If not, perhaps they could arrange to meet at Auster's bank.

Quinn entered the booth, dug into his pocket, and removed what money was left: two dimes, a quarter, and eight pennies. He dialled information for the number, got his dime back in the coin return box, deposited the dime again, and dialled. Auster picked up on the third ring.

'Quinn here,' said Quinn.

He heard a groan on the other end. 'Where the hell have you been hiding?' There was irritation in Auster's voice. 'I've called you a thousand times.'

'I've been busy. Working on the case.'

'The case?'

'The case. The Stillman case. Remember?'

'Of course I remember.'

'That's why I'm calling. I want to come for the money now. The five hundred dollars.'

'What money?'

'The cheque, remember? The cheque I gave you. The one made out to Paul Auster.'

'Of course I remember. But there is no money. That's why I've been trying to call you.'

'You had no right to spend it,' Quinn shouted, suddenly beside himself. 'That money belonged to me.'

'I didn't spend it. The cheque bounced.'

'I don't believe you.'

'You can come here and see the letter from the bank, if you want. It's sitting here on my desk. The cheque was no good.'

'That's absurd.'

'Yes, it is. But it hardly matters now, does it?'

'Of course it matters. I need the money to go on with the case.'

'But there is no case. It's all over.'

'What are you talking about?'

'The same thing you are. The Stillman case.'

'But what do you mean "it's over?" I'm still working on it.'

'I can't believe it.'

'Stop being so goddamn mysterious. I don't have the slightest idea what you're talking about.'

'I don't believe you don't know. Where the hell have you been? Don't you read the newspapers?'

'Newspapers? Goddamnit, say what you mean. I don't have time to read newspapers.'

There was a silence on the other end, and for a moment Quinn felt that the conversation was over, that he had somehow fallen asleep and had just now woken up to find the telephone in his hand.

'Stillman jumped off the Brooklyn Bridge,' Auster said. 'He committed suicide two and a half months ago.'

'You're lying.'

'It was all over the papers. You can check for yourself.'

Quinn said nothing.

'It was your Stillman,' Auster went on. 'The one who used to be a Professor at Columbia. They say he died in mid-air, before he even hit the water.'

'And Peter? What about Peter?'

'I have no idea.'

'Does anybody know?'

'Impossible to say. You'd have to find that out yourself.'

'Yes, I suppose so,' said Quinn.

Then, without saying goodbye to Auster, he hung up. He took

the other dime and used it to call Virginia Stillman. He still knew the number by heart.

A mechanical voice spoke the number back to him and announced that it had been disconnected. The voice then repeated the message, and afterwards the line went dead.

Quinn could not be sure what he felt. In those first moments, it was as though he felt nothing, as though the whole thing added up to nothing at all. He decided to postpone thinking about it. There would be time for that later, he thought. For now, the only thing that seemed to matter was going home. He would return to his apartment, take off his clothes, and sit in a hot bath. Then he would look through the new magazines, play a few records, do a little housecleaning. Then, perhaps, he would begin to think about it.

He walked back to 107th Street. The keys to his house were still in his pocket, and as he unlocked his front door and walked up the three flights to his apartment, he felt almost happy. But then he stepped into the apartment, and that was the end of that.

Everything had changed. It seemed like another place altogether, and Quinn thought he must have entered the wrong apartment by mistake. He backed into the hall and checked the number on the door. No, he had not been wrong. It was his apartment; it was his key that had opened the door. He walked back inside and took stock of the situation. The furniture had been rearranged. Where there had once been a table there was now a chair. Where there had once been a sofa there was now a table. There were new pictures on the walls, a new rug was on the floor. And his desk? He looked for it but could not find it. He studied the furniture more carefully and saw that it was not his. What had been there the last time he was in the apartment had been removed. His desk was gone, his books were gone, the child drawings of his dead son were gone. He went from the living room to the bedroom. His bed was gone, his bureau was gone. He opened the top drawer of the bureau that was there. Women's underthings lay tangled in random clumps: panties, bras, slips.

The next drawer held women's sweaters. Quinn went no further than that. On a table near the bed there was a framed photograph of a blond, beefy-faced young man. Another photograph showed the same young man smiling, standing in the snow with his arm around an insipid looking girl. She, too, was smiling. Behind them there was a ski slope, a man with two skiis on his shoulder, and the blue winter sky.

Quinn went back to the living room and sat down in a chair. He saw a half-smoked cigarette with lipstick on it in an ashtray. He lit it up and smoked it. Then he went into the kitchen, opened the refrigerator, and found some orange juice and a loaf of bread. He drank the juice, ate three slices of bread, and then returned to the living room, where he sat down in the chair again. Fifteen minutes later he heard footsteps coming up the stairs, a jangling of keys outside the door, and then the girl from the photograph entered the apartment. She was wearing a white nurse's uniform and held a brown grocery bag in her arms. When she saw Quinn, she dropped the bag and screamed. Or else she screamed first and then dropped the bag. Quinn could never be sure which. The bag ripped open when it hit the floor, and milk gurgled in a white path toward the edge of the rug.

Quinn stood up, raised his hand in a gesture of peace, and told her not to worry. He wasn't going to hurt her. The only thing he wanted to know was why she was living in his apartment. He took the key from his pocket and held it up in the air, as if to prove his good intentions. It took him a while to convince her, but at last her panic subsided.

That did not mean she had begun to trust him or that she was any less afraid. She hung by the open door, ready to make a dash for it at the first sign of trouble. Quinn held his distance, not wanting to make things worse. His mouth kept talking, explaining again and again that she was living in his house. She clearly did not believe one word of it, but she listened in order to humour him, no doubt hoping that he would talk himself out and finally leave.

'I've been living here for a month,' she said. 'It's my apartment. I signed a year's lease.'

'But why do I have the key?' Quinn asked for the seventh or eighth time. 'Doesn't that convince you?'

'There are hundreds of ways you could have got that key.'

'Didn't they tell you there was someone living here when you rented the place?'

'They said it was a writer. But he disappeared, hadn't paid his rent in months.'

'That's me!' shouted Quinn. 'I'm the writer!'

The girl looked him over coldly and laughed. 'A writer? That's the funniest thing I ever heard. Just look at you. I've never seen a bigger mess in all my life.'

'I've had some difficulties lately,' muttered Quinn, by way of explanation. 'But it's only temporary.'

'The landlord told me he was glad to get rid of you anyway. He doesn't like tenants who don't have jobs. They use too much heat and run down the fixtures.'

'Do you know what happened to my things?'

'What things?'

'My books. My furniture. My papers.'

'I have no idea. They probably sold what they could and threw the rest away. Everything was cleared out before I moved in.'

Quinn let out a deep sigh. He had come to the end of himself. He could feel it now, as though a great truth had finally dawned in him. There was nothing left.

'Do you realize what this means?' he asked.

'Frankly, I don't care,' the girl said. 'It's your problem, not mine. I just want you to get out of here. Right now. This is my place, and I want you out. If you don't leave, I'm going to call the police and have you arrested.'

It didn't matter anymore. He could stand there arguing with the girl for the rest of the day, and still he wouldn't get his apartment back. It was gone, he was gone, everything was gone. He stammered something inaudible, excused himself for taking up her time, and walked past her out the door.

13

Because it no longer mattered to him what happened, Quinn was not surprised that the front door at 69th Street opened without a key. Nor was he surprised when he reached the ninth floor and walked down the corridor to the Stillmans' apartment that that door should be open as well. Least of all did it surprise him to find the apartment empty. The place had been stripped bare, and the rooms now held nothing. Each one was identical to every other: a wooden floor and four white walls. This made no particular impression on Quinn. He was exhausted, and the only thing he could think of was closing his eyes.

He went to one of the rooms at the back of the apartment, a small space that measured no more than ten feet by six feet. It had one wire-mesh window that gave on to a view of the airshaft, and of all the rooms it seemed to be the darkest. Within this room there was a second door which led to a windowless cubicle that contained a toilet and a sink. Quinn put the red notebook on the floor, removed the deaf mute's pen from his pocket, and tossed it onto the red notebook. Then he took off his watch and put it in his pocket. After that he took off all his clothes, opened the window, and one by one dropped each thing down the airshaft: first his right shoe, then his left shoe; one sock, and then the other sock; his shirt, his jacket, his underpants, his pants. He did not look out to watch them fall, nor did he check to see where they landed. Then he closed the window, lay down in the centre of the floor, and went to sleep.

It was dark in the room when he woke up. Quinn could not be sure how much time had passed – whether it was the night of that day or the night of the next. It was even possible, he thought, that it was not night at all. Perhaps it was merely dark inside the room, and outside, beyond the window, the sun was shining. For several moments he considered getting up and going to the window to see, but then he decided it did not matter. If it was not night now, he thought, then night would come later. That was certain, and whether he looked out the window or not, the answer would be the same. On the other hand, if it was in fact night here in New York, then surely the sun was shining somewhere else. In China, for example, it was no doubt mid-afternoon, and the rice farmers were mopping sweat from their brows. Night and day were no more than relative terms; they did not refer to an absolute condition. At any given moment, it was always both. The only reason we did not know it was because we could not be in two places at the same time.

Quinn also considered getting up and going to another room, but then he realized that he was quite happy where he was. It was comfortable here in the spot he had chosen, and he found that he enjoyed lying on his back with his eyes open, looking up at the ceiling – or what would have been the ceiling, had he been able to see it. Only one thing was lacking for him, and that was the sky. He realized that he missed having it overhead, after so many days and nights spent in the open. But he was inside now, and no matter what room he chose to camp in, the sky would remain hidden, inaccessible even at the farthest limit of sight.

He thought he would stay there until he no longer could. There would be water from the sink to quench his thirst, and that would buy him some time. Eventually, he would get hungry and have to eat. But he had been working for so long now at wanting so little that he knew this moment was still several days off. He decided not to think about it until he had to. There was no sense in worrying, he thought, no sense in troubling himself with things that did not matter.

He tried to think about the life he had lived before the story began. This caused many difficulties, for it seemed so remote to him now. He remembered the books he had written under the name of William Wilson. It was strange, he thought, that he had done that, and he wondered now why he had. In his heart, he realized that Max Work was dead. He had died somewhere on the way to his next case, and Quinn could not bring himself to feel sorry. It all seemed so unimportant now. He thought back to his desk and the thousands of words he had written there. He thought back to the man who had been his agent and realized he could not remember his name. So many things were disappearing now, it was difficult to keep track of them. Quinn tried to work his way through the Mets' lineup, position by position, but his mind was beginning to wander. The centrefielder, he remembered, was Mookie Wilson, a promising young player whose real name was William Wilson. Surely there was something interesting in that. Quinn pursued the idea for a few moments but then abandoned it. The two William Wilsons cancelled each other out, and that was all. Quinn waved goodbye to them in his mind. The Mets would finish in last place again, and no one would suffer.

The next time he woke up, the sun was shining in the room. There was a tray of food beside him on the floor, the dishes steaming with what looked like a roast beef dinner. Quinn accepted this fact without protest. He was neither surprised nor disturbed by it. Yes, he said to himself, it is perfectly possible that food should have been left here for me. He was not curious to know how or why this had taken place. It did not even occur to him to leave the room to look through the rest of the apartment for an answer. Rather, he examined the food on the tray more closely and saw that in addition to two large slices of roast beef there were seven little roast potatoes, a plate of asparagus, a fresh roll, a salad, a carafe of red wine, and wedges of cheese and a pear for dessert. There was a white linen napkin, and the silverware was of the finest quality. Quinn ate the food – or half of it, which was as much as he could manage.

After his meal, he began to write in the red notebook. He continued writing until darkness returned to the room. There was a small light fixture in the middle of the ceiling and a switch for it by the door, but the thought of using it did not appeal to Quinn. Not long after that he fell asleep again. When he woke up, there was sunlight in the room and another tray of food beside him on the floor. He ate what he could of the food and then went back to writing in the red notebook.

For the most part his entries from this period consisted of marginal questions concerning the Stillman case. Quinn wondered, for example, why he had not bothered to look up the newspaper reports of Stillman's arrest in 1969. He examined the problem of whether the moon landing of that same year had been connected in any way with what had happened. He asked himself why he had taken Auster's word for it that Stillman was dead. He tried to think about eggs and wrote out such phrases as 'a good egg', 'egg on his face', 'to lay an egg', 'to be as like as two eggs'. He wondered what would have happened if he had followed the second Stillman instead of the first. He asked himself why Christopher, the patron saint of travel, had been decanonized by the Pope in 1969, just at the time of the trip to the moon. He thought through the question of why Don Quixote had not simply wanted to write books like the ones he loved – instead of living out their adventures. He wondered why he had the same initials as Don Quixote. He considered whether the girl who had moved into his apartment was the same girl he had seen in Grand Central Station reading his book. He wondered if Virginia Stillman had hired another detective after he failed to get in touch with her. He asked himself why he had taken Auster's word for it that the cheque had bounced. He thought about Peter Stillman and wondered if he had ever slept in the room he was in now. He wondered if the case was really over or if he was not somehow still working on it. He wondered what the map would look like of all the steps he had taken in his life and what word it would spell.

When it was dark, Quinn slept, and when it was light he ate the food and wrote in the red notebook. He could never be sure how much time passed during each interval, for he did not concern himself with counting the days or the hours. It seemed to him, however, that little by little the darkness had begun to win out over the light, that whereas in the beginning there had been a predominance of sunshine, the light had gradually become fainter and more fleeting. At first, he attributed this to a change of season. The equinox had surely passed already, and perhaps the solstice was approaching. But even after winter had come and the process should theoretically have started to reverse itself, Quinn observed that the periods of dark nevertheless kept gaining on the periods of light. It seemed to him that he had less and less time to eat his food and write in the red notebook. Eventually, it seemed to him that these periods had been reduced to a matter of minutes. Once, for example, he finished his food and discovered that there was only enough time to write three sentences in the red notebook. The next time there was light, he could only manage two sentences. He began to skip his meals in order to devote himself to the red notebook, eating only when he felt he could no longer hold out. But the time continued to diminish, and soon he was able to eat no more than a bite or two before the darkness came back. He did not think of turning on the electric light, for he had long ago forgotten it was there.

This period of growing darkness coincided with the dwindling of pages in the red notebook. Little by little, Quinn was coming to the end. At a certain point, he realized that the more he wrote the sooner the time would come when he could no longer write anything. He began to weigh his words with great care, struggling to express himself as economically and clearly as possible. He regretted having wasted so many pages at the beginning of the red notebook, and in fact felt sorry that he had bothered to write about the Stillman case at all. For the case was far behind him now, and he no longer bothered to think about it. It had been a bridge to another place in his life, and now that he had crossed it, its meaning had been lost. Quinn no longer had any interest in himself. He wrote about the stars, the earth, his hopes for mankind. He felt that his words had been severed from him, that now they were a part of the world at large, as real and specific as a stone, or a lake, or a flower. They no longer had anything to do with him. He remembered the moment of his birth and how he had been pulled gently from his mother's womb. He remembered the infinite kindness of the world and all the people he had ever loved. Nothing mattered now but the beauty of all this. He wanted to go on writing about it, and it pained him to know that this would not be possible. Nevertheless, he tried to face the end of the red notebook with courage. He wondered if he had it in him to write without a pen, if he could learn to speak instead, filling the darkness with his voice, speaking the words into the air, into the walls, into the city, even if the light never came back again.

The last sentence of the red notebook reads: 'What will happen when there are no more pages in the red notebook?'

At this point the story grows obscure. The information has run out, and the events that follow this last sentence will never be known. It would be foolish even to hazard a guess.

I returned home from my trip to Africa in February, just hours before a snowstorm began to fall on New York. I called my friend Auster that evening, and he urged me to come over to see him as soon as I could. There was something so insistent in his voice that I dared not refuse, even though I was exhausted.

At his apartment, Auster explained to me what little he knew about Quinn, and then he went on to describe the strange case he had accidently become involved in. He had become obsessed by it, he said, and he wanted my advice about what he should do. Having heard him out, I began to feel angry that he had treated Quinn with such indifference. I scolded him for not having taken a greater part in events, for not having done something to help a man who was so obviously in trouble.

Auster seemed to take my words to heart. In fact, he said, that was why he had asked me over. He had been feeling guilty and needed to unburden himself. He said that I was the only person he could trust.

He had spent the last several months trying to track down Quinn, but with no success. Quinn was no longer living in his apartment, and all attempts to reach Virginia Stillman had failed. It was then that I suggested that we take a look at the Stillman apartment. Somehow, I had an intuition that this was where Quinn had wound up.

We put on our coats, went outside, and took a cab to East 69th Street. The snow had been falling for an hour, and already the roads were treacherous. We had little trouble getting into the building – slipping through the door with one of the tenants who was just coming home. We went upstairs and found the door to what had once been the Stillmans' apartment. It was unlocked. We stepped in cautiously and discovered a series of bare, empty rooms. In a small room at the back, impeccably clean as all the other rooms were, the red notebook was lying on the floor. Auster picked it up, looked through it briefly, and said that it was Quinn's. Then he handed it to me and said that I should keep it. The whole business had upset him so much that he was afraid to keep it himself. I said that I would hold on to it until he was ready to read it, but he shook his head and told me that he never wanted to see it again. Then we left and walked out into the snow. The city was entirely white now, and the snow kept falling, as though it would never end.

As for Quinn, it is impossible for me to say where he is now. I have followed the red notebook as closely as I could, and any inaccuracies in the story should be blamed on me. There were moments when the text was difficult to decipher, but I have done my best with it and have refrained from any interpretations. The red notebook, of course, is only half the story, as any sensitive reader will understand. As for Auster, I am convinced that he behaved badly throughout. If our friendship has ended, he has only himself to blame. As for me, my thoughts remain with Quinn. He will be with me always. And wherever he may have disappeared to, I wish him luck.

Ghosts

First of all there is Blue. Later there is White, and then there is Black, and before the beginning there is Brown. Brown broke him in, Brown taught him the ropes, and when Brown grew old, Blue took over. That is how it begins. The place is New York, the time is the present, and neither one will ever change. Blue goes to his office every day and sits at his desk, waiting for something to happen. For a long time nothing does, and then a man named White walks through the door, and that is how it begins.

The case seems simple enough. White wants Blue to follow a man named Black and to keep an eye on him for as long as necessary. While working for Brown, Blue did many tail jobs, and this one seems no different, perhaps even easier than most.

Blue needs the work, and so he listens to White and doesn't ask many questions. He assumes it's a marriage case and that White is a jealous husband. White doesn't elaborate. He wants a weekly report, he says, sent to such and such a postbox number, typed out in duplicate on pages so long and so wide. A cheque will be sent each week to Blue in the mail. White then tells Blue where Black lives, what he looks like, and so on. When Blue asks White how long he thinks the case will last, White says he doesn't know. Just keep sending the reports, he says, until further notice.

To be fair to Blue, he finds it all a little strange. But to say that he has misgivings at this point would be going too far. Still, it's impossible for him not to notice certain things about White. The black beard, for example, and the overly bushy eyebrows. And then there is the skin, which seems inordinately white, as though covered with powder. Blue is no amateur in the art of disguise, and it's not difficult for him to see through this one. Brown was his teacher, after all, and in his day Brown was the best in the business. So Blue begins to think he was wrong, that the case has

135

nothing to do with marriage. But he gets no farther than this, for White is still speaking to him, and Blue must concentrate on following his words.

Everything has been arranged, White says. There's a small apartment directly across the street from Black's. I've already rented it, and you can move in there today. The rent will be paid for until the case is over.

Good idea, says Blue, taking the key from White. That will eliminate the legwork.

Exactly, White answers, stroking his beard.

And so it's settled. Blue agrees to take the job, and they shake hands on it. To show his good faith, White even gives Blue an advance of ten fifty-dollar bills.

That is how it begins, then. The young Blue and a man named White, who is obviously not the man he appears to be. It doesn't matter, Blue says to himself after White has left. I'm sure he has his reasons. And besides, it's not my problem. The only thing I have to worry about is doing my job.

It is 3 February 1947. Little does Blue know, of course, that the case will go on for years. But the present is no less dark than the past, and its mystery is equal to anything the future might hold. Such is the way of the world: one step at a time, one word and then the next. There are certain things that Blue cannot possibly know at this point. For knowledge comes slowly, and when it comes, it is often at great personal expense.

White leaves the office, and a moment later Blue picks up the phone and calls the future Mrs Blue. I'm going under cover, he tells his sweetheart. Don't worry if I'm out of touch for a little while. I'll be thinking of you the whole time.

Blue takes a small grey satchel down from the shelf and packs it with his thirty-eight, a pair of binoculars, a notebook, and other tools of the trade. Then he tidies his desk, puts his papers in order, and locks up the office. From there he goes to the apartment that White has rented for him. The address is unimportant. But let's say Brooklyn Heights, for the sake of argument. Some quiet, rarely travelled street not far from the bridge – Orange

Street perhaps. Walt Whitman handset the first edition of *Leaves of Grass* on this street in 1855, and it was here that Henry Ward Beecher railed against slavery from the pulpit of his red-brick church. So much for local colour.

It's a small studio apartment on the third floor of a four-storey brownstone. Blue is happy to see that it's fully equipped, and as he walks around the room inspecting the furnishings, he discovers that everything in the place is new: the bed, the table, the chair, the rug, the linens, the kitchen supplies, everything. There is a complete set of clothes hanging in the closet, and Blue, wondering if the clothes are meant for him, tries them on and sees that they fit. It's not the biggest place I've ever been in, he says to himself, pacing from one end of the room to the other, but it's cosy enough, cosy enough.

He goes back outside, crosses the street, and enters the opposite building. In the entryway he searches for Black's name on one of the mailboxes and finds it: Black – 3rd floor. So far so good. Then he returns to his room and gets down to business.

Parting the curtains of the window, he looks out and sees Black sitting at a table in his room across the street. To the extent that Blue can make out what is happening, he gathers that Black is writing. A look through the binoculars confirms that he is. The lenses, however, are not powerful enough to pick up the writing itself, and even if they were, Blue doubts that he would be able to read the handwriting upside down. All he can say for certain, therefore, is that Black is writing in a notebook with a red fountain pen. Blue takes out his own notebook and writes: 3 Feb. 3pm Black writing at his desk.

Now and then Black pauses in his work and gazes out the window. At one point, Blue thinks that he is looking directly at him and ducks out of the way. But on closer inspection he realizes that it is merely a blank stare, signifying thought rather than seeing, a look that makes things invisible, that does not let them in. Black gets up from his chair every once in a while and disappears to a hidden spot in the room, a corner Blue supposes, or perhaps the bathroom, but he is never gone for very long, always returning promptly to the desk. This goes on for several hours, and Blue is none the wiser for his efforts. At six o'clock he writes the second sentence in his notebook: This goes on for several hours.

It's not so much that Blue is bored, but that he feels thwarted. Without being able to read what Black has written, everything is a blank so far. Perhaps he's a madman, Blue thinks, plotting to blow up the world. Perhaps that writing has something to do with his secret formula. But Blue is immediately embarrassed by such a childish notion. It's too early to know anything, he says to himself, and for the time being he decides to suspend judgement.

His mind wanders from one small thing to another, eventually settling on the future Mrs Blue. They were planning to go out tonight, he remembers, and if it hadn't been for White showing up at the office today and this new case, he would be with her now. First the Chinese restaurant on 39th Street, where they would have wrestled with the chopsticks and held hands under the table, and then the double feature at the Paramount. For a brief moment he has a startlingly clear picture of her face in his mind (laughing with lowered eyes, feigning embarrassment), and he realizes that he would much rather be with her than sitting in this little room for God knows how long. He thinks about calling her up on the phone for a chat, hesitates, and then decides against it. He doesn't want to seem weak. If she knew how much he needed her, he would begin to lose his advantage, and that wouldn't be good. The man must always be the stronger one.

Black has now cleared his table and replaced the writing materials with dinner. He sits there chewing slowly, staring out the window in that abstracted way of his. At the sight of food, Blue realizes that he is hungry and hunts through the kitchen cabinet for something to eat. He settles on a meal of canned stew and soaks up the gravy with a slice of white bread. After dinner he has some hope that Black will be going outside, and he is encouraged when he sees a sudden flurry of activity in Black's room. But all comes to nothing. Fifteen minutes later, Black is sitting at his desk again, this time reading a book. A lamp is on beside him, and Blue has a clearer view of Black's face than before. Blue estimates Black's age to be the same as his, give or take a year or two. That is to say, somewhere in his late twenties or early thirties. He finds Black's face pleasant enough, with nothing to distinguish it from a thousand other faces one sees every day. This is a disappointment to Blue, for he is still secretly hoping to discover that Black is a madman. Blue looks through the binoculars and reads the title of the book that Black is reading. *Walden*, by Henry David Thoreau. Blue has never heard of it before and writes it down carefully in his notebook.

So it goes for the rest of the evening, with Black reading and Blue watching him read. As time passes, Blue grows more and more discouraged. He's not used to sitting around like this, and with the darkness closing in on him now, it's beginning to get on his nerves. He likes to be up and about, moving from one place to another, doing things. I'm not the Sherlock Holmes type, he would say to Brown, whenever the boss gave him a particularly sedentary task. Give me something I can sink my teeth into. Now, when he himself is the boss, this is what he gets: a case with nothing to do. For to watch someone read and write is in effect to do nothing. The only way for Blue to have a sense of what is happening is to be inside Black's mind, to see what he is thinking, and that of course is impossible. Little by little, therefore, Blue lets his own mind drift back to the old days. He thinks of Brown and some of the cases they worked on together, savouring the memory of their triumphs. There was the Redman Affair, for example, in which they tracked down the bank-teller who had embezzled a quarter of a million dollars. For that one Blue pretended to be a bookie and lured Redman into placing a bet with him. The money was traced back to the bills missing from the bank, and the man got what was coming to him. Even better was the Gray Case. Gray had been missing for over a year, and his wife was ready to give him up for dead. Blue searched through all the normal channels and came up empty. Then, one day, as he was about to file his final report, he stumbled on Gray in a bar, not two blocks from where the wife was sitting, convinced he would never return. Gray's name was now Green, but Blue knew it was Gray in spite of this, for he had been carrying around a photograph of the man for the past three months and knew his face by heart. It turned out to be amnesia. Blue took Gray back to his wife, and although he didn't remember her and continued to call himself Green, he found her to his liking and some days later proposed marriage. So Mrs Gray became Mrs Green, married to the same man a second time, and while Gray never remembered the past – and stubbornly refused to admit that he had forgotten anything – that did not seem to stop him from living comfortably in the present. Whereas Gray had worked as an engineer in his former life, as Green he now kept the job as bartender in the bar two blocks away. He liked mixing the drinks, he said, and talking to the people who came in, and he couldn't imagine doing anything else. I was born to be a bartender, he announced to Brown and Blue at the wedding party, and who were they to object to what a man chose to do with his life?

Those were the good old days, Blue says to himself now, as he watches Black turn off the light in his room across the street. Full of strange twists and amusing coincidences. Well, not every case can be exciting. You've got to take the good with the bad.

Blue, ever the optimist, wakes up the next morning in a cheerful mood. Outside, snow is falling on the quiet street, and everything has turned white. After watching Black eat his breakfast at the table by the window and read a few more pages of *Walden*, Blue sees him to retreat to the back of the room and then return to the window dressed in his overcoat. The time is shortly after eight o'clock. Blue reaches for his hat, his coat, his muffler and boots, hastily scrambles into them, and gets downstairs to the street less than a minute after Black. It is a windless morning, so still that he can hear the snow falling on the branches of the trees. No one else is about, and Black's shoes have made a perfect set of tracks on the white pavement. Blue follows the tracks around the corner and then sees Black ambling down the next street, as if enjoying the weather. Not the behaviour of a man about to escape, Blue thinks, and accordingly he slows his pace. Two streets later, Black enters a small grocery store, stays ten or twelve minutes, and then comes out with two heavily loaded brown paper bags. Without noticing Blue, who is standing in a doorway across the street, he begins retracing his steps towards Orange Street. Stocking up for the storm, Blue says to himself. Blue then decides to risk losing contact with Black and goes into the store himself to do the same. Unless it's a decoy, he thinks, and Black is planning to dump the groceries and take off, it's fairly certain that he's on his way home. Blue therefore does his own shopping, stops in next door to buy a newspaper and several magazines, and then returns to his room on Orange Street. Sure enough, Black is already at his desk by the window, writing in the same notebook as the day before.

Because of the snow, visibility is poor, and Blue has trouble deciphering what is happening in Black's room. Even the binoculars don't help much. The day remains dark, and through the endlessly falling snow, Black appears to be no more than a shadow. Blue resigns himself to a long wait and then settles down with his newspapers and magazines. He is a devoted reader of *True Detective* and tries never to miss a month. Now, with time on his hands, he reads the new issue thoroughly, even pausing to read the little notices and ads on the back pages. Buried among the feature stories on gangbusters and secret agents, there is one short article that strikes a chord in Blue, and even after he finishes the magazine, he finds it difficult not to keep thinking about it. Twenty-five years ago, it seems, in a patch of woods outside Philadelphia, a little boy was found murdered. Although the police promptly began work on the case, they never managed to come up with any clues. Not only did they have no suspects, they could not even identify the boy. Who he was, where he had come from, why he was there – all these questions remained unanswered. Eventually, the case was dropped from the active file, and if not for the coroner who had been assigned to do the autopsy on the boy, it would have been forgotten altogether. This man, whose name was Gold, became obsessed by the murder. Before the child was buried, he made a death mask of his face, and from then on devoted whatever time he could to the mystery. After twenty years, he reached retirement age, left his job, and began spending every moment on the case. But things did not go well. He made no headway, came not one step closer to solving the crime. The article in *True Detective* describes how he is now offering a reward of two thousand dollars to anyone who can provide information about the little boy. It also includes a grainy, retouched photograph of the man holding the death mask in his hands. The look in his eyes is so haunted and imploring that Blue can scarcely turn his own eyes away. Gold is growing old now, and he is afraid that he will die before he solves the case. Blue is deeply moved by this. If it were possible, he would like nothing better than to drop what he's doing and try to help Gold. There aren't enough men like that, he thinks. If the boy were Gold's son, then it would make sense: revenge, pure and simple, and anyone can understand that. But the boy was a complete stranger to him, and so there's nothing personal about it, no hint of a secret motive. It is this thought that so affects Blue. Gold refuses to accept a world in which the murderer of a child can go unpunished, even if the murderer himself is now dead, and he is willing to sacrifice his own life and happiness to right the wrong. Blue then thinks about the little boy for a while, trying to imagine what really happened, trying to feel what the boy must have felt, and then it dawns on him that the murderer must have been one of the parents, for otherwise the boy would have been reported as missing. That only makes it worse, Blue thinks, and as he begins to grow sick at the thought of it, fully understanding now what Gold must feel all the time, he realizes that twenty-five years ago he too was a little boy and that had the boy lived he would be Blue's age now. It could have been me, Blue thinks. I could have been that little boy. Not knowing what else to do, he cuts out the picture from the magazine and tacks it onto the wall above his bed.

So it goes for the first days. Blue watches Black, and little of anything happens. Black writes, reads, eats, takes brief strolls through the neighbourhood, seems not to notice that Blue is there. As for Blue, he tries not to worry. He assumes that Black is lying low, biding his time until the right moment comes. Since Blue is only one man, he realizes that constant vigilance is not expected of him. After all, you can't watch someone twenty-four hours a day. There has to be time for you to sleep, to eat, to do your laundry, and so on. If White wanted Black to be watched around the clock, he would have hired two or three men, not one. But Blue is only one, and more than what is possible he cannot do.

Still, he does begin to worry, in spite of what he tells himself. For if Black must be watched, then it would follow that he must be watched every hour of every day. Anything less than constant surveillance would be as no surveillance at all. It would not take much, Blue reasons, for the entire picture to change. A single moment's inattention – a glance to the side of him, a pause to scratch his head, the merest yawn – and presto, Black slips away and commits whatever heinous act he is planning to commit. And yet, there will necessarily be such moments, hundreds and even thousands of them every day. Blue finds this troubling, for no matter how often he turns this problem over inside himself, he gets no closer to solving it. But that is not the only thing that troubles him.

Until now, Blue has not had much chance for sitting still, and this new idleness has left him at something of a loss. For the first time in his life, he finds that he has been thrown back on himself, with nothing to grab hold of, nothing to distinguish one moment from the next. He has never given much thought to the world inside him, and though he always knew it was there, it has remained an unknown quantity, unexplored and therefore dark, even to himself. He has moved rapidly along the surface of things for as long as he can remember, fixing his attention on these surfaces only in order to perceive them, sizing up one and then passing on to the next, and he has always taken pleasure in the world as such, asking no more of things than that they be there. And until now they have been, etched vividly against the daylight, distinctly telling him what they are, so perfectly themselves and nothing else that he has never had to pause before them or look twice. Now, suddenly, with the world as it were removed from him, with nothing much to see but a vague shadow by the name of Black, he finds himself thinking about things that have never occurred to him before, and this, too, has begun to trouble him. If thinking is perhaps too strong a word at this point, a slightly more modest term – speculation, for example – would not be far from the mark. To speculate, from the Latin *speculatus*, meaning mirror or looking glass. For in spying out at Black across the street, it is as though Blue were looking into a mirror, and instead of merely watching another, he finds that he is also watching himself. Life has slowed down so drastically for him that Blue is now able to see things that have previously escaped his attention. The trajectory of the light that passes through the room each day, for example, and the way the sun at certain hours will reflect the snow on the far corner of the ceiling in his room. The beating of his heart, the sound of his breath, the blinking of his eyes – Blue is now aware of these tiny events, and try as he might to ignore them, they persist in his mind like a nonsensical phrase repeated over and over again. He knows it cannot be true, and yet little by little this phrase seems to be taking on a meaning.

Of Black, of White, of the job he has been hired to do, Blue now begins to advance certain theories. More than just helping to pass the time, he discovers that making up stories can be a pleasure in itself. He thinks that perhaps White and Black are brothers and that a large sum of money is at stake – an inheritance, for example, or the capital invested in a partnership. Perhaps White wants to prove that Black is incompetent, have him committed to an institution, and take control of the family fortune himself. But Black is too clever for that and has gone into hiding, waiting for the pressure to ease up. Another theory that Blue puts forward has White and Black as rivals, both of them racing toward the same goal – the solution to a scientific problem, for example – and White wants Black watched in order to be sure he isn't outsmarted. Still another story has it that White is a renegade agent from the FBI or some espionage organization, perhaps foreign, and has struck out on his own to conduct some peripheral investigation not necessarily sanctioned by his superiors. By hiring Blue to do his work for him, he can keep the surveillance of Black a secret and at the same time continue to perform his normal duties. Day by day, the list of these stories grows, with Blue sometimes returning in his mind to an early story to add certain flourishes and details and at other times starting over again with something new. Murder plots, for instance, and kidnapping schemes for giant ransoms. As the days go on, Blue realizes there is no end to the stories he can tell. For Black is no more than a kind of blankness, a hole in the texture of things, and one story can fill this hole as well as any other.

Blue does not mince words, however. He knows that more than anything else he would like to learn the real story. But at this early stage he also knows that patience is called for. Bit by bit, therefore, he begins to dig in, and with each day that passes he finds himself a little more comfortable with his situation, a little more resigned to the fact that he is in for the long haul.

Unfortunately, thoughts of the future Mrs Blue occasionally disturb his growing peace of mind. Blue misses her more than ever, but he also senses somehow that things will never be the same again. Where this feeling comes from he cannot tell. But while he feels reasonably content whenever he confines his thoughts to Black, to his room, to the case he is working on, whenever the future Mrs Blue enters his consciousness, he is seized by a kind of panic. All of a sudden, his calm turns to anguish, and he feels as though he is falling into some dark, cave-like place, with no hope of finding a way out. Nearly every day he has been tempted to pick up the phone and call her, thinking that perhaps a moment of real contact would break the spell. But the days pass, and still he doesn't call. This, too, is troubling to him, for he cannot remember a time in his life when he has been so reluctant to do a thing he so clearly wants to do. I'm changing, he says to himself. Little by little, I'm no longer the same. This interpretation reassures him somewhat, at least for a while, but in the end it only leaves him feeling stranger than before. The days pass, and it becomes difficult for him not to keep seeing pictures of the future Mrs Blue in his head, especially at night, and there in the darkness of his room, lying on his back with his eyes open, he reconstructs her body piece by piece, beginning with her feet and ankles, working his way up her legs and along her thighs, climbing from her belly toward her breasts, and then, roaming happily among the softness, dipping down to her buttocks and then up again along her back, at last finding her neck and curling forward to her round and smiling face. What is she doing now? he sometimes asks himself. And what does she think of all this? But he can never come up with a satisfactory answer. If he is able to invent a multitude of stories to fit the facts concerning Black, with the future Mrs Blue all is silence, confusion, and emptiness.

The day comes for him to write his first report. Blue is an old hand at such compositions and has never had any trouble with them. His method is to stick to outward facts, describing events as though each word tallied exactly with the thing described, and to question the matter no further. Words are transparent for him, great windows that stand between him and the world, and until now they have never impeded his view, have never even seemed to be there. Oh, there are moments when the glass gets a trifle smudged and Blue has to polish it in one spot or another, but once he finds the right word, everything clears up. Drawing on the entries he has made previously in his notebook, sifting through them to refresh his memory and to underscore pertinent remarks, he tries to fashion a coherent whole, discarding the slack and embellishing the gist. In every report he has written so far, action holds forth over interpretation. For example: The subject walked from Columbus Circle to Carnegie Hall. No references to the weather, no mention of the traffic, no stab at trying to guess what the subject might be thinking. The report confines itself to known and verifiable facts, and beyond this limit it does not try to go.

Faced with the facts of the Black case, however, Blue grows aware of his predicament. There is the notebook, of course, but when he looks through it to see what he has written, he is disappointed to find such paucity of detail. It's as though his words, instead of drawing out the facts and making them sit palpably in the world, have induced them to disappear. This has never happened to Blue before. He looks out across the street and sees Black sitting at his desk as usual. Black, too, is looking through the window at that moment, and it suddenly occurs to Blue that he can no longer depend on the old procedures. Clues, legwork, investigative routine – none of this is going to matter anymore. But then, when he tries to imagine what will replace these things, he gets nowhere. At this point, Blue can only surmise what the case is not. To say what it is, however, is completely beyond him.

Blue sets his typewriter on the table and casts about for ideas, trying to apply himself to the task at hand. He thinks that perhaps a truthful account of the past week would include the various stories he has made up for himself concerning Black. With so little else to report, these excursions into the make-believe would at least give some flavour of what has happened. But Blue brings himself up short, realizing that they have nothing really to do with Black. This isn't the story of my life, after all, he says. I'm supposed to be writing about him, not myself.

Still, it looms as a perverse temptation, and Blue must struggle with himself for some time before fighting it off. He goes back to the beginning and works his way through the case, step by step. Determined to do exactly what has been asked of him, he painstakingly composes the report in the old style, tackling each detail with such care and aggravating precision that many hours go by before he manages to finish. As he reads over the results, he is forced to admit that everything seems accurate. But then why does he feel so dissatisfied, so troubled by what he has written? He says to himself: what happened is not really what happened. For the first time in his experience of writing reports, he discovers that words do not necessarily work, that it is possible for them to obscure the things they are trying to say. Blue looks around the room and fixes his attention on various objects, one after the other. He sees the lamp and says to himself, lamp. He sees the bed and says to himself, bed. He sees the notebook and says to himself, notebook. It will not do to call the lamp a bed, he thinks, or the bed a lamp. No, these words fit snugly around the things they stand for, and the moment Blue speaks them, he feels a deep satisfaction, as though he has just proved the existence of the world. Then he looks out across the street and sees Black's window. It is dark now, and Black is asleep. That's the problem, Blue says to himself, trying to find a little courage. That and nothing else. He's there, but it's impossible to see him. And even when I do see him it's as though the lights are out.

He seals up his report in an envelope and goes outside, walks to the corner and drops it into the mailbox. I may not be the smartest person in the world, he says to himself, but I'm doing my best, I'm doing my best.

After that, the snow begins to melt. The next morning, the sun is shining brightly, clusters of sparrows are chirping in the trees, and Blue can hear the pleasant dripping of water from the edge of the roof, the branches, the lampposts. Spring suddenly does not seem far away. Another few weeks, he says to himself, and every morning will be like this one.

Black takes advantage of the weather to wander farther afield than previously, and Blue follows. Blue is relieved to be moving again, and as Black continues on his way, Blue hopes the journey will not end before he's had a chance to work out the kinks. As one would imagine, he has always been an ardent walker, and to feel his legs striding along through the morning air fills him with happiness. As they move through the narrow streets of Brooklyn Heights, Blue is encouraged to see that Black keeps increasing his distance from home. But then, his mood suddenly darkens. Black begins to climb the staircase that leads to the walkway across the Brooklyn Bridge, and Blue gets it into his head that he's planning to jump. Such things happen, he tells himself. A man goes to the top of the bridge, gives a last look to the world through the wind and the clouds, and then leaps out over the water, bones cracking on impact, his body broken apart. Blue gags on the image, tells himself to stay alert. If anything starts to happen, he decides, he will step out from his role as neutral bystander and intervene. For he does not want Black to be dead – at least not yet.

It has been many years since Blue crossed the Brooklyn Bridge on foot. The last time was with his father when he was a boy, and the memory of that day comes back to him now. He can see himself holding his father's hand and walking at his side, and as he hears the traffic moving along the steel bridge-road below, he can remember telling his father that the noise sounded like the buzzing of an enormous swarm of bees. To his left is the Statue of Liberty; to his right is Manhattan, the buildings so tall in the morning sun they seem to be figments. His father was a great one for facts, and he told Blue the stories of all the monuments and skyscrapers, vast litanies of detail – the architects, the dates, the political intrigues – and how at one time the Brooklyn Bridge was the tallest structure in America. The old man was born the same year the bridge was finished, and there was always that link in Blue's mind, as though the bridge were somehow a monument to his father. He liked the story he was told that day as he and Blue Senior walked home over the same wooden planks he was walking on now, and for some reason he never forgot it. How John Roebling, the designer of the bridge, got his foot crushed between the dock pilings and a ferry boat just days after finishing the plans and died from gangrene in less than three weeks. He didn't have to die, Blue's father said, but the only treatment he would accept was hydrotherapy, and that proved useless, and Blue was struck that a man who had spent his life building bridges over bodies of water so that people wouldn't get wet should believe that the only true medicine consisted in immersing oneself in water. After John Roebling's death, his son Washington took over as chief engineer, and that was another curious story. Washington Roebling was just thirty-one at the time, with no building experience except for the wooden bridges he designed during the Civil War, but he proved to be even more brilliant than his father. Not long after construction began on the Brooklyn Bridge, however, he was trapped for several hours during a fire in one of the underwater caissons and came out of it with a severe case of the bends, an excruciating disease in which nitrogen bubbles gather in the bloodstream. Nearly killed by the attack, he was thereafter an invalid, unable to leave the top floor room where he and his wife set up house in Brooklyn Heights. There Washington Roebling sat every day for many years, watching the progress of the bridge through a telescope, sending his wife down every morning with his instructions, drawing elaborate colour pictures for the foreign workers who spoke no English so they would understand what to do next, and the remarkable thing was that the whole bridge was literally in his head: every piece of it had been memorized, down to the tiniest bits of steel and stone, and though Washington Roebling never set foot on the bridge, it was totally present inside him, as though by the end of all those years it had somehow grown into his body.

Blue thinks of this now as he makes his way across the river, watching Black ahead of him and remembering his father and his boyhood out in Gravesend. The old man was a cop, later a detective at the 77th precinct, and life would have been good, Blue thinks, if it hadn't been for the Russo Case and the bullet that went through his father's brain in 1927. Twenty years ago, he says to himself, suddenly appalled by the time that has passed, wondering if there is a heaven, and if so whether or not he will get to see his father again after he dies. He remembers a story from one of the endless magazines he has read this week, a new monthly called *Stranger than Fiction*, and it seems somehow to follow from all the other thoughts that have just come to him. Somewhere in the French Alps, he recalls, a man was lost skiing twenty or twenty-five years ago, swallowed up by an avalanche, and his body was never recovered. His son, who was a little boy at the time, grew up and also became a skier. One day in the past year he went skiing, not far from the spot where his father was lost – although he did not know this. Through the minute and persistent displacements of the ice over the decades since his father's death, the terrain was now completely different from what it had been. All alone there in the mountains, miles away from any other human being, the son chanced upon a body in the ice – a dead body, perfectly intact, as though preserved in suspended animation. Needless to say, the young man stopped to examine it, and as he bent down and looked at the face of the corpse, he had the distinct and terrifying impression that he was looking at himself. Trembling with fear, as the article put it, he inspected the body more closely, all sealed away as it was in the ice, like someone on the other side of a thick window, and saw that it was his father. The dead man was still young, even younger than his son was now, and there was something awesome about it, Blue felt, something so odd and terrible about being older than your own father, that he actually had to fight back tears as he read the article. Now, as he nears the end of the bridge, these same feelings come back to him, and he wishes to God that his father could be there, walking over the river and telling him stories. Then. suddenly aware of what his mind is doing, he wonders why he has turned so sentimental, why all these thoughts keep coming to him, when for so many years they have never even occured to him. It's all part of it, he thinks, embarrassed at himself for being like this. That's what happens when you have no one to talk to.

He comes to the end and sees that he was wrong about Black. There will be no suicides today, no jumping from bridges, no leaps into the unknown. For there goes his man, as blithe and unperturbed as anyone can be, descending the stairs of the walkway and travelling along the street that curves around City Hall, then moving north along Centre Street past the courthouse and other municipal buildings, never once slackening his pace, continuing on through Chinatown and beyond. These divagations last several hours, and at no point does Blue have the sense that Black is walking to any purpose. He seems rather to be airing his lungs, walking for the pure pleasure of walking, and as the journey goes on Blue confesses to himself for the first time that he is developing a certain fondness for Black.

At one point Black enters a bookstore and Blue follows him in. There Black browses for half an hour or so, accumulating a small pile of books in the process, and Blue, with nothing better to do, browses as well, all the while trying to keep his face hidden from Black. The little glances he takes when Black seems not to be looking give him the feeling that he has seen Black before, but he can't remember where. There's something about the eyes, he says to himself, but that's as far as he gets, not wanting to call attention to himself and not really sure if there's anything to it.

A minute later, Blue comes across a copy of *Walden* by Henry David Thoreau. Flipping through the pages, he is surprised to discover that the name of the publisher is Black: 'Published for the Classics Club by Walter J. Black, Inc., Copyright 1942.' Blue is momentarily jarred by this coincidence, thinking that perhaps there is some message in it for him, some glimpse of meaning that could make a difference. But then, recovering from the jolt, he begins to think not. It's a common enough name, he says to himself – and besides, he knows for a fact that Black's name is not Walter. Could be a relative though, he adds, or maybe even his father. Still turning this last point over in his mind, Blue decides to buy the book. If he can't read what Black writes, at least he can read what he reads. A long shot, he says to himself, but who knows that it won't give him some hint of what the man is up to.

So far so good. Black pays for his books, Blue pays for his book, and the walk continues. Blue keeps looking for some pattern to emerge, for some clue to drop in his path that will lead him to Black's secret. But Blue is too honest a man to delude himself, and he knows that no rhyme or reason can be read into anything that's happened so far. For once, he is not discouraged by this. In fact, as he probes more deeply into himself, he realizes that on the whole he feels rather invigorated by it. There is something nice about being in the dark, he discovers, something thrilling about not knowing what is going to happen next. It keeps you alert, he thinks, and there's no harm in that, is there? Wide awake and on your toes, taking it all in, ready for anything.

A few moments after thinking this thought, Blue is finally

offered a new development, and the case takes on its first twist. Black turns a corner in midtown, walks halfway down the block, hesitates briefly, as if searching for an address, backtracks a few paces, moves on again, and several seconds later enters a restaurant. Blue follows him in, thinking nothing much of it, since it's lunchtime after all, and people have to eat, but it does not escape him that Black's hesitation seems to indicate that he's never been here before, which in turn might mean that Black has an appointment. It's a dark place inside, fairly crowded, with a group of people clustered around the bar in front, lots of chatter and the clinking of silverware and plates in the background. It looks expensive, Blue thinks, with wood panelling on the walls and white tablecloths, and he decides to keep his bill as low as he can. Tables are available, and Blue takes it as a good omen when he is seated within eyeshot of Black, not obtrusively close, but not so far as not to be able to watch what he does. Black tips his hand by asking for two menus, and three or four minutes later breaks into a smile when a woman walks across the room, approaches Black's table, and kisses him on the cheek before sitting down. The woman's not bad, Blue thinks. A bit on the lean side for his taste, but not bad at all. Then he thinks: now the interesting part begins.

Unfortunately, the woman's back is turned to Blue, so he can't watch her face as the meal progresses. As he sits there eating his Salisbury steak, he thinks that maybe his first hunch was the right one, that it's a marriage case after all. Blue is already imagining the kinds of things he will write in his next report, and it gives him pleasure to contemplate the phrases he will use to describe what he is seeing now. By having another person in the case, he knows that certain decisions have to be made. For example: should he stick with Black or divert his attention to the woman? This could possibly accelerate matters a bit, but at the same time it could mean that Black would be given the chance to slip away from him, perhaps for good. In other words, is the meeting with the woman a smoke-screen or the real thing? Is it a part of the case or not, is it an essential or contingent fact? Blue ponders these questions for a while and concludes that it's too early to tell. Yes, it could be one thing, he tells himself. But it could also be another.

About midway through the meal, things seem to take a turn for the worse. Blue detects a look of great sadness in Black's face, and before he knows it the woman seems to be crying. At least that is what he can gather from the sudden change in the position of her body: her shoulders slumped, her head leaning forward, her face perhaps covered by her hands, the slight shuddering along her back. It could be a fit of laughter, Blue reasons, but then why would Black be so miserable? It looks as though the ground has just been cut out from under him. A moment later, the woman turns her face away from Black, and Blue gets a glimpse of her in profile: tears without question, he thinks, as he watches her dab her eyes with a napkin and sees a smudge of wet mascara glistening on her cheek. She stands up abruptly and walks off in the direction of the ladies' room. Again Blue has an unobstructed view of Black, and seeing that sadness in his face, that look of absolute dejection, he almost begins to feel sorry for him. Black glances in Blue's direction, but clearly he's not seeing anything, and then, an instant later, he buries his face in his hands. Blue tries to guess what is happening, but it's impossible to know. It looks like it's over between them, he thinks, it has the feeling of something that's come to an end. And yet, for all that, it could just be a tiff.

The woman returns to the table looking a little better, and then the two of them sit there for a few minutes without saying anything, leaving their food untouched. Black sighs once or twice, looking off into the distance, and finally calls for a cheque. Blue does the same and then follows the two of them out of the restaurant. He notes that Black has his hand on her elbow, but that could just be a reflex, he tells himself, and probably means nothing. They walk down the street in silence, and at the corner Black waves down a cab. He opens the door for the woman, and before she climbs in he touches her very gently on the cheek. She gives him a brave little smile in return, but still they don't say a word. Then she sits down in the back seat, Black shuts the door, and the cab takes off.

Black walks around for a few minutes, pausing briefly in front of a travel agency window to study a poster of the White Mountains, and then climbs into a cab himself. Blue gets lucky again and manages to find another cab just seconds later. He tells the driver to follow Black's cab and then sits back as the two yellow cars make their way slowly through the traffic downtown, across the Brooklyn Bridge, and finally to Orange Street. Blue is shocked by the fare and kicks himself mentally for not following the woman instead. He should have known that Black was going home.

His mood brightens considerably when he enters his building and finds a letter in his mailbox. It can only be one thing, he tells himself, and sure enough, as he walks upstairs and opens the envelope, there it is: the first cheque, a postal money order for the exact amount settled on with White. He finds it a bit perplexing, however, that the method of payment should be anonymous. Why not a personal cheque from White? This leads Blue to toy with the thought that White is a renegade agent after all, eager to cover his tracks and therefore making sure there will be no record of the payments. Then, removing his hat and overcoat and stretching out on the bed, Blue realizes that he's a little disappointed not to have had some comment about the report. Considering how hard he struggled to get it right, a word of encouragement would have been welcomed. The fact that the money was sent means that White was not dissatisfied. But still – silence is not a rewarding response, no matter what it means. If that's the way it is, Blue says to himself, I'll just have to get used to it.

The days go by, and once again things settle down to the barest of routines. Black writes, reads, shops in the neighbourhood, visits the post office, takes an occasional stroll. The woman does not reappear, and Black makes no further excursions to Manhattan. Blue begins to think that any day he will get a letter telling him the case is closed. The woman is gone, he reasons, and that could be the end of it. But nothing of the sort happens. Blue's meticulous description of the scene in the restaurant draws no special response from White, and week after week the cheques continue to arrive on time. So much for love, Blue says to himself. The woman never meant anything. She was just a diversion.

In this early period, Blue's state of mind can best be described as one of ambivalence and conflict. There are moments when he feels so completely in harmony with Black, so naturally at one with the other man, that to anticipate what Black is going to do, to know when he will stay in his room and when he will go out, he need merely look into himself. Whole days go by when he doesn't even bother to look through the window or follow Black onto the street. Now and then, he even allows himself to make solo expeditions, knowing full well that during the time he is gone Black will not have budged from his spot. How he knows this remains something of a mystery to him, but the fact is that he is never wrong, and when the feeling comes over him, he is beyond all doubt and hesitation. On the other hand, not all moments are like these. There are times when he feels totally removed from Black, cut off from him in a way that is so stark and absolute that he begins to lose the sense of who he is. Loneliness envelops him, shuts him in, and with it comes a terror worse than anything he has ever known. It puzzles him that he should switch so rapidly from one state to another, and for a long time he goes back and forth between extremes, not knowing which one is true and which one false.

After a stretch of particularly bad days, he begins to long for some companionship. He sits down and writes a detailed letter to Brown, outlining the case and asking for his advice. Brown has retired to Florida, where he spends most of his time fishing, and Blue knows that it will take quite a while before he receives an answer. Still, the day after he mails the letter, he begins looking forward to the reply with an eagerness that soon grows to obsession. Each morning, about an hour before the mail is delivered, he plants himself by the window, watching for the postman to round the corner and come into view, pinning all his hopes on what Brown will say to him. What he is expecting from this letter is not certain. Blue does not even ask the question, but surely it is something monumental, some luminous and extra-ordinary words that will bring him back to the world of the living.

As the days and weeks go by without any letter from Brown, Blue's disappointment grows into an aching, irrational despera-tion. But that is nothing compared to what he feels when the letter finally comes. For Brown does not even address himself to what Blue wrote. It's good to hear from you, the letter begins, and good to know you're working so hard. Sounds like an interesting case. Can't say I miss any of it, though. Here it's the good life for me – get up early and fish, spend some time with the wife, read a little, sleep in the sun, nothing to complain about. The only thing I don't understand is why I didn't move down here years ago.

The letter goes on in that vein for several pages, never once broaching the subject of Blue's torments and anxieties. Blue feels betrayed by the man who was once like a father to him, and when he finishes the letter he feels empty, the stuffing all knocked out of him. I'm on my own, he thinks, there's no one to turn to anymore. This is followed by several hours of despondency and self-pity, with Blue thinking once or twice that maybe he'd be better off dead. But eventually he works his way out of the gloom. For Blue is a solid character on the whole, less given to dark thoughts than most, and if there are moments when he feels the world is a foul place, who are we to blame him for it? By the time supper rolls around, he has even begun to look on the bright side. This is perhaps his greatest talent: not that he does not despair, but that he never despairs for very long. It might be a good thing after all, he says to himself. It might be better to stand alone than to depend on anyone else. Blue thinks about his for a while and decides there is something to be said for it. He is no longer an apprentice. There is no master above him anymore. I'm my own man, he says to himself. I'm my own man, accountable to no one but myself.

Inspired by this new approach to things, he discovers that he has as last found the courage to contact the future Mrs Blue. But when he picks up the phone and dials her number, there is no answer. This is a disappointment, but he remains undaunted. I'll try again some other time, he says. Some time soon.

The days continue to pass. Once again Blue falls into step with Black, perhaps even more harmoniously than before. In doing so, he discovers the inherent paradox of his situation. For the closer he feels to Black, the less he finds it necessary to think about him. In other words, the more deeply entangled he becomes, the freer he is. What bogs him down is not involvement but separation. For it is only when Black seems to drift away from him that he must go out looking for him, and this takes time and effort, not to speak of struggle. At those moments when he feels closest to Black, however, he can even begin to lead the semblance of an independent life. At first he is not very daring in what he allows himself to do, but even so he considers it a kind of triumph, almost an act of bravery. Going outside, for example, and walking up and down the block. Small as it might be, this gesture fills him with happiness, and as he moves back and forth along Orange Street in the lovely spring weather, he is glad to be alive in a way he has not felt in years. At one end there is a view of the river, the harbour, the Manhattan skyline, the bridges. Blue finds all this beautiful, and on some days he even allows himself to sit for several minutes on one of the benches and look out at the boats. In the other direction there is the church, and sometimes Blue goes to the small grassy yard to sit for a while, studying the bronze statue of Henry Ward Beecher. Two slaves are holding on to Beecher's legs, as though begging him to help them, to make them free at last, and in the brick wall behind there is a porcelain relief of Abraham Lincoln. Blue cannot help but feel inspired by these images, and each time he comes to the churchyard his head fills with noble thoughts about the dignity of man.

Little by little, he becomes more bold in his strayings from Black. It is 1947, the year that Jackie Robinson breaks in with the Dodgers, and Blue follows his progress closely, remembering the churchyard and knowing there is more to it than just baseball. One bright Tuesday afternoon in May, he decides to make an excursion to Ebbetts Field, and as he leaves Black behind in his room on Orange Street, hunched over his desk as usual with his pen and papers, he feels no cause for worry, secure in the fact that everything will be exactly the same when he returns. He rides the subway, rubs shoulders with the crowd, feels himself lunging towards a sense of the moment. As he takes his seat at the ball park, he is struck by the sharp clarity of the colours around him: the green grass, the brown dirt, the white ball, the blue sky above. Each thing is distinct from every other thing, wholly separate and defined, and the geometric simplicity of the pattern impresses Blue with its force. Watching the game, he finds it difficult to take his eyes off Robinson, lured constantly by the blackness of the man's face, and he thinks it must take courage to do what he is doing, to be alone like that in front of so many strangers, with half of them no doubt wishing him to be dead. As the game moves along, Blue finds himself cheering whatever Robinson does, and when the black man steals a base in the third inning he rises to his feet, and later, in the seventh, when Robinson doubles off the wall in left, he actually pounds the back of the man next to him for joy. The Dodgers pull it out in the ninth with a sacrifice fly, and as Blue shuffles off with the rest of the crowd and makes his way home, it occurs to him that Black did not cross his mind even once.

But ball games are only the beginning. On certain nights, when it is clear to Blue that Black will not be going anywhere, he slips out to a bar not far away for a beer or two, enjoying the conversations he sometimes has with the bartender, whose name is Red, and who bears an uncanny resemblance to Green, the bartender from the Gray Case so long ago. A blowsy tart named Violet is often there, and once or twice Blue gets her tipsy enough to get invited back to her place around the corner. He knows that she likes him well enough because she never makes him pay for it, but he also knows that it has nothing to do with love. She calls him honey and her flesh is soft and ample, but whenever she has one drink too many she begins to cry, and then Blue has to console her, and he secretly wonders if it's worth the trouble. His guilt towards the future Mrs Blue is scant, however, for he justifies these sessions with Violet by comparing himself to a soldier at war in another country. Every man needs a little comfort, especially when his number could be up tomorrow. And besides, he isn't made of stone, he says to himself.

More often than not, however, Blue will bypass the bar and go to the movie theatre several blocks away. With summer coming on now and the heat beginning to hover uncomfortably in his little room, it's refreshing to be able to sit in the cool theatre and watch the feature show. Blue is fond of the movies, not only for the stories they tell and the beautiful women he can see in them, but for the darkness of the theatre itself, the way the pictures on the screen are somehow like the thoughts inside his head whenever he closes his eyes. He is more or less indifferent to the kinds of movies he sees, whether comedies or dramas, for example, or whether the film is shot in black and white or in colour, but he has a particular weakness for movies about detectives, since there is a natural connection, and he is always gripped by these stories more than by others. During this period he sees a number of such movies and enjoys them all: *Lady in the Lake*, *Fallen Angel*, *Dark Passage*, *Body and Soul*, *Ride the Pink Horse*, *Desperate*, and so on. But for Blue there is one that stands out from the rest, and he likes it so much that he actually goes back the next night to see it again.

It's called *Out of the Past*, and it stars Robert Mitchum as an ex-private eye who is trying to build a new life for himself in a small town under an assumed name. He has a girl friend, a sweet country girl named Ann, and runs a gas station with the help of a deaf-and-dumb boy, Jimmy, who is firmly devoted to him. But the past catches up with Mitchum, and there's little he can do about it. Years ago, he had been hired to look for Jane Greer, the mistress of gangster Kirk Douglas, but once he found her they fell in love and ran off together to live in secret. One thing led to another – money was stolen, a murder was committed – and eventually Mitchum came to his senses and left Greer, finally understanding the depth of her corruption. Now he is being blackmailed by Douglas and Greer into committing a crime, which itself is merely a set-up, for once he figures out what is happening, he sees that they are planning to frame him for another murder. A complicated story unfolds, with Mitchum desperately trying to extricate himself from the trap. At one point, he returns to the small town where he lives, tells Ann that he's innocent, and again persuades her of his love. But it's really too late, and Mitchum knows it. Towards the end, he manages to convince Douglas to turn in Greer for the murder she committed, but at that moment Greer enters the room, calmly takes out a gun, and kills Douglas. She tells Mitchum that they belong to each other, and he, fatalistic to the last, appears to go along. They decide to escape the country together, but as Greer goes to pack her bag, Mitchum picks up the phone and calls the police. They get into the car and drive off, but soon they come to a police roadblock. Greer, seeing that she's been double-crossed, pulls a gun from her bag and shoots Mitchum. The police then open fire on the car and Greer is killed as well. After that, there's one last scene – the next morning, back in the small town of Bridgeport. Jimmy is sitting on a bench outside the gas station, and Ann walks over and sits down beside him. Tell me one thing, Jimmy, she says, I've got to know this one thing: was he running away with her or not? The boy thinks for a moment, trying to decide between truth and kindness. Is it more important to preserve his friend's good name or to spare the girl? All this happens in no more than an instant. Looking into the girl's eyes, he nods his head, as if to say yes, he was in love with Greer after all. Ann pats Jimmy's arm and thanks him, then walks off to her former boyfriend, a straight-arrow local policeman who always despised Mitchum. Jimmy looks up at the gas station sign with Mitchum's name on it, gives a little salute of friendship, and then turns away and walks down the road. He is the only one who knows the truth, and he will never tell.

For the next few days, Blue goes over this story many times in his head. It's a good thing, he decides, that the movie ends with the deaf mute boy. The secret is buried, and Mitchum will remain an outsider, even in death. His ambition was simple enough: to become a normal citizen in a normal American town, to marry the girl next door, to live a quiet life. It's strange, Blue thinks, that the new name Mitchum chooses for himself is Jeff Bailey. This is remarkably close to the name of another character in a movie he saw the previous year with the future Mrs Blue – George Bailey, played by James Stewart in *It's a Wonderful Life*. That story was also about small town America, but from the opposite point of view: the frustrations of a man who spends his whole life trying to escape. But in the end he comes to understand that his life has been a good one, that he has done the right thing all along. Mitchum's Bailey would no doubt like to be the same man as Stewart's Bailey. But in his case the name is false, a product of wishful thinking. His real name is Markham – or, as Blue sounds it out to himself, mark him – and that is the whole point. He has been marked by the past, and once that happens, nothing can be done about it. Something happens, Blue thinks, and then it goes on happening forever. It can never be changed, can never be otherwise. Blue begins to be haunted by this thought, for he sees it as a kind of warning, a message delivered up from within himself, and try as he does to push it away, the darkness of this thought does not leave him.

One night, therefore, Blue finally turns to his copy of *Walden*. The time has come, he says to himself, and if he doesn't make an effort now, he knows that he never will. But the book is not a simple business. As Blue begins to read, he feels as though he is entering an alien world. Trudging through swamps and brambles, hoisting himself up gloomy screes and treacherous cliffs, he feels like a prisoner on a forced march, and his only thought is to escape. He is bored by Thoreau's words and finds it difficult to concentrate. Whole chapters go by, and when he comes to the end of them he realizes that he has not retained a thing. Why would anyone want to go off and live alone in the woods? What's all this about planting beans and not drinking coffee or eating meat? Why all these interminable descriptions of birds? Blue thought that he was going to get a story, or at least have something like a story, but this is no more than blather, an endless harangue about nothing at all.

It would be unfair to blame him, however. Blue has never read much of anything except newspapers and magazines, and an occasional adventure novel when he was a boy. Even experienced and sophisticated readers have been known to have trouble with *Walden*, and no less a figure than Emerson once wrote in his journal that reading Thoreau made him feel nervous and wretched. To Blue's credit, he does not give up. The next day he begins again, and this second go-through is somewhat less rocky than the first. In the third chapter he comes across a sentence that finally says something to him – Books must be read as deliberately and reservedly as they were written – and suddenly he understands that the trick is to go slowly, more slowly than he has ever gone with the words before. This helps to some extent, and certain passages begin to grow clear: the business about clothes in the beginning, the battle between the red ants and the black ants, the argument against work. But Blue still finds it painful, and though he grudgingly admits that Thoreau is perhaps not as stupid as he thought, he begins to resent Black for putting him through this torture. What he does not know is that were he to find the patience to read the book in the spirit in which it asks to be read, his entire life would begin to change, and little by little he would come to a full understanding of his situation – that is to say, of Black, of White, of the case, of everything that concerns him. But lost chances are as much a part of life as chances taken, and a story cannot dwell on what might have been. Throwing the book aside in disgust, Blue puts on his coat (for it is fall now) and goes out for a breath of air. Little does he realize that this is the beginning of the end. For something is about to happen, and once it happens, nothing will ever be the same again.

He goes to Manhattan, wandering farther from Black than at any time before, venting his frustration in movement, hoping to calm himself down by exhausting his body. He walks north, alone in his thoughts, not bothering to take in the things around him. On East 26th Street his left shoelace comes undone, and it is precisely then, as he bends down to tie it, crouching on one knee, that the sky falls on top of him. For who should he glimpse at just that moment but the future Mrs Blue. She is coming up the street with her two arms linked through the right arm of a man Blue has never seen before, and she is smiling radiantly, engrossed in what the man is saying to her. For several moments Blue is so at a loss that he doesn't know whether to bend his head farther down and hide his face or stand up and greet the woman whom he now understands – with a knowledge as sudden and irrevocable as the slamming of a door – will never be his wife. As it turns out, he manages neither – first ducking his head, but then discovering a second later that he wants her to recognize him, and when he sees she will not, being so wrapped up in her companion's talk, Blue abruptly rises from the pavement when they are no more than six feet away from him. It is as though some spectre has suddenly materialized in front of her, and the ex-future Mrs Blue gives out a little gasp, even before she sees who the spectre is. Blue speaks her name, in a voice that seems strange to him, and she stops dead in her tracks. Her face registers the shock of seeing Blue – and then, rapidly, her expression turns to one of anger.

You! she says to him. You!

Before he has the chance to say a word, she disentangles herself from her companion's arm and begins pounding Blue's chest with her fists, screaming insanely at him, accusing him of one foul crime after another. It is all Blue can do to repeat her name over and over, as though trying desperately to distinguish between the woman he loves and the wild beast who is now attacking him. He feels totally defenceless, and as the onslaught continues, he begins to welcome each new blow as just punishment for his behaviour. The other man soon puts a stop to it, however, and though Blue is tempted to take a swing at him, he is too stunned to act quickly enough, and before he knows it the man has led away the weeping ex-future Mrs Blue down the street and around the corner, and that's the end of it.

This brief scene, so unexpected and devastating, turns Blue

inside out. By the time he regains his composure and manages to return home, he realizes that he has thrown away his life. It's not her fault, he says to himself, wanting to blame her but knowing he can't. He might have been dead for all she knew, and how can he hold it against her for wanting to live? Blue feels tears forming in his eyes, but more than grief he feels anger at himself for being such a fool. He has lost whatever chance he might have had for happiness, and if that is the case, then it would not be wrong to say that this is truly the beginning of the end.

Blue gets back to his room on Orange Street, lies down on his bed, and tries to weigh the possibilities. Eventually, he turns his face to the wall and encounters the photograph of the coroner from Philadelphia, Gold. He thinks of the sad blankness of the unsolved case, the child lying in his grave with no name, and as he studies the death mask of the little boy, he begins to turn an idea over in his mind. Perhaps there are ways of getting close to Black, he thinks, ways that need not give him away. God knows there must be. Moves that can be made, plans that can be set in motion – perhaps two or three at the same time. Never mind the rest, he tells himself. It's time to turn the page.

His next report is due the day after tomorrow, and so he sits down to it now in order to get it mailed off on schedule. For the past few months his reports have been exceedingly cryptic, no more than a paragraph or two, giving the bare bones and nothing else, and this time he does not depart from the pattern. However, at the bottom of the page he interjects an obscure comment as a kind of test, hoping to elicit something more than silence from White: Black seems ill. I'm afraid he might be dying. Then he seals up the report, saying to himself that this is only the beginning.

Two days hence, Blue hastens early in the morning to the Brooklyn Post Office, a great castle of a building within eyeshot of the Manhattan Bridge. All of Blue's reports have been addressed to box number one thousand and one, and he walks over to it now as though by accident, sauntering past it and unobtrusively peeking inside to see if the report has come. It has. Or at least a letter is there – a solitary white envelope tilted at a forty-five degree angle in the narrow cubby – and Blue has no reason to suspect it's any letter other than his own. He then begins a slow circular walk around the area, determined to remain until White or someone working for White appears, his eyes fixed on the huge wall of numbered boxes, each box with a different combination, each one holding a different secret. People come and go, open boxes and close them, and Blue keeps wandering in his circle, pausing every now and then in some random spot and then moving on. Everything seems brown to him, as though the fall weather outside has penetrated the room, and the place smells pleasantly of cigar smoke. After several hours he begins to get hungry, but he does not give in to the call of his stomach, telling himself it's now or never and therefore holding his ground. Blue watches everyone who approaches the bank of post boxes, zeroing in on each person who skirts the vicinity of one thousand and one, aware of the fact that if it's not White who comes for the reports it could be anyone – an old woman, a young child, and consequently he must take nothing for granted. But none of these possibilities comes to anything, for the box remains untouched throughout, and though Blue momentarily and successively spins a story for each candidate who comes near, trying to imagine how that person might be connected to White and or Black, what role he or she might play in the case, and so on, one by one he is forced to dismiss them back into the oblivion from which they have come.

Just past noon, at a moment when the post office begins to get crowded – an influx of people on their lunch break rushing through to mail letters, buy stamps, attend to business of one sort or another – a man with a mask on his face walks through the door. Blue doesn't notice him at first, what with so many others coming through the door at the same time, but as the man separates himself from the crowd and begins walking toward the numbered post boxes, Blue finally catches sight of the mask – a mask of the sort that children wear on Hallowe'en, made of rubber and portraying some hideous monster with gashes in his forehead and bleeding eyeballs and fangs for teeth. The rest of him is perfectly ordinary (grey tweed overcoat, red scarf wrapped around his neck), and Blue senses in this first moment that the man behind the mask is White. As the man continues walking toward the area of box one thousand and one, this sense grows to conviction. At the same time, Blue also feels that the man is not really there, that even though he knows he is seeing him, it is more than likely that he is the only one who can. On this point, however, Blue is wrong, for as the masked man continues moving across the vast marble floor, Blue sees a number of people laughing and pointing at him – but whether this is better or worse he cannot say. The masked man reaches box one thousand and one, spins the combination wheel back and forth and back again, and opens the box. As soon as Blue sees that this is definitely his man, he begins making a move toward him, not really sure of what he is planning to do, but in the back of his mind no doubt intending to grab hold of him and tear the mask of his face. But the man is too alert, and once he has pocketed the envelope and locked the box, he gives a quick glance around the room, sees Blue approaching, and makes a dash for it, heading for the door as fast as he can. Blue runs after him, hoping to catch him from behind and tackle him, but he gets tangled momentarily in a crowd of people at the door, and by the time he manages to get through it, the masked man is bounding down the stairs, landing on the sidewalk, and running down the street. Blue continues in pursuit, even feels he is gaining ground, but then the man reaches the corner, where a bus just happens to be pulling out from a stop, and so he conveniently leaps aboard, and Blue is left in the lurch, all out of breath and standing there like an idiot.

Two days later, when Blue receives his cheque in the mail, there is finally a word from White. No more funny business, it says, and though it's not much of a word, for all that Blue is glad to have received it, happy to have cracked White's wall of silence at last. It's not clear to him, however, whether the message refers to the last report or to the incident in the post office. After thinking it over for a while, he decides that it makes no

difference. One way or another, the key to the case is action.
He must go on disrupting things wherever he can, a little here,
a little there, chipping away at each conundrum until the
whole structure begins to weaken, until one day the whole
rotten business comes toppling to the ground.

Over the next few weeks, Blue returns to the post office
several times, hoping to catch another glimpse of White. But
nothing comes of it. Either the report is already gone from the
box when he gets there, or White does not show up. The fact
that this area of the post office is open twenty-four hours a day
leaves Blue with few options. White is on to him now, and he
will not make the same mistake twice. He will simply wait until
Blue is gone before going to the box, and unless Blue is willing
to spend his entire life in the post office, there's no way he can
expect to sneak up on White again.

The picture is far more complicated than Blue ever imagined.
For almost a year now, he has thought of himself as essentially
free. For better or worse he had been doing his job, looking
straight ahead of him and studying Black, waiting for a possible opening, trying to stick with it, but through it all he has
not given a single thought to what might be going on behind
him. Now, after the incident with the masked man and the
further obstacles that have ensued, Blue no longer knows what
to think. It seems perfectly plausible to him that he is also
being watched, observed by another in the same way that he
has been observing Black. If that is the case, then he has never
been free. From the very start he has been the man in the
middle, thwarted in front and hemmed in on the rear. Oddly
enough, this thought reminds him of some sentences from
Walden, and he searches through his notebook for the exact
phrasing, fairly certain that he has written them down. We are
not where we are, he finds, but in a false position. Through an
infirmity of our natures, we suppose a case, and put ourselves
into it, and hence are in two cases at the same time, and it is
doubly difficult to get out. This makes sense to Blue, and
though he is beginning to feel a little frightened, he thinks that

perhaps it is not too late for him to do something about it.

The real problem boils down to identifying the nature of the problem itself. To start with, who poses the greater threat to him, White or Black? White has kept up his end of the bargain: the cheques have come on time every week, and to turn against him now, Blue knows, would be to bite the hand that feeds him. And yet White is the one who set the case in motion – thrusting Blue into an empty room, as it were, and then turning off the light and locking the door. Ever since, Blue has been groping about in the darkness, feeling blindly for the light switch, a prisoner of the case itself. All well and good, but why would White do such a thing? When Blue comes up against this question, he can no longer think. His brain stops working, he can get no farther than this.

Take Black, then. Until now he has been the entire case, the apparent cause of all his troubles. But if White is really out to get Blue and not Black, then perhaps Black has nothing to do with it, perhaps he is no more than an innocent bystander. In that case, it is Black who occupies the position Blue has assumed all along to be his, and Blue who takes the role of Black. There is something to be said for this. On the other hand, it is also possible that Black is somehow working in league with White and that together they have conspired to do Blue in.

If so, what are they doing to him? Nothing very terrible, finally – at least not in any absolute sense. They have trapped Blue into doing nothing, into being so inactive as to reduce his life to almost no life at all. Yes, says Blue to himself, that's what it feels like: like nothing at all. He feels like a man who has been condemned to sit in a room and go on reading a book for the rest of his life. This is strange enough – to be only half alive at best, seeing the world only through words, living only through the lives of others. But if the book were an interesting one, perhaps it wouldn't be so bad. He could get caught up in the story, so to speak, and little by little begin to forget himself. But this book offers him nothing. There is no story, no plot, no action – nothing but a man sitting alone in a room and writing a book. That's all there is, Blue realizes, and he no longer wants any part of it. But how to get out? How to get out of the room that is the book that will go on being written for as long as he stays in the room?

As for Black, the so-called writer of this book, Blue can no longer trust what he sees. Is it possible that there really is such a man – who does nothing, who merely sits in his room and writes? Blue has followed him everywhere, has tracked him down into the remotest corners, has watched him so hard that his eyes seem to be failing him. Even when he does leave his room, Black never goes anywhere, never does much of anything: grocery shopping, an occasional haircut, a trip to the movies, and so on. But mostly he just wanders around the streets, looking at odd bits of scenery, clusters of random data, and even this happens only in spurts. For a while it will be buildings – craning his neck to catch a glimpse of the roofs, inspecting doorways, running his hands slowly over the stone façades. And then, for a week or two, it will be public statues, or the boats in the river, or the signs in the street. Nothing more than that, with scarcely a word to anyone, and no meetings with others except for that one lunch with the woman in tears by now so long ago. In one sense, Blue knows everything there is to know about Black: what kind of soap he buys, what newspapers he reads, what clothes he wears, and each of these things he has faithfully recorded in his notebook. He has learned a thousand facts, but the only thing they have taught him is that he knows nothing. For the fact remains that none of this is possible. It is not possible for such a man as Black to exist.

Consequently, Blue begins to suspect that Black is no more than a ruse, another one of White's hirelings, paid by the week to sit in that room and do nothing. Perhaps all that writing is merely a sham – page after page of it: a list of every name in the phone book, for example, or each word from the dictionary in alphabetical order, or a handwritten copy of *Walden*. Or perhaps they are not even words, but senseless scribbles, random marks of a pen, a growing heap of nonsense and confusion. This would make White the real writer then – and Black no more than his stand-in, a fake, an actor with no substance of his own. Then there are the times, following through with this thought, that Blue believes the only logical explanation is that Black is not one man but several. Two, three, four look-alikes who play the role of Black for Blue's benefit, each one putting in his allotted time and then going back to the comforts of hearth and home. But this is a thought too monstrous for Blue to contemplate for very long. Months go by, and at last he says to himself out loud: I can't breathe anymore. This is the end. I'm dying.

It is midsummer, 1948. Finally mustering the courage to act, Blue reaches into his bag of disguises and casts about for a new identity. After dismissing several possibilities, he settles on an old man who used to beg on the corners of his neighbourhood when he was a boy – a local character by the name of Jimmy Rose – and decks himself out in the garb of tramphood: tattered woollen clothes, shoes held together with string to prevent the soles from flapping, a weathered carpetbag to hold his belongings, and then, last of all, a flowing white beard and long white hair. These final details give him the look of an Old Testament prophet. Blue as Jimmy Rose is not a scrofulous down-and-outer so much as a wise fool, a saint of penury living in the margins of society. A trifle daft perhaps, but harmless: he exudes a sweet indifference to the world around him, for since everything has happened to him already, nothing can disturb him anymore.

Blue posts himself in a suitable spot across the street, takes a fragment of a broken magnifying glass from his pocket, and begins reading a crumpled day-old newspaper that he has salvaged from one of the nearby garbage cans. Two hours later, Black appears, walking down the steps of his house and then turning in Blue's direction. Black pays no attention to the bum – either lost in his own thoughts or ignoring him on purpose – and so as he begins to approach, Blue addresses him in a pleasant voice.

Can you spare some change, mister?

Black stops, looks over the dishevelled creature who has just spoken, and gradually relaxes into a smile as he realizes he is not in danger. Then he reaches into his pocket, pulls out a coin, and puts it in Blue's hand.

Here you are, he says.

God bless you, says Blue.

Thank you, answers Black, touched by the sentiment.

Never fear, says Blue. God blesses all.

And with that word of reassurance, Black tips his hat to Blue and continues on his way.

The next afternoon, once again in bum's regalia, Blue waits for Black in the same spot. Determined to keep the conversation going a little longer this time, now that he has won Black's confidence, Blue finds that the problem is taken out of his hands when Black himself shows an eagerness to linger. It is late in the day by now, not yet dusk but no longer afternoon, the twilight hour of slow changes, of glowing bricks and shadows. After greeting the bum cordially and giving him another coin, Black hesitates a moment, as though debating whether to take the plunge, and then says:

Has anyone ever told you that you look just like Walt Whitman?

Walt who? answers Blue, remembering to play his part.

Walt Whitman. A famous poet.

No, says Blue. I can't say I know him.

You wouldn't know him, says Black. He's not alive anymore. But the resemblance is remarkable.

Well, you know what they say, says Blue. Every man has his double somewhere. I don't see why mine can't be a dead man.

The funny thing, continues Black, is that Walt Whitman used to work on this street. He printed his first book right here, not far from where we're standing.

You don't say, says Blue, shaking his head pensively. It makes you stop and think, doesn't it?

There are some odd stories about Whitman, Black says, gesturing to Blue to sit down on the stoop of the building behind them, which he does, and then Black does the same, and suddenly it's just the two of them out there in the summer light together, chatting away like two old friends about this and that.

Yes, says Black, settling in comfortably to the langour of the moment, a number of very curious stories. The one about Whitman's brain, for example. All his life Whitman believed in the science of phrenology – you know, reading the bumps on the skull. It was very popular at the time.

Can't say I've ever heard of it, replies Blue.

Well, that doesn't matter, says Black. The main thing is that Whitman was interested in brains and skulls – thought they could tell you everything about a man's character. Anyway, when Whitman lay dying over there in New Jersey about fifty or sixty years ago, he agreed to let them perform an autopsy on him after he was dead.

How could he agree to it after he was dead?

Ah, good point. I didn't say it right. He was still alive when he agreed. He just wanted them to know that he didn't mind if they opened him up later. What you might call his dying wish.

Famous last words.

That's right. A lot of people thought he was a genius, you see, and they wanted to take a look at his brain to find out if there was anything special about it. So, the day after he died, a doctor removed Whitman's brain – cut it right out of his head – and had it sent to the American Anthropometric Society to be measured and weighed.

Like a giant cauliflower, interjects Blue.

Exactly. Like a big grey vegetable. But this is where the story gets interesting. The brain arrives at the laboratory, and just as they're about to work on it, one of the assistants drops it on the floor.

Did it break?

Of course it broke. A brain isn't very tough, you know. It splattered all over the place, and that was that. The brain of America's greatest poet got swept up and thrown out with the garbage.

Blue, remembering to respond in character, emits several wheezing laughs – a good imitation of an old codger's mirth. Black laughs, too, and by now the atmosphere has thawed to such an extent that no one could ever know they were not lifelong chums.

It's sad to think of poor Walt lying in his grave, though, says Black. All alone and without any brains.

Just like that scarecrow, says Blue.

Sure enough, says Black. Just like the scarecrow in the land of Oz.

After another good laugh, Black says: And then there's the story of the time Thoreau came to visit Whitman. That's a good one, too.

Was he another poet?

Not exactly. But a great writer just the same. He's the one who lived alone in the woods.

Oh yes, says Blue, not wanting to carry his ignorance too far. Someone once told me about him. Very fond of nature he was. Is that the man you mean?

Precisely, answers Black. Henry David Thoreau. He came down from Massachusetts for a little while and paid a call on Whitman in Brooklyn. But the day before that he came right here to Orange Street.

Any particular reason?

Plymouth Church. He wanted to hear Henry Ward Beecher's sermon.

A lovely spot, says Blue, thinking of the pleasant hours he has spent in the grassy yard. I like to go there myself.

Many great men have gone there, says Black. Abraham Lincoln, Charles Dickens – they all walked down this street and went into the church.

Ghosts.

Yes, there are ghosts all around us.

And the story?

It's really very simple. Thoreau and Bronson Alcott, a friend of his, arrived at Whitman's house on Myrtle Avenue, and Walt's mother sent them up to the attic bedroom he shared with his mentally retarded brother, Eddy. Everything was just fine. They shook hands, exchanged greetings, and so on. But then, when they sat down to discuss their views of life, Thoreau and Alcott noticed a full chamber pot right in the middle of the floor. Walt was of course an expansive fellow and paid no attention, but the two New Englanders found it hard to keep talking with a bucket of excrement in front of them. So eventually they went downstairs to the parlour and continued the conversation there. It's a minor detail, I realize. But still, when two great writers meet, history is made, and it's important to get all the facts straight. That chamber pot, you see, somehow reminds me of the brains on the floor. And when you stop to think about it, there's a certain similarity of form. The bumps and convolutions, I mean. There's a definite connection. Brains and guts, the insides of a man. We always talk about trying to get inside a writer to understand his work better. But when you get right down to it, there's not much to find in there – at least not much that's different from what you'd find in anyone else.

You seem to know a lot about these things, says Blue, who's beginning to lose the thread of Black's argument.

It's my hobby, says Black. I like to know how writers live, especially American writers. It helps me to understand things.

I see, says Blue, who sees nothing at all, for with each word Black speaks, he finds himself understanding less and less.

Take Hawthorne, says Black. A good friend of Thoreau's, and probably the first real writer America ever had. After he graduated from college, he went back to his mother's house in Salem, shut himself up in his room, and didn't come out for twelve years.

What did he do in there?

He wrote stories.

Is that all? He just wrote?

Writing is a solitary business. It takes over your life. In some sense, a writer has no life of his own. Even when he's there, he's not really there.

Another ghost.

Exactly.

Sounds mysterious.

It is. But Hawthorne wrote great stories, you see, and we still read them now, more than a hundred years later. In one of them, a man named Wakefield decides to play a joke on his wife. He tells her that he has to go away on a business trip for a few days, but instead of leaving the city, he goes around the corner, rents a room, and just waits to see what will happen. He can't say for sure why he's doing it, but he does it just the same. Three or four days go by, but he doesn't feel ready to return home yet, and so he stays on in the rented room. The days turn into weeks, the weeks turn into months. One day Wakefield walks down his old street and sees his house decked out in mourning. It's his own funeral, and his wife has become a lonely widow. Years go by. Every now and then he crosses paths with his wife in town, and once, in the middle of a large crowd, he actually brushes up against her. But she doesn't recognize him. More years pass, more than twenty years, and little by little Wakefield has become an old man. One rainy night in autumn, as he's taking a walk through the empty streets, he happens to pass by his old house and peeks through the window. There's a nice warm fire burning in the fireplace, and he thinks to himself: how pleasant it would be if I were in there right now, sitting in one of those cosy chairs by the hearth instead of standing out here in the rain. And so, without giving it any more thought than that, he walks up the steps of the house and knocks on the door.

And then?

That's it. That's the end of the story. The last thing we see is the door opening and Wakefield going inside with a crafty smile on his face.

And we never know what he says to his wife?

No. That's the end. Not another word. But he moved in again, we know that much, and remained a loving spouse until death.

By now the sky has begun to darken overhead, and night is fast approaching. A last glimmer of pink remains in the west, but the day is as good as done. Black, taking his cue from the darkness, stands up from his spot and extends his hand to Blue.

It's been a pleasure talking to you, he says. I had no idea we'd been sitting here so long.

The pleasure's been mine, says Blue, relieved that the

conversation is over, for he knows that it won't be long now before his beard begins to slip, what with the summer heat and his nerves making him perspire into the glue.

My name is Black, says Black, shaking Blue's hand.

Mine's Jimmy, says Blue. Jimmy Rose.

I'll remember this little talk of ours for a long time, Jimmy, says Black.

I will, too, says Blue. You've given me a lot to think about.

God bless you, Jimmy Rose, says Black.

And God bless you, sir, says Blue.

And then, with one last handshake, they walk off in opposite directions, each one accompanied by his own thoughts.

Later that night, when Blue returns to his room, he decides that he had best bury Jimmy Rose now, get rid of him for good. The old tramp has served a purpose, but beyond this point it would not be wise to go.

Blue is glad to have made this initial contact with Black, but the encounter did not quite have the desired effect, and all in all he feels rather shaken by it. For even though the talk had nothing to do with the case, Blue cannot help feeling that Black was actually referring to it all along – talking in riddles, so to speak, as though trying to tell Blue something, but not daring to say it out loud. Yes, Black was more than friendly, his manner was altogether pleasant, but still Blue cannot get rid of the thought that the man was on to him from the start. If so, then Black is surely one of the conspirators – for why else would he have gone on talking to Blue as he did? Not from loneliness, certainly. Assuming that Black is for real, then loneliness cannot be an issue. Everything about his life to this point has been part of a determined plan to remain alone, and it would be absurd to read his willingness to talk as an effort to escape the throes of solitude. Not at this late date, not after more than a year of avoiding all human contact. If Black is finally resolved to break out of his hermetic routine, then why would he begin by talking to a broken-down old man on a street corner? No, Black knew that he was talking to Blue. And if he knew that, then he knows who Blue is. No two ways about it, Blue says to himself: he knows everything.

When the time comes for him to write his next report, Blue is forced to confront this dilemma. White never said anything about making contact with Black. Blue was to watch him, no more, no less, and he wonders now if he has not in fact broken the rules of his assignment. If he includes the conversation in his report, then White might object. On the other hand, if he does not put it in, and if Black is indeed working with White, then White will know immediately that Blue is lying. Blue mulls this over for a long time, but for all that he gets no closer to finding a solution. He's stuck, one way or the other, and he knows it. In the end, he decides to leave it out, but only because he still puts some meagre hope in the fact that he has guessed wrong and that White and Black are not in it together. But this last little stab at optimism comes to naught. Three days after sending in the sanitized report, his weekly cheque comes in the mail, and inside the envelope there is also a note that says, Why do you lie?, and then Blue has proof beyond any shadow of a doubt. And from that moment on, Blue lives with the knowledge that he is drowning.

The next night he follows Black into Manhattan on the subway, dressed in his normal clothes, no longer feeling he has to hide anything. Black gets off at Times Square and wanders around for a while in the bright lights, the noise, the crowds of people surging this way and that. Blue, watching him as though his life depended on it, is never more than three or four steps behind him. At nine o'clock, Black enters the lobby of the Algonquin Hotel, and Blue follows him in. There's quite a crowd milling about, and tables are scarce, so when Black sits down in a corner nook that just that moment has become free, it seems perfectly natural for Blue to approach and politely ask if he can join him. Black has no objection and gestures with an indifferent shrug of the shoulders for Blue to take the chair opposite. For several minutes they say nothing to each other, waiting for someone to take their orders, in the meantime watching the women walk by in their summer dresses, inhaling the different perfumes that flit behind them in the air, and Blue feels no rush to jump into things, content to bide his time and let the business take its course. When the waiter at last comes to ask their pleasure, Black orders a Black and White on the rocks, and Blue cannot help but take this as a secret message that the fun is about to begin, all the while marvelling at Black's effrontery, his crassness, his vulgar obsession. For the sake of symmetry Blue orders the same drink. As he does so, he looks Black in the eyes, but Black gives nothing away, looking back at Blue with utter blankness, dead eyes that seem to say there is nothing behind them and that no matter how hard Blue looks, he will never find a thing.

This gambit nevertheless breaks the ice, and they begin by discussing the merits of various brands of scotch. Plausibly enough, one thing leads to another, and as they sit there chatting about the inconveniences of the New York summer season, the decor of the hotel, the Algonquin Indians who lived in the city long ago when it was all woods and fields, Blue slowly evolves into the character he wants to play for the night, settling on a jovial blowhard by the name of Snow, a life insurance salesman from Kenosha, Wisconsin. Play dumb, Blue tells himself, for he knows that it would make no sense to reveal who he is, even though he knows that Black knows. It's got to be hide and seek, he says, hide and seek to the end.

They finish their first drink and order another round, followed by yet another, and as the talk ambles from actuarial tables to the life expectancies of men in different professions, Black lets fall a remark that turns the conversation in another direction.

I suppose I wouldn't be very high up on your list, he says.

Oh? says Blue having no idea what to expect. What kind of work do you do?

I'm a private detective, says Black, point blank, all cool and collected, and for a brief moment Blue is tempted to throw his drink in Black's face, he's that peeved, that burned at the man's gall.

You don't say! Blue exclaims, quickly recovering and managing to feign a bumpkin's surprise. A private detective. Imagine that.

In the flesh. Just think of what the wife will say when I tell her. Me in New York having drinks with a private eye. She'll never believe it.

What I'm trying to say, says Black rather abruptly, is that I don't imagine my life expectancy is very great. At least not according to your statistics.

Probably not, Blue blusters on. But think of the excitement! There's more to life than living a long time, you know. Half the men in America would give ten years off their retirement to live the way you do. Cracking cases, living by your wits, seducing women, pumping bad guys full of lead – God, there's a lot to be said for it.

That's all make-believe, says Black. Real detective work can be pretty dull.

Well, every job has its routines, Blue continues. But in your case at least you know that all the hard work will eventually lead to something out of the ordinary.

Sometimes yes, sometimes no. But most of the time it's no. Take the case I'm working on now. I've been at it for more than a year already, and nothing could be more boring. I'm so bored that sometimes I think I'm losing my mind.

How so?

Well, figure it out yourself. My job is to watch someone, no one in particular as far as I can tell, and send in a report about him every week. Just that. Watch this guy and write about it. Not one damned thing more.

What's so terrible about that?

He doesn't do anything, that's what. He just sits in his room all day and writes. It's enough to drive you crazy.

It could be that he's leading you along. You know, lulling you to sleep before springing into action.

That's what I thought at first. But now I'm sure that nothing's going to happen – not ever. I can feel it in my bones.

That's too bad, says Blue sympathetically. Maybe you should resign from the case.

I'm thinking about it. I'm also thinking that maybe I should chuck the whole business and go into something else. Some other line of work. Sell insurance, maybe, or run off to join the circus.

I never realized it could get as bad as that, says Blue, shaking his head. But tell me, why aren't you watching your man now? Shouldn't you be keeping an eye on him?

That's just the point, answers Black, I don't even have to bother anymore. I've been watching him for so long now that I know him better than I know myself. All I have to do is think about him, and I know what he's doing, I know where he is, I know everything. It's come to the point that I can watch him with my eyes closed.

Do you know where he is now?

At home. The same as usual. Sitting in his room and writing.

What's he writing about?

I'm not sure, but I have a pretty good idea. I think he's writing about himself. The story of his life. That's the only possible answer. Nothing else would fit.

So why all the mystery?

I don't know, says Black, and for the first time his voice betrays some emotion, catching ever so slightly on the words.

It all boils down to one question, then, doesn't it? says Blue, forgetting all about Snow now and looking Black straight in the eyes. Does he know you're watching him or not?

Black turns away, unable to look at Blue anymore, and says with a suddenly trembling voice: Of course he knows. That's the whole point, isn't it? He's got to know, or else nothing makes sense.

Why?

Because he needs me, says Black, still looking away. He needs my eye looking at him. He needs me to prove he's alive.

Blue sees a tear fall down Black's cheek, but before he can say anything, before he can begin to press home his advantage, Black stands up hastily and excuses himself, saying that he has to make a telephone call. Blue waits in his chair for ten or fifteen minutes, but he knows that he's wasting his time. Black won't be back. The conversation is over, and no matter how long he sits there, nothing more will happen tonight.

Blue pays for the drinks and then heads back to Brooklyn. As he turns down Orange Street, he looks up at Black's window and sees that everything is dark. No matter, says Blue, he'll return before long. We haven't come to the end yet. The party is only beginning. Wait until the champagne is opened, and then we'll see what's what.

Once inside, Blue paces back and forth, trying to plot his next move. It seems to him that Black has finally made a mistake, but he is not quite certain. For in spite of the evidence, Blue cannot shrug the feeling that it was all done on purpose, and that Black has now begun to call out to him, leading him along, so to speak, urging him on towards whatever end he is planning.

Still, he has broken through to something, and for the first time since the case began he is no longer standing where he was. Ordinarily, Blue would be celebrating this little triumph of his, but it turns out that he is in no mood for patting himself on the back tonight. More than anything else, he feels sad, he feels drained of enthusiasm, he feels disappointed in the world. Somehow, the facts have finally let him down, and he finds it hard not to take it personally, knowing full well that however he might present the case to himself, he is a part of it, too. Then he walks to the window, looks out across the street, and sees that the lights are now on in Black's room.

He lies down on his bed and thinks: goodbye, Mr White. You were never really there, were you? There never was such a man as White. And then: poor Black. Poor soul. Poor blighted no one. And then, as his eyes grow heavy and sleep begins to wash over him, he thinks how strange it is that everything has its own colour. Everything we see, everything we touch – everything in the world has its own colour. Struggling to stay awake a little longer, he begins to make a list. Take blue for example, he says. There are bluebirds and blue jays and blue herons. There are cornflowers and periwinkles. There is noon over New York. There are blueberries, huckleberries, and the Pacific Ocean.

There are blue devils and blue ribbons and blue bloods. There is a voice singing the blues. There is my father's police uniform. There are blue laws and blue movies. There are my eyes and my name. He pauses, suddenly at a loss for more blue things, and then moves on to white. There are seagulls, he says, and terns and storks and cockatoos. There are the walls of this room and the sheets on my bed. There are lilies-of-the-valley, carnations, and the petals of daisies. There is the flag of peace and Chinese death. There is mother's milk and semen. There are my teeth. There are the whites of my eyes. There are white bass and white pines and white ants. There is the President's house and white rot. There are white lies and white heat. Then, without hesitating, he moves on to black, beginning with black books, the black market, and the Black Hand. There is night over New York, he says. There are the Chicago Black Sox. There are blackberries and crows, blackouts and black marks, Black Tuesday and the Black Death. There is blackmail. There is my hair. There is the ink that comes out of a pen. There is the world a blind man sees. Then, finally growing tired of the game, he begins to drift, saying to himself that there is no end to it. He falls asleep, dreams of things that happened long ago, and then, in the middle of the night, wakes up suddenly and begins pacing the room again, thinking about what he will do next.

Morning comes, and Blue starts busying himself with another disguise. This time it's the Fuller brush man, a trick he has used before, and for the next two hours he patiently goes about giving himself a bald head, a moustache, and age lines around his eyes and mouth, sitting in front of his little mirror like an old-time vaudevillian on tour. Shortly after eleven o'clock, he gathers up his case of brushes and walks across the street to Black's building. Picking the lock on the front door is child's play for Blue, no more than a matter of seconds, and as he slips into the hallway he can't help feeling something of the old thrill. No tough stuff, he reminds himself, as he starts climbing the stairs to Black's floor. This visit is only to get a look inside, to stake out the room for future reference. Still, there's an excitement to the moment that

Blue can't quite suppress. For it's more than just seeing the room, he knows – it's the thought of being there himself, of standing inside those four walls, of breathing the same air as Black. From now on, he thinks, everything that happens will affect everything else. The door will open, and after that Black will be inside of him forever.

He knocks, the door opens, and suddenly there is no more distance, the thing and the thought of the thing are one and the same. Then it's Black who is there, standing in the doorway with an uncapped fountain pen in his right hand, as though interrupted in his work, and yet with a look in his eyes that tells Blue he's been expecting him, resigned to the hard truth, but no longer seeming to care.

Blue launches into his patter about the brushes, pointing to the case, offering apologies, asking admittance, all in the same breath, with that rapid salesman's pitch he's done a thousand times before. Black calmly lets him in, saying he might be interested in a toothbrush, and as Blue steps across the sill, he goes rattling on about hair brushes and clothes brushes, anything to keep the words flowing, for in that way he can leave the rest of himself free to take in the room, observe the observable, think, all the while diverting Black from his true purpose.

The room is much as he imagined it would be, though perhaps even more austere. Nothing on the walls, for example, which surprises him a little, since he always thought there would be a picture or two, an image of some kind just to break the monotony, a nature scene perhaps, or else a portrait of someone Black might once have loved. Blue was always curious to know what the picture would be, thinking it might be a valuable clue, but now that he sees there is nothing, he understands that this is what he should have expected all along. Other than that, there's precious little to contradict his former notions. It's the same monk's cell he saw in his mind: the small, neatly made bed in one corner, the kitchenette in another corner, everything spotless, not a crumb to be seen. Then, in the centre of the room facing the window, the wooden table with a single stiffbacked wooden chair. Pencils, pens, a typewriter. A bureau, a night table, a lamp. A bookcase on the north wall, but no more than several books in it: *Walden, Leaves of Grass, Twice-Told Tales*, a few others. No telephone, no radio, no magazines. On the table, neatly stacked around the edges, piles of paper: some blank, some written on, some typed, some in longhand. Hundreds of pages, perhaps thousands. But you can't call this a life, thinks Blue. You can't really call it anything. It's a no man's land, the place you come to at the end of the world.

They look through the toothbrushes, and Black finally chooses a red one. From there they start examining the various clothes brushes, with Blue giving demonstrations on his own suit. For a man as neat as yourself, says Blue, I should think you'd find it indispensable. But black says he's managed so far without one. On the other hand, maybe he'd like to consider a hair brush, and so they go through the possibilities in the sample case, discussing the different sizes and shapes, the different kinds of bristles, and so on. Blue is already done with his real business, of course, but he goes through the motions nevertheless, wanting to do the thing right, even if it doesn't matter. Still, after Black has paid for the brushes and Blue is packing up his case to go, he can't resist making one little remark. You seem to be a writer, he says, gesturing to the table, and Black says yes, that's right, he's a writer.

It looks like a big book, Blue continues.

Yes, says Black. I've been working on it for many years.

Are you almost finished?

I'm getting there, Black says thoughtfully. But sometimes it's hard to know where you are. I think I'm almost done, and then I realize I've left out something important, and so I have to go back to the beginning again. But yes, I do dream of finishing it one day. One day soon, perhaps.

I hope I get a chance to read it, says Blue.

Anything is possible, says Black. But first of all, I've got to finish it. There are days when I don't even know if I'll live that long.

Well, we never know, do we? says Blue, nodding philosophically. One day we're alive, and the next day we're dead. It happens to all of us.

Very true, says Black. It happens to all of us.

They're standing by the door now, and something in Blue wants to go on making inane remarks of this sort. Playing the buffoon is enjoyable, he realizes, but at the same time there's an urge to toy with Black, to prove that nothing has escaped him – for deep down Blue wants Black to know that he's just as smart as he is, that he can match wits with him every step of the way. But Blue manages to fight back the impulse and hold his tongue, nodding politely in thanks for the sales, and then makes his exit. That's the end of the Fuller brush man, and less than an hour later he is discarded into the same bag that holds the remains of Jimmy Rose. Blue knows that no more disguises will be needed. The next step is inevitable, and the only thing that matters now is to choose the right moment.

But three nights later, when he finally gets his chance, Blue realizes that he's scared. Black goes out at nine o'clock, walks down the street, and vanishes around the corner. Although Blue knows that this is a direct signal, that Black is practically begging him to make his move, he also feels that it could be a set-up, and now, at the last possible moment, when only just before he was filled with confidence, almost swaggering with a sense of his own power, he sinks into a fresh torment of self-doubt. Why should he suddenly begin to trust Black? What earthly cause could there be for him to think they are both working on the same side now? How has this happened, and why does he find himself so obsequiously at Black's bidding once again? Then, from out of the blue, he begins to consider another possibility. What if he just simply left? What if he stood up, went out the door, and walked away from the whole business? He ponders this thought for a while, testing it out in his mind, and little by little he begins to tremble, overcome by terror and happiness, like a slave stumbling onto a vision of his own freedom. He imagines himself somewhere else, far away from here, walking through the woods and swinging an axe over his shoulder. Alone and free, his own man at last. He would build his life from the bottom up, an exile, a pioneer, a pilgrim in the new world. But that is as far as he gets. For no sooner does he begin to walk through these woods in the middle of nowhere than he feels that Black is there too, hiding behind some tree, stalking invisibly through some thicket, waiting for Blue to lie down and close his eyes before sneaking up on him and slitting his throat. It goes on and on, Blue thinks. If he doesn't take care of Black now, there will never be any end to it. This is what the ancients called fate, and every hero must submit to it. There is no choice, and if there is anything to be done, it is only the one thing that leaves no choice. But Blue is loath to acknowledge it. He struggles against it, he rejects it, he grows sick at heart. But that is only because he already knows, and to fight it is already to have accepted it, to want to say no is already to have said yes. And so Blue gradually comes round, at last giving in to the necessity of the thing to be done. But that is not to say he does not feel afraid. From this moment on, there is only one word that speaks for Blue, and that word is fear.

He has wasted valuable time, and now he must rush forth onto the street, hoping feverishly it is not too late. Black will not be gone forever, and who knows if he is not lurking around the corner, just waiting for the moment to pounce? Blue races up the steps of Black's building, fumbles awkwardly as he picks the front door lock, continually glancing over his shoulder, and then goes up the stairs to Black's floor. The second lock gives him more trouble than the first, though theoretically it should be simpler, an easy job even for the rawest beginner. This clumsiness tells Blue that he's losing control, letting it all get the better of him; but even though he knows it, there's little he can do but ride it out and hope that his hands will stop shaking. But it goes from bad to worse, and the moment he sets foot in Black's room, he feels everything go dark inside him, as though the night were pressing through his pores, sitting on top of him with a tremendous weight, and at the same time his head seems to be growing, filling with air as though about to detach itself from his body and float away. He takes one more step into the room and then blacks out, collapsing to the floor like a dead man.

His watch stops with the fall, and when he comes to he doesn't know how long he's been out. Dimly at first, he regains consciousness with a sense of having been here before, perhaps long ago, and as he sees the curtains fluttering by the open window and the shadows moving strangely on the ceiling, he thinks that he is lying in bed at home, back when he was a little boy, unable to sleep during the hot summer nights, and he imagines that if he listens hard enough he will be able to hear the voices of his mother and father talking quietly in the next room. But this lasts only a moment. He begins to feel the ache in his head, to register the disturbing queasiness in his stomach, and then, finally seeing where he is, to relive the panic that gripped him the moment he entered the room. He scrambles shakily to his feet, stumbling once or twice in the process, and tells himself he can't stay here, he's got to be going, yes, and right away. He grabs hold of the doorknob, but then, remembering suddenly why he came here in the first place, snatches the flashlight from his pocket and turns it on, waving it fitfully around the room until the light falls by chance on a pile of papers stacked neatly at the edge of Black's desk. Without thinking twice, Blue gathers up the papers with his free hand, saying to himself it doesn't matter, this will be a start, and then makes his way to the door.

Back in his room across the street, Blue pours himself a glass of brandy, sits down on his bed, and tells himself to be calm. He drinks off the brandy sip by sip and then pours himself another glass. As his panic begins to subside, he is left with a feeling of shame. He's botched it, he tells himself, and that's the long and the short of it. For the first time in his life he has not been equal to the moment, and it comes as a shock to him – to see himself as a failure, to realize that at bottom he's a coward.

He picks up the papers he has stolen, hoping to distract himself from these thoughts. But this only compounds the problem, for once he begins to read them, he sees they are nothing more than his own reports. There they are, one after the other, the weekly accounts, all spelled out in black and white, meaning nothing, saying nothing, as far from the truth of the case as silence would have been. Blue groans when he sees them, sinking down deep within himself, and then, in the face of what he finds there, begins to laugh, at first faintly, but with growing force, louder and louder, until he is gasping for breath, almost choking on it, as though trying to obliterate himself once and for all. Taking the papers firmly in his hand, he flings them up to the ceiling and watches the pile break apart, scatter, and come fluttering to the ground, page by miserable page.

It is not certain that Blue ever really recovers from the events of this night. And even if he does, it must be noted that several days go by before he returns to a semblance of his former self. In that time he does not shave, he does not change his clothes, he does not even contemplate stirring from his room. When the day comes for him to write his next report, he does not bother. It's finished now, he says, kicking one of the old reports on the floor, and I'll be damned if I ever write one of those again.

For the most part, he either lies on his bed or paces back and forth in his room. He looks at the various pictures he has tacked onto the walls since starting the case, studying each one in its turn, thinking about it for as long as he can, and then passing on to the next. There is the coroner from Philadelphia, Gold, with the death mask of the little boy. There is a snow-covered mountain, and in the upper right hand corner of the photograph, an inset of the French skier, his face enclosed in a small box. There is the Brooklyn Bridge, and next to it the two Roeblings, father and son. There is Blue's father, dressed in his police uniform and receiving a medal from the mayor of New York, Jimmy Walker. Again there is Blue's father, this time in his street clothes, standing with his arm around Blue's mother in the early days of their marriage, the two of them smiling brightly into the camera. There is a picture of Brown with his arm around Blue, taken in front of their office on the day Blue was made a partner. Below it there is an action shot of Jackie Robinson sliding into second base. Next to that there is a portrait of Walt Whitman. And finally, directly to the poet's left, there is a movie still of Robert Mitchum from one of the fan magazines: gun in hand, looking as though the world is about to cave in on him. There is no picture of the ex-future Mrs Blue, but each time Blue makes a tour of his little gallery, he pauses in front of a certain blank spot on the wall and pretends that she, too, is there.

For several days, Blue does not bother to look out the window. He has enclosed himself so thoroughly in his own thoughts that Black no longer seems to be there. The drama is Blue's alone, and if Black is in some sense the cause of it, it's as though he has already played his part, spoken his lines, and made his exit from the stage. For Blue at this point can no longer accept Black's existence, and therefore he denies it. Having penetrated Black's room and stood there alone, having been, so to speak, in the sanctum of Black's solitude, he cannot respond to the darkness of that moment except by replacing it with a solitude of his own. To enter Black, then, was the equivalent of entering himself, and once inside himself, he can no longer conceive of being anywhere else. But this is precisely where Black is, even though Blue does not know it.

One afternoon, therefore, as if by chance, Blue comes closer to the window than he has in many days, happens to pause in front of it, and then, as if for old time's sake, parts the curtains and looks outside. The first thing he sees is Black – not inside his room, but sitting on the stoop of his building across the street, looking up at Blue's window. Is he finished, then? Blue wonders. Does this mean it's over?

Blue retrieves his binoculars from the back of the room and returns to the window. Bringing them into focus on Black, he studies the man's face for several minutes, first one feature and then another, the eyes, the lips, the nose, and so on, taking the face apart and then putting it back together. He is moved by the depth of Black's sadness, the way the eyes looking up at him seem so devoid of hope, and in spite of himself, caught unawares by this image, Blue feels compassion rising up to him, a rush of pity for that forlorn figure across the street. He wishes it were not so, however, wishes he had the courage to load his gun, take aim at Black, and fire a bullet through his head. He'd never know what hit him, Blue thinks, he'd be in heaven before he touched the ground. But as soon as he has played out this little scene in his mind, he begins to recoil from it. No, he realizes, that's not what he wishes at all. If not that, then – what? Still struggling against the surge of tender feelings, saying to himself that he wants to be left alone, that all he wants is peace and quiet, it gradually dawns on him that he has in fact been standing there for several minutes wondering if there is not some way that he might help Black, if it would not be possible for him to offer his hand in friendship. That would certainly turn the tables, Blue thinks, that would certainly stand the whole business on its head. But why not? Why not do the unexpected? To knock on the door, to erase the whole story – it's no less absurd than anything else. For the fact of the matter is, all the fight has been taken out of Blue. He no longer has the stomach for it. And, to all appearances, neither does Black. Just look at him, Blue says to himself. He's the saddest creature in the world. And then, the moment he says these words, he understands that he's also talking about himself.

Long after Black leaves the steps, therefore, turning around and re-entering the building, Blue goes on staring at the vacant spot. An hour or two before dusk, he finally turns from the window, sees the disorder he has allowed his room to fall into, and spends the next hour straightening things up – washing the dishes, making the bed, putting away his clothes, removing the old reports from the floor. Then he goes into the bathroom, takes a long shower, shaves, and puts on fresh clothes, selecting his best blue suit for the occasion. Everything is different for him now, suddenly and irrevocably different. There is no more dread, no more trembling. Nothing but a calm assurance, a sense of rightness in the thing he is about to do.

Shortly after nightfall, he adjusts his tie one last time before the mirror and then leaves the room, going outside, crossing the street, and entering Black's building. He knows that Black is there, since a small lamp is on in his room, and as he walks up the stairs he tries to imagine the expression that will come over Black's face when he tells him what he has in mind. He knocks twice on the door, very politely, and then hears Black's voice from within: The door's open. Come in.

It is difficult to say exactly what Blue was expecting to find – but in all events, it was not this, not the thing that confronts him the moment he steps into the room. Black is there, sitting on his bed, and he's wearing the mask again, the same one Blue saw on the man in the post office, and in his right hand he's holding a gun, a thirty-eight revolver, enough to blow a man apart at such close range, and he's pointing it directly at Blue. Blue stops in his tracks, says nothing. So much for burying the hatchet, he thinks. So much for turning the tables.

Sit down in the chair, Blue, says Black, gesturing with the gun to the wooden desk chair. Blue has no choice, and so he sits – now facing Black, but too far away to make a lunge at him, too awkwardly positioned to do anything about the gun.

I've been waiting for you, says Black. I'm glad you finally made it.

I figured as much, answers Blue.

Are you surprised?

Not really. At least not at you. Myself maybe – but only because I'm so stupid. You see, I came here tonight in friendship.

But of course you did, says Black, in a slightly mocking voice. Of course we're friends. We've been friends from the beginning, haven't we? The very best of friends.

If this is how you treat your friends, says Blue, then lucky for me I'm not one of your enemies.

Very funny.

That's right, I'm the original funny man. You can always count on a lot of laughs when I'm around.

And the mask – aren't you going to ask me about the mask?

I don't see why. If you want to wear that thing, it's not my problem.

But you have to look at it, don't you?

Why ask questions when you already know the answer?

It's grotesque, isn't it?

Of course it's grotesque.

And frightening to look at.

Yes, very frightening.

Good. I like you, Blue. I always knew you were the right one for me. A man after my own heart.

If you stopped waving that gun around, maybe I'd start feeling the same about you.

I'm sorry, I can't do that. It's too late now.

Which means?

I don't need you anymore, Blue.

It might not be so easy to get rid of me, you know. You got me into this, and now you're stuck with me.

No, Blue, you're wrong. Everything is over now.

Stop the doubletalk.

It's finished. The whole thing is played out. There's nothing more to be done.

Since when?

Since now. Since this moment.

You're out of your mind.

No, Blue. If anything, I'm in my mind, too much in my mind. It's used me up, and now there's nothing left. But you know that, Blue, you know that better than anyone.

So why don't you just pull the trigger?

When I'm ready, I will.

And then walk out of here leaving my body on the floor? Fat chance.

Oh no, Blue. You don't understand. It's going to be the two of us together, just like always.

But you're forgetting something, aren't you?

Forgetting what?

You're supposed to tell me the story. Isn't that how it's supposed to end? You tell me the story, and then we say goodbye.

You know it already, Blue. Don't you understand that? You know the story by heart.

Then why did you bother in the first place?

Don't ask stupid questions.

And me – what was I there for? Comic relief?

No, Blue, I've needed you from the beginning. If it hadn't been for you, I couldn't have done it.

Needed me for what?

To remind me of what I was supposed to be doing. Every time I looked up, you were there, watching me, following me, always in sight, boring into me with your eyes. You were the whole world to me, Blue, and I turned you into my death. You're the one thing that doesn't change, the one thing that turns everything inside out.

And now there's nothing left. You've written your suicide note, and that's the end of it.

Exactly.

You're a fool. You're a goddamned, miserable fool.

I know that. But no more than anyone else. Are you going to sit there and tell me that you're smarter than I am? At least I know what I've been doing. I've had my job to do, and I've done it. But you're nowhere, Blue. You've been lost from the first day.

Why don't you pull the trigger, then, you bastard? says Blue, suddenly standing up and pounding his chest in anger, daring Black to kill him. Why don't you shoot me now and get it over with?

Blue then takes a step towards Black, and when the bullet doesn't come, he takes another, and then another, screaming at the masked man to shoot, no longer caring if he lives or dies. A moment later, he's right up against him. Without hesitating he swats the gun out of Black's hand, grabs him by the collar, and yanks him to his feet. Black tries to resist, tries to struggle against Blue, but Blue is too strong for him, all crazy with the passion of his anger, as though turned into someone else, and as the first blows begin to land on Black's face and groin and stomach, the man can do nothing, and not long after that he's out cold on the floor. But that does not prevent Blue from continuing the assault, batttering the unconscious Black with his feet, picking him up and banging his head on the floor, pelting his body with one punch after another. Eventually, when Blue's fury begins to abate and he sees what he has done, he cannot say for certain whether Black is alive or dead. He removes the mask from Black's face and puts his ear against his mouth, listening for the sound of Black's breath. There seems to be something, but he can't tell if it's coming from Black or himself. If he's alive now, Blue thinks, it won't be for long. And if he's dead, then so be it.

Blue stands up, his suit all in tatters, and begins collecting the pages of Black's manuscript from the desk. This takes several minutes. When he has all of them, he turns off the lamp in the corner and leaves the room, not even bothering to give Black a last look.

It's past midnight when Blue gets back to his room across the street. He puts the manuscript down on the table, goes into the bathroom, and washes the blood off his hands. Then he changes his clothes, pours himself a glass of Scotch, and sits down at the table with Black's book. Time is short. They'll be coming before he knows it, and then there will be hell to pay. Still, he does not let this interfere with the business at hand.

He reads the story right through, every word of it from beginning to end. By the time he finishes, dawn has come, and the room has begun to brighten. He hears a bird sing, he hears footsteps going down the street, he hears a car driving across the Brooklyn Bridge. Black was right, he says to himself. I knew it all by heart.

But the story is not yet over. There is still the final moment, and that will not come until Blue leaves the room. Such is the way of the world: not one moment more, not one moment less. When Blue stands up from his chair, puts on his hat, and walks through the door, that will be the end of it.

Where he goes after that is not important. For we must remember that all this took place more than thirty years ago, back in the days of our earliest childhood. Anything is possible, therefore. I myself prefer to think that he went far away, boarding a train that morning and going out West to start a new life. It is even possible that America was not the end of it. In my secret dreams, I like to think of Blue booking passage on some ship and sailing to China. Let it be China, then, and we'll leave it at that. For now is the moment that Blue stands up from his chair, puts on his hat, and walks through the door. And from this moment on, we know nothing.

The Locked Room

1

It seems to me now that Fanshawe was always there. He is the place where everything begins for me, and without him I would hardly know who I am. We met before we could talk, babies crawling through the grass in diapers, and by the time we were seven we had pricked our fingers with pins and made ourselves blood brothers for life. Whenever I think of my childhood now, I see Fanshawe. He was the one who was with me, the one who shared my thoughts, the one I saw whenever I looked up from myself.

But that was a long time ago. We grew up, went off to different places, drifted apart. None of that is very strange, I think. Our lives carry us along in ways we cannot control, and almost nothing stays with us. It dies when we do, and death is something that happens to us every day.

Seven years ago this November, I received a letter from a woman named Sophie Fanshawe. 'You don't know me,' the letter began, 'and I apologize for writing to you like this out of the blue. But things have happened, and under the circumstances I don't have much choice.' It turned out that she was Fanshawe's wife. She knew that I had grown up with her husband, and she also knew that I lived in New York, since she had read many of the articles I had published in magazines.

The explanation came in the second paragraph, very bluntly, without any preamble. Fanshawe had disappeared, she wrote, and it was more than six months since she had last seen him. Not a word in all that time, not the slightest clue as to where he might be. The police had found no trace of him, and the private detective she hired to look for him had come up empty-handed. Nothing was sure, but the facts seemed to speak for themselves: Fanshawe was probably dead; it was pointless to think he would be coming back. In the light of all this, there was something important she needed to discuss with me, and she wondered if I would agree to see her.

This letter caused a series of little shocks in me. There was too much information to absorb all at once; too many forces were pulling me in different directions. Out of nowhere, Fanshawe had suddenly reappeared in my life. But no sooner was his name mentioned than he had vanished again. He was married, he had been living in New York – and I knew nothing about him any more. Selfishly, I felt hurt that he had not bothered to get in touch with me. A phone call, a post card, a drink to catch up on old times – it would not have been difficult to arrange. But the fault was equally my own. I knew where Fanshawe's mother lived, and if I had wanted to find him, I could easily have asked her. The fact was that I had let go of Fanshawe. His life had stopped the moment we went our separate ways, and he belonged to the past for me now, not to the present. He was a ghost I carried around inside me, a prehistoric figment, a thing that was no longer real. I tried to remember the last time I had seen him, but nothing was clear. My mind wandered for several minutes and then stopped short, fixing on the day his father died. We were in high school then and could not have been more than seventeen years old.

I called Sophie Fanshawe and told her I would be glad to see her whenever it was convenient. We decided on the following day, and she sounded grateful, even though I explained to her that I had not heard from Fanshawe and had no idea where he was.

She lived in a red-brick tenement in Chelsea, an old walk-up building with gloomy stairwells and peeling paint on the walls. I climbed the five flights to her floor, accompanied by the sounds of radios and squabbles and flushing toilets that came from the apartments on the way up, paused to catch my breath, and then knocked. An eye looked through the peephole in the door, there was a clatter of bolts being turned, and then Sophie Fanshawe was standing before me, holding a small baby in her left arm. As she smiled at me and invited me in, the baby tugged at her long brown hair. She ducked away gently from the attack, took hold of her child with her two hands, and turned him face front towards me. This was Ben, she said, Fanshawe's son, and he had been born just three-and-a-half months ago. I pretended to admire the baby, who was waving his arms and drooling whitish spittle down his chin, but I was more interested in his mother. Fanshawe had been lucky. The woman was beautiful, with dark, intelligent eyes, almost fierce in their steadiness. Thin, not more than average height, and with something slow in her manner, a thing that made her both sensual and watchful, as though she looked out on the world from the heart of a deep inner vigilance. No man would have left this woman of his own free will – especially not when she was about to have his child. That much was certain to me. Even before I stepped into the apartment, I knew that Fanshawe had to be dead.

It was a small railroad flat with four rooms, sparsely furnished, with one room set aside for books and a work table, another that served as the living room, and the last two for sleeping. The place was well-ordered, shabby in its details, but on the whole not uncomfortable. If nothing else, it proved that Fanshawe had not spent his time making money. But I was not one to look down my nose at shabbiness. My own apartment was even more cramped and dark than this one, and I knew what it was to struggle each month to come up with the rent.

Sophie Fanshawe gave me a chair to sit in, made me a cup of coffee, and then sat down on the tattered blue sofa. With the baby on her lap, she told me the story of Fanshawe's disappearance.

They had met in New York three years ago. Within a month they had moved in together, and less than a year after that they were married. Fanshawe was not an easy man to live with, she said, but she loved him, and there had never been anything in his behaviour to suggest that he did not love her. They had been happy together; he had been looking forward to the birth of the baby; there was no bad blood between them. One day in April he told her that he was going to New Jersey for the afternoon to see his mother, and then he did not come back. When Sophie called her mother-in-law late that night, she learned that Fanshawe had never made the visit. Nothing like this had ever happened before, but Sophie decided to wait it out. She didn't want to be one of those wives who panicked whenever her husband failed to show up, and she knew that Fanshawe needed more breathing room than most men. She even decided not to ask any questions when he returned home. But then a week went by, and then another week, and at last she went to the police. As she expected, they were not overly concerned about her problem. Unless there was evidence of a crime, there was little they could do. Husbands, after all, deserted their wives every day, and most of them did not want to be found. The police made a few routine inquiries, came up with nothing, and then suggested that she hire a private detective. With the help of her mother-in-law, who offered to pay the costs, she engaged the services of a man named Quinn. Quinn worked doggedly on the case for five or six weeks, but in the end he begged off, not wanting to take any more of their money. He told Sophie that Fanshawe was most likely still in the country, but whether alive or dead he could not say. Quinn was no charlatan. Sophie found him sympathetic, a man who genuinely wanted to help, and when he came to her that last day she realized it was impossible to argue against his verdict. There was nothing to be done. If Fanshawe had decided to leave her, he would not have stolen off without a word. It was not like him to shy away from the truth, to back down from unpleasant confrontations. His disappearance could therefore mean only one thing: that some terrible harm had come to him.

Still, Sophie went on hoping that something would turn up. She had read about cases of amnesia, and for a while this took hold of her as a desperate possibility: the thought of Fanshawe staggering around somewhere not knowing who he was, robbed of his life but nevertheless alive, perhaps on the verge of returning to himself at any moment. More weeks passed and then the end of her pregnancy began to approach. The baby was due in less than a month – which meant that it could come at any time –

and little by little the unborn child began to take up all her thoughts, as though there was no more room inside her for Fanshawe. These were the words she used to describe the feeling – no more room inside her – and then she went on to say that this probably meant that in spite of everything she was angry at Fanshawe, angry at him for having abandoned her, even though it wasn't his fault. This statement struck me as brutally honest. I had never heard anyone talk about personal feelings like that – so unsparingly, with such disregard for conventional pieties – and as I write this now, I realize that even on that first day I had slipped through a hole in the earth, that I was falling into a place where I had never been before.

One morning, Sophie continued, she woke up after a difficult night and understood that Fanshawe would not be coming back. It was a sudden, absolute truth, never again to be questioned. She cried then, and went on crying for a week, mourning Fanshawe as though he were dead. When the tears stopped, however, she found herself without regrets. Fanshawe had been given to her for a number of years, she decided, and that was all. Now there was the child to think about, and nothing else really mattered. She knew this sounded rather pompous – but the fact was that she continued to live with this sense of things, and it continued to make life possible for her.

I asked her a series of questions, and she answered each one calmly, deliberately, as though making an effort not to colour the responses with her own feelings. How they had lived, for example, and what work Fanshawe had done, and what had happened to him in the years since I had last seen him. The baby started fussing on the sofa, and without any pause in the conversation, Sophie opened her blouse and nursed him, first on one breast and then on the other.

She could not be sure of anything prior to her first meeting with Fanshawe, she said. She knew that he had dropped out of college after two years, had managed to get a deferment from the army, and wound up working on a ship of some sort for a while. An oil tanker, she thought, or perhaps a freighter. After that, he had lived in France for several years – first in Paris, then as the caretaker of a farmhouse in the South. But all this was quite dim to her, since Fanshawe had never talked much about the past. At the time they met, he had not been back in America more than eight or ten months. They literally bumped into each other – the two of them standing by the door of a Manhattan bookshop one wet Saturday afternoon, looking through the window and waiting for the rain to stop. That was the beginning, and from that day until the day Fanshawe disappeared, they had been together nearly all the time.

Fanshawe had never had any regular work, she said, nothing that could be called a real job. Money didn't mean much to him, and he tried to think about it as little as possible. In the years before he met Sophie, he had done all kinds of things – the stint in the merchant marine, working in a warehouse, tutoring, ghost writing, waiting on tables, painting apartments, hauling furniture for a moving company – but each job was temporary, and once he had earned enough to keep himself going for a few months, he would quit. When he and Sophie began living together, Fanshawe did not work at all. She had a job teaching music in a private school, and her salary could support them both. They had to be careful, of course, but there was always food on the table, and neither of them had any complaints.

I did not interrupt. It seemed clear to me that this catalogue was only a beginning, details to be disposed of before turning to the business at hand. Whatever Fanshawe had done with his life, it had little connection with this list of odd jobs. I knew this immediately, in advance of anything that was said. We were not talking about just anyone, after all. This was Fanshawe, and the past was not so remote that I could not remember who he was.

Sophie smiled when she saw that I was ahead of her, that I knew what was coming. I think she had expected me to know, and this merely confirmed that expectation, erasing any doubts she might have had about asking me to come. I knew without having to be told, and that gave me the right to be there, to be listening to what she had to say.

'He went on with his writing,' I said. 'He became a writer, didn't he?'

Sophie nodded. That was exactly it. Or part of it, in any case. What puzzled me was why I have never heard of him. If Fanshawe was a writer, then surely I would have run across his name somewhere. It was my business to know about these things, and it seemed unlikely that Fanshawe, of all people, would have escaped my attention. I wondered if he had been unable to find a publisher for his work. It was the only question that seemed logical.

No, Sophie said, it was more complicated than that. He had never tried to publish. At first, when he was very young, he was too timid to send anything out, feeling that his work was not good enough. But even later, when his confidence had grown, he discovered that he preferred to stay in hiding. It would distract him to start looking for a publisher, he told her, and when it came right down to it, he would much rather spend his time on the work itself. Sophie was upset by this indifference, but whenever she pressed him about it, he would answer with a shrug: there's no rush, sooner or later he would get around to it.

Once or twice, she actually thought of taking matters into her own hands and smuggling a manuscript out to a publisher, but she never went through with it. There were rules in a marriage that couldn't be broken, and no matter how wrong-headed his attitude was, she had little choice but to go along with him. There was a great quantity of work, she said, and it maddened her to think of it just sitting there in the closet, but Fanshawe deserved her loyalty, and she did her best to say nothing.

One day, about three or four months before he disappeared, Fanshawe came to her with a compromise gesture. He gave her his word that he would do something about it within a year, and to prove that he meant it, he told her that if for any reason he failed to keep up his end of the bargain, she was to take all his manuscripts to me and put them in my hands. I was the guardian of his work, he said, and it was up to me to decide what should happen to it. If I thought it was worth publishing, he would give in to my judgement. Furthermore, he said, if anything should happen to him in the meantime, she was to give me the manuscripts at once and allow me to make all the arrangements, with the understanding that I would receive twenty-five per cent of any money the work happened to earn. If I thought his writings were not worth publishing, however, then I should return the manuscripts to Sophie, and she was to destroy them, right down to the last page.

These pronouncements startled her, Sophie said, and she almost laughed at Fanshawe for being so solemn about it. The whole scene was out of character for him, and she wondered if it didn't have something to do with the fact that she had just become pregnant. Perhaps the idea of fatherhood had sobered him into a new sense of responsibility; perhaps he was so determined to prove his good intentions that he had overstated the case. Whatever the reason, she found herself glad that he had changed his mind. As her pregnancy advanced, she even began to have secret dreams of Fanshawe's success, hoping that she would be able to quit her job and raise the child without any financial pressure. Everything had gone wrong, of course, and Fanshawe's work was soon forgotten, lost in the turmoil that followed his disappearance. Later, when the dust began to settle, she had resisted carrying out his instructions – for fear that it would jinx any chance she had of seeing him again. But eventually she gave in, knowing that Fanshawe's word had to be respected. That was why she had written to me. That was why I was sitting with her now.

For my part, I didn't know how to react. The proposition had caught me off guard, and for a minute or two I just sat there, wrestling with the enormous thing that had been thrust at me. As far as I could tell, there was no earthly reason for Fanshawe to have chosen me for this job. I had not seen him in more than ten years, and I was almost surprised to learn that he still remembered who I was. How could I be expected to take on such a responsibility – to stand in judgement of a man and say whether his life had been worth living? Sophie tried to explain. Fanshawe had not been in touch, she said, but he had often talked to her about me, and each time my name had been mentioned, I was described as his best friend in the world – the one true friend he had ever had. He had also managed to keep up with my work, always buying the magazines in which my articles appeared, and sometimes even reading the pieces aloud to her. He admired what I did, Sophie said; he was proud of me, and he felt that I had it in me to do something great.

All this praise embarrassed me. There was so much intensity in Sophie's voice, I somehow felt that Fanshawe was speaking through her, telling me these things with his own lips. I admit that I was flattered, and no doubt that was a natural feeling under the circumstances. I was having a hard time of it just then, and the fact was that I did not share this high opinion of myself. I had written a great many articles, it was true, but I did not see that as a cause for celebration, nor was I particularly proud of it. As far as I was concerned, it was just a little short of hack work. I had begun with great hopes, thinking that I would become a novelist, thinking that I would eventually be able to write something that would touch people and make a difference in their lives. But time went on, and little by little I realized that this was not going to happen. I did not have such a book inside me, and at a certain point I told myself to give up my dreams. It was simpler to go on writing articles in any case. By working hard, by moving steadily from one piece to the next, I could more or less earn a living – and, for whatever it was worth, I had the pleasure of seeing my name in print almost constantly. I understood that things could have been far more dismal than they were. I was not quite thirty, and already I had something of a reputation. I had begun with reviews of poetry and novels, and now I could write about nearly anything and do a creditable job. Movies, plays, art shows, concerts, books, even baseball games – they had only to ask, and I would do it. The world saw me as a bright young fellow, a new critic on the rise, but inside myself I felt old, already used up. What I had done so far amounted to a mere fraction of nothing at all. It was so much dust, and the slightest wind would blow it away.

Fanshawe's praise, therefore, left me with mixed feelings. On the one hand, I knew that he was wrong. On the other hand (and this is where it gets murky), I wanted to believe that he was right. I thought: is it possible that I've been too hard on myself? And once I began to think that, I was lost. But who wouldn't jump at the chance to redeem himself – what man is strong enough to reject the possibility of hope? The thought flickered through me that I could one day be resurrected in my own eyes, and I felt a sudden burst of friendship for Fanshawe across the years, across all the silence of the years that had kept us apart.

That was how it happened. I succumbed to the flattery of a man who wasn't there, and in that moment of weakness I said yes. I'll be glad to read the work, I said, and do whatever I can to help. Sophie smiled at this – whether from happiness or disappointment I could never tell – and then stood up from the sofa and carried the baby into the next room. She stopped in front of a tall oak cupboard, unlatched the door, and let it swing open on its hinges. There you are, she said. There were boxes and binders and folders and notebooks cramming the shelves – more things than I would have thought possible. I remember laughing with embarrassment and making some feeble joke. Then, all business, we discussed the best way for me to carry the manuscripts out of the apartment, eventually deciding on two large suitcases. It took the better part of an hour, but in the end we managed to squeeze everything in. Clearly, I said, it was going to take me some time to sift through all the material. Sophie told me not to worry, and then she apologized for burdening me with such a job. I said that I understood, that there was no way she could have refused to carry out Fanshawe's request. It was all very dramatic, and at the same time gruesome, almost comical. The beautiful Sophie delicately put the baby down on the floor, gave me a great hug of thanks, and then kissed me on the cheek. For a moment I thought she was going to cry, but the moment passed and there were no tears. Then I hauled the two suitcases slowly down the stairs and onto the street. Together, they were as heavy as a man.

2

The truth is far less simple than I would like it to be. That I loved Fanshawe, that he was my closest friend, that I knew him better than anyone else – these are facts, and nothing I say can ever diminish them. But that is only a beginning, and in my struggle to remember things as they really were, I see now that I also held back from Fanshawe, that a part of me always resisted him. Especially as we grew older, I do not think I was ever entirely comfortable in his presence. If envy is too strong a word for what I am trying to say, then I would call it a suspicion, a secret feeling that Fanshawe was somehow better than I was. All this was unknown to me at the time, and there was never anything specific that I could point to. Yet the feeling lingered that there was more innate goodness in him than in others, that some unquenchable fire was keeping him alive, that he was more truly himself than I could ever hope to be.

Early on, his influence was already quite pronounced. This extended even to very small things. If Fanshawe wore his belt buckle on the side of his pants, then I would move my belt into the same position. If Fanshawe came to the playground wearing black sneakers, then I would ask for black sneakers the next time my mother took me to the shoe store. If Fanshawe brought a copy of *Robinson Crusoe* with him to school, then I would begin reading *Robinson Crusoe* that same evening at home. I was not the only one who behaved like this, but I was perhaps the most devoted, the one who gave in most willingly to the power he held over us. Fanshawe himself was not aware of that power, and no doubt that was the reason he continued to hold it. He was indifferent to the attention he received, calmly going about his business, never using his influence to manipulate others. He did not play the pranks the rest of us did; he did not make mischief; he did not get into trouble with the teachers. But no one held this against him. Fanshawe stood apart from us, and yet he was the one who held us together, the one we approached to arbitrate our disputes, the one we could count on to be fair and to cut through our petty quarrels. There was something so attractive about him that you always wanted him beside you, as if you could live within his sphere and be touched by what he was. He was there for you, and yet at the same time he was inaccessible. You felt there was a secret core in him that could never be penetrated, a mysterious centre of hiddenness. To imitate him was somehow to participate in that mystery, but it was also to understand that you could never really know him.

I am talking about our very early childhood – as far back as five, six, seven years old. Much of it is buried now, and I know that even memories can be false. Still, I don't think I would be wrong in saying that I have kept the aura of those days inside me, and to the extent that I can feel what I felt then, I doubt those feelings can lie. Whatever it was that Fanshawe eventually became, my sense is that it started for him back then. He formed himself very quickly, was already a sharply defined presence by the time we started school. Fanshawe was visible, whereas the rest of us were creatures without shape, in the throes of constant tumult, floundering blindly from one moment to the next. I don't mean to say that he grew up fast – he never seemed older than he was – but that he was already himself before he grew up. For one reason or another, he never became subject to the same upheavals as the rest of us. His dramas were of a different order – more internal, no doubt more brutal – but with none of the abrupt changes that seemed to punctuate everyone else's life.

One incident is particularly vivid to me. It concerns a birthday party that Fanshawe and I were invited to in the first or second grade, which means that it falls at the very beginning of the period I am able to talk about with any precision. It was a Saturday afternoon in spring, and we walked to the party with another boy, a friend of ours named Dennis Walden. Dennis had a much harder life than either of us did: an alcoholic mother, an overworked father, innumerable brothers and sisters. I had been to his house two or three times – a great, dark ruin of a place – and I can remember being frightened by his mother, who made me think of a fairy-tale witch. She would spend the whole day behind the closed door of her room, always in her bathrobe, her pale face a nightmare of wrinkles, poking her head out every now and then to scream something at the children. On the day of the party, Fanshawe and I had been duly equipped with presents to give the birthday boy, all wrapped in coloured paper and tied with ribbons. Dennis, however, had nothing, and he felt bad about it. I can remember trying to console him with some empty phrase or other: it didn't matter, no one really cared, in all the confusion it wouldn't be noticed. But Dennis did care, and that was what Fanshawe immediately understood. Without any explanation, he turned to Dennis and handed him his present. Here, he said, take this one – I'll tell them I left mine at home. My first reaction was to think that Dennis would resent the gesture, that he would feel insulted by Fanshawe's pity. But I was wrong. He hesitated for a moment, trying to absorb this sudden change of fortune, and then nodded his head, as if acknowledging the wisdom of what Fanshawe had done. It was not an act of charity so much as an act of justice, and for that reason Dennis was able to accept it without humiliating himself. The one thing had been turned into the other. It was a piece of magic, a combination of offhandedness and total conviction, and I doubt that anyone but Fanshawe would have pulled it off.

After the party, I went back with Fanshawe to his house. His mother was there, sitting in the kitchen, and she asked us about the party and whether the birthday boy had liked the present she had bought for him. Before Fanshawe had a chance to say anything, I blurted out the story of what he had done. I had no intention of getting him into trouble, but it was impossible for me to keep it to myself. Fanshawe's gesture had opened up a whole new world for me: the way someone could enter the feelings of another and take them on so completely that his own were no longer important. It was the first truly moral act I had witnessed, and nothing else seemed worth talking about. Fanshawe's mother was not so enthusiastic, however. Yes, she said, that was a kind and generous thing to do, but it was also wrong. The present had cost her money, and by giving it away Fanshawe had in some sense stolen that money from her. On top of that, Fanshawe had acted impolitely by showing up without a present – which reflected badly on her, since she was the one responsible for his actions. Fanshawe listened carefully to his mother and did not say a word. After she was finished, he still did not speak, and she asked him if he understood. Yes, he said, he understood. It probably would have ended there, but then, after a short pause, Fanshawe went on to say that he still thought he was right. It didn't matter to him how she felt: he would do the same thing again the next time. A scene followed this little exchange. Mrs Fanshawe became angry at his impertinence, but Fanshawe stuck to his guns, refusing to budge under the barrage of her reprimands. Eventually, he was ordered to his room and I was told to leave the house. I was appalled by his mother's unfairness, but when I tried to speak up in his defence, Fanshawe waved me off. Rather than protest any more, he took his punishment silently and disappeared into his room.

The whole episode was pure Fanshawe: the spontaneous act of goodness, the unswerving belief in what he had done, and the mute, almost passive giving in to its consequences. No matter how remarkable his behaviour was, you always felt that he was detached from it. More than anything else, it was this quality that sometimes scared me away from him. I would get so close to Fanshawe, would admire him so intensely, would want so desperately to measure up to him – and then, suddenly, a moment would come when I realized that he was alien to me, that the way he lived inside himself could never correspond to the way I needed to live. I wanted too much of things, I had too many desires, I lived too fully in the grip of the immediate ever to attain such indifference. It mattered to me that I do well, that I impress people with the empty signs of my ambition: good grades, varsity letters, awards for whatever it was they were judging us on that week. Fanshawe remained aloof from all that, quietly standing in his corner, paying no attention. If he did well, it was always in spite of himself, with no struggle, no effort, no stake in the thing he had done. This posture could be unnerving, and it took me a long time to learn that what was good for Fanshawe was not necessarily good for me.

I do not want to exaggerate, however. If Fanshawe and I eventually had our differences, what I remember most about our childhood is the passion of our friendship. We lived next door to each other, and our fenceless backyards merged into an unbroken stretch of lawn, gravel, and dirt, as though we belonged to the same household. Our mothers were close friends, our fathers were tennis partners, neither one of us had a brother: ideal conditions therefore, with nothing to stand between us. We were born less than a week apart and spent our babyhoods in the backyard together, exploring the grass on all fours, tearing apart the flowers, standing up and taking our first steps on the same day. (There are photographs to document this.) Later, we learned baseball and football in the backyard together. We built our forts, played our games, invented our worlds in the backyard, and still later, there were our rambles through the town, the long afternoons on our bicycles, the endless conversations. It would be impossible, I think, for me to know anyone as well as I knew Fanshawe then. My mother recalls that we were so attached to each other that once, when we were six, we asked her if it was possible for men to get married. We wanted to live together when we grew up, and who else but married people did that? Fanshawe was going to be an astronomer, and I was going to be a vet. We were thinking of a big house in the country – a place where the sky would be dark enough at night to see all the stars and where there would be no shortage of animals to take care of.

In retrospect, I find it natural that Fanshawe should have

become a writer. The severity of his inwardness almost seemed to demand it. Even in grammar school he was composing little stories, and I doubt there was ever a time after the age of ten or eleven when he did not think of himself as a writer. In the beginning, of course, it didn't seem to mean much. Poe and Stevenson were his models, and what came out of it was the usual boyish claptrap. 'One night, in the year of our Lord seventeen hundred and fifty-one, I was walking through a murderous blizzard toward the house of my ancestors, when I chanced upon a spectre-like figure in the snow.' That kind of thing, filled with overblown phrases and extravagant turns of plot. In the sixth grade, I remember, Fanshawe wrote a short detective novel of about fifty pages, which the teacher let him read to the class in ten-minute installments each day at the end of school. We were all proud of Fanshawe and surprised by the dramatic way he read, acting out the parts of each of the characters. The story escapes me now, but I recall that it was infinitely complex, with the outcome hinging on something like the confused identities of two sets of twins.

Fanshawe was not a bookish child, however. He was too good at games for that, too central a figure among us to retreat into himself. All through those early years, one had the impression there was nothing he did not do well, nothing he did not do better than everyone else. He was the best baseball player, the best student, the best looking of all the boys. Any one of these things would have been enough to give him special status – but together they made him seem heroic, a child who had been touched by the gods. Extraordinary as he was, however, he remained one of us. Fanshawe was not a boy-genius or a prodigy; he did not have any miraculous gift that would have set him apart from the children his own age. He was a perfectly normal child – but more so, if that is possible, more in harmony with himself, more ideally a normal child than any of the rest of us.

At heart, the Fanshawe I knew was not a bold person. Nevertheless, there were times when he shocked me by his willingness to jump into dangerous situations. Behind all the surface composure, there seemed to be a great darkness: an urge to test himself, to take risks, to haunt the edges of things. As a boy, he had a passion for playing around construction sites, clambering up ladders and scaffolds, balancing on planks over an abyss of machinery, sandbags, and mud. I would hover in the background as Fanshawe performed these stunts, silently imploring him to stop, but never saying anything – wanting to go, but afraid to lest he should fall. As time went on, these impulses became more articulate. Fanshawe would talk to me about the importance of 'tasting life'. Making things hard for yourself, he said, searching out the unknown – this was what he wanted, and more and more as he got older. Once, when we were about fifteen, he persuaded me to spend the weekend with him in New York – roaming the streets, sleeping on a bench in the old Penn Station, talking to bums, seeing how long we could last without eating. I remember getting drunk at seven o'clock on Sunday morning in Central Park and puking all over the grass. For Fanshawe this was essential business – another step toward proving oneself – but for me it was only sordid, a miserable lapse into something I was not. Still, I continued to go along with him, a befuddled witness, sharing in the quest but not quite part of it, an adolescent Sancho astride my donkey, watching my friend do battle with himself.

A month or two after our weekend on the bum, Fanshawe took me to a brothel in New York (a friend of his arranged the visit), and it was there that we lost our virginity. I remember a small brownstone apartment on the Upper West Side near the river – a kitchenette and one dark bedroom with a flimsy curtain hanging between them. There were two black women in the place, one fat and old, the other young and pretty. Since neither one of us wanted the older woman, we had to decide who would go first. If memory serves, we actually went into the hall and flipped a coin. Fanshawe won, of course, and two minutes later I found myself sitting in the little kitchen with the fat madam. She called me sugar, reminding me every so often that

she was still available, in case I had a change of heart. I was too
nervous to do anything but shake my head, and then I just sat
there, listening to Fanshawe's intense and rapid breathing on
the other side of the curtain. I could only think about one thing:
that my dick was about to go into the same place that Fanshawe's was now. Then it was my turn, and to this day I have
no idea what the girl's name was. She was the first naked
woman I had seen in the flesh, and she was so casual and
friendly about her nakedness that things might have gone well
for me if I hadn't been distracted by Fanshawe's shoes – visible
in the gap between the curtain and the floor, shining in the light
of the kitchen, as if detached from his body. The girl was sweet
and did her best to help me, but it was a long struggle, and even
at the end I felt no real pleasure. Afterward, when Fanshawe
and I walked out into the twilight, I didn't have much to say for
myself. Fanshawe, however, seemed rather content, as if the
experience had somehow confirmed his theory about tasting
life. I realized then that Fanshawe was much hungrier than I
could ever be.

We led a sheltered life out there in the suburbs. New York
was only twenty miles away, but it could have been China for all
it had to do with our little world of lawns and wooden houses.
By the time he was thirteen or fourteen, Fanshawe became a
kind of internal exile, going through the motions of dutiful
behaviour, but cut off from his surroundings, contemptuous of
the life he was forced to live. He did not make himself difficult
or outwardly rebellious, he simply withdrew. After command-
ing so much attention as a child, always standing at the exact
centre of things, Fanshawe almost disappeared by the time we
reached high school, shunning the spotlight for a stubborn
marginality. I knew that he was writing seriously by then
(although by the age of sixteen he had stopped showing his
work to anyone), but I take that more as a symptom than as a
cause. In our sophomore year, for example, Fanshawe was the
only member of our class to make the varsity baseball team. He
played extremely well for several weeks, and then, for no

apparent reason, quit the team. I remember listening to him describe the incident to me the day after it happened: walking into the coach's office after practice and turning in his uniform. The coach had just taken his shower, and when Fanshawe entered the room he was standing by his desk stark naked, a cigar in his mouth and his baseball cap on his head. Fanshawe took pleasure in the description, dwelling on the absurdity of the scene, embellishing it with details about the coach's squat, pudgy body, the light in the room, the puddle of water on the grey concrete floor – but that was all it was, a description, a string of words divorced from anything that might have concerned Fanshawe himself. I was disappointed that he had quit, but Fanshawe never really explained what he had done, except to say that he found baseball boring.

As with many gifted people, a moment came when Fanshawe was no longer satisfied with doing what came easily to him. Having mastered all that was demanded of him at an early age, it was probably natural that he should begin to look for challenges elsewhere. Given the limitations of his life as a high school student in a small town, the fact that he found that elsewhere inside himself is neither surprising nor unusual. But there was more to it than that, I believe. Things happened around that time in Fanshawe's family that no doubt made a difference, and it would be wrong not to mention them. Whether they made an essential difference is another story, but I tend to think that everything counts. In the end, each life is no more than the sum of contingent facts, a chronicle of chance intersections, of flukes, of random events that divulge nothing but their own lack of purpose.

When Fanshawe was sixteen, it was discovered that his father had cancer. For a year and a half he watched his father die, and during that time the family slowly unravelled. Fanshawe's mother was perhaps hardest hit. Stoically keeping up appearances, attending to the business of medical consultations, financial arrangements, and trying to maintain the household, she swung fitfully between great optimism over the chances of recovery and a kind of paralytic despair. According to Fanshawe, she was never able to accept the one inevitable fact that kept staring her in the face. She knew what was going to happen, but she did not have the strength to admit that she knew, and as time went on she began to live as though she were holding her breath. Her behaviour became more and more eccentric: all-night binges of manic house-cleaning, a fear of being in the house alone (combined with sudden, unexplained absences from the house), and a whole range of imagined ailments (allergies, high blood pressure, dizzy spells). Toward the end, she started taking an interest in various crackpot theories – astrology, psychic phenomena, vague spiritualist notions about the soul – until it became impossible to talk to her without being worn down to silence as she lectured on the corruption of the human body.

Relations between Fanshawe and his mother became tense. She clung to him for support, acting as though the family's pain belonged only to her. Fanshawe had to be the solid one in the house; not only did he have to take care of himself, he had to assume responsibility for his sister, who was just twelve at the time. But this brought with it another set of problems – for Ellen was a troubled, unstable child, and in the parental void that ensued from the illness she began to look to Fanshawe for everything. He became her father, her mother, her bastion of wisdom and comfort. Fanshawe understood how unhealthy her dependence on him was, but there was little he could do about it short of hurting her in some irreparable way. I remember how my own mother would talk about 'poor Jane' (Mrs Fanshawe) and how terrible the whole thing was for the 'baby'. But I knew that in some sense it was Fanshawe who suffered the most. It was just that he never got a chance to show it.

As for Fanshawe's father, there is little I can say with any certainty. He was a cipher to me, a silent man of abstracted benevolence, and I never got to know him well. Whereas my father tended to be around a lot, especially on the weekends, Fanshawe's father was rarely to be seen. He was a lawyer of some prominence, and at one time he had had political ambitions – but these had ended in a series of disappointments. He usually worked until late, pulling into the driveway at eight or nine o'clock, and often spent Saturday and part of Sunday at his office. I doubt that he ever knew quite what to make of his son, for he seemed to be a man with little feeling for children, someone who had lost all memory of having been a child himself. Mr Fanshawe was so thoroughly adult, so completely immersed in serious, grown-up matters, that I imagine it was hard for him not to think of us as creatures from another world.

He was not yet fifty when he died. For the last six months of his life, after the doctors had given up hope of saving him, he lay in the spare bedroom of the Fanshawe house, watching the yard through the window, reading an occasional book, taking his pain-killers, dozing. Fanshawe spent most of his free time with him then, and though I can only speculate on what happened, I assume that things changed between them. At the very least, I know how hard he worked at it, often staying home from school to be with him, trying to make himself indispensable, nursing him with unflinching attentiveness. It was a grim thing for Fanshawe to go through, too much for him perhaps, and though he seemed to take it well, summoning up the bravery that is possible only in the very young, I sometimes wonder if he ever managed to get over it.

There is only one more thing I want to mention here. At the end of this period – the very end, when no one expected Fanshawe's father to last more than a few days – Fanshawe and I went for a drive after school. It was February, and a few minutes after we started, a light snow began to fall. We drove aimlessly, looping through some of the neighbouring towns, paying little attention to where we were. Ten or fifteen miles from home, we came upon a cemetery; the gate happened to be open, and for no particular reason we decided to drive in. After a while, we stopped the car and began to wander around on foot. We read the inscriptions on the stones, speculated on what each of those lives might have been, fell silent, walked some more, talked, fell silent again. By now the snow was coming down heavily, and the ground was turning white. Somewhere in the middle of the cemetery there was a freshly dug grave, and Fanshawe and I stopped at the edge and looked down into it. I can remember how quiet it was, how far away the world seemed to be from us. For a long time neither one of us spoke, and then Fanshawe said that he wanted to see what it was like at the bottom. I gave him my hand and held on tightly as he lowered himself into the grave. When his feet touched the ground he looked back up at me with a half-smile, and then lay down on his back, as though pretending to be dead. It is still completely vivid to me: looking down at Fanshawe as he looked up at the sky, his eyes blinking furiously as the snow fell onto his face.

By some obscure train of thought, it made me think back to when we were very small – no more than four or five years old. Fanshawe's parents had bought some new appliance, a television perhaps, and for several months Fanshawe kept the cardboard box in his room. He had always been generous in sharing his toys, but this box was off limits to me, and he never let me go in it. It was his secret place, he told me, and when he sat inside and closed it up around him, he could go wherever he wanted to go, could be wherever he wanted to be. But if another person ever entered his box, then its magic would be lost for good. I believed this story and did not press him for a turn, although it nearly broke my heart. We would be playing in his room, quietly setting up soldiers or drawing pictures, and then, out of the blue, Fanshawe would announce that he was going into his box. I would try to go on with what I had been doing, but it was never any use. Nothing interested me so much as what was happening to Fanshawe inside the box, and I would spend those minutes desperately trying to imagine the adventures he was having. But I never learned what they were, since it was also against the rules for Fanshawe to talk about them after he climbed out.

Something similar was happening now in that open grave in the snow. Fanshawe was alone down there, thinking his thoughts, living through those moments by himself, and though I was present, the event was sealed off from me, as though I was not really there at all. I understood that this was Fanshawe's way of imagining his father's death. Again, it was a matter of pure chance: the open grave was there, and Fanshawe had felt it calling out to him. Stories happen only to those who are able to tell them, someone once said. In the same way, perhaps, experiences present themselves only to those who are able to have them. But this is a difficult point, and I can't be sure of any of it. I stood there waiting for Fanshawe to come up, trying to imagine what he was thinking, for a brief moment trying to see what he was seeing. Then I turned my head up to the darkening winter sky – and everything was a chaos of snow, rushing down on top of me.

By the time we started walking back to the car, the sun had set. We stumbled our way through the cemetery, not saying anything to each other. Several inches of snow had fallen, and it kept coming down, more and more heavily, as though it would never stop. We reached the car, climbed in, and then, against all our expectations, couldn't get moving. The back tyres were stuck in a shallow ditch, and nothing we did made any difference. We pushed, we jostled, and still the tyres spun with that horrible, futile noise. Half an hour went by, and then we gave up, reluctantly deciding to abandon the car. We hitchhiked home in the storm, and another two hours went by before we finally made it back. It was only then that we learned that Fanshawe's father had died during the afternoon.

3

Several days went by before I found the courage to open the suitcases. I finished the article I was working on, I went to the movies, I accepted invitations I normally would have turned down. These tactics did not fool me, however. Too much depended on my response, and the possibility of being disappointed was something I did not want to face. There was no difference in my mind between giving the order to destroy Fanshawe's work and killing him with my own hands. I had been given the power to obliterate, to steal a body from its grave and tear it to pieces. It was an intolerable position to be in, and I wanted no part of it. As long as I left the suitcases untouched, my conscience would be spared. On the other hand, I had made a promise, and I knew that I could not delay forever. It was just at this point (gearing myself up, getting ready to do it) that a new dread took hold of me. If I did not want Fanshawe's work to be bad, I discovered, I also did not want it to be good. This is a difficult feeling for me to explain. Old rivalries no doubt had something to do with it, a desire not to be humbled by Fanshawe's brilliance – but there was also a feeling of being trapped. I had given my word. Once I opened the suitcases, I would become Fanshawe's spokesman – and I would go on speaking for him, whether I liked it or not. Both possibilities frighened me. To issue a death sentence was bad enough, but working for a dead man hardly seemed better. For several days I moved back and forth between these fears, unable to decide which one was worse. In the end, of course, I did open the suitcases. But by then it probably had less to do with Fanshawe than it did with Sophie. I wanted to see her again, and the sooner I got to work, the sooner I would have a reason to call her.

I am not planning to go into any details here. By now, everyone knows what Fanshawe's work is like. It has been read and discussed, there have been articles and studies, it has become public property. If there is anything to be said, it is only that it took me no more than an hour or two to understand that my feelings were quite beside the point. To care about words, to have a stake in what is written, to believe in the power of books – this overwhelms the rest, and beside it one's life becomes very small. I do not say this in order to congratulate myself or to put my actions in a better light. I was the first, but beyond that I see nothing to set me apart from anyone else. If Fanshawe's work had been any less than it was, my role would have been different – more important, perhaps, more crucial to the outcome of the story. But as it was, I was no more than an invisible instrument. Something had happened, and short of denying it, short of pretending I had not opened the suitcases, it would go on happening, knocking down whatever was in front of it, moving with a momentum of its own.

It took me about a week to digest and organize the material, to divide finished work from drafts, to gather the manuscripts into some semblance of chronological order. The earliest piece was a poem, dating from 1963 (when Fanshawe was sixteen), and the last was from 1976 (just one month before he disappeared). In all there were over a hundred poems, three novels (two short and one long), and five one-act plays – as well as thirteen notebooks, which contained a number of aborted pieces, sketches, jottings, remarks on the books Fanshawe was reading, and ideas for future projects. There were no letters, no diaries, no glimpses into Fanshawe's private life. But that was something I had expected. A man does not spend his time hiding from the world without making sure to cover his tracks. Still, I had thought that somewhere among all the papers there might be some mention of me – if only a letter of instruction or a notebook entry naming me his literary executor. But there was nothing. Fanshawe had left me entirely on my own.

I telephoned Sophie and arranged to have dinner with her the following night. Because I suggested a fashionable French restaurant (way beyond what I could afford), I think she was able to guess my response to Fanshawe's work. But beyond this hint of a celebration, I said as little as I could. I wanted everything to advance at its own pace – no abrupt moves, no premature gestures. I was already certain about Fanshawe's work, but I was afraid to rush into things with Sophie. Too much hinged on how I acted, too much could be destroyed by blundering at the start. Sophie and I were linked now, whether she knew it or not – if only to the extent that we would be partners in promoting Fanshawe's work. But I wanted more than that, and I wanted Sophie to want it as well. Struggling against my eagerness, I urged caution on myself, told myself to think ahead.

She wore a black silk dress, tiny silver earrings, and had swept back her hair to show the line of her neck. As she walked into the restaurant and saw me sitting at the bar, she gave me a warm, complicitous smile, as though telling me she knew how beautiful she was, but at the same time commenting on the weirdness of the occasion – savouring it somehow, clearly alert to the outlandish implications of the moment. I told her that she was stunning, and she answered almost whimsically that this was her first night out since Ben had been born – and that she had wanted to 'look different'. After that, I stuck to business, trying to hang back within myself. When we were led to our table and given our seats (white tablecloth, heavy silverware, a red tulip in a slender vase between us), I responded to her second smile by talking about Fanshawe.

She did not seem surprised by anything I said. It was old news for her, a fact that she had already come to terms with, and what I was telling her merely confirmed what she had known all along. Strangely enough, it did not seem to excite her. There was a wariness in her attitude that confused me, and for several minutes I was lost. Then, slowly, I began to understand that her feelings were not very different from my own. Fanshawe had disappeared from her life, and I saw that she might have good reason to resent the burden that had been imposed on her. By publishing Fanshawe's work, by devoting herself to a man who was no longer there, she would be forced to live in the past, and whatever future she might want to build for herself would be tainted by the role she had to play: the official widow, the dead writer's muse, the beautiful heroine in a tragic story. No one wants to be part of a fiction, and even less so if that fiction is real. Sophie was just twenty-six years old. She was too young to live through someone else, too intelligent not to want a life that was completely her own. The fact that she had loved Fanshawe was not the point. Fanshawe was dead, and it was time for her to leave him behind.

None of this was said in so many words. But the feeling was there, and it would have been senseless to ignore it. Given my own reservations, it was odd that I should have been the one to carry the torch, but I saw that if I didn't take hold of the thing and get it started, the job would never get done.

'You don't really have to get involved,' I said. 'We'll have to consult, of course, but that shouldn't take up much of your time. If you're willing to leave the decisions to me, I don't think it will be very bad at all.'

'Of course I'll leave them to you,' she said. 'I don't know the first thing about any of this. If I tried to do it myself, I'd get lost within five minutes.'

'The important thing is to know that we're on the same side,' I said. 'In the end, I suppose it boils down to whether or not you can trust me.'

'I trust you,' she said.

'I haven't given you any reason to,' I said. 'Not yet, in any case.'

'I know that. But I trust you anyway.'

'Just like that?'

'Yes. Just like that.'

She smiled at me again, and for the rest of the dinner we said nothing more about Fanshawe's work. I had been planning to discuss it in detail – how best to begin, what publishers might be interested, what people to contact, and so on – but this no longer seemed important. Sophie was quite content not to think about it, and now that I had reassured her that she didn't have to, her playfulness gradually returned. After so many difficult months, she finally had a chance to forget some of it for a while, and I could see how determined she was to lose herself in the very simple pleasures of this moment: the restaurant, the food, the laughter of the people around us, the fact that she was here and not anywhere else. She wanted to be indulged in all this, and who was I not to go along with her?'

I was in good form that night. Sophie inspired me, and it didn't take long for me to get warmed up. I cracked jokes, told stories, performed little tricks with the silverware. The woman was so beautiful that I had trouble keeping my eyes off her. I wanted to see her laugh, to see how her face would respond to what I said, to watch her eyes, to study her gestures. God knows what absurdities I came out with, but I did my best to detach myself, to bury my real motives under this onslaught of charm. That was the hard part. I knew that Sophie was lonely, that she wanted the comfort of a warm body beside her – but a quick roll in the hay was not what I was after, and if I moved too fast that was probably all it would turn out to be. At this early stage, Fanshawe was still there with us, the unspoken link, the invisible force that had brought us together. It would take some time before he disappeared, and until that happened, I found myself willing to wait.

All this created an exquisite tension. As the evening progressed, the most casual remarks became tinged with erotic overtones. Words were no longer simply words, but a curious code of silences, a way of speaking that continually moved around the thing that was being said. As long as we avoided the real subject, the spell would not be broken. We both slipped naturally into this kind of banter, and it became all the more powerful because neither one of us abandoned the charade. We knew what we were doing, but at the same time we pretended not to. Thus my courtship of Sophie began – slowly, decorously, building by the smallest of increments.

After dinner we walked for twenty minutes or so in the late

November darkness, then finished up the evening with drinks in a bar downtown. I smoked one cigarette after another, but that was the only clue to my tumult. Sophie talked for a while about her family in Minnesota, her three younger sisters, her arrival in New York eight years ago, her music, her teaching, her plan to go back to it next fall – but we were so firmly entrenched in our jocular mode by then that each remark became an excuse for additional laughter. It would have gone on, but there was the babysitter to think about, and so we finally cut it short at around midnight. I took her to the door of her apartment and made my last great effort of the evening.

'Thank you, doctor,' Sophie said. 'The operation was a success.'

'My patients always survive,' I said. 'It's the laughing gas. I just turn on the valve, and little by little they get better.'

'That gas might be habit-forming.'

'That's the point. The patients keep coming back for more – sometimes two or three operations a week. How do you think I paid for my Park Avenue apartment and the summer place in France?'

'So there's a hidden motive.'

'Absolutely. I'm driven by greed.'

'Your practice must be booming.'

'It was. But I'm more or less retired now. I'm down to one patient these days – and I'm not sure if she'll be coming back.'

'She'll be back,' Sophie said, with the coyest, most radiant smile I had ever seen. 'You can count on it.'

'That's good to hear,' I said. 'I'll have my secretary call her to schedule the next appointment.'

'The sooner the better. With these long-term treatments, you can't waste a moment.'

'Excellent advice. I'll remember to order a new supply of laughing gas.'

'You do that, doctor. I really think I need it.'

We smiled at each other again, and then I wrapped her up in a big bear hug, gave her a brief kiss on the lips, and got down the stairs as fast as I could.

I went straight home, realized that bed was out of the question, and then spent two hours in front of the television, watching a movie about Marco Polo. I finally conked out at around four, in the middle of the *Twilight Zone* rerun.

My first move was to contact Stuart Green, an editor at one of the larger publishing houses. I didn't know him very well, but we had grown up in the same town, and his younger brother, Roger, had gone through school with me and Fanshawe. I guessed that Stuart would remember who Fanshawe was, and that seemed like a good way to get started. I had run into Stuart at various gatherings over the years, perhaps three or four times, and he had always been friendly, talking about the good old days (as he called them) and always promising to send my greetings to Roger the next he saw him. I had no idea what to expect from Stuart, but he sounded happy enough to hear from me when I called. We arranged to meet at his office one afternoon that week.

It took him a few moments to place Fanshawe's name. It was familiar to him, he said, but he didn't know from where. I prodded his memory a bit, mentioned Roger and his friends, and then it suddenly came back to him. 'Yes, yes, of course,' he said. 'Fanshawe. That extraordinary little boy. Roger used to insist that he would grow up to be President.' That's the one, I said, and then I told him the story.

Stuart was a rather prissy fellow, a Harvard type who wore bow ties and tweed jackets, and though at bottom he was little more than a company man, in the publishing world he was what passed for an intellectual. He had done well for himself so far – a senior editor in his early thirties, a solid and responsible young worker – and there was no question that he was on the rise. I say all this only to prove that he was not someone who would be automatically susceptible to the kind of story I was telling. There was very little romance in him, very little that was not cautious and business-like – but I could feel that he was interested, and as I went on talking, he even seemed to become excited.

He had nothing to lose, of course. If Fanshawe's work didn't appeal to him, it would be simple enough for him to turn it down. Rejections were the heart of his job, and he wouldn't have to think twice about it. On the other hand, if Fanshawe was the writer I said he was, then publishing him could only help Stuart's reputation. He would share in the glory of having discovered an unknown American genius, and he would be able to live off this coup for years.

I handed him the manuscript of Fanshawe's big novel. In the end, I said, it would have to be all or nothing – the poems, the plays, the other two novels – but this was Fanshawe's major work, and it was logical that it should come first. I was referring to *Neverland*, of course. Stuart said that he liked the title, but when he asked me to describe the book, I said that I'd rather not, that I thought it would be better if he found out for himself. He raised an eyebrow in response (a trick he had probably learned during his year at Oxford), as if to imply that I shouldn't play games with him. I wasn't, as far as I could tell. It was just that I didn't want to coerce him. The book could do the work itself, and I saw no reason to deny him the pleasure of entering it cold: with no map, no compass, no one to lead him by the hand.

It took three weeks for him to get back to me. The news was neither good nor bad, but it seemed hopeful. There was probably enough support among the editors to get the book through, Stuart said, but before they made the final decision they wanted to have a look at the other material. I had been expecting that – a certain prudence, playing it close to the vest – and told Stuart that I would come around to drop off the manuscripts the following afternoon.

'It's a strange book,' he said, pointing to the copy of *Neverland* on his desk. 'Not at all your typical novel, you know. Not your typical anything. It's still not clear that we're going ahead with it, but if we do, publishing it will be something of a risk.'

'I know that,' I said. 'But that's what makes it interesting.'

'The real pity is that Fanshawe isn't around. I'd love to be able to work with him. There are things in the book that should be changed, I think, certain passages that should be cut. It would make the book even stronger.'

'That's just editor's pride,' I said. 'It's hard for you to see a manuscript and not want to attack it with a red pencil. The fact is, I think the parts you object to now will eventually make sense to you, and you'll be glad you weren't able to touch them.'

'Time will tell,' said Stuart, not ready to concede the point. 'But there's no question,' he went on, 'no question that the man could write. I read the book more than two weeks ago, and it's been with me ever since. I can't get it out of my head. It keeps coming back to me, and always at the strangest moments. Stepping out of the shower, walking down the street, crawling into bed at night – whenever I'm not consciously thinking about anything. That doesn't happen very often, you know. You read so many books in this job that they all tend to blur together. But Fanshawe's book stands out. There's something powerful about it, and the oddest thing is that I don't even know what it is.'

'That's probably the real test,' I said. 'The same thing happened to me. The book gets stuck somewhere in the brain, and you can't get rid of it.'

'And what about the other stuff?'

'Same thing,' I said. 'You can't stop thinking about it.'

Stuart shook his head, and for the first time I saw that he was honestly impressed. It lasted no more than a moment, but in that moment his arrogance and posturing suddenly disappeared, and I almost found myself wanting to like him.

'I think we might be on to something,' he said. 'If what you say is true, then I really think we might be on to something.'

We were, and as things turned out, perhaps even more than Stuart had imagined. *Neverland* was accepted later that month, with an option on the other books as well. My quarter of the advance was enough to buy me some time, and I used it to work on an edition of the poems. I also went to a number of directors to see if there was any interest in doing the plays. Eventually, this came off, too, and a production of three one-acts was planned for a small downtown theatre – to open about six weeks after *Neverland* was published. In the meantime, I persuaded the editor of one of the bigger magazines I occasionally wrote for to let me do an article on Fanshawe. It turned out to be a long, rather exotic piece, and at the time I felt it was one of the best things I had ever written. The article was scheduled to appear two months before the publication of *Neverland* – and suddenly it seemed as though everything was happening at once.

I admit that I got caught up in it all. One thing kept leading to another, and before I knew it a small industry had been set in motion. It was a kind of delirium, I think. I felt like an engineer, pushing buttons and pulling levers, scrambling from valve chambers to circuit boxes, adjusting a part here, devising an improvement there, listening to the contraption hum and chug and purr, oblivious to everything but the din of my brainchild. I was the mad scientist who had invented the great hocus-pocus machine, and the more smoke that poured from it, the more noise it produced, the happier I was.

Perhaps that was inevitable; perhaps I needed to be a little mad in order to get started. Given the strain of reconciling myself to the project, it was probably necessary for me to equate Fanshawe's success with my own. I had stumbled onto a cause, a thing that justified me and made me feel important, and the more fully I disappeared into my ambitions for Fanshawe, the more sharply I came into focus for myself. This is not an excuse; it is merely a description of what happened. Hindsight tells me that I was looking for trouble, but at the time I knew nothing about it. More important, even if I had known, I doubt that it would have made a difference.

Underneath it all was the desire to stay in touch with Sophie. As time went on, it became perfectly natural for me to call her three or four times a week, to see her for lunch, to stop by for an afternoon stroll through the neighbourhood with Ben. I introduced her to Stuart Green, invited her along to meet the theatre director, found her a lawyer to handle contracts and other legal matters. Sophie took all this in her stride, treating these encounters more as social occasions than as business talks, making it clear to the people we saw that I was the one in charge. I sensed that she was determined not to feel indebted to Fanshawe, that whatever happened or did not happen, she would continue to keep her distance from it. The money made her happy, of course, but she never really connected it to Fanshawe's work. It was an unlikely gift, a winning lottery ticket that had dropped from the sky, and that was all. Sophie saw through the whirlwind from the very start. She understood the fundamental absurdity of the situation, and because there was no greed in her, no impulse to press her own advantage, she did not lose her head.

I worked hard at courting her. No doubt my motives were transparent, but perhaps that was to the good. Sophie knew that I had fallen in love with her, and the fact that I did not pounce on her, that I did not force her to declare her feelings for me, probably did more to convince her of my seriousness than anything else. Still, I could not wait forever. Discretion has its role, but too much of it can be fatal. A moment came when I could feel that we were no longer jousting with each other, that things between us had already been settled. In thinking about this moment now, I am tempted to use the traditional language of love. I want to talk in metaphors of heat, of burning, of barriers melting down in the face of irresistible passions. I am aware of how overblown these terms might sound, but in the end I believe they are accurate. Everything had changed for me, and words that I had never understood before suddenly began to make sense. This came as a revelation, and when I finally had time to absorb it, I wondered how I had managed to live so long without learning this simple thing. I am not talking about desire so much as knowledge, the discovery that two people, through desire, can create a thing more powerful than either of them can create alone. This knowledge changed me, I think, and actually made me feel more human. By belonging to Sophie, I began to feel as though I belonged to everyone else as well. My true place in the world, it turned out, was somewhere beyond myself, and if that place was inside me, it was also unlocatable. This was the tiny hole between self and not-self, and for the first time in my life I saw this nowhere as the exact centre of the world.

It happened to be my thirtieth birthday. I had known Sophie

for about three months by then, and she insisted on making an evening of it. I was reluctant at first, never having paid much attention to birthdays, but Sophie's sense of occasion finally won me over. She bought me an expensive, illustrated edition of *Moby Dick*, took me to dinner in a good restaurant, and then ushered me along to a performance of *Boris Godunov* at the Met. For once, I let myself go with it, not trying to second-guess my happiness, not trying to stay ahead of myself or outmanoeuvre my feelings. Perhaps I was beginning to sense a new boldness in Sophie; perhaps she was making it known to me that she had decided things for herself, that it was too late now for either one of us to back off. Whatever it was, that was the night when everything changed, when there was no longer any question of what we were going to do. We returned to her apartment at eleven-thirty, Sophie paid the drowsy babysitter, and then we tiptoed into Ben's room and stood there for a while watching him as he slept in his crib. I remember distinctly that neither one of us said anything, that the only sound I could hear was the faint gurgling of Ben's breath. We leaned over the bars and studied the shape of his little body – lying on his stomach, legs tucked under him, ass in the air, two or three fingers stuck in his mouth. It seemed to go on for a long time, but I doubt it was more than a minute or two. Then, without any warning, we both straightened up, turned towards each other, and began to kiss. After that, it is difficult for me to speak of what happened. Such things have little to do with words, so little, in fact, that it seems almost pointless to try to express them. If anything, I would say that we were falling into each other, that we were falling so fast and so far that nothing could catch us. Again, I lapse into metaphor. But that is probably beside the point. For whether or not I can talk about it does not change the truth of what happened. The fact is, there never was such a kiss, and in all my life I doubt there can ever be such a kiss again.

4

I spent that night in Sophie's bed, and from then on it became impossible to leave it. I would go back to my own apartment during the day to work, but every evening I would return to Sophie. I became a part of the household – shopping for dinner, changing Ben's diapers, taking out the garbage – living more intimately with another person than I had ever lived before. Months went by, and to my constant bewilderment, I discovered that I had a talent for this kind of life. I had been born to be with Sophie, and little by little I could feel myself becoming stronger, could feel her making me better than I had been. It was strange how Fanshawe had brought us together. If not for his disappearance, none of this would have happened. I owed him a debt, but other than doing what I could for his work, I had no chance to pay it back.

My article was published, and it seemed to have the desired effect. Stuart Green called to say that it was a 'great boost' – which I gathered to mean that he felt more secure now in having accepted the book. With all the interest the article had generated, Fanshawe no longer seemed like such a long shot. Then *Neverland* came out, and the reviews were uniformly good, some of them extraordinary. It was all that one could have hoped for. This was the fairy tale that every writer dreams about, and I admit that even I was a little shocked. Such things are not supposed to happen in the real world. Only a few weeks after publication, sales were greater than had been expected for the whole edition. A second printing eventually went to press, there were ads placed in newspapers and magazines, and then the book was sold to a paperback company for republication the following year. I don't mean to imply that the book was a bestseller by commercial standards or that Sophie was on her way to becoming a millionaire, but given the seriousness and difficulty of Fanshawe's work, and given the public's tendency to stay away from such work, it was a success beyond anything we had imagined possible.

In some sense, this is where the story should end. The young genius is dead, but his work will live on, his name will be remembered for years to come. His childhood friend has rescued the beautiful young widow, and the two of them will live happily ever after. That would seem to wrap it up, with nothing left but a final curtain call. But it turns out that this is only the beginning. What I have written so far is no more than a prelude, a quick synopsis of everything that comes before the story I have to tell. If there were no more to it than this, there would be nothing at all – for nothing would have compelled me to begin. Only darkness has the power to make a man open his heart to the world, and darkness is what surrounds me whenever I think of what happened. If courage is needed to write about it, I also know that writing about it is the one chance I have to escape. But I doubt this will happen, not even if I manage to tell the truth. Stories without endings can do nothing but go on forever, and to be caught in one means that you must die before your part in it is played out. My only hope is that there is an end to what I am about to say, that somewhere I will find a break in the darkness. This hope is what I define as courage, but whether there is reason to hope is another question entirely.

It was about three weeks after the plays had opened. I spent the night at Sophie's apartment as usual, and in the morning I went uptown to my place to do some work. I remember that I was supposed to be finishing a piece on four or five books of poetry – one of those frustrating, hodge-podge reviews – and I was having trouble concentrating. My mind kept wandering away from the books on my desk, and every five minutes or so I would pop up from my chair and pace about the room. A strange story had been reported to me by Stuart Green the day before, and it was hard for me to stop thinking about it.

According to Stuart, people were beginning to say that there was no such person as Fanshawe. The rumour was that I had invented him to perpetrate a hoax and had actually written the books myself. My first response was to laugh, and I made some crack about how Shakespeare hadn't written any plays either. But now that I had given some thought to it, I didn't know whether to feel insulted or flattered by this talk. Did people not trust me to tell the truth? Why would I go to the trouble of creating an entire body of work and then not want to take credit for it? And yet – did people really think I was capable of writing a book as good as *Neverland*? I realized that once all of Fanshawe's manuscripts had been published, it would be perfectly possible for me to write another book or two under his name – to do the work myself and yet pass it off as his. I was not planning to do this, of course, but the mere thought of it opened up certain bizarre and intriguing notions to me: what it means when a writer puts his name on a book, why some writers choose to hide behind a pseudonym, whether or not a writer has a real life anyway. It struck me that writing under another name might be something I would enjoy – to invent a secret identity for myself – and I wondered why I found this idea so attractive. One thought kept leading me to another, and by the time the subject was exhausted, I discovered that I had squandered most of the morning.

Eleven-thirty rolled around – the hour of the mail – and I made my ritual excursion down the elevator to see if there was anything in my box. This was always a crucial moment of the day for me, and I found it impossible to approach it calmly. There was always the hope that good news would be sitting there – an unexpected cheque, an offer of work, a letter that would somehow change my life – and by now the habit of anticipation was so much a part of me that I could scarcely look at my mailbox without getting a rush. This was my hiding place, the one spot in the world that was purely my own. And yet it linked me to the rest of the world, and in its magic darkness there was the power to make things happen.

There was only one letter for me that day. It came in a plain white envelope with a New York postmark and had no return address. The handwriting was unfamiliar to me (my name and address were printed out in block letters), and I couldn't even begin to guess who it was from. I opened the envelope in the elevator – and it was then, standing there on my way to the ninth floor, that the world fell on top of me.

'Don't be angry with me for writing to you,' the letter began. 'At the risk of causing you heart failure, I wanted to send you one last word – to thank you for what you have done. I knew that you were the person to ask, but things have turned out even better than I thought they would. You have gone beyond the possible, and I am in your debt. Sophie and the child will be taken care of, and because of that I can live with a clear conscience.

'I'm not going to explain myself here. In spite of this letter, I want you to go on thinking of me as dead. Nothing is more important that that, and you must not tell anyone that you've heard from me. I am not going to be found, and to speak of it would only lead to more trouble than it's worth. Above all, say nothing to Sophie. Make her divorce me, and then marry her as soon as you can. I trust you to do that – and I give you my blessings. The child needs a father, and you're the only one I can count on.

'I want you to understand that I haven't lost my mind. I made certain decisions that were necessary, and though people have suffered, leaving was the best and kindest thing I have ever done.

'Seven years from the day of my disappearance will be the day of my death. I have passed judgement on myself, and no appeals will be heard.

'I beg you not to look for me. I have no desire to be found, and it seems to me that I have the right to live the rest of my life as I see fit. Threats are repugnant to me – but I have no choice but to give you this warning: if by some miracle you manage to track me down, I will kill you.

'I'm pleased that so much interest has been taken in my writing. I never had the slightest inkling that anything like this could happen. But it all seems so far away from me now. Writing books belongs to another life, and to think about it now leaves me cold. I will never try to claim any of the money – and I gladly give it to you and Sophie. Writing was an illness that plagued me for a long time, but now I have recovered from it.

'Rest assured that I won't be in touch again. You are free of me now, and I wish you a long and happy life. How much better that everything should come to this. You are my friend, and my one hope is that you will always be who you are. With me it's another story. Wish me luck.'

There was no signature at the bottom of the letter, and for the next hour or two I tried to persuade myself that it was a prank. If Fanshawe had written it, why would he have neglected to sign his name? I clung to this as evidence of a trick, desperately looking for an excuse to deny what had happened. But this optimism did not last very long, and little by little I forced myself to face the facts. There could be any number of reasons for the name to be left out, and the more I thought about it, the more clearly I saw that this was precisely why the letter should be considered genuine. A prankster would make a special point of including the name, but the real person would not think twice about it: only someone not out to deceive would have the self-assurance to make such an apparent mistake. And then there were the final sentences of the letter: '. . . remain who you are. With me it's another story.' Did this mean that Fanshawe had become someone else? Unquestionably he was living under another name – but how was he living – and where? The New York postmark was something of a clue, perhaps, but it just as easily could have been a blind, a bit of false information to throw me off his track. Fanshawe had been extremely careful. I read the letter over and over, trying to pull it apart, looking for an opening, a way to read between the lines – but nothing came of it. The letter was opaque, a block of darkness that thwarted every attempt to get inside it. In the end I gave up, put the letter in a drawer of my desk, and admitted that I was lost, that nothing would ever be the same for me again.

What bothered me most, I think, was my own stupidity. Looking back on it now, I saw that all the facts had been given to me at the start – as early as my first meeting with Sophie. For years Fanshawe publishes nothing, then he tells his wife what to do if anything should happen to him (contact me, get his work published), and then he vanishes. It was all so obvious. The man wanted to leave, and he left. He simply got up one day and walked out on his pregnant wife, and because she trusted him, because it was inconceivable to her that he would do such a thing, she had no choice but to think he was dead. Sophie had deluded herself, but given the situation, it was hard to see how she could have done otherwise. I had no such excuse. Not once from the very beginning had I thought things through for myself. I had jumped right in with her, had rejoiced in accepting her misreading of the facts, and then had stopped thinking altogether. People have been shot for smaller crimes than that.

The days went by. All my instincts told me to confide in Sophie, to share the letter with her, and yet I couldn't bring myself to do it. I was too afraid, too uncertain as to how she would react. In my stronger moods, I argued to myself that keeping silent was the only way to protect her. What possible good would it do for her to know that Fanshawe had walked out on her? She would blame herself for what had happened, and I didn't want her to be hurt. Underneath this noble silence, however, there was a second silence of panic and fear. Fanshawe was alive – and if I let Sophie know it, what would this knowledge do to us? The thought that Sophie might want him back was too much for me, and I did not have the courage to risk finding out. This was perhaps my greatest failure of all. If I had believed enough in Sophie's love for me, I would have been willing to risk anything. But at the time there seemed to be no other choice, and so I did what Fanshawe had asked me to do – not for him, but for myself. I locked up the secret inside me and learned to hold my tongue.

A few more days went by, and then I proposed marriage to Sophie. We had talked about it before, but this time I took it out of the realm of talk, making it clear to her that I meant business. I realized that I was acting out of character (humourless, inflexible), but I couldn't help myself. The uncertainty of the situation was impossible to live with, and I felt that I had to resolve things right then and there. Sophie noticed this change in me, of course, but since she didn't know the reason for it, she interpreted it as an excess of passion – the behaviour of a nervous, overly ardent male, panting after the thing he wanted most (which was also true). Yes, she said, she would marry me. Did I ever really think she would turn me down?

'And I want to adopt Ben, too,' I said. 'I want him to have my name. It's important that he grow up thinking of me as his father.'

Sophie answered that she wouldn't have it any other way. It was the only thing that made sense – for all three of us.

'And I want it to happen soon,' I went on, 'as soon as possible. In New York, you couldn't get a divorce for a year – and that's too long, I couldn't stand waiting that long. But there are other places, Alabama, Nevada, Mexico, God knows where. We could go off on a vacation, and by the time we got back, you'd be free to marry me.'

Sophie said that she liked the way that sounded – 'free to marry me'. If it meant going somewhere for a while, she would go, she said, she would go anywhere I wanted.

'After all,' I said, 'he's been gone for more than a year now, almost a year and a half. It takes seven years before a dead person can be declared officially dead. Things happen, life moves on. Just think: we've known each other for almost a year.'

'To be precise,' Sophie answered, 'you walked through that door for the first time on November twenty-fifth, nineteen-seventy-six. In eight more days it will be exactly a year.'

'You remember.'

'Of course I remember. It was the most important day of my life.'

We took a plane to Birmingham, Alabama on November twenty-seventh and were back in New York by the first week of December. On the eleventh we were married in City Hall, and afterward we went to a drunken dinner with about twenty of our friends. We spent that night at the Plaza, ordered a room service breakfast in the morning, and later that day flew to Minnesota with Ben. On the eighteenth, Sophie's parents gave us a wedding party at their house, and on the night of the twenty-fourth we celebrated Norwegian Christmas. Two days later, Sophie and I left the snow and went to Bermuda for a week and a half, then returned to Minnesota to fetch Ben. Our plan was to start looking for a new apartment as soon as we got back to New York. Somewhere over western Pennsylvania, about an hour into the flight, Ben peed through his diapers onto my lap. When I showed him the large dark spot on my pants, he laughed, clapped his hands together, and then, looking straight into my eyes, called me Da for the first time.

5

I dug into the present. Several months passed, and little by little it began to seem possible that I would survive. This was life in a foxhole, but Sophie and Ben were down there with me, and that was all I really wanted. As long as I remembered not to look up, the danger could not touch us.

We moved to an apartment on Riverside Drive in February. Settling in carried us through to mid-spring, and I had little chance to dwell on Fanshawe. If the letter did not vanish from my thoughts altogether, it no longer posed the same threat. I was secure with Sophie now, and I felt that nothing could break us apart – not even Fanshawe, not even Fanshawe in the flesh. Or so it appeared to me then, whenever I happened to think of it. I understand now how badly I was deceiving myself, but I did not find that out until much later. By definition, a thought is something you are aware of. The fact that I did not once stop thinking about Fanshawe, that he was inside me day and night for all those months, was unknown to me at the time. And if you are not aware of having a thought, is it legitimate to say that you are thinking? I was haunted, perhaps, I was even possessed – but there were no signs of it, no clues to tell me what was happening.

Daily life was full for me now. I hardly noticed that I was doing less work than I had in years. I had no job to go off to in the morning, and since Sophie and Ben were in the apartment with me, it was not very difficult to find excuses for avoiding my desk. My work schedule grew slack. Instead of beginning at nine sharp every day, I sometimes didn't make it to my little room until eleven or eleven-thirty. On top of that, Sophie's presence in the house was a constant temptation. Ben still took one or two naps a day, and in those quiet hours while he slept, it was hard for me not to think about her body. More often than not, we wound up making love. Sophie was just as hungry for it as I was, and as the weeks passed, the house was slowly eroticized, transformed into a domain of sexual possibilities. The nether world rose up to the surface. Each room acquired its own memory, each spot evoked a different moment, so that even in the calm of practical life, a particular patch of carpet, say, or the threshold of a particular door, was no longer strictly a thing but a sensation, an echo of our erotic life. We had entered the paradox of desire. Our need for each other was inexhaustible, and the more it was fulfilled, the more it seemed to grow.

Every now and then, Sophie talked of looking for a job, but neither one of us felt any urgency about it. Our money was holding up well, and we even managed to put away quite a bit. Fanshawe's next book, *Miracles*, was in the works, and the advance from the contract had been heftier than the one from *Neverland*. According to the schedule that Stuart and I had charted out, the poems would come six months after *Miracles*, then Fanshawe's earliest novel, *Blackouts*, and last of all the plays. Royalties from *Neverland* started coming in that March, and with cheques suddenly arriving for one thing and another, all money problems evaporated. Like everything else that seemed to be happening, this was a new experience for me. For the past eight or nine years, my life had been a constant scrambling act, a frantic lunge from one paltry article to the next, and I had considered myself lucky whenever I could see ahead for more than a month or two. Care was embedded inside me; it was part of my blood, my corpuscles, and I hardly knew what it was to breathe without wondering if I could afford to pay the gas bill. Now, for the first time since I had gone out on my own, I realized that I didn't have to think about these things anymore. One morning, as I sat at my desk struggling over the final sentence of an article, groping for a phrase that was not there, it gradually dawned on me that I had been given a second chance. I could give this up and start again. I no longer had to write articles. I could move on to other things, begin to do the work I had always wanted to do. This was my chance to save myself, and I decided I'd be a fool not to take it.

More weeks passed. I went into my room every morning, but nothing happened. Theoretically, I felt inspired, and whenever I was not working, my head was filled with ideas. But each time I sat down to put something on paper, my thoughts seemed to vanish. Words died the moment I lifted my pen. I started a number of projects, but nothing really took hold, and one by one I dropped them. I looked for excuses to explain why I couldn't get going. That was no problem, and before long I had come up with a whole litany: the adjustment to married life, the responsibilities of fatherhood, my new workroom (which seemed too cramped), the old habit of writing for a deadline, Sophie's body, the sudden windfall – everything. For several days, I even toyed with the idea of writing a detective novel, but then I got stuck with the plot and couldn't fit all the pieces together. I let my mind drift without purpose, hoping to persuade myself that idleness was proof of gathering strength, a sign that something was about to happen. For more than a month, the only thing I did was copy out passages from books. One of them, from Spinoza, I tacked onto my wall: 'And when he dreams he does not want to write, he does not have the power to dream he wants to write; and when he dreams he wants to write, he does not have the power to dream he does not want to write.'

It's possible that I would have worked my way out of this slump. Whether it was a permanent condition or a passing phase is still unclear to me. My gut feeling is that for a time I was truly lost, floundering desperately inside myself, but I do not think this means my case was hopeless. Things were happening to me. I was living through great changes, and it was still too early to tell where they were going to lead. Then, unexpectedly, a solution presented itself. If that is too favourable a word, I will call it a compromise. Whatever it was, I put up very little resistance to it. It came at a vulnerable time for me, and my judgement was not all it should have been. This was my second crucial mistake, and it followed directly from the first.

I was having lunch with Stuart one day near his office on the Upper East Side. Midway through the meal, he brought up the Fanshawe rumours again, and for the first time it occurred to me that he was actually beginning to have doubts. The subject was so fascinating to him that he couldn't stay away from it. His manner was arch, mockingly conspiratorial, but underneath the pose I began to suspect that he was trying to trap me into a confession. I played along with him for a while, and then, growing tired of the game, said that the one foolproof method of settling the question was to commission a biography. I made this remark in all innocence (as a logical point, not as a suggestion), but it seemed to strike Stuart as a splendid idea. He began to gush: of course, of course, the Fanshawe myth explained, perfectly obvious, of course, the true story at last. In a matter of minutes he had the whole thing figured out. I would write the book. It would appear after all of Fanshawe's work had been published, and I could have as much time as I wanted – two years, three years, whatever. It would have to be an extraordinary book, Stuart added, a book equal to Fanshawe himself, but he had great confidence in me, and he knew I could do the job. The proposal caught me off guard, and I treated it as a joke. But Stuart was serious; he wouldn't let me turn him down. Give it some thought, he said, and then tell me how you feel. I remained sceptical, but to be polite I told him I would think about it. We agreed that I would give him a final answer by the end of the month.

I discussed it with Sophie that night, but since I couldn't talk to her honestly, the conversation was not much help to me.

'It's up to you,' she said. 'If you want to do it, I think you should go ahead.'

'It doesn't bother you?'

'No. At least I don't think so. It's already occurred to me that sooner or later there would be a book about him. If it had to happen, then better it should be by you than by someone else.'

'I'd have to write about you and Fanshawe. It might be strange.'

'A few pages will be enough. As long as you're the one who's writing them, I'm not really worried.'

'Maybe,' I said, not knowing how to continue. 'The toughest question, I suppose, is whether I want to get so involved in thinking about Fanshawe. Maybe it's time to let him fade away.'

'It's your decision. But the fact is, you could do this book better than anyone else. And it doesn't have to be a straight biography, you know. You could do something more interesting.'

'Like what?'

'I don't know, something more personal, more gripping. The story of your friendship. It could be as much about you as about him.'

'Maybe. At least it's an idea. The thing that puzzles me is how you can be so calm about it.'

'Because I'm married to you and I love you, that's how. If you decide it's something you want to do, then I'm for it. I'm not blind, after all. I know you've been having trouble with your work, and I sometimes feel that I'm to blame for it. Maybe this is the kind of project you need to get started again.'

I had secretly been counting on Sophie to make the decision for me, assuming she would object, assuming we would talk about it once and that would be the end of it. But just the opposite had happened. I had backed myself into a corner, and my courage suddenly failed me. I let a couple of days go by, and then I called Stuart and told him I would do the book. This got me another free lunch, and after that I was on my own.

There was never any question of telling the truth. Fanshawe had to be dead, or else the book would make no sense. Not only would I have to leave the letter out, but I would have to pretend that it had never been written. I make no bones about what I was planning to do. It was clear to me from the beginning, and I plunged into it with deceit in my heart. The book was a work of fiction. Even though it was based on facts, it could tell nothing but lies. I signed the contract, and afterwards I felt like a man who had signed away his soul.

I wandered in my mind for several weeks, looking for a way to begin. Every life is inexplicable, I kept telling myself. No matter how many facts are told, no matter how many details are given, the essential thing resists telling. To say that so and so was born here and went there, that he did this and did that, that he married this woman and had these children, that he lived, that he died, that he left behind these books or this battle or that bridge – none of that tells us very much. We all want to be told stories, and we listen to them in the same way we did when we were young. We imagine the real story inside the words, and to do this we substitute ourselves for the person in the story, pretending that we can understand him because we understand ourselves. This is a deception. We exist for ourselves, perhaps, and at times we even have a glimmer of who we are, but in the end we can never be sure, and as our lives go on, we become more and more opaque to ourselves, more and more aware of our own incoherence. No one can cross the boundary into another – for the simple reason that no one can gain access to himself.

I thought back to something that had happened to me eight years earlier, in June of 1970. Short of money, and with no immediate prospects for the summer, I took a temporary job as a census-taker in Harlem. There were about twenty of us in the group, a commando corps of field workers hired to track down people who had not responded to the questionnaires sent out in the mail. We trained for several days in a dusty second-floor loft across from the Apollo Theatre, and then, having mastered the intricacies of the forms and the basic rules of census-taker etiquette, dispersed into the neighbourhood with our red, white, and blue shoulder bags to knock on doors, ask questions, and return with the facts. The first place I went to turned out to be the headquarters of a numbers operation. The door opened a sliver, a head poked out (behind it I could see a dozen men in a

bare room writing on long picnic tables), and I was politely told
that they weren't interested. That seemed to set the tone. In one
apartment I talked with a half-blind woman whose parents had
been slaves. Twenty minutes into the interview, it finally
dawned on her that I wasn't black, and she started cackling with
laughter. She had suspected it all long, she said, since my voice
was funny, but she had trouble believing it. I was the first white
person who had ever been inside her house. In another apartment, I came upon a household of eleven people, none of them
older than twenty-two. But for the most part no one was there.
And when they were, they wouldn't talk to me or let me in.
Summer came, and the streets grew hot and humid, intolerable
in the way that only New York can be. I would begin my rounds
early, blundering stupidly from house to house, feeling more
and more like a man from the moon. I finally spoke to the
supervisor (a fast-talking black man who wore silk ascots and a
sapphire ring) and explained my problem to him. It was then
that I learned what was really expected of me. This man was
paid a certain amount for each form a member of his crew
turned in. The better our results, the more money would go into
his pocket. 'I'm not telling you what to do,' he said, 'but it seems
to me that if you've given it an honest shot, then you shouldn't
feel too bad.'

'Just give up?' I asked.

'On the other hand,' he continued philosophically, 'the
government wants completed forms. The more forms they get,
the better they're going to feel. Now I know you're an intelligent
boy, and I know you don't get five when you put two and two
together. Just because a door doesn't open when you knock on
it doesn't mean that nobody's there. You've got to use your
imagination, my friend. After all, we don't want the government to be unhappy, do we?'

The job became considerably easier after that, but it was no
longer the same job. My field work had turned into desk work,
and instead of an investigator I was now an inventor. Every day
or two, I stopped by the office to pick up a new batch of forms

and turn in the ones I had finished, but other than that I didn't have to leave my apartment. I don't know how many people I invented – but there must have been hundreds of them, perhaps thousands. I would sit in my room with the fan blowing in my face and a cold towel wrapped around my neck, filling out questionnaires as fast as my hand could write. I went in for big households – six, eight, ten children – and took special pride in concocting odd and complicated networks of relationships, drawing on all the possible combinations: parents, children, cousins, uncles, aunts, grandparents, common law spouses, stepchildren, half-brothers, half-sisters, and friends. Most of all, there was the pleasure of making up names. At times I had to curb my impulse towards the outlandish – the fiercely comical, the pun, the dirty word – but for the most part I was content to stay within the bounds of realism. When my imagination flagged, there were certain mechanical devices to fall back on: the colours (Brown, White, Black, Green, Grey, Blue), the Presidents (Washington, Adams, Jefferson, Fillmore, Pierce), fictional characters (Finn, Starbuck, Dimmsdale, Budd). I liked names associated with the sky (Orville Wright, Amelia Earhart), with silent humour (Keaton, Langdon, Lloyd), with long homeruns (Killebrew, Mantle, Mays), and with music (Schubert, Ives, Armstrong). Occasionally, I would dredge up the names of distant relatives or old school friends, and once I even used an anagram of my own.

It was a childish thing to be doing, but I had no qualms. Nor was it hard to justify. The supervisor would not object; the people who actually lived at the addresses on the forms would not object (they did not want to be bothered, especially not by a white boy snooping into their personal business); and the government would not object, since what it did not know could not hurt it, and certainly no more than it was already hurting itself. I even went so far as to defend my preference for large families on political grounds: the greater the poor population, the more obligated the government would feel to spend money on it. This was the dead souls scam with an American twist, and my conscience was clear.

That was on one level. At the heart of it was the simple fact that I was enjoying myself. It gave me pleasure to pluck names out of thin air, to invent lives that had never existed, that never would exist. It was not precisely like making up characters in a story, but something grander, something far more unsettling. Everyone knows that stories are imaginary. Whatever effect they might have on us, we know they are not true, even when they tell us truths more important than the ones we can find elsewhere. As opposed to the story writer, I was offering my creations directly to the real world, and therefore it seemed possible to me that they could affect this real world in a real way, that they could eventually become a part of the real itself. No writer could ask for more than that.

All this came back to me when I sat down to write about Fanshawe. Once, I had given birth to a thousand imaginary souls. Now, eight years later, I was going to take a living man and put him in his grave. I was the chief mourner and officiating clergyman at this mock funeral, and my job was to speak the right words, to say the thing that everyone wanted to hear. The two actions were opposite and identical, mirror images of one another. But this hardly consoled me. The first fraud had been a joke, no more than a youthful adventure, whereas the second fraud was serious, a dark and frightening thing. I was digging a grave, after all, and there were times when I began to wonder if I was not digging my own.

Lives make no sense, I argued. A man lives and then he dies, and what happens in between makes no sense. I thought of the story of La Chère, a soldier who took part in one of the earliest French expeditions to America. In 1562, Jean Ribaut left behind a number of men at Port Royal (near Hilton Head, South Carolina) under the command of Albert de Pierra, a madman who ruled through terror and violence. 'He hanged with his own hands a drummer who had fallen under his displeasure,' Francis Parkman writes, 'and banished a soldier, named La Chère, to a solitary island, three leagues from the fort, where he left him to starve.' Albert was eventually murdered in an uprising by his men, and the half-dead La Chère was rescued from the island. One would think that La Chère was now safe, that having lived through his terrible punishment he would be exempt from further catastrophe. But nothing is that simple. There are no odds to beat, no rules to set a limit on bad luck, and at each moment we begin again, as ripe for a low blow as we were the moment before. Things collapsed at the settlement. The men had no talent for coping with the wilderness, and famine and homesickness took over. Using a few makeshift tools, they spent all their energies on building a ship 'worthy of Robinson Crusoe' to get them back to France. On the Atlantic, another catastrophe: there was no wind, their food and water ran out. The men began to eat their shoes and leather jerkins, some drank sea water in desperation, and several died. Then came the inevitable descent into cannibalism. 'The lot was cast,' Parkman notes, 'and it fell on La Chère, the same wretched man whom Albert had doomed to starvation on a lonely island. They killed him, and with ravenous avidity portioned out his flesh. The hideous repast sustained them till land rose in sight, when, it is said, in a delirium of joy, they could no longer steer their vessel, but let her drift at the will of tide. A small English bark bore down upon them, took them all on board, and, after landing the feeblest, carried the rest prisoners to Queen Elizabeth.'

I use La Chère only as an example. As destinies go, his is by no means strange – perhaps it is even blander than most. At least he travelled along a straight line, and that in itself is rare, almost a blessing. In general, lives seem to veer abruptly from one thing to another, to jostle and bump, to squirm. A person heads in one direction, turns sharply in mid-course, stalls, drifts, starts up again. Nothing is ever known, and inevitably we come to a place quite different from the one we set out for. In my first year as a student at Columbia, I walked by a bust of Lorenzo Da Ponte every day on my way to class. I knew him vaguely as Mozart's librettist, but then I learned that he had also been the first Italian professor at Columbia. The one thing seemed incompatible with the other, and so I decided to look into it, curious to know how one man could wind up living two such different lives. As it turned out, Da Ponte lived five or six. He was born Emmanuele Conegliano in 1749, the son of a Jewish leather merchant. After the death of his mother, his father made a second marriage to a Catholic and decided that he and his children should be baptized. The young Emmanuele showed promise as a scholar, and by the time he was fourteen, the Bishop of Cenada (Monsignore Da Ponte) took the boy under his wing and paid all the costs of his education for the priesthood. As was the custom of the time, the disciple was given his benefactor's name. Da Ponte was ordained in 1773 and became a seminary teacher, with a special interest in Latin, Italian, and French literature. In addition to becoming a follower of the Enlightenment, he involved himself in a number of complicated love affairs, took up with a Venetian noblewoman, and secretly fathered a child. In 1776, he sponsored a public debate at the seminary in Treviso which posed the question whether civilization had succeeded in making mankind any happier. For this affront to Church principles, he was forced to take flight – first to Venice, then to Gorizia, and finally to Dresden, where he began his new career as a librettist. In 1782, he went to Vienna with a letter of introduction to Salieri and was eventually hired as 'poeta dei teatri imperiali', a position he held for almost ten years. It was during this period that he met Mozart and collaborated on the three operas that have preserved his name from oblivion. In 1790, however, when Leopold II curbed musical activities in Vienna because of the Turkish war, Da Ponte found himself out of a job. He went to Trieste and fell in love with an English woman named Nancy Grahl or Krahl (the name is still disputed). From there the two of them went to Paris, and then on to London, where they remained for thirteen years. Da Ponte's musical work was restricted to writing a few libretti for undistinguished composers. In 1805, he and Nancy emigrated to America, where he lived out the last thirty-three years of his

life, for a time working as a shopkeeper in New Jersey and
Pennsylvania, and dying at the age of eighty-nine – one of the
first Italians to be buried in the New World. Little by little,
everything had changed for him. From the dapper, unctuous
ladies' man of his youth, an opportunist steeped in the political
intrigues of both Church and court, he became a perfectly
ordinary citizen of New York, which in 1805 must have looked
like the end of the world to him. From all that to this: a hard-
working professor, a dutiful husband, the father of four. When
one of his children died, it is said, he was so distraught with
grief that he refused to leave his house for almost a year. The
point being that, in the end, each life is irreducible to anything
other than itself. Which is as much as to say: lives make no
sense.

I don't mean to harp on any of this. But the circumstances
under which lives shift course are so various that it would seem
impossible to say anything about a man until he is dead. Not
only is death the one true arbiter of happiness (Solon's remark),
it is the only measurement by which we can judge life itself. I
once knew a bum who spoke like a Shakespearean actor, a
battered, middle-aged alcoholic with scabs on his face and rags
for clothes, who slept on the street and begged money from me
constantly. Yet he had once been the owner of an art gallery on
Madison Avenue. There was another man I knew who had once
been considered the most promising young novelist in America.
At the time I met him, he had just inherited fifteen thousand
dollars from his father and was standing on a New York street
corner passing out hundred dollar bills to strangers. It was all
part of a plan to destroy the economic system of the United
States, he explained to me. Think of what happens. Think of
how lives burst apart. Goffe and Whalley, for example, two of
the judges who condemned Charles I to death, came to Connec-
ticut after the Restoration and spent the rest of their lives in a
cave. Or Mrs Winchester, the widow of the rifle manufacturer,
who feared that the ghosts of the people killed by her husband's
rifles were coming to take her soul – and therefore continually

added rooms onto her house, creating a monstrous labyrinth of corridors and hideouts, so that she could sleep in a different room every night and thereby elude the ghosts, the irony being that during the San Francisco earthquake of 1906 she was trapped in one of those rooms and nearly starved to death because she couldn't be found by the servants. There is also M. M. Bakhtin, the Russian critic and literary philosopher. During the German invasion of Russia in World War II, he smoked the only copy of one of his manuscripts, a book-length study of German fiction that had taken him years to write. One by one, he took the pages of his manuscript and used the paper to roll his cigarettes, each day smoking a little more of the book until it was gone. These are true stories. They are also parables, perhaps, but they mean what they mean only because they are true.

In his work, Fanshawe shows a particular fondness for stories of this kind. Especially in the notebooks, there is a constant retelling of little anecdotes, and because they are so frequent – and more so toward the end – one begins to suspect that Fanshawe felt they could somehow help him to understand himself. One of the very last (from February 1976, just two months before he disappeared) strikes me as significant.

'In a book I once read by Peter Freuchen,' Fanshawe writes, 'the famous Arctic explorer describes being trapped by a blizzard in northern Greenland. Alone, his supplies dwindling, he decided to build an igloo and wait out the storm. Many days passed. Afraid, above all, that he would be attacked by wolves – for he heard them prowling hungrily on the roof of his igloo – he would periodically step outside and sing at the top of his lungs in order to frighten them away. But the wind was blowing fiercely, and no matter how hard he sang, the only thing he could hear was the wind. If this was a serious problem, however, the problem of the igloo itself was much greater. For Freuchen began to notice that the walls of his little shelter were gradually closing in on him. Because of the particular weather conditions outside, his breath was literally freezing to the walls, and with each breath the walls became that much thicker, the igloo became that much smaller, until eventually there was almost no room left for his body. It is surely a frightening thing, to imagine breathing yourself into a coffin of ice, and to my mind considerably more compelling than, say, *The Pit and the Pendulum* by Poe. For in this case it is the man himself who is the agent of his own destruction, and further, the instrument of that destruction is the very thing he needs to keep himself alive. For surely a man cannot live if he does not breathe. But at the same time, he will not live if he does breathe. Curiously, I do not remember how Freuchen managed to escape his predicament. But needless to say, he did escape. The title of the book, if I recall, is *Arctic Adventure*. It has been out of print for many years.'

6

In June of that year (1978), Sophie, Ben, and I went out to New Jersey to see Fanshawe's mother. My parents no longer lived next door (they had retired to Florida), and I had not been back in years. As Ben's grandmother, Mrs Fanshawe had stayed in touch with us, but relations were somewhat difficult. There seemed to be an undercurrent of hostility in her toward Sophie, as though she secretly blamed her for Fanshawe's disappearance, and this resentment would surface every now and then in some offhand remark. Sophie and I invited her to dinner at reasonable intervals, but she accepted only rarely, and then, when she did come, she would sit there fidgeting and smiling, rattling on in that brittle way of hers, pretending to admire the baby, paying Sophie inappropriate compliments and saying what a lucky girl she was, and then leave early, always getting up in the middle of a conversation and blurting out that she had forgotten an appointment somewhere else. Still, it was hard to hold it against her. Nothing had gone very well in her life, and by now she had more or less stopped hoping it would. Her husband was dead; her daughter had gone through a long series of mental breakdowns and was now living on tranquillizers in a halfway house; her son had vanished. Still beautiful at fifty (as a boy, I thought she was the most ravishing woman I had ever seen), she kept herself going with a number of intricate love affairs (the roster of men was always in flux), shopping sprees in New York, and a passion for golf. Fanshawe's literary success had taken her by surprise, but now that she had adjusted to it, she was perfectly willing to assume responsibility for having given birth to a genius. When I called to tell her about the biography, she sounded eager to help. She had letters and photographs and documents, she said, and would show me whatever I wanted to see.

We got there by mid-morning, and after an awkward start, followed by a cup of coffee in the kitchen and a long talk about the weather, we were taken upstairs to Fanshawe's old room. Mrs Fanshawe had prepared quite thoroughly for me, and all the materials were laid out in neat piles on what had been Fanshawe's desk. I was stunned by the accumulation. Not knowing what to say, I thanked her for being so helpful – but in fact I was frightened, overwhelmed by the sheer bulk of what was there. A few minutes later, Mrs Fanshawe went downstairs and out into the backyard with Sophie and Ben (it was a warm, sunny day), and I was left there alone. I remember looking out the window and catching a glimpse of Ben as he waddled across the grass in his diaper-padded overalls, shrieking and pointing as a robin skimmed overhead. I tapped on the window, and when Sophie turned around and looked up, I waved to her. She smiled, blew me a kiss, and then walked off to inspect a flower bed with Mrs Fanshawe.

I settled down behind the desk. It was a terrible thing to be sitting in that room, and I didn't know how long I would be able to take it. Fanshawe's baseball glove lay on a shelf with a scuffed-up baseball inside it; on the shelves above it and below it were the books he had read as a child; directly behind me was the bed, with the same blue-and-white checkered quilt I remembered from years before. This was the tangible evidence, the remains of a dead world. I had stepped into the museum of my own past, and what I found there nearly crushed me.

In one pile: Fanshawe's birth certificate, Fanshawe's report cards from school, Fanshawe's Cub Scout badges, Fanshawe's high school diploma. In another pile: photographs. An album of Fanshawe as a baby; an album of Fanshawe and his sister; an album of the family (Fanshawe as a two-year-old smiling in his father's arms, Fanshawe and Ellen hugging their mother on the backyard swing, Fanshawe surrounded by his cousins). And then the loose pictures – in folders, in envelopes, in little boxes: dozens of Fanshawe and me together (swimming, playing catch, riding bikes, mugging in the yard; my father with the two of us on his back; the short haircuts, the baggy jeans, the ancient cars behind us: a Packard, a DeSoto, a wood-pannelled Ford station wagon). Class pictures, team pictures, camp pictures. Pictures of races, of games. Sitting in a canoe, pulling on a rope in a tug-of-war. And then, toward the bottom, a few from later years: Fanshawe as I had never seen him. Fanshawe standing in Harvard Yard; Fanshawe on the deck of an Esso oil tanker; Fanshawe in Paris, in front of a stone fountain. Last of all, a single picture of Fanshawe and Sophie – Fanshawe looking older, grimmer; and Sophie so terribly young, so beautiful, and yet somehow distracted, as though unable to concentrate. I took a deep breath and then started to cry, all of a sudden, not aware until the last moment that I had those tears inside me – sobbing hard, shuddering with my face in my hands.

A box to the right of the pictures was filled with letters, at least a hundred of them, beginning at the age of eight (the clumsy writing of a child, smudged pencil marks and erasures) and continuing on through the early seventies. There were letters from college, letters from the ship, letters from France. Most of them were addressed to Ellen, and many were quite long. I knew immediately that they were valuable, no doubt more valuable than anything else in the room – but I didn't have the heart to read them there. I waited ten or fifteen minutes, then went downstairs to join the others.

Mrs Fanshawe did not want the originals to leave the house, but she had no objection to having the letters photocopied. She even offered to do it herself, but I told her not to bother: I would come out again another day and take care of it.

We had a picnic lunch in the yard. Ben dominated the scene by dashing to the flowers and back again between each bite of his sandwich, and by two o'clock we were ready to go home. Mrs Fanshawe drove us to the bus station and kissed all three of us goodbye, showing more emotion than at any other time during the visit. Five minutes after the bus started up, Ben fell asleep in my lap, and Sophie took hold of my hand.

'Not such a happy day, was it?' she said.

'One of the worst,' I said.

'Imagine having to make conversation with that woman for four hours. I ran out of things to say the moment we got there.'

'She probably doesn't like us very much.'

'No, I wouldn't think so.'

'But that's the least of it.'

'It was hard being up there alone, wasn't it?'

'Very hard.'

'Any second thoughts?'

'I'm afraid so.'

'I don't blame you. The whole thing is getting pretty spooky.'

'I'll have to think it through again. Right now, I'm beginning to feel I've made a big mistake.'

Four days later, Mrs Fanshawe telephoned to say that she was going to Europe for a month and that perhaps it would be a good idea for us to take care of our business now (her words). I had been planning to let the matter slide, but before I could think of a decent excuse for not going out there, I heard myself agreeing to make the trip the following Monday. Sophie backed off from accompanying me, and I didn't press her to change her mind. We both felt that one family visit had been enough.

Jane Fanshawe met me at the bus station, all smiles and affectionate hellos. From the moment I climbed into her car, I sensed that things were going to be different this time. She had made an effort with her appearance (white pants, a red silk blouse, her tanned, unwrinkled neck exposed), and it was hard not to feel that she was enticing me to look at her, to acknowledge the fact that she was still beautiful. But there was more to it than that: a vaguely insinuating tone to her voice, an assumption that we were somehow old friends, on an intimate footing because of the past, and wasn't it lucky that I had come by myself, since now we were free to talk openly with each other. I found it all rather distasteful and said no more than I had to.

'That's quite a little family you have there, my boy,' she said, turning to me as we stopped for a red light.

'Yes,' I said. 'Quite a little family.'

'The baby is adorable, of course. A regular heart-throb. But a bit on the wild side, wouldn't you say?'

'He's only two. Most children tend to be high-spirited at that age.'

'Of course. But I do think that Sophie dotes on him. She seems so amused all the time, if you know what I mean. I'm not arguing against laughter, but a little discipline wouldn't hurt either.'

'Sophie acts that way with everyone,' I said. 'A lively woman is bound to be a lively mother. As far as I can tell, Ben has no complaints.'

A slight pause, and then, as we started up again, cruising along a broad commercial avenue, Jane Fanshawe added: 'She's a lucky girl, that Sophie. Lucky to have landed on her feet. Lucky to have found a man like you.'

'I usually think of it the other way around,' I said.

'You shouldn't be so modest.'

'I'm not. It's just that I know what I'm talking about. So far, all the luck has been on my side.'

She smiled at this briefly, enigmatically, as though judging me a dunce, and yet somehow conceding the point, aware that I wasn't going to give her an opening. By the time we reached her house a few minutes later, she seemed to have dropped her initial tactics. Sophie and Ben were no longer mentioned, and she became a model of solicitude, telling me how glad she was that I was writing the book about Fanshawe, acting as though her encouragement made a real difference – an ultimate sort of approval, not only of the book but of who I was. Then, handing me the keys to her car, she told me how to get to the nearest photocopy store. Lunch, she said, would be waiting for me when I got back.

It took more than two hours to copy the letters, which made it nearly one o'clock by the time I returned to the house. Lunch was indeed there, and it was an impressive spread: asparagus, cold salmon, cheese, white wine, the works. It was all set out on the dining table, accompanied by flowers and what were clearly the best dishes. The surprise must have shown on my face.

'I wanted to make it festive,' Mrs Fanshawe said. 'You have no idea how good it makes me feel to have you here. All the memories that come back. It's as though the bad things never happened.'

I suspected that she had already started drinking while I was gone. Still in control, still steady in her movements, there was a certain thickening that had crept into her voice, a wavering, effusive quality that had not been there before. As we sat down to the table, I told myself to watch it. The wine was poured in liberal doses, and when I saw her paying more attention to her glass than to her plate, merely picking at her food and eventually ignoring it altogether, I began to expect the worst. After some idle talk about my parents and my two younger sisters, the conversation lapsed into a monologue.

'It's strange,' she said, 'strange how things in life turn out. From one moment to the next, you never know what's going to happen. Here you are, the little boy who lived next door. You're the same person who used to run through this house with mud on his shoes – all grown up now, a man. You're the father of my grandson, do you realize that? You're married to my son's wife. If someone had told me ten years ago that this was the future, I would have laughed. That's what you finally learn from life: how strange it is. You can't keep up with what happens. You can't even imagine it.

'You even look like him, you know. You always did, the two of you – like brothers, almost like twins. I remember how when you were both small I would sometimes confuse you from a distance. I couldn't even tell which one of you was mine.

'I know how much you loved him, how you looked up to him. But let me tell you something, my dear. He wasn't half the boy you were. He was cold inside. He was all dead in there, and I don't think he ever loved anyone – not once, not ever in his life. I'd sometimes watch you and your mother across the yard – the way you would run to her and throw your arms around her neck, the way you would let her kiss you – and right there, smack in front of me, I could see everything I didn't have with my own son. He wouldn't let me touch him, you know. After the age of four or five, he'd cringe every time I got near him. How do you think that makes a woman feel – to have her own son despise her? I was so damned young back then. I wasn't even twenty when he was born. Imagine what it does to you to be rejected like that.

'I'm not saying that he was bad. He was a separate being, a child without parents. Nothing I said ever had an effect on him. The same with his father. He refused to learn anything from us. Robert tried and tried, but he could never get through to the boy. But you can't punish someone for a lack of affection, can you? You can't force a child to love you just because he's your child.

'There was Ellen, of course. Poor, tortured Ellen. He was good to her, we both know that. But too good somehow, and in the end it wasn't good for her at all. He brainwashed her. He made her so dependent on him that she began to think twice before turning to us. He was the one who understood her, the one who gave her advice, the one who could solve her problems. Robert and I were no more than figureheads. As far as the children were concerned, we hardly existed. Ellen trusted her brother so much that she finally gave up her soul to him. I'm not saying that he knew what he was doing, but I still have to live with the results. The girl is twenty-seven years old, but she acts as though she were fourteen – and that's when she's doing well. She's so confused, so panicked inside herself. One day she thinks I'm out to destroy her, the next day she calls me thirty times on the telephone. Thirty times. You can't even begin to imagine what it's like.

'Ellen's the reason why he never published any of his work, you know. She's why he quit Harvard after his second year. He was writing poetry back then, and every few weeks he would send her a batch of manuscripts. You know what those poems are like. They're almost impossible to understand. Very passionate, of course, filled with all that ranting and exhortation, but so obscure you'd think they were written in code. Ellen would spend hours puzzling over them, acting as if her life depended on it, treating the poems as secret messages, oracles written directly to her. I don't think he had any idea what was happening. Her brother was gone, you see, and these poems were all she had left of him. The poor baby. She was only fifteen at the time, and already falling to pieces anyway. She would pore over those pages until they were all crumpled and dirty, lugging them around with her wherever she went. When she got really bad, she would go up to perfect strangers on the bus and force them into their hands. "Read these poems," she'd say. "They'll save your life."

'Eventually, of course, she had that first breakdown. She wandered off from me in the supermarket one day, and before I knew it she was taking those big jugs of apple juice off the shelves and smashing them on the floor. One after another, like someone in a trance, standing in all that broken glass, her ankles bleeding, the juice running everywhere. It was horrible. She got so wild, it took three men to restrain her and carry her off.

'I'm not saying that her brother was responsible. But those damned poems certainly didn't help, and rightly or wrongly he blamed himself. From then on, he never tried to publish anything. He came to visit Ellen in the hospital, and I think it was too much for him, seeing her like that, totally beside herself, totally crazy – screaming at him and accusing him of hating her. It was a real schizoid break, you know, and he wasn't able to deal with it. That's when he took the vow not to publish. It was a kind of penance, I think, and he stuck to it for the rest of his life, didn't he, he stuck to it in that stubborn, brutal way of his, right to the end.

'About two months later, I got a letter from him informing me that he had quit college. He wasn't asking my advice, mind you, he was telling me what he'd done. Dear mother, and so on and so forth, all very noble and impressive. I'm dropping out of school to relieve you of the financial burden of supporting me. What with Ellen's condition, the huge medical costs, the blankety x and y and z, and so on and so forth.

'I was furious. A boy like that throwing his education away for nothing. It was an act of sabotage, but there wasn't anything I could do about it. He was already gone. A friend of his at Harvard had a father who had some connection with shipping – I think he represented the seamen's union or something – and he managed to get his papers through that man. By the time the letter reached me, he was in Texas somewhere, and that was that. I didn't see him again for more than five years.

'Every month or so a letter or postcard would come for Ellen, but there was never any return address. Paris, the south of France, God knows where, but he made sure that we didn't have any way of getting in touch with him. I found this behaviour despicable. Cowardly and despicable. Don't ask me why I saved the letters. I'm sorry I didn't burn them. That's what I should have done. Burned the whole lot of them.'

She went on like this for more than an hour, her words gradually mounting in bitterness, at some point reaching a moment of sustained clarity, and then, following the next glass of wine, gradually losing coherence. Her voice was hypnotic. As long as she went on speaking, I felt that nothing could touch me anymore. There was a sense of being immune, of being protected by the words that came from her mouth. I scarcely bothered to listen. I was floating inside that voice, I was surrounded by it, buoyed up by its persistence, going with the flow of syllables, the rise and fall, the waves. As the afternoon light came streaming through the windows onto the table, sparkling in the sauces, the melting butter, the green wine bottles, everything in the room became so radiant and still that I began to find it unreal that I should be sitting there in my own body. I'm melting, I said to myself, watching the butter soften in its dish, and once or twice I even thought that I mustn't let this go on, that I mustn't allow the moment to slip away from me, but in the end I did nothing about it, feeling somehow that I couldn't.

I make no excuses for what happened. Drunkenness is never more than a symptom, not an absolute cause, and I realize that it would be wrong for me to try to defend myself. Nevertheless, there is at least the possibility of an explanation. I am fairly certain now that the things that followed had as much to do with the past as with the present, and I find it odd, now that I have some distance from it, to see how a number of ancient feelings finally caught up with me that afternoon. As I sat there listening to Mrs Fanshawe, it was hard not to remember how I had seen her as a boy, and once this began to happen, I found myself stumbling onto images that had not been visible to me in years. There was one in particular that struck me with great force: an afternoon in August when I was thirteen or fourteen, looking through my bedroom window into the yard next door and seeing Mrs Fanshawe walk out in a red two-piece bathing suit, casually unhook the top half, and lie down on a lawn chair with her back to the sun. All this happened by chance. I had been sitting by my window day-dreaming, and then, unexpectedly, a beautiful woman comes sauntering into my field of vision, almost naked, unaware of my presence, as though I had conjured her myself. This image stayed with me for a long time, and I returned to it often during my adolescence: a little boy's lust, the quick of late-night fantasies. Now that this woman was apparently in the act of seducing me, I hardly knew what to think. On the one hand, I found the scene grotesque. On the other hand, there was something natural about it, even logical, and I sensed that if I didn't use all my strength to fight it, I was going to allow it to happen.

There's no question that she made me pity her. Her version of Fanshawe was so anguished, so fraught with the signs of genuine unhappiness, that I gradually weakened to her, fell into her trap. What I still don't understand, however, is to what extent she was conscious of what she was doing. Had she planned it in advance, or did the thing just happen by itself? Was her rambling speech a ploy to wear down my resistance, or was it a spontaneous burst of true feeling? I suspect that she was telling the truth about Fanshawe, her own truth at any rate, but that is not enough to convince me – for even a child knows that the truth can be used for devious ends. More importantly, there is the question of motive. Close to six years after the fact, I still haven't come up with an answer. To say that she found me irresistible would be far-fetched, and I am not willing to delude myself about that. It was much deeper, much more sinister. Recently, I've begun to wonder if she didn't somehow sense a hatred in me for Fanshawe that was just as strong as her own. Perhaps she felt this unspoken bond between us, perhaps it was the kind of bond that could be proved only through some perverse, extravagant act. Fucking me would be like fucking Fanshawe – like fucking her own son – and in the darkness of this sin, she would have him again – but only in order to destroy him. A terrible revenge. If this is true, then I do not have the luxury of calling myself her victim. If anything, I was her accomplice.

It began not long after she started to cry – when she finally exhausted herself and the words broke apart, crumbling into tears. Drunk, filled with emotion, I stood up, walked over to where she was sitting, and put my arms around her in a gesture of comfort. This carried us across the threshold. Mere contact was enough to trigger a sexual response, a blind memory of other bodies, of other embraces, and a moment later we were kissing, and then, not many moments after that, lying naked on her bed upstairs.

Although I was drunk, I was not so far gone that I didn't know what I was doing. But not even guilt was enough to stop me. This moment will end, I said to myself, and no one will be hurt. It has nothing to do with my life, nothing to do with Sophie. But then, even as it was happening, I discovered there was more to it than that. For the fact was that I liked fucking Fanshawe's mother – but in a way that had nothing to do with pleasure. I was consumed, and for the first time in my life I found no tenderness inside me. I was fucking out of hatred, and I turned it into an act of violence, grinding away at this woman as though I wanted to pulverize her. I had entered my own darkness, and it was there that I learned the one thing that is more terrible than anything else: that sexual desire can also be the desire to kill, that a moment comes when it is possible for a man to choose death over life. This woman wanted me to hurt her, and I did, and I found myself revelling in my cruelty. But even then I knew that I was only halfway home, that she was no more than a shadow, and that I was using her to attack Fanshawe himself. As I came into her the second time – the two of us covered with sweat, groaning like creatures in a nightmare – I finally understood this. I wanted to kill Fanshawe. I wanted Fanshawe to be dead, and I was going to do it. I was going to track him down and kill him.

I left her in the bed asleep, crept out of the room, and called for a taxi from the phone downstairs. Half an hour later I was on the bus back to New York. At the Port Authority Terminal, I went into the men's room and washed my hands and face, then took the subway uptown. I got home just as Sophie was setting the table for dinner.

7

The worst of it began then. There were so many things to hide from Sophie, I could barely show myself to her at all. I turned edgy, remote, shut myself up in my little work-room, craved only solitude. For a long time Sophie bore with me, acting with a patience I had no right to expect, but in the end even she began to wear out, and by the middle of the summer we had started quarrelling, picking at each other, squabbling over things that meant nothing. One day I walked into the house and found her crying on the bed, and I knew then that I was on the verge of smashing my life.

For Sophie, the problem was the book. If only I would stop working on it, then things would return to normal. I had been too hasty, she said. The project was a mistake, and I should not be stubborn about admitting it. She was right, of course, but I kept arguing the other side to her: I had committed myself to the book, I had signed a contract for it, and it would be cowardly to back out. What I didn't tell her was that I no longer had any intention of writing it. The book existed for me now only in so far as it could lead me to Fanshawe, and beyond that there was no book at all. It had become a private matter for me, something no longer connected to writing. All the research for the biography, all the facts I would uncover as I dug into his past, all the work that seemed to belong to the book – these were the very things I would use to find out where he was. Poor Sophie. She never had the slightest notion of what I was up to – for what I claimed to be doing was in fact no different from what I actually did. I was piecing together the story of a man's life. I was gathering information, collecting names, places, dates, establishing a chronology of events. Why I persisted like this still baffles me. Everything had been reduced to a single impulse: to find Fanshawe, to speak to Fanshawe, to confront Fanshawe one last time. But I could never take it farther than that, could never pin down an image of what I was hoping to achieve by such an encounter. Fanshawe had written that he would kill me, but that threat did not scare me off. I knew that I had to find him – that nothing would be settled until I did. This was the given, the first principle, the mystery of faith: I acknowledged it, but I did not bother to question it.

In the end, I don't think that I really intended to kill him. The murderous vision that had come to me with Mrs Fanshawe did not last, at least not on any conscious level. There were times when little scenes would flash through my head – of strangling Fanshawe, of stabbing him, of shooting him in the heart – but others had died similar deaths inside me over the years, and I did not pay much attention to them. The strange thing was not that I might have wanted to kill Fanshawe, but that I sometimes imagined he *wanted* me to kill him. This happened only once or twice – at moments of extreme lucidity – and I became convinced that this was the true meaning of the letter he had written. Fanshawe was waiting for me. He had chosen me as his executioner, and he knew that he could trust me to carry out the job. But that was precisely why I wasn't going to do it. Fanshawe's power had to be broken, not submitted to. The point was to prove to him that I no longer cared – that was the crux of it: to treat him as a dead man, even though he was alive. But before I proved this to Fanshawe, I had to prove it to myself, and the fact that I needed to prove it was proof that I still cared too much. It was not enough for me to let things take their course. I had to shake them up, bring them to a head. Because I still doubted myself, I needed to run risks, to test myself before the greatest possible danger. Killing Fanshawe would mean nothing. The point was to find him alive – and then to walk away from him alive.

The letters to Ellen were useful. Unlike the notebooks, which tended to be speculative and devoid of detail, the letters were highly specific. I sensed that Fanshawe was making an effort to entertain his sister, to cheer her up with amusing stories, and consequently the references were more personal than elsewhere. Names, for example, were often mentioned – of college friends, of shipmates, of people he knew in France. And if there were no return addresses on the envelopes, there were nevertheless many places discussed: Baytown, Corpus Christi, Charleston, Baton Rouge, Tampa, different neighbourhoods in Paris, a village in southern France. These things were enough to get me started, and for several weeks I sat in my room making lists, correlating people with places, places with times, times with people, drawing maps and calendars, looking up addresses, writing letters. I was hunting for leads, and anything that held even the slightest promise I tried to pursue. My assumption was that somewhere along the line Fanshawe had made a mistake – that someone knew where he was, that someone from the past had seen him. This was by no means sure, but it seemed like the only plausible way to begin.

The college letters are rather plodding and sincere – accounts of books read, discussions with friends, descriptions of dormitory life – but these come from the period before Ellen's breakdown, and they have an intimate, confidential tone that the future letters abandon. On the ship, for example, Fanshawe rarely says anything about himself – except as it might pertain to an anecdote he has chosen to tell. We see him trying to fit into his new surroundings, playing cards in the dayroom with an oiler from Louisiana (and winning), playing pool in various low-life bars ashore (and winning), and then explaining his success as a fluke: 'I'm so geared up not to fall on my face, I've somehow gone beyond myself. A surge of adrenalin, I think.' Descriptions of working overtime in the engine room, 'a hundred and forty degrees, if you can believe it – my sneakers filled up with so much sweat, they squished as though I'd been walking in puddles'; of having a wisdom tooth pulled by a drunken dentist in Baytown, Texas, 'blood all over the place, and little bits of tooth cluttering the hole in my gums for a week.' As a newcomer with no seniority, Fanshawe was moved from job to job. At each port there were crew members who left the ship to go home and others who came aboard to take their places, and if one of these fresh arrivals preferred Fanshawe's job to the one that was open, the Kid (as he was called) would be bumped to something else. Fanshawe therefore worked variously as an ordinary seaman (scraping and painting the deck), as a utility man (mopping floors, making beds, cleaning toilets), and as a messman (serving food and washing dishes). This last job was the hardest, but it was also the most interesting, since ship life chiefly revolves around the subject of food: the great appetites nurtured by boredom, the men literally living from one meal to the next, the surprising delicacy of some of them (fat, coarse men judging dishes with the haughtiness and disdain of eighteenth-century French dukes). But Fanshawe was given good advice by an old-timer the day he started the job: 'Don't take no shit from no one,' the man said. 'If a guy complains about the food, tell him to button it. If he keeps it up, act like he's not there and serve him last. If that don't do the trick, tell him you'll put ice water in his soup the next time. Even better, tell him you'll piss in it. You gotta let them know who's boss.'

We see Fanshawe carrying the captain his breakfast one morning after a night of violent storms off Cape Hatteras: Fanshawe putting the grapefruit, the scrambled eggs, and the toast on a tray, wrapping the tray in tinfoil, then further wrapping it in towels, hoping the plates will not blow off into the water when he reaches the bridge (since the wind is holding at seventy miles per hour); Fanshawe then climbing up the ladder, taking his first steps on the bridge, and then, suddenly, as the wind hits him, doing a wild pirouette – the ferocious air shooting under the tray and pulling his arms up over his head, as though he were holding on to a primitive flying machine, about to launch himself over the water; Fanshawe, summoning all his strength to pull down the tray, finally wrestling it to a position flat against his chest, the plates miraculously not slipping, and then, step by struggling step, walking the length of the bridge, a tiny figure dwarfed by the havoc of the air around him; Fanshawe, after how many minutes, making it to the other end, entering the forecastle, finding the plump captain behind the wheel, saying, 'Your breakfast, captain', and the helmsman turning, giving him the briefest glance of recognition and replying, in a distracted voice, 'Thanks, kid. Just put it on the table over there.'

Not everything was so amusing to Fanshawe, however. There is mention of a fight (no details given) that seems to have disturbed him, along with several ugly scenes he witnessed ashore. An instance of nigger-baiting in a Tampa bar, for example: a crowd of drunks ganging up on an old black man who had wandered in with a large American flag – wanting to sell it – and the first drunk opening the flag and saying there weren't enough stars on it – 'this flag's a fake' – and the old man denying it, almost grovelling for mercy, as the other drunks start grumbling in support of the first – the whole thing ending when the old man is pushed out the door, landing flat on the sidewalk, and the drunks nodding approval, dismissing the matter with a few comments about making the world safe for democracy. 'I felt humiliated,' Fanshawe wrote, 'ashamed of myself for being there.'

Still, the letters are basically jocular in tone ('Call me Redburn', one of them begins), and by the end one senses that Fanshawe has managed to prove something to himself. The ship is no more than an excuse, an arbitrary otherness, a way to test himself against the unknown. As with any initiation, survival itself is the triumph. What begin as possible liabilities – his Harvard education, his middle-class background – he eventually turns to his advantage, and by the end of his stint he is the acknowledged intellectual of the crew, no longer just the 'Kid' but at times also the 'Professor', brought in to arbitrate disputes (who was the twenty-third President, what is the population of Florida, who played left field for the 1947 Giants) and consulted regularly as a source of obscure information. Crew members ask his help in filling out bureaucratic forms (tax schedules, insurance questionnaires, accident reports), and some even ask him to write letters for them (in one case, seventeen love letters for Otis Smart to his girlfriend Sue-Ann in Dido, Louisiana). The point is not that Fanshawe becomes the centre of attention, but that he manages to fit in, to find a place for himself. The true test, after all, is to be like everyone else. Once that happens, he no longer has to question his singularity. He is free – not only of others, but of himself. The ultimate proof of this, I think, is that when he leaves the ship, he says goodbye to no one. He signs off one night in Charleston, collects his pay from the captain, and then just disappears. Two weeks later he arrives in Paris.

No word for two months. And then, for the next three months, nothing but postcards. Brief, elliptical messages scrawled on the back of commonplace tourist shots: Sacré Coeur, the Eiffel Tower, the Conciergerie. When the letters do begin to come, they arrive fitfully, and say nothing of any great importance. We know that by now Fanshawe is deep into his work (numerous early poems, a first draft of *Blackouts*), but the letters give no real sense of the life he is leading. One feels that he is in conflict, unsure of himself in regard to Ellen, not wanting to lose touch with her and yet unable to decide how much or how little to tell her. (And the fact is that most of these letters are not even read by Ellen. Addressed to the house in New Jersey, they are of course opened by Mrs Fanshawe, who screens them before showing them to her daughter – and more often than not, Ellen does not see them. Fanshawe, I think, must have known this would happen, at least would have suspected it. Which further complicates the matter – since in some way these letters are not written to Ellen at all. Ellen, finally, is no more than a literary device, the medium through which Fanshawe communicates with his mother. Hence her anger. For even as he speaks to her, he can pretend to ignore her.)

For about a year the letters dwell almost exclusively on objects (buildings, streets, descriptions of Paris), hashing out meticulous catalogues of things seen and heard, but Fanshawe himself is barely present. Then, gradually, we begin to see some of his acquaintances, to sense a slow gravitation towards the anecdote – but still, the stories are divorced from any context, which gives them a floating, disembodied quality. We see, for example, an old Russian composer by the name of Ivan Wyshnegradsky, now nearly eighty years old – impoverished, a widower, living alone in a shabby apartment on the rue Mademoiselle. 'I see this man more than anyone else,' Fanshawe declares. Then not a word about their friendship, not a glimmer of what they say to each other. Instead, there is a lengthy description of the quarter-tone piano in the apartment, with its enormous bulk and multiple keyboards (built for Wyshnegradsky in Prague almost fifty years before, and one of only three quarter-tone pianos in Europe), and then, making no further allusions to the composer's career, the story of how Fanshawe gives the old man a refrigerator. 'I was moving to another apartment last month,' Fanshawe writes. 'Since the place was furnished with a new refrigerator, I decided to give the old one to Ivan as a present. Like many people in Paris, he has never had a refrigerator – storing his food for all these years in a little box in the wall of his kitchen. He seemed quite pleased by the offer, and I made all the arrangements to have it delivered to his house – carrying it upstairs with the help of the man who drove the truck. Ivan greeted the arrival of this machine as an important event in his life – bubbling over like a small child – and yet he was wary, I could see that, even a bit daunted, not quite sure what to make of this alien object. "It's so big," he kept saying, as we worked it into place, and then, when we plugged it in and the motor started up – "Such a lot of noise." I assured him that he would get used to it, pointing out all the advantages of this modern convenience, all the ways in which his life would be improved. I felt like a missionary: big Father Know-It-All, redeeming the life of this stone-age man by showing him the true religion. A week or so went by, and Ivan called me nearly every day to tell me how happy he was with the refrigerator, describing all the new foods he was able to buy and keep in his house. Then disaster.

"I think it's broken," he said to me one day, sounding very contrite. The little freezer section on top had apparently filled up with frost, and not knowing how to get rid of it, he had used a hammer, banging away not only at the ice but at the coils below it. "My dear friend," he said, "I'm very sorry." I told him not to fret – I would find a repair man to fix it. A long pause on the other end. "Well," he said at last, "I think maybe it's better this way. The noise, you know. It makes it very hard to concentrate. I've lived so long with my little box in the wall, I feel rather attached to it. My dear friend, don't be angry. I'm afraid there's nothing to be done with an old man like me. You get to a certain point in life, and then it's too late to change." '

Further letters continue this trend, with various names mentioned, various jobs alluded to. I gather that the money Fanshawe earned on the ship lasted for about a year and that afterwards he scrambled as best he could. For a time it seems that he translated a series of art books; at another time there is evidence that he worked as an English tutor for several lycée students; still again, it seems that he worked the graveyard shift one summer at the *New York Times* Paris office as a switchboard operator (which, if nothing else, indicates that he had become fluent in French); and then there is a rather curious period during which he worked off and on for a movie producer – revising treatments, translating, preparing script synopses. Although there are few autobiographical allusions in any of Fanshawe's works, I believe that certain incidents in *Neverland* can be traced back to this last experience (Montag's house in chapter seven; Flood's dream in chapter thirty). 'The strange thing about this man,' Fanshawe writes (referring to the movie producer in one of his letters), 'is that while his financial dealings with the rich border on the criminal (cutthroat tactics, outright lying), he is quite gentle with those down on their luck. People who owe him money are rarely sued or taken to court – but are given a chance to work off their debts by rendering him services. His chauffeur, for example, is a destitute marquis who drives around in a white Mercedes. There is an old baron who does nothing but xerox papers. Every time I visit the apartment to turn in my work, there is some new lackey standing in the corner, some decrepit nobleman hiding behind the curtains, some elegant financier who turns out to be the messenger boy. Nor does anything go to waste. When the ex-director who had been living in the maid's room on the sixth floor committed suicide last month, I inherited his overcoat – and have been wearing it ever since. A long black affair that comes down almost to my ankles. It makes me look like a spy.'

As for Fanshawe's private life, there are only the vaguest hints. A dinner party is referred to, a painter's studio is described, the name Anne sneaks out once or twice – but the nature of these connections is obscure. This was the kind of thing I needed, however. By doing the necessary legwork, by going out and asking enough questions, I figured I would eventually be able to track some of these people down.

Besides a three-week trip to Ireland (Dublin, Cork, Limerick, Sligo), Fanshawe seems to have remained more or less fixed. The final draft of *Blackouts* was completed at some point during his second year in Paris; *Miracles* was written during the third, along with forty or fifty short poems. All this is rather easy to determine – since it was around this time that Fanshawe developed the habit of dating his work. Still unclear is the precise moment when he left Paris for the country, but I believe it falls somewhere between June and September of 1971. The letters become sparse just then, and even the notebooks give no more than a list of the books he was reading (Raleigh's *History of the World* and *The Journeys* of Cabeza de Vaca). But once he is ensconced in the country house, he gives a fairly elaborate account of how he wound up there. The details are unimportant in themselves, but one crucial thing emerges: while living in France Fanshawe did not hide the fact that he was a writer. His friends knew about his work, and if there was ever any secret, it was only meant for his family. This is a definite slip on his part – the only time in any of the letters he gives himself away. 'The Dedmons, an American couple I know in Paris,' he writes, 'are unable to visit their country house for the next year (they're going to Japan). Since the place has been broken into once or twice, they're reluctant to leave it empty – and have offered me the job of caretaker. Not only do I get it rent-free, but I'm also given the use of a car and a small salary (enough to get by on if I'm very careful). This is a lucky break. They said they would much rather pay me to sit in the house and write for a year than rent it out to strangers.' A small point, perhaps, but when I came across it in the letter, I was heartened. Fanshawe had momentarily let down his guard – and if it happened once, there was no reason to assume it could not happen again.

As examples of writing, the letters from the country surpass all the others. By now, Fanshawe's eye has become incredibly sharp, and one senses a new availability of words inside him, as though the distance between seeing and writing had been narrowed, the two acts now almost identical, part of a single, unbroken gesture. Fanshawe is preoccupied by the landscape, and he keeps returning to it, endlessly watching it, endlessly recording its changes. His patience before these things is never less than remarkable, and there are passages of nature writing in both the letters and notebooks as luminous as any I have read. The stone house he lives in (walls two feet thick) was built during the Revolution: on one side is a small vineyard, on the other side is a meadow where sheep graze; there is a forest behind (magpies, rooks, wild boar), and in front, across the road, are the cliffs that lead up to the village (population forty). On these same cliffs, hidden in a tangle of bushes and trees, are the ruins of a chapel that once belonged to the Knights Templar. Broom, thyme, scrub oak, red soil, white clay, the Mistral – Fanshawe lives amidst these things for more than a year, and little by little they seem to alter him, to ground him more deeply in himself. I hesitate to talk about a religious or mystical experience (these terms mean nothing to me), but from all the evidence it seems that Fanshawe was alone for the whole time, barely seeing anyone, barely even opening his mouth. The stringency of this life disciplined him. Solitude became a passageway into the self, an instrument of discovery. Although he was still quite young at the time, I believe this period marked the beginning of his maturity as a writer. From now on, the work is no longer promising – it is fulfilled, accomplished, unmistakably his own. Starting with the long sequence of poems written in the country (*Ground Work*), and then on through the plays and *Neverland* (all written in New York), Fanshawe is in full flower. One looks for traces of madness, for signs of the thinking that eventually turned him against himself – but the work reveals nothing of the sort. Fanshawe is no doubt an unusual person, but to all appearances he is sane, and when he returns to America in the fall of 1972, he seems totally in command of himself.

My first answers came from the people Fanshawe had known at Harvard. The word *biography* seemed to open doors for me, and I had no trouble getting appointments to see most of them. I saw his freshman roommate; I saw several of his friends; I saw two or three of the Radcliffe girls he had dated. Nothing much came of it, however. Of all the people I met, only one said anything of interest. This was Paul Schiff, whose father had made the arrangements for Fanshawe's job on the oil tanker. Schiff was now a paediatrician in Westchester County, and we spoke in his office one evening until quite late. There was an earnestness about him that I liked (a small, intense man, his hair already thinning, with steady eyes and a soft, resonant voice), and he talked openly, without any prodding. Fanshawe had been an important person in his life, and he remembered their friendship well. 'I was a diligent boy,' Schiff said. 'Hard-working, obedient, without much imagination. Fanshawe wasn't intimidated by Harvard the way the rest of us were, and I think I was in awe of that. He had read more than anyone else – more poets, more philosophers, more novelists – but the business of school seemed to bore him. He didn't care about grades, cut class a lot, just seemed to go his own way. In freshman year, we lived down the hall from each other, and for some reason he picked me out to be his friend. After that, I sort of tagged along after him. Fanshawe had so many ideas about everything, I think I learned more from him than from any of my classes. It was a bad case of hero-worship, I suppose – but Fanshawe helped me, and I haven't forgotten it. He was the one who taught me to think for myself, to make my own choices. If it hadn't been for him, I never would have become a doctor. I switched to pre-med because he convinced me to do what I wanted to do, and I'm still grateful to him for it.

'Midway through our second year, Fanshawe told me that he was going to quit school. It didn't really surprise me. Cambridge wasn't the right place for Fanshawe, and I knew that he was restless, itching to get away. I talked to my father, who represented the seamen's union, and he worked out that job for Fanshawe on the ship. It was arranged very neatly. Fanshawe was whisked through all the paperwork, and a few weeks later he was off. I heard from him several times – postcards from here and there. Hi, how are you, that kind of thing. It didn't bother me though, and I was glad that I'd been able to do something for him. But then, all those good feelings eventually blew up in my face. I was in the city one day about four years ago, walking along Fifth Avenue, and I ran into Fanshawe, right there on the street. I was delighted to see him, really surprised and happy, but he hardly even talked to me. It was as though he'd forgotten who I was. Very stiff, almost rude. I had to force my address and phone number into his hand. He promised to call, but of course he never did. It hurt a lot, I can tell you. The son-of-a-bitch, I thought to myself, who does he think he is? He wouldn't even tell me what he was doing – just evaded my questions and sauntered off. So much for college days, I thought. So much for friendship. It left an ugly taste in my mouth. Last year, my wife bought one of his books and gave it to me as a birthday present. I know it's childish, but I haven't had the heart to open it. It just sits there on the shelf collecting dust. It's very strange, isn't it? Everyone says it's a masterpiece, but I don't think I can ever bring myself to read it.'

This was the most lucid commentary I got from anyone. Some of the oil tanker shipmates had things to say, but nothing that really served my purpose. Otis Smart, for example, remembered the love letters Fanshawe had written for him. When I reached him by telephone in Baton Rouge, he went on about them at great length, even quoting some of the phrases Fanshawe had made up ('my darling twinkle-toes', 'my pumpkin squash woman', 'my wallow-dream wickedness', and so on), laughing as he spoke. The damndest thing was, he said, that the whole time he was sending those letters to Sue-Ann, she was fooling around with someone else, and the day he got home she announced to him that she was getting married. 'It's just as well,' Smart added. 'I ran into Sue-Ann back home last year, and she's up to about three hundred pounds now. She looks like a cartoon fat lady – strutting down the street in orange stretch pants with a mess of brats bawling around her. It made me laugh, it did – remembering the letters. That Fanshawe really cracked me up. He'd get going with some of those lines of his, and I'd start rolling on the floor like a monkey. It's too bad about what happened. You hate to hear about a guy punching his ticket so young.'

Jeffrey Brown, now a chef in a Houston restaurant, had been the assistant cook on the ship. He remembered Fanshawe as the one white crew member who had been friendly to him. 'It wasn't easy,' Brown said. 'The crew was mostly a bunch of rednecks, and they'd just as soon spit at me as say hello. But Fanshawe stuck by me, didn't care what anyone thought. When we got into Baytown and places like that, we'd go ashore together for drinks, for girls, whatever. I knew those towns better than Fanshawe did, and I told him that if he wanted to stick with me, we couldn't go into the regular sailors' bar. I knew what my ass would be worth in places like that, and I didn't want trouble. No problem, Fanshawe said, and off we'd go to the black sections, no problem at all. Most of the time, things were pretty calm on the ship – nothing I couldn't handle. But then this rough customer came on for a few weeks. A guy named Cutbirth, if you can believe it, Roy Cutbirth. He was a stupid honky oiler who finally got thrown off the ship when the Chief Engineer figured out he didn't know squat about engines. He'd cheated on his oiler's test to get the job – just the man to have down there if you want to blow up the ship. This Cutbirth was dumb, mean and dumb. He had those tattoos on his knuckles – a letter on each finger: L-O-V-E on the right hand, H-A-T-E on the left. When you see that kind of crazy shit, you just want to keep away. This guy once bragged to Fanshawe about how he used to spend his Saturday nights back home in Alabama – sitting on a hill over the interstate and shooting at cars. A charming fellow, no matter how you put it. And then there was this sick eye he had, all bloodshot and messed up. But he liked to brag about that, too. Seems he got it one day when a piece of glass flew into it. That was in Selma, he said, throwing bottles at Martin Luther King. I don't have to tell you that this Cutbirth wasn't my bosom buddy. He used to give me a lot of stares, muttering under his breath and nodding to himself, but I paid no attention. Things went on like that for a while. Then he tried it with Fanshawe around, and the way it came out, it was just a little too loud for Fanshawe to ignore. He stops, turns to Cutbirth, and says, "What did you say?" And Cutbirth, all tough and cocky, says something like "I was just wondering when you and the jungle bunny are getting married, sweetheart." Well, Fanshawe was always peaceable and friendly, a real gentleman, if you know what I mean, and so I wasn't expecting what happened. It was like watching that hulk on the TV, the man who turns into a beast. All of a sudden he got angry, I mean raging, damned near *beside* himself with anger. He grabbed Cutbirth by the shirt and just threw him against the wall, just pinned him there and held on, breathing right into his face. "Don't ever say that again," Fanshawe says, his eyes all on fire. "Don't ever say that again, or I'll kill you." And damned if you didn't believe him when he said it. The guy was ready to kill, and Cutbirth knew it. "Just joking," he says. "Just making a little joke." And that was the end of it – real fast. The whole thing didn't take more than half a blink. About two days later, Cutbirth got fired. A lucky thing, too. If he'd stayed around any longer, there's no telling what might have happened.'

I got dozens of statements like this one – from letters, from phone conversations, from interviews. It went on for months, and each day the material expanded, grew in geometric surges, accumulating more and more associations, a chain of contacts that eventually took on a life of its own. It was an infinitely hungry organism, and in the end I saw that there was nothing to prevent it from becoming as large as the world itself. A life touches one life, which in turn touches another life, and very quickly the links are innumerable, beyond calculation. I knew about a fat woman in a small Louisiana town; I knew about a demented racist with tattoos on his fingers and a name that defied understanding. I knew about dozens of people I had never heard of before, and each one had been a part of Fanshawe's life. All well and good, perhaps, and one might say that this surplus of knowledge was the very thing that proved I was getting somewhere. I was a detective, after all, and my job was to hunt for clues. Faced with a million bits of random information, led down a million paths of false inquiry, I had to find the one path that would take me where I wanted to go. So far, the essential fact was that I hadn't found it. None of these people had seen or heard from Fanshawe in years, and short of doubting everything they told me, short of beginning an investigation into each one of them, I had to assume they were telling the truth.

What it boiled down to, I think, was a question of method. In some sense, I already knew everything there was to know about Fanshawe. The things I learned did not teach me anything important, did not go against any of the things I already knew. Or, to put it another way: the Fanshawe I had known was not the same Fanshawe I was looking for. There had been a break somewhere, a sudden, incomprehensible break – and the things I was told by the various people I questioned did not account for it. In the end, their statements only confirmed that what happened could not possibly have happened. That Fanshawe was kind, that Fanshawe was cruel – this was an old story, and I already knew it by heart. What I was looking for was something different, something I could not even imagine: a purely irrational act, a thing totally out of character, a contradiction of everything Fanshawe had been up to the moment he vanished. I kept trying to leap into the unknown, but each time I landed, I found myself on home ground, surrounded by what was most familiar to me.

The farther I went, the more the possibilities narrowed. Perhaps that was a good thing, I don't know. If nothing else, I knew that each time I failed, there would be one less place to look. Months went by, more months than I would like to admit. In February and March I spent most of my time looking for Quinn, the private detective who had worked for Sophie. Strangely enough, I couldn't find a trace of him. It seemed that he was no longer in business – not in New York, not anywhere. For a while I investigated reports of unclaimed bodies, questioned people who worked at the city morgue, tried to track down his family – but nothing came of it. As a last resort, I considered hiring another private detective to look for him, but then decided not to. One missing man was enough, I felt, and then, little by little, I used up the possibilities that were left. By mid-April, I was down to the last one. I held out for a few more days, hoping I would get lucky, but nothing developed. On the morning of the twenty-first, I finally walked into a travel agency and booked a flight to Paris.

I was supposed to leave on a Friday. On Tuesday, Sophie and I went shopping for a record player. One of her younger sisters was about to move to New York, and we were planning to give her our old record player as a present. The idea of replacing it had been in the air for several months, and this finally gave us an excuse to go looking for a new one. So we went downtown that Tuesday, bought the thing, and then lugged it home in a cab. We hooked it up in the same spot where the old one had been and then packed away the old one in the new box. A clever solution, we thought. Karen was due to arrive in May, and in the mean time we wanted to keep it somewhere out of sight. That was when we ran into a problem.

Storage space was limited, as it is in most New York apartments, and it seemed that we didn't have any left. The one closet that offered any hope was in the bedroom, but the floor was already crammed with boxes – three deep, two high, four across and there wasn't enough room on the shelf above. These were the cartons that held Fanshawe's things (clothes, books, odds and ends), and they had been there since the day we moved in. Neither Sophie nor I had known what to do with them when she cleaned out her old place. We didn't want to be surrounded by memories of Fanshawe in our new life, but at the same time it seemed wrong just to throw the things away. The boxes had been a compromise, and eventually we no longer seemed to notice them. They became a part of the domestic landscape – like the broken floorboard under the living room rug, like the crack in the wall above our bed – invisible in the flux of daily life. Now, as Sophie opened the door of the closet and looked inside, her mood suddenly changed.

'Enough of this,' she said, squatting down in the closet. She pushed away the clothes that were draped over the boxes, clicking hangers against each other, parting the jumble in frustration. It was an abrupt anger, and it seemed to be directed more at herself than at me.

'Enough of what?' I was standing on the other side of the bed, watching her back.

'All of it,' she said, still flinging the clothes back and forth. 'Enough of Fanshawe and his boxes.'

'What do you want to do with them?' I sat down on the bed and waited for an answer, but she didn't say anything. 'What do you want to do with them, Sophie?' I asked again.

She turned around and faced me, and I could see that she was on the point of tears. 'What good is a closet if you can't even use it?' she said. Her voice was trembling, losing control. 'I mean

284

he's dead, isn't he? And if he's dead, why do we need all this
. . . all this' – gesturing, groping for the word – 'garbage. It's like
living with a corpse.'

'If you want, we can call the Salvation Army today,' I said.

'Call them now. Before we say another word.'

'I will. But first we'll have to open the boxes and sort through
them.'

'No. I want it to be everything, all at once.'

'It's fine for clothes,' I said. 'But I wanted to hold on to the
books for a while. I've been meaning to make a list, and I
wanted to check for any notes in the margins. I could finish in
half an hour.'

Sophie looked at me in disbelief. 'You don't understand anything, do you?' she said. And then, as she stood up, the tears
finally came out of her eyes – child's tears, tears that held
nothing back, falling down her cheeks as if she didn't know they
were there. 'I can't get through to you anymore. You just don't
hear what I'm saying.'

'I'm doing my best, Sophie.'

'No, you're not. You think you are, but you're not. Don't you
see what's happening? Your bringing him back to life.'

'I'm writing a book. That's all – just a book. But if I don't take
it seriously, how can I hope to get it done?'

'There's more to it than that. I know it, I can feel it. If the two
of us are going to last, he's got to be dead. Don't you understand that? Even if he's alive, he's got to be dead.'

'What are you talking about? Of course he's dead.'

'Not for much longer. Not if you keep it up.'

'But you were the one who got me started. You wanted me to
do the book.'

'That was a hundred years ago, my darling. I'm so afraid I'm
going to lose you. I couldn't take it if that happened.'

'It's almost finished, I promise. This trip is the last step.'

'And then what?'

'We'll see. I can't know what I'm getting into until I'm in it.'

'That's what I'm afraid of.'

'You could go with me.'

'To Paris?'

'To Paris. The three of us could go together.'

'I don't think so. Not the way things are now. You go alone. At least then, if you come back, it will be because you want to.'

'What do you mean "if"?'

'Just that. "If". As in, "if you come back." '

'You can't believe that.'

'But I do. If things go on like this, I'm going to lose you.'

'Don't talk like that, Sophie.'

'I can't help it. You're so close to being gone already. I sometimes think I can see you vanishing before my eyes.'

'That's nonsense.'

'You're wrong. We're coming to the end, my darling, and you don't even know it. You're going to vanish, and I'll never see you again.'

8

Things felt oddly bigger to me in Paris. The sky was more present than in New York, its whims more fragile. I found myself drawn to it, and for the first day or two I watched it constantly – sitting in my hotel room and studying the clouds, waiting for something to happen. These were northern clouds, the dream clouds that are always changing, massing up into huge grey mountains, discharging brief showers, dissipating, gathering again, rolling across the sun, refracting the light in ways that always seem different. The Paris sky has its own laws, and they function independently of the city below. If the buildings appear solid, anchored in the earth, indestructible, the sky is vast and amorphous, subject to constant turmoil. For the first week, I felt as though I had been turned upside-down. This was an old-world city, and it had nothing to do with New York – with its slow skies and chaotic streets, its bland clouds and aggressive buildings. I had been displaced, and it made me suddenly unsure of myself. I felt my grip loosening, and at least once an hour I had to remind myself why I was there.

My French was neither good nor bad. I had enough to understand what people said to me, but speaking was difficult, and there were times when no words came to my lips, when I struggled to say even the simplest things. There was a certain pleasure in this, I believe – to experience language as a collection of sounds, to be forced to the surface of words where meanings vanish – but it was also quite wearing, and it had the effect of shutting me up in my thoughts. In order to understand what people were saying, I had to translate everything silently into English, which meant that even when I understood, I was understanding at one remove – doing twice the work and getting half the result. Nuances, subliminal associations, undercurrents – all these things were lost on me. In the end, it would probably not be wrong to say that everything was lost on me.

Still, I pushed ahead. It took me a few days to get the investigation started, but once I made my first contact, others followed. There were a number of disappointments, however. Wyshnegradsky was dead; I was unable to locate any of the people Fanshawe had tutored in English; the woman who had hired Fanshawe at the *New York Times* was gone, had not worked there in years. Such things were to be expected, but I took them hard, knowing that even the smallest gap could be fatal. These were empty spaces for me, blanks in the picture, and no matter how successful I was in filling the other areas, doubts would remain, which meant that the work could never be truly finished.

I spoke to the Dedmons, I spoke to the art book publishers Fanshawe had worked for, I spoke to the woman named Anne (a girlfriend, it turned out), I spoke to the movie producer. 'Odd jobs,' he said to me, in Russian-accented English, 'that's what he did. Translations, script summaries, a little ghost-writing for my wife. He was a smart boy, but too stiff. Very literary, if you know what I'm saying. I wanted to give him a chance to act – even offered to give him fencing and riding lessons for a picture we were going to do. I liked his looks, thought we could make something of him. But he wasn't interested. I've got other eggs to fry, he said. Something like that. It didn't matter. The picture made millions, and what do I care if the boy wants to act or not?'

There was something to be pursued here, but as I sat with this man in his monumental apartment on the Avenue Henri Martin, waiting for each sentence of his story between phone calls, I suddenly realized that I didn't need to hear any more. There was only one question that mattered, and this man couldn't answer it for me. If I stayed and listened to him, I would be given more details, more irrelevancies, yet another pile of useless notes. I had been pretending to write a book for too long now, and little by little I had forgotten my purpose. Enough, I said to myself, consciously echoing Sophie, enough of this, and then I stood up and left.

The point was that no one was watching me anymore. I no longer had to put up a front as I had at home, no longer had to delude Sophie by creating endless busy-work for myself. The charade was over. I could discard my non-existent book at last. For about ten minutes, walking back to my hotel across the river, I felt happier than I had in months. Things had been simplified, reduced to the clarity of a single problem. But then, the moment I absorbed this thought, I understood how bad the situation really was. I was coming to the end now, and I still hadn't found him. The mistake I was looking for had never surfaced. There were no leads, no clues, no tracks to follow. Fanshawe was buried somewhere, and his whole life was buried with him. Unless he wanted to be found, I didn't have a ghost of a chance.

Still, I pushed ahead, trying to come to the end, to the very end, burrowing blindly through the last interviews, not willing to give up until I had seen everyone. I wanted to call Sophie. One day, I even went so far as to walk to the post office and wait in line for the foreign operator, but I didn't go through with it. Words were failing me constantly now, and I panicked at the thought of losing my nerve on the phone. What was I supposed to say, after all? Instead, I sent her a postcard with a photograph of Laurel and Hardy on it. On the back I wrote: 'True marriages never make sense. Look at the couple on the other side. Proof that anything is possible, no? Perhaps we should start wearing derbies. At the very least, remember to clean out the closet before I return. Hugs to Ben.'

I saw Anne Michaux the following afternoon, and she gave a little start when I entered the café where we had arranged to meet (Le Rouquet, Boulevard Saint Germain). What she told me about Fanshawe is not important: who kissed who, what happened where, who said what, and so on. It comes down to more of the same. What I will mention, however, is that her initial double take was caused by the fact that she mistook me for

Fanshawe. Just the briefest flicker, as she put it, and then it was gone. The resemblance had been noticed before, of course, but never so viscerally, with such immediate impact. I must have shown my reaction, for she quickly apologized (as if she had done something wrong) and returned to the point several times during the two or three hours we spent together – once even going out of her way to contradict herself: 'I don't know what I was thinking. You don't look at all like him. It must have been the American in both of you.'

Nevertheless, I found it disturbing, could not help feeling appalled. Something monstrous was happening, and I had no control over it anymore. The sky was growing dark inside – that much was certain; the ground was trembling. I found it hard to sit still, and I found it hard to move. From one moment to the next, I seemed to be in a different place, to forget where I was. Thoughts stop where the world begins, I kept telling myself. But the self is also in the world, I answered, and likewise the thoughts that come from it. The problem was that I could no longer make the right distinctions. This can never be that. Apples are not oranges, peaches are not plums. You feel the difference on your tongue, and then you know, as if inside yourself. But everything was beginning to have the same taste to me. I no longer felt hungry, I could no longer bring myself to eat.

As for the Dedmons, there is perhaps even less to say. Fanshawe could not have chosen more fitting benefactors, and of all the people I saw in Paris, they were the kindest, the most gracious. Invited to their apartment for drinks, I stayed on for dinner, and then, by the time we reached the second course, they were urging me to visit their house in the Var – the same house where Fanshawe had lived, and it needn't be a short visit, they said, since they were not planning to go there themselves until August. It had been an important place for Fanshawe and his work, Mr Dedmon said, and no doubt my book would be enhanced if I saw it myself. I couldn't disagree with him, and no sooner were these words out of my mouth than Mrs Dedmon was on the phone making arrangements for me in her precise and elegant French.

There was nothing to hold me in Paris anymore, and so I took the train the following afternoon. This was the end of the line for me, my southward trek to oblivion. Whatever hope I might have had (the faint possibility that Fanshawe had returned to France, the illogical thought that he had found refuge in the same place twice) evaporated by the time I got there. The house was empty; there was no sign of anyone. On the second day, examining the rooms on the upper floor, I came across a short poem Fanshawe had written on the wall – but I knew that poem already, and under it there was a date: 25 August 1972. He had never come back. I felt foolish now even for thinking it.

For want of anything better to do, I spent several days talking to people in the area: the nearby farmers, the villagers, the people of surrounding towns. I introduced myself by showing them a photograph of Fanshawe, pretending to be his brother, but feeling more like a down-and-out private eye, a buffoon clutching at straws. Some people remembered him, others didn't, still others weren't sure. It made no difference. I found the southern accent impenetrable (with its rolling 'r's and nasalized endings) and barely understood a word that was said to me. Of all the people I saw, only one had heard from Fanshawe since his departure. This was his closest neighbour – a tenant farmer who lived about a mile down the road. He was a peculiar little man of about forty, dirtier than anyone I had ever met. His house was a dank, crumbling seventeenth-century structure, and he seemed to live there by himself, with no companions but his truffle dog and hunting rifle. He was clearly proud of having been Fanshawe's friend, and to prove how close they had been he showed me a white cowboy hat that Fanshawe had sent to him after returning to America. There was no reason not to believe his story. The hat was still in its original box and apparently had never been worn. He explained that he was saving it for the right moment, and then launched into a political harangue that I had trouble following. The revolution was coming, he said, and when it did, he was going to buy a white horse and a machine gun, put on his hat, and ride down the main street in town, plugging all the shopkeepers who had collaborated with the Germans during the War. Just like in America, he added. When I asked him what he meant, he delivered a rambling, hallucinatory lecture about cowboys and Indians. But that was a long time ago, I said, trying to cut him short. No, no, he insisted, it still goes on today. Didn't I know about the shootouts on Fifth Avenue? Hadn't I heard of the Apaches? It was pointless to argue. In defence of my ignorance, I told him that I lived in another neighbourhood.

I stayed on in the house for a few more days. My plan was to do nothing for as long as I could, to rest up. I was exhausted, and I needed a chance to regroup before going back to Paris. A day or two went by. I walked through the fields, visited the woods, sat out in the sun reading French translations of American detective novels. It should have been the perfect cure: holing up in the middle of nowhere, letting my mind float free. But none of it really helped. The house wouldn't make room for me, and by the third day I sensed that I was no longer alone, that I could never be alone in that place. Fanshawe was there, and no matter how hard I tried not to think about him, I couldn't escape. This was unexpected, galling. Now that I had stopped looking for him, he was more present to me than ever before. The whole process had been reversed. After all these months of trying to find him, I felt as though I was the one who had been found. Instead of looking for Fanshawe, I had actually been running away from him. The work I had contrived for myself – the false book, the endless detours – had been no more than an attempt to ward him off, a ruse to keep him as far away from me as possible. For if I could convince myself that I was looking for him, then it necessarily followed that he was somewhere else – somewhere beyond me, beyond the limits of my life. But I had been wrong. Fanshawe was exactly where I was, and he had been there since the beginning. From the moment his letter arrived, I had been struggling to imagine him, to see him as he might have been – but my mind had always conjured a blank. At best, there was one impoverished image: the door of a locked room. That was the extent of it: Fanshawe alone in that room, condemned to a mythical solitude – living perhaps, breathing perhaps, dreaming God knows what. This room, I now discovered, was located inside my skull.

Strange things happened to me after that. I returned to Paris, but once there I found myself with nothing to do. I didn't want to look up any of the people I had seen before, and I didn't have the courage to go back to New York. I became inert, a thing that could not move, and little by little I lost track of myself. If I am able to say anything about this period at all, it is only because I have certain documentary evidence to help me. The visa stamps in my passport, for example; my airplane ticket, my hotel bill, and so on. These things prove to me that I remained in Paris for more than a month. But that is very different from remembering, and in spite of what I know, I still find it impossible. I see things that happened, I encounter images of myself in various places, but only at a distance, as though I were watching someone else. None of it feels like memory, which is always anchored within; it's out there beyond what I can feel or touch, beyond anything that has to do with me. I have lost a month from my life, and even now it is a difficult thing for me to confess, a thing that fills me with shame.

A month is a long time, more than enough time for a man to come apart. Those days come back to me in fragments when they come at all, bits and pieces that refuse to add up. I see myself falling down drunk on the street one night, standing up, staggering towards a lamppost, and then vomiting all over my shoes. I see myself sitting in a movie theatre with the lights on and watching a crowd of people file out around me, unable to remember the film I had just seen. I see myself prowling the rue Saint-Denis at night, picking out prostitutes to sleep with, my head burning with the thought of bodies, an endless jumble of naked breasts, naked thighs, naked buttocks. I see my cock being sucked, I see myself on a bed with two girls kissing each other, I see an enormous black woman spreading her legs on a bidet and washing her cunt. I will not try to say that these things are not real, that they did not happen. It's just that I can't account for them. I was fucking the brains out of my head, drinking myself into another world. But if the point was to obliterate Fanshawe, then my binge was a success. He was gone – and I was gone along with him.

The end, however, is clear to me. I have not forgotten it, and I feel lucky to have kept that much. The entire story comes down to what happened at the end, and without that end inside me now, I could not have started this book. The same holds for the two books that come before it, *City of Glass* and *Ghosts*. These three stories are finally the same story, but each one represents a different stage in my awareness of what it is about. I don't claim to have solved any problems. I am merely suggesting that a moment came when it no longer frightened me to look at what had happened. If words followed, it was only because I had no choice but to accept them, to take them upon myself and go where they wanted me to go. But that does not necessarily make the words important. I have been struggling to say goodbye to something for a long time now, and this struggle is all that really matters. The story is not in the words; it's in the struggle.

One night, I found myself in a bar near the Place Pigalle. *Found* is the term I wish to use, for I have no idea of how I got there, no memory of entering the place at all. It was one of those clip joints that are common in the neighbourhood: six or eight girls at the bar, the chance to sit at a table with one of them and buy an exorbitantly priced bottle of champagne, and then, if one is so inclined, the possibility of coming to a certain financial agreement and retiring to the privacy of a room in the hotel next door. The scene begins for me as I'm sitting at one of the tables with a girl, just having received the bucket of champagne. The girl was Tahitian, I remember, and she was beautiful: no more than nineteen or twenty, very small, and wearing a dress of white netting with nothing underneath, a crisscross of cables over her smooth brown skin. The effect was superbly erotic. I remember her round breasts visible in the diamond-shaped openings, the overwhelming softness of her neck when I leaned over and kissed it. She told me her name, but I insisted on calling her Fayaway, telling her that she was an exile from Typee and that I was Herman Melville, an American sailor who had come all the way from New York to rescue her. She hadn't the vaguest idea of what I was talking about, but she continued to smile, no doubt thinking me crazy as I rambled on in my sputtering French, unperturbed, laughing when I laughed, allowing me to kiss her wherever I liked.

We were sitting in an alcove in the corner, and from my seat I was able to take in the rest of the room. Men came and went, some popping their heads through the door and leaving, some staying for a drink at the bar, one or two going to a table as I had done. After about fifteen minutes, a young man came in who was obviously American. He seemed nervous to me, as if he had never been in such a place before, but his French was surprisingly good, and as he fluently ordered a whiskey at the bar and started talking to one of the girls, I saw that he meant to stay for a while. I studied him from my little nook, continuing to run my hand along Fayaway's leg and to nuzzle her with my face, but the longer he stood there, the more distracted I became. He was tall, athletically built, with sandy hair and an open, somewhat boyish manner. I guessed his age at twenty-six or twenty-seven – a graduate student, perhaps, or else a young lawyer working for an American firm in Paris. I had never seen this man before, and yet there was something familiar about him, something that stopped me from turning away: a brief scald, a weird synapse of recognition. I tried out various names on him, shunted him through the past, unravelled the spool of associations – but nothing happened. He's no one, I said to myself, finally giving up. And then, out of the blue, by some muddled chain of reasoning, I finished the thought by adding: and if he's no one, then he must be Fanshawe. I laughed out loud at my joke. Ever on the alert, Fayaway laughed with me. I knew that nothing could be more absurd, but I said it again: Fanshawe. And then again: Fanshawe. And the more I said it, the more it pleased me to say it. Each time the word came out of my mouth, another burst of laughter followed. I was intoxicated by the sound of it; it drove me to a pitch of raucousness, and little by little Fayaway seemed to grow confused. She had probably thought I was referring to some sexual practice, making some joke she couldn't understand, but my repetitions had gradually robbed the word of its meaning, and she began to hear it as a threat. I looked at the man across the room and spoke the word again. My happiness was immeasurable. I exulted in the sheer falsity of my assertion, celebrating the new power I had just bestowed upon myself. I was the sublime alchemist who could change the world at will. This man was Fanshawe because I said he was Fanshawe, and that was all there was to it. Nothing could stop me anymore. Without even pausing to think, I whispered into Fayaways's ear that I would be right back, disengaged myself from her wonderful arms, and sauntered over to the pseudo-Fanshawe at the bar. In my best imitation of an Oxford accent, I said:

'Well, old man, fancy that. We meet again.'

He turned around and looked at me carefully. The smile that had been forming on his face slowly diminished into a frown. 'Do I know you?' he finally asked.

'Of course you do,' I said, all bluster and good humour. 'The name's Melville. Herman Melville. Perhaps you've read some of my books.'

He didn't know whether to treat me as a jovial drunk or a dangerous psychopath, and the confusion showed on his face. It was a splendid confusion, and I enjoyed it thoroughly.

'Well,' he said at last, forcing out a little smile, 'I might have read one or two.'

'The one about the whale, no doubt.'

'Yes. The one about the whale.'

'I'm glad to hear it,' I said, nodding pleasantly, and then put my arm around his shoulder. 'And so, Fanshawe,' I said, 'what brings you to Paris this time of year?'

The confusion returned to his face. 'Sorry,' he said, 'I didn't catch that name.'

'Fanshawe.'

'Fanshawe?'

'Fanshawe. F-A-N-S-H-A-W-E.'

'Well,' he said, relaxing into a broad grin, suddenly sure of himself again, 'that's the problem right there. You've mixed me up with someone else. My name isn't Fanshawe. It's Stillman. Peter Stillman.'

'No problem,' I answered, giving him a little squeeze. 'If you want to call yourself Stillman, that's fine with me. Names aren't important, after all. What matters is that I know who you really are. You're Fanshawe. I knew it the moment you walked in. "There's the old devil himself," I said. "I wonder what he's doing in a place like this?" '

He was beginning to lose patience with me now. He removed my arm from his shoulder and backed off. 'That's enough,' he said. 'You've made a mistake, and let's leave it at that. I don't want to talk to you anymore.'

'Too late,' I said. 'Your secret's out, my friend. There's no way to hide from me now.'

'Leave me alone,' he said, showing anger for the first time. 'I don't talk to lunatics. Leave me alone, or there'll be trouble.'

The other people in the bar couldn't understand what we were saying, but the tension had become obvious, and I could feel myself being watched, could feel the mood shift around me. Stillman suddenly seemed to panic. He shot a glance at the woman behind the bar, looked apprehensively at the girl beside him, and then made an impulsive decision to leave. He pushed me out of his way and started for the door. I could have let it go at that, but I didn't. I was just getting warmed up, and I didn't want my inspiration to be wasted. I went back to where Faya-way was sitting and put a few hundred francs on the table. She feigned a pout in response. 'C'est mon frère,' I said. 'Il est fou. Je dois le poursuivre.' And then, as she reached for the money, I blew her a kiss, turned around, and left.

Stillman was twenty or thirty yards ahead of me, walking quickly down the street. I kept pace with him, hanging back to avoid being noticed, but not letting him move out of sight. Every now and then he looked back over his shoulder, as though expecting me to be there, but I don't think he saw me until we were well out of the neighbourhood, away from the crowds and commotion, slicing through the quiet, darkened core of the Right Bank. The encounter had spooked him, and he behaved like a man running for his life. But that was not difficult to understand. I was the thing we all fear most: the belligerent stranger who steps out from the shadows, the knife that stabs us in the back, the speeding car that crushes us to death. He was right to be running, but his fear only egged me on, goaded me to pursue him, made me rabid with determination. I had no plan, no idea of what I was going to do, but I followed him without the slightest doubt, knowing that my whole life hinged on it. It is important to stress that by now I was completely lucid – no wobbling, no drunkenness, utterly clear in my head. I realized that I was acting outrageously. Stillman was not Fanshawe – I knew that. He was an arbitrary choice, totally innocent and blank. But that was the thing that thrilled me – the randomness of it, the vertigo of pure chance. It made no sense, and because of that, it made all the sense in the world.

A moment came when the only sounds in the street were our footsteps. Stillman looked back again and finally saw me. He began moving faster, breaking into a trot. I called after him: 'Fanshawe.' I called after him again: 'It's too late. I know who you are, Fanshawe.' And then, on the next street: 'It's all over, Fanshawe. You'll never get away.' Stillman said nothing in response, did not even bother to turn around. I wanted to keep talking to him, but by now he was running, and if I tried to talk, it would only have slowed me down. I abandoned my taunts and went after him. I have no idea how long we ran, but it seemed to go on for hours. He was younger than I was, younger and stronger, and I almost lost him, almost didn't make it. I pushed myself down the dark street, passing the point of exhaustion, of sickness, frantically hurtling toward him, not allowing myself to stop. Long before I reached him, long before I even knew I was going to reach him, I felt as though I was no longer inside myself. I can think of no other way to express it. I couldn't feel myself anymore. The sensation of life had dribbled out of me, and in its place there was a miraculous euphoria, a sweet poison rushing through my blood, the undeniable odour of nothingness. This is the moment of my death, I said to myself, this is when I die. A second later, I caught up to Stillman and tackled him from behind. We went crashing to the pavement, the two of us grunting on impact. I had used up all my strength, and by now I was too short of breath to defend myself, too drained to struggle. Not a word was said. For several seconds we grappled on the sidewalk, but then he managed to break free of my grip, and after that there was nothing I could do. He started pounding me with his fists, kicking me with the points of his shoes, pummelling me all over. I remember trying to protect my face with my hands; I remember the pain and how it stunned me, how much it hurt and how desperately I wanted not to feel it anymore. But it couldn't have lasted very long, for nothing else comes back to me. Stillman tore me apart, and by the time he was finished, I was out cold. I can remember waking up on the sidewalk and being surprised that it was still night, but that's the extent of it. Everything else is gone.

For the next three days I didn't move from my hotel room. The shock was not so much that I was in pain, but that it would not be strong enough to kill me. I realized this by the second or third day. At a certain moment, lying there on the bed and looking at the slats of the closed shutters, I understood that I had lived through it. It felt strange to be alive, almost incomprehensible. One of my fingers was broken; both temples were gashed; it ached even to breathe. But that was somehow beside the point. I was alive, and the more I thought about it, the less I understood. It did not seem possible that I had been spared.

Later that same night, I wired Sophie that I was coming home.

9

I am nearly at the end now. There is one thing left, but that did not happen until later, until three more years had passed. In the mean time, there were many difficulties, many dramas, but I do not think they belong to the story I am trying to tell. After my return to New York, Sophie and I lived apart for almost a year. She had given up on me, and there were months of confusion before I finally won her back. From the vantage point of this moment (May 1984), that is the only thing that matters. Beside it, the facts of my life are purely incidental.

On 23 February 1981, Ben's baby brother was born. We named him Paul, in memory of Sophie's grandfather. Several months later (in July) we moved across the river, renting the top two floors of a brownstone house in Brooklyn. In September, Ben started kindergarten. We all went to Minnesota for Christmas, and by the time we got back, Paul was walking on his own. Ben, who had gradually taken him under his wing, claimed full credit for the development.

As for Fanshawe, Sophie and I never talked about him. This was our silent pact, and the longer we said nothing, the more we proved our loyalty to each other. After I returned the advance money to Stuart Green and officially stopped writing the biography, we mentioned him only once. That came on the day we decided to live together again, and it was couched in strictly practical terms. Fanshawe's books and plays had continued to produce a good income. If we were going to stay married, Sophie said, then using the money for ourselves was out of the question. I agreed with her. We found other ways to earn what we had to and placed the royalty money in trust for Ben – and subsequently for Paul as well. As a final step, we hired a literary agent to manage the business of Fanshawe's work: requests to perform plays, reprint negotiations, contracts, whatever needed to be done. To the extent that we were able to act, we did. If Fanshawe still had the power to destroy us, it would only be because we wanted him to, because we wanted to destroy ourselves. That was why I never bothered to tell Sophie the truth – not because it frightened me, but because the truth was no longer important. Our strength was in our silence, and I had no intention of breaking it.

Still, I knew that the story wasn't over. My last month in Paris had taught me that, and little by little I learned to accept it. It was only a matter of time before the next thing happened. This seemed inevitable to me, and rather than deny it anymore, rather than delude myself with the thought that I could ever get rid of Fanshawe, I tried to prepare myself for it, tried to make myself ready for anything. It is the power of this *anything*, I believe, that has made the story so difficult to tell. For when anything can happen – that is the precise moment when words begin to fail. To the degree that Fanshawe became inevitable, that was the degree to which he was no longer there. I learned to accept this. I learned to live with him in the same way I lived with the thought of my own death. Fanshawe himself was not death – but he was like death, and he functioned as a trope for death inside me. If not for my breakdown in Paris, I never would have understood this. I did not die there, but I came close, and there was a moment, perhaps there were several moments, when I tasted death, when I saw myself dead. There is no cure for such an encounter. Once it happens, it goes on happening; you live with it for the rest of your life.

The letter came early in the spring of 1982. This time the postmark was from Boston, and the message was terse, more urgent than before. 'Impossible to hold out any longer,' it said. 'Must talk to you. 9 Columbus Square, Boston; April 1st. This is where it ends, I promise.'

I had less than a week to invent an excuse for going to Boston. This turned out to be more difficult than it should have been. Although I persisted in not wanting Sophie to know anything (feeling that it was the least I could do for her), I somehow balked at telling another lie, even though it had to be done. Two or three days slipped by without any progress, and in the end I concocted some lame story about having to consult papers in the Harvard Library. I can't even remember what papers they were supposed to be. Something to do with an article I was going to write, I think, but that could be wrong. The important thing was that Sophie did not raise any objections. Fine, she said, go right ahead, and so on. My gut feeling is that she suspected something was up, but that is only a feeling, and it would be pointless to speculate about it here. Where Sophie is concerned, I tend to believe that nothing is hidden.

I booked a seat for April first on the early train. On the morning of my departure, Paul woke up a little before five and climbed into bed with us. I roused myself an hour later and crept out of the room, pausing briefly at the door to watch Sophie and the baby in the dim grey light – sprawled out, impervious, the bodies I belonged to. Ben was in the kitchen upstairs, already dressed, eating a banana and drawing pictures. I scrambled some eggs for the two of us and told him that I was about to take a train to Boston. He wanted to know where Boston was.

'About two hundred miles from here,' I said.

'Is that as far away as space?'

'If you went straight up, you'd be getting close.'

'I think you should go to the moon. A rocket ship is better than a train.'

'I'll do that on the way back. They have regular flights from Boston to the moon on Fridays. I'll reserve a seat the moment I get there.'

'Good. Then you can tell me what it's like.'

'If I find a moon rock, I'll bring one back for you.'

'What about Paul?'

'I'll get one for him, too.'

'No thanks.'

'What does that mean?'

302

'I don't want a moon rock. Paul would put his in his mouth and choke.'

'What would you like instead?'

'An elephant.'

'There aren't any elephants in space.'

'I know that. But you aren't going to space.'

'True.'

'And I bet there are elephants in Boston.'

'You're probably right. Do you want a pink elephant or a white elephant?'

'A grey elephant. A big fat one with lots of wrinkles.'

'No problem. Those are the easiest ones to find. Would you like it wrapped up in a box, or should I bring it home on a leash?'

'I think you should ride it home. Sitting on top with a crown on your head. Just like an emperor.'

'The emperor of what?'

'The emperor of little boys.'

'Do I get to have an empress?'

'Of course. Mommy is the empress. She'd like that. Maybe we should wake her up and tell her.'

'Let's not. I'd rather surprise her with it when I get home.'

'Good idea. She won't believe it until she sees it anyway.'

'Exactly. And we don't want her to be disappointed. In case I can't find the elephant.'

'Oh, you'll find it, Dad. Don't worry about that.'

'How can you be so sure?'

'Because you're the emperor. An emperor can get anything he wants.'

It rained the whole way up, the sky even threatening snow by the time we reached Providence. In Boston, I bought myself an umbrella and covered the last two or three miles on foot. The streets were gloomy in the piss-grey air, and as I walked to the South End, I saw almost no one: a drunk, a group of teenagers, a telephone man, two or three stray mutts. Columbus Square consisted of ten or twelve houses in a row, fronting on a cobbled island that cut it off from the main thoroughfare. Number nine was the most dilapidated of the lot – four stories like the others, but sagging, with boards propping up the entranceway and the brick façade in need of mending. Still, there was an impressive solidity to it, a nineteenth-century elegance that continued to show through the cracks. I imagined large rooms with high ceilings, comfortable ledges by the bay window, moulded ornaments in the plaster. But I did not get to see any of these things. As it turned out, I never got beyond the front hall.

There was a rusted metal clapper in the door, a half-sphere with a handle in the centre, and when I twisted the handle, it made the sound of someone retching – a muffled, gagging sound that did not carry very far. I waited, but nothing happened. I twisted the bell again, but no one came. Then, testing the door with my hand, I saw that it wasn't locked – pushed it open, paused, and went in. The front hall was empty. To my right was the staircase, with its mahogany banister and bare wooden steps: to my left were closed double doors, blocking off what was no doubt the parlour; straight ahead there was another door, also closed, that probably led to the kitchen. I hesitated for a moment, decided on the stairs, and was about to go up when I heard something from behind the double doors – a faint tapping, followed by a voice I couldn't understand. I turned from the staircase and looked at the door, listening for the voice again. Nothing happened.

A long silence. Then, almost in a whisper, the voice spoke again. 'In here,' it said.

I went to the doors and pressed my ear against the crack between them. 'Is that you, Fanshawe?'

'Don't use that name,' the voice said, more distinctly this time. 'I won't allow you to use that name.' The mouth of the person inside was lined up directly with my ear. Only the door was between us, and we were so close that I felt as if the words were being poured into my head. It was like listening to a man's heart beating in his chest, like searching a body for a pulse. He stopped talking, and I could feel his breath slithering through the crack.

'Let me in,' I said. 'Open the door and let me in.'

'I can't do that,' the voice answered. 'We'll have to talk like this.'

I grabbed hold of the door knob and shook the doors in frustration. 'Open up,' I said. 'Open up, or I'll break the door down.'

'No,' said the voice. 'The door stays closed.' By now I was convinced that it was Fanshawe in there. I wanted it to be an impostor, but I recognized too much in that voice to pretend it was anyone else. 'I'm standing here with a gun,' he said, 'and it's pointed right at you. If you come through the door, I'll shoot.'

'I don't believe you.'

'Listen to this,' he said, and then I heard him turn away from the door. A second later a gun went off, followed by the sound of plaster falling to the floor. I tried to peer through the crack in the mean time, hoping to catch a glimpse of the room, but the space was too narrow. I could see no more than a thread of light, a single grey filament. Then the mouth returned, and I could no longer see even that.

'All right,' I said, 'you have a gun. But if you don't let me see you, how will I know you are who you say you are?'

'I haven't said who I am.'

'Let me put it another way. How can I know I'm talking to the right person?'

'You'll have to trust me.'

'At this late date, trust is about the last thing you should expect.'

'I'm telling you that I'm the right person. That should be enough. You've come to the right place, and I'm the right person.'

'I thought you wanted to see me. That's what you said in your letter.'

'I said that I wanted to talk to you. There's a difference.'

'Let's not split hairs.'

'I'm just reminding you of what I wrote.'

'Don't push me too far, Fanshawe. There's nothing to stop me from walking out.'

I heard a sudden intake of breath, and then a hand slapped violently against the door. 'Not Fanshawe!' he shouted. 'Not Fanshawe – ever again!'

I let a few moments pass, not wanting to provoke another outburst. The mouth withdrew from the crack, and I imagined that I heard groans from somewhere in the middle of the room – groans or sobs, I couldn't tell which. I stood there waiting, not knowing what to say next. Eventually, the mouth returned, and after another long pause Fanshawe said, 'Are you still there?'

'Yes.'

'Forgive me. I didn't want it to begin like this.'

'Just remember,' I said, 'I'm only here because you asked me to come.'

'I know that. And I'm grateful to you for it.'

'It might help if you explained why you invited me.'

'Later. I don't want to talk about that yet.'

'Then what?'

'Other things. The things that have happened.'

'I'm listening.'

'Because I don't want you to hate me. Can you understand that?'

'I don't hate you. There was a time when I did, but I'm over that now.'

'Today is my last day, you see. And I had to make sure.'

'Is this where you've been all along?'

'I came here about two years ago, I think.'

'And before that?'

'Here and there. That man was after me, and I had to keep moving. It gave me a feeling for travel, a real taste for it. Not at all what I had expected. My plan had always been to sit still and let the time run out.'

'You're talking about Quinn?'

'Yes. The private detective.'

'Did he find you?'

'Twice. Once in New York. The next time down South.'

'Why did he lie about it?'

'Because I scared him to death. He knew what would happen to him if anyone found out.'

'He disappeared, you know. I couldn't find a trace of him.'

'He's somewhere. It's not important.'

'How did you manage to get rid of him?'

'I turned everything around. He thought he was following me, but in fact I was following him. He found me in New York, of course, but I got away – wriggled right through his arms. After that, it was like playing a game. I led him along, leaving clues for him everywhere, making it impossible for him not to find me. But I was watching him the whole time, and when the moment came, I set him up, and he walked straight into my trap.'

'Very clever.'

'No. It was stupid. But I didn't have any choice. It was either that or get hauled back – which would have meant being treated like a crazy man. I hated myself for it. He was only doing his job, after all, and it made me feel sorry for him. Pity disgusts me, especially when I find it in myself.'

'And then?'

'I couldn't be sure if my trick had really worked. I thought Quinn might come after me again. And so I kept on moving, even when I didn't have to. I lost about a year like that.'

'Where did you go?'

'The South, the Southwest. I wanted to stay where it was warm. I travelled on foot, you see, slept outside, tried to go where there weren't many people. It's an enormous country, you know. Absolutely bewildering. At one point, I stayed in the desert for about two months. Later, I lived in a shack at the edge of a Hopi reservation in Arizona. The Indians had a tribal council before giving me permission to stay there.'

'You're making this up.'

'I'm not asking you to believe me. I'm telling you the story, that's all. You can think anything you want.'

'And then?'

'I was somewhere in New Mexico. I went into a diner along the road one day to get a bite to eat, and someone had left a nespaper on the counter. So I picked it up and read it. That's when I found out that a book of mine had been published.'

'Were you surprised?'

'That's not quite the word I would use.'

'What, then?'

'I don't know. Angry, I think. Upset.'

'I don't understand.'

'I was angry because the book was garbage.'

'Writers never know how to judge their work.'

'No, the book was garbage, believe me. Everything I did was garbage.'

'Then why didn't you destroy it?'

'I was too attached to it. But that doesn't make it good. A baby is attached to his caca, but no one fusses about it. It's strictly his own business.'

'Then why did you make Sophie promise to show me the work?'

'To appease her. But you know that already. You figured that out a long time ago. That was my excuse. My real reason was to find a new husband for her.'

'It worked.'

'It had to work. I didn't pick just anyone, you know.'

'And the manuscripts?'

'I thought you would throw them away. It never occurred to me that anyone would take the work seriously.'

'What did you do after you read that the book had been published?'

'I went back to New York. It was an absurd thing to do, but I was a little beside myself, not thinking clearly anymore. The book trapped me into what I had done, you see, and I had to wrestle with it all over again. Once the book was published, I couldn't turn back.

'I thought you were dead.'

'That's what you were supposed to think. If nothing else, it proved to me that Quinn was no longer a problem. But this new problem was much worse. That's when I wrote you the letter.'

'That was a vicious thing to do.'

'I was angry at you. I wanted you to suffer, to live with the same things I had to live with. The instant after I dropped it in the mailbox, I regretted it.'

'Too late.'

'Yes. Too late.'

'How long did you stay in New York?'

'I don't know. Six or eight months, I think.'

'How did you live? How did you earn the money to live?'

'I stole things.'

'Why don't you tell the truth?'

'I'm doing my best. I'm telling you everything I'm able to tell.'

'What else did you do in New York?'

'I watched you. I watched you and Sophie and the baby. There was even a time when I camped outside your apartment building. For two or three weeks, maybe a month. I followed you everywhere you went. Once or twice, I even bumped into you on the street, looked you straight in the eye. But you never noticed. It was fantastic the way you didn't see me.'

'You're making all this up.'

'I must not look the same anymore.'

'No one can change that much.'

'I think I'm unrecognizable. But that was a lucky thing for you. If anything had happened, I probably would have killed you. That whole time in New York, I was filled with murderous thoughts. Bad stuff. I came close to a kind of horror there.'

'What stopped you?'

'I found the courage to leave.'

'That was noble of you.'

'I'm not trying to defend myself. I'm just giving you the story.'

'Then what?'

'I shipped out again. I still had my merchant seaman's card, and I signed on with a Greek freighter. It was disgusting, truly repulsive from beginning to end. But I deserved it; it was exactly what I wanted. The ship went everywhere – India, Japan, all over the world. I didn't get off once. Every time we came to a port, I would go down to my cabin and lock myself in. I spent two years like that, seeing nothing, doing nothing, living like a dead man.'

'While I was trying to write the story of your life.'

'Is that what you were doing?'

'So it would seem.'

'A big mistake.'

'You don't have to tell me. I found that out for myself.'

'The ship pulled into Boston one day, and I decided to get off. I had saved a tremendous amount of money, more than enough to buy this house. I've been here ever since.'

'What name have you been using?'

'Henry Dark. But no one knows who I am. I never go out. There's a woman who comes twice a week and brings me what I need, but I never see her. I leave her a note at the foot of the stairs, along with the money I owe her. It's a simple and effective arrangement. You're the first person I've spoken to in two years.'

'Do you ever think that you're out of your mind?'

'I know it looks like that to you – but I'm not, believe me. I don't even want to waste my breath talking about it. What I need for myself is very different from what other people need.'

'Isn't this house a bit big for one person?'

'Much too big. I haven't been above the ground floor since the day I moved in.'

'Then why did you buy it?'

'It cost almost nothing. And I liked the name of the street. It appealed to me.'

'Columbus Square?'

'Yes.'

'I don't follow.'

'It seemed like a good omen. Coming back to America – and then finding a house on a street named after Columbus. There was a certain logic to it.'

'And this is where you're planning to die.'

'Exactly.'

'Your first letter said seven years. You still have a year to go.'

'I've proved the point to myself. There's no need to go on with it. I'm tired. I've had enough.'

'Did you ask me to come here because you thought I would stop you?'

'No. Not at all. I'm not expecting anything from you.'

'Then what do you want?'

'I have some things to give you. At a certain point, I realized that I owed you an explanation for what I did. At least an attempt. I've spent the past six months trying to get it down on paper.'

'I thought you gave up writing for good.'

'This is different. It has no connection with what I used to do.'

'Where is it?'

'Behind you. On the floor of the closet under the stairs. A red notebook.'

I turned around, opened the closet door, and picked up the notebook. It was a standard spiral affair with two hundred ruled pages. I gave a quick glance at the contents and saw that all the pages had been filled: the same familiar writing, the same black ink, the same small letters. I stood up and returned to the crack between the doors.

'What now?' I asked.

'Take it home with you. Read it.'

'What if I can't?'

'Then save it for the boy. He might want to see it when he grows up.'

'I don't think you have any right to ask that.'

'He's my son.'

'No, he's not. He's mine.'

311

'I won't insist. Read it yourself, then. It was written for you anyway.'

'And Sophie?'

'No. You mustn't tell her.'

'That's the one thing I'll never understand.'

'Sophie?'

'How you could walk out on her like that. What did she ever do to you?'

'Nothing. It wasn't her fault. You must know that by now. It's just that I wasn't meant to live like other people.'

'How were you meant to live?'

'It's all in the notebook. Whatever I managed to say now would only distort the truth.'

'Is there anything else?'

'No, I don't think so. We've probably come to the end.'

'I don't believe you have the nerve to shoot me. If I broke down the door now, you wouldn't do a thing.'

'Don't risk it. You'd die for nothing.'

'I'd pull the gun out of your hand. I'd knock you senseless.'

'There's no point to that. I'm already dead. I took poison hours ago.'

'I don't believe you.'

'You can't possibly know what's true or not true. You'll never know.'

'I'll call the police. They'll chop down the door and drag you off to the hospital.'

'One sound at the door – and a bullet goes through my head. There's no way you can win.'

'Is death so tempting?'

'I've lived with it for so long now, it's the only thing I have left.'

I no longer knew what to say. Fanshawe had used me up, and as I heard him breathing on the other side of the door, I felt as if the life were being sucked out of me. 'You're a fool,' I said, unable to think of anything else. 'You're a fool, and you deserve to die.' Then, overwhelmed by my own weakness and stupidity, I started pounding the door like a child, shaking and sputtering, on the point of tears.

'You'd better go now,' Franshawe said. 'There's no reason to drag this out.'

'I don't want to go,' I said. 'We still have things to talk about.'

'No, we don't. It's finished. Take the notebook and go back to New York. That's all I ask of you.'

I was so exhausted that for a moment I thought I was going to fall down. I clung to the doorknob for support, my head going black inside, struggling not to pass out. After that, I have no memory of what happened. I found myself outside, in front of the house, the umbrella in one hand and the red notebook in the other. The rain had stopped, but the air was still raw, and I could feel the dankness in my lungs. I watched a large truck clatter by in the traffic, following its red tail-light until I couldn't see it anymore. When I looked up, I saw that it was almost night. I started walking away from the house, mechanically putting one foot in front of the other, unable to concentrate on where I was going. I think I fell down once or twice. At one point, I remember waiting on a corner and trying to get a cab, but no one stopped for me. A few minutes after that, the umbrella slipped from my hand and fell into a puddle. I didn't bother to pick it up.

It was just after seven o'clock when I arrived at South Station. A train for New York had left fifteen minutes earlier, and the next one wasn't scheduled until eight-thirty. I sat down on one of the wooden benches with the red notebook on my lap. A few late commuters straggled in; a janitor slowly moved across the marble floor with a mop; I listened in as two men talked about the Red Sox behind me. After ten minutes of fighting off the impulse, I at last opened the notebook. I read steadily for almost an hour, flipping back and forth among the pages, trying to get a sense of what Fanshawe had written. If I say nothing about what I found there, it is because I understood very little. All the words were familiar to me, and yet they seemed to have been put together strangely, as though their final purpose was to cancel each other out. I can think of no other way to express it. Each sentence erased the sentence before it, each paragraph made the next paragraph impossible. It is odd, then, that the feeling that survives from this notebook is one of great lucidity. It is as if Fanshawe knew his final work had to subvert every expectation I had for it. These were not the words of a man who regretted anything. He had answered the question by asking another question, and therefore everything remained open, unfinished, to be started again. I lost my way after the first word, and from then on I could only grope ahead, faltering in the darkness, blinded by the book that had been written for me. And yet, underneath this confusion, I felt there was something too willed, something too perfect, as though in the end the only thing he had really wanted was to fail – even to the point of failing himself. I could be wrong, however. I was hardly in a condition to be reading anything at that moment, and my judgement is possibly askew. I was there, I read those words with my own eyes, and yet I find it hard to trust in what I am saying.

I wandered out to the tracks several minutes in advance. It was raining again, and I could see my breath in the air before me, leaving my mouth in little bursts of fog. One by one, I tore the pages from the notebook, crumpled them in my hand, and dropped them into a trash bin on the platform. I came to the last page just as the train was pulling out.